VITAL SIGNS

Cape Breton is the Thought-Control Centre of Canada
RAY SMITH

A Night at the Opera
RAY SMITH

Going Down Slow
JOHN METCALF

Century
RAY SMITH

Quickening
TERRY GRIGGS

Moody Food
RAY ROBERTSON

Alphabet
KATHY PAGE

Lunar Attractions
CLARK BLAISE

An Aesthetic Underground
JOHN METCALF

Lord Nelson Tavern
RAY SMITH

Heroes
RAY ROBERTSON

A History of Forgetting
CAROLINE ADDERSON

The Camera Always Lies
HUGH HOOD

Canada Made Me
NORMAN LEVINE

Vital Signs (a reSet Original)
JOHN METCALF

For Hannah —

happy reading —

John Metcalf

Vital Signs

JOHN METCALF

BIBLIOASIS

Library and Archives Canada Cataloguing in Publication

Metcalf, John, 1938–
[Novellas]
Vital signs : collected novellas / John Metcalf.

(reSet books)
Issued in print and electronic formats.
ISBN 978-1-77196-052-6 (paperback). — ISBN 978-1-77196-053-3 (ebook)

I. Title.

PS8576.E83V5 2016 C813'.54 C2015-907398-7
C2015-907399-5

Readied for the press by Daniel Wells
Copy-edited by Emily Donaldson
Cover and text design by Gordon Robertson

Biblioasis acknowledges the ongoing financial support of the Government of Canada through the Canada Council for the Arts, Canadian Heritage, the Canada Book Fund; and the Government of Ontario through the Ontario Arts Council.

PRINTED AND BOUND IN CANADA

MIX
Paper from responsible sources
FSC® C004071

METCALF THE NOVELLAIST

by Jeet Heer

FOR LOVERS of well-wrought fiction, a small community that always has to huddle together to fend off extinction, John Metcalf is known as a short-story writer and man of letters. The two facets of his achievement are inextricable, since he's not only written such classic stories as "The Years in Exile" and "Single Gents Only" but has also been tireless in championing the short story as a form with its own special properties and excellence.

Through the dozens of anthologies he's edited, through his eloquent and forceful critical advocacy, and most especially through his mentoring and editing of scores of short-story writers ranging from Caroline Adderson to Stephen Heighton to Kathleen Winter, Metcalf has done more than anyone to make the short story the defining Canadian literary genre, a form both innovative and worthy of an international readership. Like his peers Alice Munro, Mavis Gallant, and Clark Blaise, Metcalf has written stories that will be read as long as humanity cherishes prose narrative. But he is also articulate about why the short story is the perfect laboratory for narrative experiment, the form where the immemorial human need to tell tales can be fused with the most advanced techniques of linguistic inventiveness.

To see John Metcalf simply as a short-story writer, however, is to sell him short; to define his best work, you have to resort to an awkward nonce word: novellaist.

The novella is Metcalf's métier, the form where his fiction-making facility finds its fullest fruition. This book, gathering together his entire output in the form, is essential for appreciating not just how fine a writer Metcalf can be but also how alert he is to the possibilities of literary form, finding, as he does, in the boundaries of the novella, an ample field for his various gifts—verbal precision, comic performance, narrative juxtaposition—not just to flourish but to create a beautiful completeness, the way the flowers in a well-tended garden exist not in isolation but in the service of the whole.

The novella is a betwixt-and-between form, sitting halfway between the novel and the short story. Novels have long been the most popular narrative vessel, engaging readers in an extended immersive experience. But the pleasures novels offer, more often than not, come at a price. Henry James's indictment of the Victorian triple-decker as "large, loose baggy monsters" applies, alas, to all but the finest novels. Masterpieces aside, the novel's cardinal sin is that its narrative length leads to verbal slackness, longueurs, loss of focus. It's a rare novel that earns every word it uses.

Conversely, as Metcalf has taught us, the strength of the short story is that it can be perfect, just as poems can be perfect. In a great story, every paragraph, every sentence, every phrase, every word, exists for a reason. Yet the short story's very shortness can also be problematic, depriving it of the expansiveness and amplitude of the novel, the novel's ability to encompass multiple perspectives and the interplay of tones.

For Metcalf, the novella provides the best of both worlds: the linguistic exactness of the story and the broad canvas of the novel. As he wrote in his 2003 memoir *An Aesthetic Under-*

ground, "The novella form fascinated me because it could be tightly controlled—page by page—as a short story could, yet at the same time was expansive enough to allow for theatrical effects. Individual scenes could be built with lyric intensity and then juxtaposed with broad comedy. Broad comedy could be tempered to become intensely moving. Writing novellas was a particularly joyful kind of playing."

The novella has had few masters. Among the classic writers, there is Melville and Conrad. More recently, and much closer to Metcalf's own writing practices, Alice Munro and Mavis Gallant, two "short-story writers" whose peak work was done in the novella form. Munro and Metcalf have been reading each others' work for decades, and the literary scholars of the future will find a rich topic in studying how their careers cross-fertilized. In particular, one of Metcalf's innovations in "Private Parts"—the unreliable narrator who is aware of his own unreliability—might well have informed Munro's masterful "Meneseteung." But more broadly, Metcalf and Munro have both given us a new kind of novella—not the extended "tale" of Melville and Conrad but something closer to a condensed novel, a work that is polyphonic in the way of the best novels but with a short-story-like tautness.

Literary forms are constraints that liberate: they push a writer to discipline language and narrative to maximum effect. Just as Shakespeare's language bloomed in the rule-bound enclosure of the sonnet, the novella has been an enabling form for Metcalf, allowing him to hone his craft at both a micro and macro level.

The micro level is language itself, the macro level the shape of the unfolding story. For Metcalf, steeped in high modernism, fiction isn't only a matter of *le mot juste*, but of language at the even more molecular level of syllable and punctuation. To be a true Metcalf reader you have to savour what he does with commas and italics, as well as with words. Here is a typical Metcalf paragraph from "Polly Ongle":

> It was Happy Hour in the bar on the main floor of the Chateau Laurier. People drifting in were pantomiming distress and amazement as they eased out of sodden raincoats or used the edge of their hands to wipe rain from eyebrows and foreheads. Men were seating themselves gingerly and loosening from their knees the cling of damp cloth; women were being casually dangerous with umbrellas. Necks were being mopped with handkerchiefs; spectacles were being polished with bar napkins.

This is a typical Metcalf paragraph, not one with particularly heightened language or a set-piece. Yet attend to how much craft there is even in a paragraph devoted to simple stage setting.

There's the puckish play of the adjectives: "gingerly" is carefully placed after "men were seating themselves" so as to mimic the very movement being described. "Casually dangerous" is impishly oxymoronic.

There's the texture of the words themselves. The phrase "loosening from their knees the cling of damp cloth" has a nice dance between the "n" and "m" sounds with the hard-c sound of "cling" and "cloth" which, to my ears, evokes the distant clang of cutlery heard at a restaurant. The "i" in "cling" and the "a" and "p" in "damp" capture *in sound* the lifting of damp cloth away from skin.

There's the delicious evocativeness of the diction: "pantomiming," "sodden," and "mopped" all sharpening our perception.

Finally, the use of the semi-colon in the last two sentences gives an orderly shape. The semi-colons serve as a scale, suggesting a balanced symmetry of nouns and actions on either side ("men" balanced with "women" and "necks" balanced with "spectacles," for example). "Men" and "Women" are the camera in the middle shot; "necks" and "spectacles" are the camera in the close-up. The close-up *intensifies* what is seen—the realness of the rainstorm they have escaped.

What this random paragraph of everyday Metcalf shows is that even when being casual he is hyper-alert; demands that we pay as much attention to his language as he has devoted to its writing.

The Metcalf who writes with microscopic exactness is easier to analyze than the macro Metcalf who gives equal care to how he structures his narratives. To talk about structure is to talk, in part, about plot. And Metcalf is very careful in these stories to surprise his readers; surprises that only the most knavish critic would spoil.

In lieu of summarizing Metcalf's plots, I will offer a few suggestions with regard to how readers might best appreciate their structures. In reading, and especially in rereading these novellas, pay attention to shifts in tone and repetition of events and characters. The tonal variety of the novella is one of the chief reasons Metcalf finds the form so empowering. He can be incredibly funny, creating characters and scenes that rival those of his heroes Evelyn Waugh and P.G. Wodehouse. But in all these novellas, antic scenes of merriment and mischief are juxtaposed with and enriched by other scenes that are more somber, ruminative, and inward, that display Wordsworthian "Intimations of Immortality" seen in the beauty of the natural world.

His ability to contrast moods speaks to Metcalf's deepest feelings about what it is to be alive. Alice Munro once wrote, "John Metcalf often comes as close to the baffling, painful comedy of human experience as a writer can get." The inherent contradiction of "painful comedy" is acute: for Metcalf life is both a comedy and a tragedy. The novella allows him to show both sides of the equation.

It's when he's dealing with intimacy that Metcalf is at his most painfully comedic. Indeed, all of these novellas are about coupling: the way men and women come together and separate, the loneliness that causes us to seek the warmth of another person's flesh, and the loss caused by distance and separation.

John Metcalf is one of the finest writers of our time and these novellas are his finest work.

PRIVATE PARTS

A Memoir

PART ONE

1

One of my earliest sexual memories, more vivid and perhaps more important than any subsequent sexual memory, is of my Uncle Fred and the idiot. I must have been then six or seven years old, evacuated to my Uncle Fred's farm in what was then called Cumberland to escape the bombing of the Yorkshire industrial town in which my father worked. Auntie Lizzie even then seemed strange to me. She had what people called a "nutcracker" face, a nose and chin that threatened to meet, and the chin barbed with bristles. The countless farm cats fled under sofa and settle to escape her harsh caress. Her voice was so dreadful it could arrest the agricultural activities of men two and a half fields away. I learned years later that it was to escape Aunt Lizzie that my Uncle Fred trudged daily to the top field where he sat for hours smoking his pipe in a hen hut. It was there that they found him face-down dead in the litter and hen shit.

Looking back now to those childhood times, I see their faces wrinkled and seamed, Uncle Fred always in corduroy worn smooth, Aunt Lizzie in faded pinafores and laceless, clopping shoes, her hands permanently reddened, the pair of them like illustrations in a history of rural life. They are, in later memory, like the crabbed, spiky drawings of Edward Ardizzone.

Whenever I think of them, words come to my mind of whose meanings I am not exactly sure, haunting words like "fustian" and "coulter," "stoup" and "flitch," words redolent of another age. It seems scarcely possible that as submarines cruised beneath the seas and tanks ground forward over the rubble of Europe, as Dresden burned and Hiroshima melted, my Uncle Fred and his day labourers were leading in the cornfields with scythes, stooking sheaves, and the women bringing dinner down to the field in cloth-covered baskets and bearing the earthenware pitchers of beer over the stubble. It is a scene that Brueghel painted.

Uncle Fred's farm lay in the lush dairy land of the Eden valley from which rose the wild and endless fells whose lower slopes were grazed by sheep but whose heights climbed to thinning bracken, boulders, bare rock, and the circling hawks.

That farm and farmyard enchanted me, the cathedral gloom of the vast barn where the silent tractor stood, its wheels nearly as high as my head, machines with spikes and tines and gleaming discs, the workbench with old biscuit tins with pretty ladies on the lids—tins full of nuts and bolts, washers, nails, screws, staples, cotter pins, fuses, spark plugs, coils of special wire. I would rummage there for hours, bend things in the vice, pound nails. The feedshed, too, was gloomy but a warm gloom, rich with the smells of meal and bran, metal scoops in the rolled-down sacks, rolled down like Aunt Lizzie's lisle stockings, crusted paddles for stirring the mash.

I thought that lisle stockings, a word I'd heard Aunt Lizzie say, were somehow connected with Golden Syrup, a green and gold tin with a lion lying down on it and lots of flies buzzing around the lion and on the tin it said Tate and Lyle's Golden Syrup: "Hold your noise!" my Uncle often said when I spoke at table asking questions, so I did not ask but I thought that stockings and syrup had some obvious connection that everyone understood in that world where bombs were falling and my father was being brave.

And I promised myself that when they'd finished evacuating me, I would go back to the bomb world where you could watch the soldiers marching, and when I was there I would understand everything.

I loved my Uncle Fred but I was frightened of him too. He killed things and didn't care and he sometimes bellowed and slapped my head. He called Gyp, the one-eyed collie, "Bugger-Lugs" and when the cows leaned against him as he was milking, the milk *rin . . . rin . . . rin* in the pail, he called them "whoring buggers" and sometimes he did very long shouts when they kicked the pail over, shouts that always started "You would, would you, you shitarse! Get over you cockstruck twat, you . . ." I tried to learn them and practised them in bed.

But I was confused by this, too, because he never said interesting things near Auntie Lizzie, bad things, and he was a Methodist laypreacher, and on Sundays would put on a suit and shirt and tie, which on him looked as preposterous as a dress and hat looked on Aunt Lizzie, and conducted fervent services for small congregations in the parlours of neighbour farms.

When he was in a good mood, when he'd got the tractor mended, or the vet had been and it wasn't mastitis, he always used to sing the same song very loudly and sometimes he sang it over and over and sometimes he just hummed most of it but burst out with single lines of words.

From the oppressive power of sin
My struggling spirit free;

Perfect righteousness bring in,
Unspotted purity;

Then with a final heave on the wrench, a final twist of the screwdriver, or the last bash on the shackle pin, he'd stand back and bellow,

Speak, and all this war shall cease,
And sin shall give its raging o'er:
Love me freely, seal my peace,
And bid me sin no more.

But he frightened me also, because his jokes and tricks were rough and sometimes painful. He it was who always squirted me with milk when stripping the cows, who urged me to touch electric fences, who advised me to wash paint off my face with petrol drawn from the tractor so that I had to be taken to the doctor for ointment, who put salt instead of sugar on my porridge, who encouraged me to pick up the body of a fox he'd shot so that I stank for a week of its musk and suffered daily scrubbings in the tin tub in front of the fire with Aunt Lizzie's emery wash cloths.

Uncle Fred employed an idiot, the son of a widow woman who lived in the village. The idiot's name was Bobby. I was frightened of him because of his potato face, and I could never understand anything he said. Uncle Fred employed him, I realize now, more from charity than for his usefulness. Mucking out the stables and balancing the wheelbarrow on its perilous trip to the midden took him all the day.

Bobby stank. He never changed his clothes. He always wore the same boots, green cord trousers, leggings, and khaki battledress top, on which his mother had stitched all the buttons, crests, badges, and ribbons that the Italian prisoners of war who worked on my Uncle's and neighbouring farms had given him. They had taught him to march up and down the yard with his pitchfork on his shoulder like a rifle and he liked to do that more than mucking-out and when Uncle Fred saw him he'd yell, "Get out of that, you girt softie! Get down the barn, you daft lummox!" and then he'd yell, "Move yourself, bollock-brains!" but the funny thing was that he called him all the same things when he was pleased with him, when the barn was finished early or he hadn't tipped over the wheelbarrow in the yard.

Uncle Fred's Italians slept in bunks in one of the barns. He called them all Albert. He was fond of them and they of him, and after the war two of them refused repatriation and stayed on with him until he died. Uncle Fred had lent them a twelve-bore shotgun to shoot rabbits and they let me go with them. They shot thrushes and blackbirds, too, and ate them and Uncle Fred said foreigners were different.

I knew my Uncle was a man of power because he preached to other grown-ups on Sundays and told them what to do but I learned one day that he was so powerful that even Policemen obeyed him.

We were doing something to the tractor and I was holding a tin can of grease with a stick in it when into the yard cycled the Policeman.

"It has come to my attention, Mr. Moore," he said, "that you have given a shotgun to them Eyetalians."

"Is that right?" said my Uncle Fred.

"Them, they're the Enemy," said the Policeman.

"Is that right?" said my Uncle Fred again.

"You have supplied arms and ammunition," said the Policeman, "to the enemies of England."

"Mr. Moore?" said my Uncle. "*Mr. Moore!*" he shouted. "I've been Fred to you since your arse was wet, George Voules, so you bugger off and play blackouts or I'll be having a word with your mum."

And then the big Policeman got on his bike and my Uncle started to walk away and then he turned and shouted.

“At least they were *fighting* before they were taken!”

And then when the big Policeman was at the yard gate, my Uncle Fred shouted,

“Flat feet, my arse!”

Behind the farmhouse is an apple tree in full blossom. Not a simple apple tree—an apple tree explosive in blossom, such an apple tree as Samuel Palmer saw. Beside the tree, a brook runs down behind the house, across the bottom fields, through the bed of wild watercress, to join the River Eden. Its rock-strewn shallowness and sound widens near the apple tree into a silent pool. The sun is bright. It is not hot but Uncle Fred insists it is. He persuades Bobby to unlace his boots and paddle in the pool. He winks at me. The joke, the wink seems to say, is coming soon. Uncle Fred next persuades Bobby to take off all his clothes and play in the water. Bobby struggles awkwardly with buttons and sleeves and the second he is naked Uncle Fred snatches away the clothes and runs off shouting with laughter towards the yard.

Bobby is making his angry face and shouting angry-sounding things. He is pointing towards the yard and he is crying. I cannot understand a word. I feel guilty and sorry but it is one of Uncle Fred’s jokes and Uncle Fred is grown-up and preaches and shouts at Policemen.

I am staring at Bobby’s thing. It hangs down from a bush of black hair and it reaches nearly to his knee. It is as fat as my arm. His ballbag is huge like the Hereford in the dark stall.

I stare and stare.

* * *

“WHEN WE HEAR the words *penis* and *vagina*, the pictures we have in our minds (known as *mental images*) tell us a lot about our true feelings,” writes Dr. Ethel Fawce, author of *Sex and the Adjusted You*. “These *mental images,*” she goes on, “can be approving or disapproving. Favourable female childhood images of the penis may be of: a banana, an ice cream cone, a mushroom, a musical instrument, or a Tootsie Roll." But what of me, whose *mental image* is of Bobby?

There's an essential rightness about this image for me, brought up as I was a hardcore Yorkshire Nonconformist. Not for me sly serpents whispering intelligences, the temptations of an Eve, but a subhuman figure in the Garden with a cock like a malignant growth.

The world of my parents and of most of the adults with whom I came in contact was pious, sour, and thin. They had married better not to burn—a fire soon damped. Gripeguts Wesley was their God.

I have a very early memory of myself a tiny child, standing in the back garden of that Yorkshire manse gazing upon rows of crucifixes, which were stuck in a special plot of earth near the door of the coal cellar. I made the crosses with kindling. Pinned to each cross was a worm. They wriggled for a long time, but then they just drooped, and then they went flat and brittle.

Poor Billy Blake, so misunderstood. To those choirs that sang in chapel and tabernacle, those grimy, mean, industrial towns of the north of England with their fortitude under the grey rain were Jerusalem.

My evacuation was of short duration.

When I came back I was given a gasmask with a Mickey Mouse face on it.

Cod-liver oil in huge bottles was supplied free of charge to children; as with all else, my mother equated nastiness with virtue.

Our way of life was like the enactment of a set of improving proverbs. Early to bed and early to rise, we wasted not, we stitched in time, took care of the pence, made sure our hands were never idle, received the reward of virtue which is its own. "Cleanliness," as Wesley remarked in one of his sermons, "is indeed next to Godliness"—and ours was carbolic.

My mother's conversation was a compendium of homely cliché; our drink was Adam's ale or "the cup that cheers," all activities were powered by "elbow grease," all locomotion by "Shanks' pony"; if at first we didn't succeed, we tried and tried and tried again; supper was always Hobson's choice.

At some ungodly hour in the morning, my mother daily holystoned the front doorstep and polished the brass doorknocker and the brass flap of the letterbox. If we were to set out on an infrequent journey, she would arise in the morning dark to prepare sandwiches because to eat in a restaurant was to waste money and she would then clean the oven and polish the toilet bowl, because, as she always said, were we to be killed in a car crash or derailment, she wouldn't like people thinking she hadn't kept a clean house.

The war years, with their strawberry jam made of turnips and their powdered eggs, were, for my mother, the happiest years of her life. The suffering was total. There was grim joy in her response to an inadequate diet and perpetual cold, to stretching out meagre scraps into meals and "making do." Something went out of her when rationing ended.

People in my world actually used such expressions as "Antichrist," "The Great Beast," and "Whore of Babylon." "Scarlet Woman" was sometimes Rome and "Whore of Babylon" was sometimes Rome and "Scarlet Woman" was sometimes not Rome but Mrs. Henderson who "carried on" with soldiers. The Book of Revelation is the source of much Nonconformist imagery; its threats of apocalyptic destruction appeal to the Nonconformist temperament. I naturally understood it to be an anti-Catholic diatribe. My world of missionary boxes, Sunday School, and sin was violent in its anti-Catholicism. Faith versus Good Works, the Thirty-nine Articles, and the fallacy of Transubstantiation, were as ABC to me. But I soon penetrated this historical obfuscation and grasped that the essence of the wickedness was that Catholicism pretended to *forgive*. Which was not *only* wicked but *silly*. For God alone could forgive and the only person I knew who claimed to have been forgiven was a man who stood up in church and said so during one of my father's sermons but my father said later the man was drunk.

In my world, guilt was personal and permanent; atonement, though demanded, was understood to be a hollow gesture.

The world beyond my world was made up of drunkards, fornicators, lewd people, those who used the King's English incorrectly, backsliders, vulgar people, sots, adulterers, those who took the Name of the Lord in Vain, who ate things in the streets, were spendthrift, who used foul language, and who carried on.

I naturally imagined Rome to be the centre of these activities and even then envied the Allied troops who were actually there seeing it all.

The abstract meanings of "the Flesh" did not have to be explained to me. The antithesis between Spirit and Flesh was in the very air I breathed. The Flesh existed to be subdued; this was accomplished by a wide range of prohibitions: silence, soap, whitened doorsteps at dawn, and whatever other mortifications my mother could invent.

The lewdest story my mother ever told, and that perhaps when I was fifteen or sixteen, was of standing beside a man in a bus queue during the war and chatting about the previous night's raid. The man said:

"I were that frightened, Mrs., you couldn't have got a needle up me bum."

What it was about this story that appealed to her I don't quite know; it couldn't have been the humour.

I retain vivid, pre-evacuation memories of our dog, Sandy, on whom I lavished all my love. My mother disliked dogs because she said they were dirty; my father said dogs were good for children and were not dirty; my mother said he didn't have to clean up after them or bear their habits; my father regarded her and then retired to the silence of his study. My mother could invest an apparently innocent word like "habits" with such intensity that even if her meaning was not clear to me; her loathing nipped questions in the bud.

If Sandy, lying on her mat, raised a hind leg to lick what my mother called her "parts," she was immediately shooed out of doors.

One morning I noticed spots of blood on the kitchen floor. Sandy was not spanked for this, which made me curious. At the same time, I noticed that her thing was more visible: red, swollen like a tulip.

I hoped it would heal up.

"It is her Time," said my mother mysteriously.

During her Time she was not allowed to go outside except on the leash but one day I forgot and she escaped to gambol with the next door mongrel. Later, I saw them on the lawn fighting, pumping, heaving, tongues lolling. I ran to find my mother who was vacuuming, somewhere on the third floor. By the time she arrived, Sandy and Rex were no longer fighting but were standing disconsolate in the middle of the lawn with their behinds mysteriously stuck together. Sandy, seeing us, tried to pull towards us but she was stuck to Rex and when she pulled, Rex yowled as if someone had stepped on his paw and Sandy whimpered. I knew they were in pain, there had been fighting, blood, and I didn't understand why my mother did not do whatever had to be done to help.

"It's too late," she said tonelessly.

This incident made me very anxious, but I knew better than to ask questions: this, I somehow knew, was the World of the Flesh.

At exactly this time, it might have been that very week, I found a hedgehog in the garden and put it in a big cardboard box to keep as a pet. My mother would not allow it in the house because she said it was dirty. She shook a box of DDT over it until it was white. Next morning it was dead.

These events somehow fused in my mind.

Much later than this, after I'd come back from being evacuated, I became aware of the other meaning of "self," and managed, in a confused way, to understand the nature of the Holy Ghost.

Every bath night, my mother washed me and then rinsed off all the soap and then washed my hair and when she'd finished, she'd hand me the cloth and say,

"Wash yourself."

When she returned to the bathroom minutes later, she would brutally towel me until I was bright red and then give me the towel, saying as she left the room,

"Dry yourself."

I understood the Trinity as being three people who were not actually people but parts of one person. I understood "yourself" in the commands to wash and dry as meaning one's thing, one's parts. The Holy Ghost was part of God and I felt I now knew *which* part.

And it was unfortunate that it was at precisely this time that I heard of something called The Sin Against the Holy Ghost. I was very anxious about this sin, not being able to discover its exact nature. All I could learn was that it was the worst sin of all, a sin too horrendous to even talk about. The one subject never talked about in my house was "that kind of thing," and it therefore seemed obvious that sex and The Sin Against the Holy Ghost were one and the same thing.

And I had done it.

Had miniature erections like the dog, seen Bobby naked and bestial, played with myself, said words, and given a girl called Marie a threepenny bit to let me watch her pee.

I knew myself to be unforgivable, of the damned, one from whom God's Face was averted for eternity.

This burden of guilt and conviction of sin tortured me for years—dirtiness, death, disapproval, impurity—and eventually became the front line of the ravaged battlefield of my adolescence.

(This will not do. The paragraphs flow too evenly, the sequence of statements rounds off the subject too neatly, leading too comfortably to the next asterisk and the beginning of another sequence of anecdote and reflection.

To reread these last paragraphs nauseates me. They remind me of cute stories of children mistakenly praying "Harold Be Thy Name," such anecdotes as grace the pages of *Reader's Digest.*

And what can you understand by my use of the word "tortured"?

Did you think I mean—"troubled"?

The fault is mine. I have pictured my mother as a joyless puritan. But this is not the whole truth. The fault lies in my writing, feelings hidden behind humour, pain distanced by genteel irony. The truth is ugly and otherwise. My father was merely eccentric; my mother was mad.

Her mind festered. It was a pit of unimaginable filth—a contagion I did not escape. I hated her. I am happy she is dead.

Had I not been stronger, had I not battled her every day of my life, I could well have joined my brothers in institutions the world over, those who mutilated their genitals with shards of glass, or worse, the ones who came in judgement and cut off tits with butchers' knives, carved cunts with cleavers.)

As I grew older and sinned more, as my reading revealed to me a larger world than the loveless world of chapel and grey rain, I vowed that my life would be filled with laughter, beautiful women, warm flesh; my life would be lived in the sun.

It's a common enough story.

At eighteen I left home forever.
At twenty-one I emigrated to Canada.

* * *

AT ABOUT the age of seven I had my first encounter with Art—an event central to this memoir and as dramatic as Paul's conversion on the Damascus Road.

Art played no part in the life of my parents or their society. The only occasion vaguely artistic was the annual performance of the *Messiah*; for this, professional soloists were imported and backed by several choirs combined. The music was supplied by a merging of brass bands. I remember a colliery band and the uniforms of the Fire Brigade.

The visual arts were not encouraged; even the old masters had too much thigh and breast about them for my mother's taste. There may have been the occasional *Laughing Cavalier* but walls were usually decorated with anonymous landscapes and calendars.

One morning my father had left the newspaper lying on the breakfast table. There was a photograph in it of a painting that had just been cleaned of the dinge and varnish of centuries and which revealed that the naked lady was not merely pointing her breast at the sky but was squirting from it a jet of milk which, as it streamed across the canvas, became stars in the Milky Way.

I asked my mother what the picture was in the paper for.

"It's a picture by an old painter that's in a museum."

"Is it beautiful?"

"Handsome is as handsome does," said my mother.

She took the paper away.

"Why is the lady...?"

"If you ask me," she said, "and I don't mind who hears me say it, people who painted that sort of thing were no better than they should be."

She rattled the dishes in the sink.

"I wouldn't give *that sort of thing* house room."

She sniffed.

"I wouldn't give you tuppence for the lot of them."

But of all the arts, the theatre was the most wicked; the word "actress" carried much the same suggestiveness as the word "model" did a few years ago. Wesley had fulminated against the theatre in the spirit of his puritan forebears and the historical disapproval was still strong in the north. Not only was my family Methodist, the whole area was an ardent Methodist stronghold. The town in which we lived was only a few miles from Haworth Parsonage and the moors. Mrs. Gaskell, in her *Life of Charlotte Brontë*, described among the books at Haworth "some mad Methodist Magazines full of miracles and apparitions, and preternatural warnings, ominous dreams, and frenzied fanaticism . . ."

A later biographer, Margaret Lane, wrote: "On the Brontë children the effects of such intimacy with Methodism were various. . . On Anne it laid its most unhappy behest, infecting her with the morbid fear of personal damnation which darkened her youth. . . On Branwell the pressure of so much religious emphasis was to destroy belief"

And my intimacy with Methodism was more intimate than theirs.

I was once taken to a pantomime at Christmas in Leeds and I remember being removed tearfully halfway through because my mother said it was vulgar and full of "that sort of thing"; I had liked it very much indeed because one of the Broker's Men had played a trombone solo and with every note his trousers had fallen lower and lower and he was wearing red underpants with big flowers on them.

There existed, however, varieties of approved entertainment that were carried on in church halls and basements. Documentary films about wildlife, the postal service, or deep-sea fishing were sometimes shown; professional itinerants such as Grey Owl sometimes appeared; missionaries gave lectures with magic-lantern slides of lepers. These church halls also provided a fourth-rate circuit for professional monologuists, a profession surely now extinct.

I can remember the monologuist who brought the certainty of art into my life. I can even remember his name; it was Mr. Montague. A large, florid, middle-aged man wearing the kind of checked suit of which characters in English novels say, "No gentleman would wear a suit like that."

He came to our house for tea. He was a flamboyant and welcome change from the usual pursed and mealy visitors such as Sanitary Inspectors and Church Stewards. Across his paunch was a looped gold chain. His voice was boomy and fruity. He called my mother "Dear Lady," which I thought was very grand, and he called my father "Sir" and he asked me if I found shaving painful. When offered a ninth or tenth scone, he patted the wide check of his waistcoat and said,

"Spare, Dear Lady, these grey hairs."

We later conducted him to the church hall. Everything was ordinary; the same boys and girls, the same ladies of the church who made much of me because I was my father's son, the same stage curtains that didn't quite close, a stage familiar to me because in dressing gown and tea towel headcloth I had trodden it as Third Shepherd or Orient King.

But Mr. Montague, when he appeared, was a Mr. Montague quite different from the Mr. Montague of the tea table. He was wearing mutton-chop whiskers, violent eyebrows, and what must have been a smoking jacket. He did different people by moving about the stage in different voices. There was a lady's voice and a terrible, stern father's voice, and a younger man's voice. The story, I had been told, was called *The Barretts of Wimpole Street*. It seemed magical to me that when he was the father you could see quite clearly the non-existent lady he was speaking to, and when he was the lady you could see him standing where he'd been before he'd moved to become the lady.

I was entranced. Any sense of being in an audience vanished. Only he and I existed. Suddenly he began to pace and shout terribly at the lady who was frightened too, and I felt so frightened I felt sick. Then I was. On Miss Moseby. Then I fainted clear away.

I was carried out and revived and afterwards I was taken back to the closet where the hymn books and extra tea cups were stored, and which he was using as a dressing room. Beads of sweat were standing on his face. I watched him peeling off the whiskers and wiping off the grease paint.

I don't remember his saying anything to me or my saying anything to him, but I knew from that moment on that when I was grown up I would be like him, become other people, be applauded, be magical. I didn't know how this would happen or what had to be done to make it happen, but standing in that cramped closet where his smell of sweat and vanishing cream was stronger than the smell of the maroon hymn books I was filled with certainty that happen it would.

* * *

EVERY FIVE YEARS or so my father was required to move to a new church and usually to a new circuit. Shortly after Mr. Montague, we moved from the north of England to the south, from baths pronounced "baths" to "barthes," a more gentle climate.

These years were marked by other transitions, from elementary to secondary school, to an intensification of the warfare with my mother, to the first counter-moves of my self-shaping.

Because my father was a Minister of Religion (the words I had to write on forms at school, or worse, say in front of the class) I was forced to demonstrate that I was not easy prey. I was perhaps the only boy in the schoolyard who never pulled a punch; I once tried to finish off a fallen opponent with a rock but some older boys grabbed me in time. Nor was this wickedness merely assumed; I seemed drawn towards all that was bad and sinful. The word "drunkard" had the same sort of allure for me that the word "buccaneer" might have for a normal child.

As complaints trickled in, fist-fights, raids on fruit trees, smoking, goldfish speared from an ornamental pond, my mother wept and prayed and assured me that I had been born for the gallows. At the end of each tearful session, she made me kneel with her and pray aloud for salvation.

In sexual terms, these years from nine to eleven were marked by an increase in masturbation and guilt. Sin had claimed me utterly. My most intense desire at that time was to be able to ejaculate. I have vague memories of group masturbation though this had no particular homosexual overtones. Certain older boys would demonstrate for those younger but much in the spirit of an old-timer passing on wisdom to a greenhorn.

My two most vivid memories of those years are both rather odd. One is of a boy called Malcolm, two or three years older than us, in the second form of the grammar school, who for a fee—candy, a penny, a general whipround—would demonstrate how when he came, sperm appeared not only from the tip of his organ *but from a hole in the side halfway up*.

When released from chores, homework, and other such nonsense, all the boys in my area took their bicycles and foregathered in a small wood about a mile from my house. There, by the ruins of an old house, we smoked cigarettes, practised throwing our sheath knives into trees, wrestled, gossiped, set fires, and swapped stolen merchandise. Malcolm smoked cheroots.

Regularly, about every three days, the local pervert appeared, much to our joy. What benefit he derived from these performances was beyond our comprehension but we were grateful to him.

The place where we played was in a clearing about halfway down a steep path. The top end of the path was close to the main road; the bottom end, screened by bushes, led out onto a quiet residential street. The path itself was a winding, beaten track, bumpy, crossed by tree roots, rutted. It was dangerous at speed and one of our more frightening games was to time bicycle runs down it.

The pervert's ritual was unchanging. He would trudge down the path wheeling his bicycle until he was about a hundred yards above us. Then he would prop his bicycle up on its little stand, turn his back, then turn again, mount, and pedal furiously down the steep hill. Just before he was level with us, he would swerve from the track onto the grass at high speed, coming to within five yards of us. By this time he was steering with one hand on the handlebars. In his other hand he gripped his member, which he attempted to wave.

Then he would veer back onto the path and wobble down the hill to crash down through the bushes at the bottom and debouch onto Gladstone Avenue.

His progress was unsteady and hazardous, rather like the charge of an inept knight whose visor has suddenly obscured vision.

When he neared us, we'd shout,

"Let's have a look at it, then!" and "My sister's is bigger than that!"

And as he careered away from us almost out of control down the bumpy hill, he'd yell, "You bastards!" and then, faintly, *Rotten bastards*, and then the crash as he engaged the bushes.

* * *

HAD THERE BEEN any truth in the myths about masturbation, I and all the other boys I knew would have been blind, deaf, dumb, hairy as the Ainu, and so debilitated as to have needed hospitalization. We dismissed these bromides as fit only for Boy Scouts. It was, however, an article of faith among us that an emission was the equivalent in exertion to a ten-mile run. Some boys did a hundred miles a day.

We masturbated, not for fun, but from overwhelming need for release. At school, and by now I was in the first form of grammar school, boys masturbated at recess, lunch hour, during the welcome darkness of educational films, some even, driven by indescribable urges, during lessons. A glance revealed those so engaged, their faces red from exertion and frustration. It was difficult to sustain the necessary rhythm and increasing speed and concentration if some fool decided to pace the aisles or ask questions about the staple products of China.

Those who had achieved success were also immediately recognizable; their faces softened into that dreamy expression which I've noted in infants who are completing a bowel movement.

Masturbation was known as "wanking" or "wanking off"; one young master endeared himself to us by pretended pedantry. He affected not to know the meaning of "wank" and always addressed a boy called Stoughton, a frenzied self-abuser, in the following way:

"Stoughton. Your attention, please. Can you enlighten us as to the nature of the feudal levy? Or may I, as your chums appear to do, address you as 'Wanker'?"

This compulsive masturbation was not, as far as I can recall, related to any external object; it was not accompanied by sexual fantasies or even imaginings of sexual intercourse. It was more in the nature of a raging unscratchable itch.

Some idea of the state might be suggested by observing a colony of monkeys.

At home, and in privacy, apart from the usual masturbations before going to sleep and on awakening, we all devised more elaborate forms of gratification. Some boys coated their penises and hands with a rich soap lather which was pleasing but had one drawback; soap was likely to enter one's organ so that ejaculation was accompanied by a stinging pain much like getting soap in one's eye. Other boys used Vaseline but it was difficult to remove afterwards. Pond's Vanishing Cream and hand-lotions were other favourites.

But as time went by, these solitary acts were turned to focus on sexual images of the outer world. Our main source of these was a magazine which could be rented for three pence per lunch hour from a newsagent's near the school. The newsagent was called Mr. Albert. The magazine was called *Health and Efficiency* and featured photographs of ungainly, nude people having picnics and playing ping-pong.

It was, perhaps, these images which drove us to the desire to stick our members *into* things. Vacuum cleaners were widely discussed and I went so far as to switch ours on one day when my mother was out shopping, but the roar and pluck of it against the cloth of my trousers frightened me. One boy I knew described to me putting his organ into a thermos flask full of warm tea. He had done this while his member was only semi-erect but the warmth rising from the tea and the constriction, and what he described as a kind of suction, aroused him in a second and he was agonizingly trapped in the flask's narrow neck. His peril was doubled because his parents were upstairs, his sister playing just outside, and he was in the kitchen. Another boy in my class swore by oranges. Another inserted himself between the furry legs held tight of a younger brother's teddy bear. One boy who played in the wood every night claimed to have fucked a hen but everyone knew he was a liar.

My own invention was the cardboard core of a toilet roll liberally coated inside with Brylcreem. The only drawback was that the Brylcreem was cold and took some time to warm up. Ejaculations were so fearsome and overwhelming that I sometimes tottered about the bathroom close to fainting.

These acts of ferocious self-abuse were of course attended by agonies of guilt. Every night I knelt by my bed, until I was cold and my knees hurt, asking Jesus' forgiveness for my lies, impurity, smoking, foul language, and constant abuse of the Temple of the Holy Spirit. And every night after my prayers, warmed, reviewing the day, my mind would fill with the image of the hairy thatch of a lady ping-pong player and my hand would sidle down to grasp my heated member and guilt would temporarily be driven out in a fresh burst of sweaty friction.

It was something of a problem to know what to do with what eventually must have amounted to pints of sperm. I tried handkerchiefs but what would happen if I forgot to remove it from under my pillow one morning and my mother discovered this yellow, rigid rag? And besides, it would have been difficult to explain the loss of a handkerchief every two or three days. Eventually I took to lifting the carpet round the edges and dribbling onto the felt underlay. My bedroom began to smell like the corridor of an extremely sleazy hotel. After some months the carpet and underlay were so tightly bonded that I began to worry about what possible explanation I could give when spring cleaning occurred.

* * *

SEXOLOGISTS STATE that males reach a peak of sexual energy at about eighteen, while females reach a peak of sexual desire in their thirties. Inaccurate, as usual. Boys achieve a peak of sexual energy at about thirteen or fourteen and by eighteen are, comparatively, quiescent, if not in decline. A boy of thirteen lives possessed, and I use the word in its biblical sense. Such words as "desire" or "lust" are pallid counters for the raw actuality. *Frenzy*, or *fever*, with their medical connotations, are more appropriate.

Everything in the physical world promoted excesses of deranged desire. Erections occurred without volition, induced by the vibrations of buses, store dummies being dressed in passing windows, the hair or an earring of the lady passenger in the seat in front. Washing hung out on a line sometimes proved unbearable. Even the texture of velvet, fresh-planed wood, or the curve of a highly glazed vase was enough to induce a voluptuous state necessitating a hasty trip to a locked bathroom.

We fought our way onto double-decker buses in order to be behind some particularly attractive woman in the hope that she might go upstairs and we could hang back on the platform perhaps to glimpse an ascending stocking seam, a froth of lacy slip or petticoat. We believed that women who wore highly shined shoes mirrored onto that polished surface visions of what was above and stared intently in the always-disappointed hope.

The words, "Thank you. Come again," from shop assistants caused us to reel about the pavement in paroxysms of hysterical laughter.

We stood as close as possible over seated women in the hope of being able to peer down blouses; when free of homework we haunted parks and wasteland at twilight in the hope of observing lovers engaged in sexual acts; in shops we asked to see items on high shelves; we peered at night through every lighted window. Housewives were stalked in the constricted aisles of G.R. Lumley and Son: Grocers, until the erection had to be concealed by stooping, as if in consideration over the Huntley and Palmers Assorted Creams, knowing that our naked lusts were marked on our brows for all to see. Being dragged through department stores by mothers where lingerie was flaunted and panties strewn about in casual heaps *while pretending to ignore it all* was anguish. Other boys' sisters and mothers were assessed; even grandmothers were eyed.

Ours was, of course, an all-male school. The girls' grammar school was about a mile away. We were forbidden to speak to them. The sight of these maidens in their plum-pudding hats and blazers, serge skirts, ankle socks and brown Oxfords drove us to the mindless frenzy of piranhas scenting blood. Our weekly trip to the nearby municipal baths was hallowed by the knowledge that the day before those very girls had used the same cubicles, hung their clothing on the same hooks, immersed their bodies in the same water. We could have drunk it, chlorine and all, in homage and desire.

The power of words need hardly be mentioned. The father of a boy who lived near me had a Navarre Society edition of the *Decameron* with sepia-tinted illustrations. Although I didn't like the boy, I cultivated him so that I could gaze at these pictures of wenches, breasts boiling over their bodices, seated on the knees of jolly friars. We gazed together, transfixed with lust. The word itself, "bodice," was only just bearable; such a word as "nipple" was beyond endurance; the black letters on the white page blurred into an aura, an aureole of shimmering desire so intense that further reading was impossible and we would stare into space bereft of our wits.

Much of my early reading was merely the search for erotic incident. Two fragments lodge in my mind yet. One, "he toyed with her bubbies" was presumably from some eighteenth-century novel. The other, "she made him free of her narrow loins," was the first of many intense pleasures given me by Evelyn Waugh.

Nightly, I crouched beneath the windowsill of my bedroom with my telescope trained on the bedroom window of a girl two houses away; once I saw her pick her nose.

I longed for a sister so that I could commit incest.

My masturbatory practices grew more fanciful and more desperate; I did it with a cylindrical pencil case filled with warm porridge and violated my younger brother's kaleidoscope.

On Sundays, I walked with my mother to church. In the winter, she wore fur gloves; in the summer, white gloves of some sort of netting stuff. I was embarrassed to be seen with her and these white gloves, worn even in extremes of heat, served as a focus for all my hatred of her and our way of life. Those net gloves were everything from which I wanted to escape.

On Sundays, she invariably smelled of lavender, a scent which even now makes me feel irritable, reminds me of piety and death.

At the close of each service, Holy Communion was celebrated. Although I always attended the sacrament I have never, in fact, partaken of it. During this most solemn rite I prayed with desperation to be forgiven my manifold sins and wickednesses. I evoked Christ's Passion, He who had died for *me*, but the harder I prayed the more my mind crowded with narrow loins, nipples, thighs, and buttocks. And although I was slowly coming to an active rejection of Christianity, I felt nervous about receiving the sacrament because, being in a state of sin, something bad *might* happen, and there was no point in going around *asking* for trouble. I had read in some anti-Semitic work of a woman in the Middle Ages who had contracted with some wicked Jews to steal a wafer by retaining it in her mouth until after mass and then handed it over to them; the Lord, however, caused the Host to turn to flesh and grow immediately to the roof of her mouth in a vast lump. My theory was that if you *hadn't* swallowed it you hadn't really *done* it, so it was my practice to swallow the wine (that didn't count; it was non-alcoholic grape juice) but push the cube of bread into my cheek and flatten it. This slimy mess I then coughed later into my handkerchief or spat out unnoticed.

On the walk home, my mother, softened perhaps by Communion, would often take my unwilling hand with her netted glove and say,

"You're still my little boy, aren't you?"

* * *

AT THE END of my first year in grammar school came my first Annual Report and the subsequent parent-teacher interview evening. My report was mediocre but my main fear was what might be said.

It seems, looking back, that I lived in a world of constant guilt, anxiety, and self-loathing; they were my mother's handmaidens. When I was a small boy, she had even managed to make me assume guilt for the sufferings of the Eighth Army. I had been playing with an outdoor tap in the garden, enjoying the splash and sparkle of it, and she'd grabbed me from behind, shaking me and shouting,

"You *wicked* boy! You're wasting water while soldiers are *dying* in the desert."

Even at the victory celebrations, when they lit a huge bonfire right in the middle of our street and the road melted and someone shot the grocer's shop, a secret worm of guilt gnawed at my pleasure.

My anxiety extended from myself to a distrust even of the inevitable processes of nature.

I had been convinced that in my case sperm would never flow.

I had despaired of growing pubic hair.

I had thought it likely that when my voice broke it would later break back again.

I was consciously kind to a ginger-coloured boy called Probert, who had an undescended testicle, because I felt that there but for the Grace of God.

But, always, it was my mother who instilled in me the deepest sense of failure and despair. I can still hear her voice in its litany of sorrows:

"You're breaking my heart."

"You were born for the gallows."

"How can we love a boy who . . ."

"I'll try to find it in my heart to forgive . . ."

"You're breaking Jesus' heart..."

"I never thought a boy of mine..."

"You've let down everyone who loves you..."

When my mother returned in the evening from the parent-teacher interviews, I was in bed reading. I heard her footsteps coming upstairs. She was wearing her Sunday clothes, a turquoise costume with a horrible turquoise hat which was bandaged with sort of turquoise net stuff and stuck through with a hatpin with a big turquoise lump on it. She said nothing. She closed the door.

Her face was set; she had that deadly calmness about her which is more frightening and dangerous than rage. She opened her handbag, groped in it without taking her eyes from mine, and then dropped on the coverlet a copy of *Health and Efficiency*.

It lay on my stomach like a lead block. It had been confiscated from me during music the week before.

She pulled up the chair and sat beside the bed.

In a quiet, almost conversational voice, she started. She could scarcely credit that a boy of hers had deliberately set fire to another boy in the metalwork shop. Why had I not told her I had broken the bench drill? I had broken the drill by disobeying orders. Rules were made to be obeyed. Had I considered what would have happened had the broken drill bit killed, maimed, or blinded another child? My father, impoverished as we were, would buy a new drill and a new apron for the boy whose apron was burned. Even if I did hate algebra so much, was it really manly to hide in the lavatories? Was that facing up to my responsibilities? Mr. Dodds had seemed evasive; was there anything I wished to tell her about geography? Anything I had not confessed? I would feel better if my conscience were clear. Her heart was sore that I had been detected smoking behind the bicycle sheds. Mastery of Latin could not be expected if I frittered away my time passing surreptitious notes. What was in the notes? Some lewdness, she had no doubt. And what wickedness could have possessed me to trace *that word* in the dust on Mr. Taylor's car?

I didn't deny doing that?

Did I know the meaning of that word?

Did I?

The true and unspeakable meaning of that word?

If I did not throw myself on God's mercy and mend my ways, if I did not apply myself to my studies, if I did not shun evil companions, and if my heart was not contrite, she had no doubt that I would end up as a common labourer with no future but the gallows.

All this, however, was of little importance.

The sacrifices that she and my father were making to give me a good education were nothing, merely duty done. She could bear the shame I had brought upon her and my father and my brother. She was, by now, used to such shame. She loved me deeply; my father loved me; my brother loved me; my uncles and aunts loved me. But it was obvious that there was no love in my heart. Actions speak louder than words. Was it not obvious from my actions that I did not return the love so freely given? If I loved others, then I would not wound them.

This *was* obvious, wasn't it?

My heart was a heart of stone.

That pain, that mother's sorrow, too, she could bear.

But it cut her to the quick—

She pointed to *Health and Efficiency* and tears started to roll down her cheeks. She was unable to express, heartbreak, inner wounds, shame, the defilement, the revulsion in her that *this*, this filth, this degradation, wallowing vile filthy nastiness, this lewd and sinful filth—did I *wish* to kill her? She would die of a broken heart. She could never raise her head again. She was heartsick that she'd lived to see this day.

For those who gave themselves to *this* there was no salvation. Christ Himself would shun them and condemn them to suffering eternal.

Her face was blotchy with tears. She gripped one of my hands in hers. Her grip was so fierce that the stone in her ring was cutting into my flesh. She brought her face closer to mine.

"If I had known," she said, "on the day that you were born what I now know, if I had known that that baby was to become what you *are*, do you know what I'd have done?

"Do you?

"Do you?"

Spittle was flecking my face.

"With joy in my heart," she said, "with *joy*, I'd have had you taken from my arms and put you out for adoption."

Still gripping my hand, she knelt by the bed pulling me down towards her.

"Oh God," she prayed, "forgive me my sins and wickedness. I am weak but Thou art strong. Take from me this bitter cup. Make known unto me wherein I have transgressed that Thou shouldst punish me by making bitter unto me the fruit of my womb. Wreak upon *me*, Oh Lord, Thy wrath, but spare, I beseech Thee, this boy . . ."

There was a lot of this stuff and it went on for quite a long time. She was rocking herself backwards and forwards in its rhythms and pulling me with her. By the end of it, she'd reduced me to a shuddering, tear-racked hysteria. She eventually left me to my tears and the glow of the reading lamp.

In the doorway, she turned and half-whispered,

"Do you know what I'm going to do now?"

I shook my head.

"Do you?"

Her eyes moved from mine, glancing at the magazine.

"*I'm going to wash my hands.*"

I cried until I could cry no more. I felt empty, exhausted, sick. I turned my pillow to the dry side. I hated myself. I looked with loathing through *Health and Efficiency*, which had been left on the bed in accusation.

I stared at the roses on the wallpaper grouping them into different patterns.

Mournfully, I wanked myself to sleep.

* * *

WHEN I WAS FOURTEEN we moved again to a new church in a different circuit—this time not far from London. By now I could hardly contain my hatred of my mother and her comfortable world of teas, scones, Agatha Christie, and missionary boxes. The Night of the Annual Report was, in memory, the turning point, though in fact the whole process must have been more complex, drawn-out, and guilt-sodden. But the feeling was hardening that if for the gallows I was born then to the gallows I would go, but I'd give the crowd a tune and a jig on the way to the Tyburn Tree.

It was with this move and in this new house that I started the daily practice of dipping my mother's toothbrush in the lavatory.

Between the years of twelve and fifteen I was building for myself a new identity. I did no more than pass at school; I was absorbed in more important tasks. My reading had always been wide and precocious but now I read so much and secretly late into the night that in school I was pale and lethargic and could hardly bring myself to go through the motions with Bunsen burners and balances and x and y and contour maps from which one was supposed to draw bumpy hills. My reading in non-fiction was mainly of rationalist history, theology, and studies of religious deviation. I devoured the works of H. G. Wells, Professor Joad, and the popular essays of Bertrand Russell. I became something of an authority on witchcraft, heresies major and minor, and the rites of the Copts. I was particularly pleased to discover that in Ethiopia, Judas Iscariot was worshipped as a saint.

I started to carry the fight to my mother by introducing the unspeakable under the guise of religious knowledge. At the tea table, I would offer such topics as the derivation of the word "bugger" from "Bulgarian," explaining to her the Manichean background until my father cleared his throat for silence or my mother said, "Though I speak with the tongues of men and of angels, and have not charity, I am become as sounding brass, or a tinkling cymbal."

I read *The Voyage of the Beagle* because I understood that Darwin had totally undermined Christianity, but the book was not helpful; *The Golden Bough*, equally heralded, was equally disappointing, but it was enlivened by accounts of some sexual customs which I would never have imagined.

Father and Son by Edmund Gosse was a particular joy.

I also managed to irritate and hurt my mother by insisting on going to churches of other denominations; I presented this as a religious and ecumenical enthusiasm. I goaded her with a show of great interest in the Roman Catholic church and invented a priest called Father O'Neil with whom I claimed to be having fascinating conversations; I managed to intimate that Father O'Neil was bent on conversion.

One of my greater triumphs in the first months of that new church was with yaws. A missionary campaign was being carried on to collect money to relieve our African brothers. A missionary had shown a colour film at church of these disgusting raspberry-like sores and skin lesions. I looked "yaws" up in the library, as I looked up everything, and could scarcely contain my pleasure.

At the tea table, I enquired as to the success of the campaign; my mother was out every night with a collecting box. The campaign, it seemed, was going well.

"I was reading about yaws today in the library," I said.

"Poor things," said my mother.

"In a book by Dr. Schweitzer."

(Actually a brief paragraph in a medical encyclopedia, but the saintly Schweitzer was better for my purposes.)

"Some more tea?" said my mother.

"It seems," I said, "that yaws is a form of venereal disease."

A cup clinked on a saucer in the silence.

"What's venereal disease?" said my brother.

"Pass this to your father," my mother said to him.

"If unchecked," I said, "it has much the same effects as syphilis and . . ."

"*Cake?*" said my mother. "It's got raisins in it."

". . . and like syphilis is caused . . ."

"*Would anyone like another cup of tea?*"

". . . caused by a spirochete. A spirochete of the same family."

"I don't think," said my mother, "that the tea-table . . ."

"*Dr. Schweitzer*," I said, "didn't actually say if yaws was contracted in the same way as syphilis but if the spirochete . . ."

My father cleared his throat and I busied myself with a slice of cake.

She was badly shaken.

But it was fiction that sustained me and offered models of subversion. And what a strange hodgepodge of books it was. I cannot remember even a fraction of them but I do recall the effects on me of *Tono-Bungay*, *Sons and Lovers*, *The Moon and Sixpence*, *Wuthering Heights*, *The Constant Nymph*, and the opening sections of *David Copperfield* and *Oliver Twist*.

My favourite poet was Keats, my favourite poem "The Eve of St. Agnes." I was bewildered that a poem so patently lubricious was endorsed for school consumption. Swinburne earned my allegiance with the lines:

Thou hast conquered, O pale Galilean; the world
has grown grey from thy breath,

Sentiments which accorded exactly with my own.

I read the plays of Christopher Marlowe because I'd heard he was an atheist and was murdered in a pub; I identified strongly with Tamburlaine.

I haunted the local library in my quest for knowledge. Not only was it a very good library, but I lusted after one of the younger librarians who had a nice smile and breasts that gave the impression of great solidity. I spent hours wondering how much they weighed, what one would feel like hot and unconfined.

It was in the library that I found one day a book called *The March of the Moderns* by the art historian William Gaunt. I have never seen or read the book since. It struck me with the radiance and power of revelation. The mundane world fell away; I was oblivious to the smell of floorpolish and damp raincoats, the click of the date stamp, the passage of other browsers along the shelves. I read standing up until closing time and then took the book home and finished it in bed.

It was like the Second Coming of Mr. Montague.

The book revealed to me a world where brilliant but persecuted people drank champagne for breakfast and were pissed by lunch, took lobsters for walks on leashes, shaved off half their moustaches, sliced off their ears and gave them to prostitutes, possessed women by the score, consorted with syphilitic dwarves, lived in brothels, and were allowed to go mad.

Somewhere in the sun, D.H. Lawrence was at it.

Hemingway was giving them both barrels.

Ezra was suffering for the faith in an American bin.

Painters everywhere were possessing their exotic Javanese models.

I, meanwhile, was in Croydon.

But Art was obviously the answer; it was just a question of finding my medium. The problem with the novel was that writing one took a long time and nothing interesting had happened to me. I tried poetry for a time, being particularly drawn to the imagists because they were very short, and seemed easiest to imitate. H.D. was one of my favourites. Painting, because of the models, attracted me the most but I couldn't draw anything that looked like anything; abstraction was the answer, of course, but secretly I thought abstraction not quite honest. I had a go at a few linocuts but gouged my hand rather badly. Drama was soured for me by memories of endless pageants and nativity plays where kids tripped over the frayed carpet and I had to say:

"I bring you tidings of Great Joy."

But I was not depressed.

I settled down to wait. I lived in the manse, ate scones, and went to school, but I was charged with a strange certainty that I was somehow different, chosen, special; my Muse, in her own good time, would descend and translate me from Croydon to that richer world where women and applause were waiting.

The calm of this newfound certainty soon began to fray; though I had no doubts about my calling, it was bringing me no immediate relief; it was bringing me no closer to an actual girl. Being new to the area I had no friends. And I had no idea of how I could approach girls. I envied the boys at school who could indulge in easy badinage at the bus stop or tobacconist. For all its crudity, it seemed to work. I would have liked to say to the girls, as they did,

"Carry your bag, Miss?" or "When are you going to wash your hair, then?" but it was not simple shyness or fear of rebuff which prevented me. I felt myself to be so other, that had I offered such pleasantries, I knew they'd just stare or be frightened or call a policeman.

Girls obsessed me, but apart from being shy I was also frightened of them. Not frightened of humiliation, though that would have been bad enough, but frightened of other things less realized, fears I was scarcely able to formulate—that contagion with which my mother had infected me. Although intellectually I rejected all her attitudes and ideas, I still somewhere felt the flesh to be sinful, obscene, disgusting. I'd once asked a boy who'd done it what it was like and he said, "hot and slimy"; this had only confirmed what I knew instinctively to be the truth. And jokes boys told about the smell of kippers. I feared, also, the disease they might carry; the word "lues" was more than a word I'd found in a dictionary; it was a physical horror. And then there was all this menstrual business. For all my lust and desire, some puritan cancer sat in my heart.

(A few years ago, I read a biography of Ruskin that recounted the debacle of his wedding night. Ruskin, intense, pure, and idealistic, was acquainted with the female form only through sculpture and paintings; his first sight of pubic hair brought him to the verge of nervous collapse; the marriage was annulled. His situation then, and mine at fourteen and fifteen, had much in common.)

For all my strange reading and precocity, another thing troubled me, something impossible to talk about with another boy, however close, a type of ignorance impossible to admit to. I had studied diagrams of female apparatus many times, followed the arrows that pointed to the various parts, read the labels, but still did not really understand the layout. Much as in botany, it was simple to learn the diagrams of a cross-section of a stem, flower, or trunk, and label the neat pencil lines "stamen," "carpels," "vascular bundles" etc., but it was a completely different matter working from an actual specimen. My specimens always turned out quite differently from the way the book said they ought to be. How much worse, then, with girls where I couldn't even follow the diagram to start with. And the possible vagaries of an actual specimen didn't bear thinking about.

For some unremembered reason I had become convinced that, within a small area, were three orifices, each capable of receiving a penis. *But only one was the right one.* I imagined dreadful scenes ranging from a contemptuous "That's my urethra, dear," to shrieks of protest and pain. Nor did I much like the sound of labia majors and labia minors which, medical works informed me, "covered and guarded" the entrance to the vagina. One presumably had to get past them first before even standing a chance of finding the right place.

It all made me very anxious.

I still pinned my hopes on Art; I bought a book called *Teach Yourself How to Draw in Pencil and Charcoal* and the largest size sketching pad that Reeves manufactured. I laboriously traced with tracing paper from the *Teach Yourself* book two nudes and some drawings of leaves and twigs. I transferred the tracings into the sketching pad and then hung about the local park and stared intently at things, pencil poised or measuring whenever girls went past. The impression I gave, alone and palely loitering by bench and drinking fountain, was, I hoped, Byronic. What was supposed to happen was this: a girl, attracted by my artistic absorption and obvious sensitivity, would approach me and say,

"Are you an artist?"

A nod.

"Yes."

"Can I look at your picture?"

"If you like. They're only sketches."

She would be overcome. She admits she's always wanted to be drawn by a real artist. I offer to sketch her. She says she lives near, and her dad's at work, and her mum's out shopping. We are in her bedroom. She is rather shy at first.

This scenario never did take place; even the ducks which surged to everyone else in the hope of bread learned to ignore me.

* * *

AND THEN I met Tony.

The circumstances of our meeting were comic; we were introduced by our mothers. Tony's mother attended my father's church. Tony had not been in Croydon when we first arrived because he had been away at boarding school, but his parents had now brought him home because he'd been so terribly unhappy there. Tony, my mother assured me, was "such a nice boy." He would be a nice friend for me and a good influence. Any boy my mother considered "nice" was obviously a twit and an undesirable of the first water, and I have no doubt he felt the same way about me. When I first saw him, I saw an extremely handsome boy, dark, with black curly hair. He was wearing a suit; his manners were impeccable. When left alone, we sniffed around each other like rigid-legged dogs. I made the first move by offering him a Player's; he declined with thanks, taking out his own Craven A *and fitting one into an amber cigarette-holder*.

We were soon inseparable. In a rush of communion, we exchanged our most valued pieces of information. He told me about sexual acts between women and animals in the Roman gladiatorial shows. He explained that, as human scent would not arouse an animal, the trainers had cloths, which had been wiped over the parts of a female animal in heat, and then sealed in airtight boxes. Just before the act was to take place, the cloth was rubbed on the woman so that the animal would think the woman of its own species. He spoke of donkeys and panthers. I told him the real name of "sucking off" was fellatio and gave him my copy of *The Picture of Dorian Gray*. I got *The March of the Moderns* from the library for him; he lent me a book called *Venus in Furs* which was really very boring but I liked it. I told him I'd never done it; he said he had done it in a rowing boat with his cousin who was nineteen, but then confessed he was lying.

We bought snuff together and tried it; it was horrible.

He told me he hadn't been withdrawn from the boarding school but expelled for writing an anonymous letter to the matron.

I confided in him my fears about the three holes and which was the right one and he said he was pretty sure there were only two. He said he had *seen* his cousin's in the rowing boat but he couldn't tell about the labia majors and minors because it was just hairy, but from the sound of it he thought they were probably part of being a virgin and were inside.

He said you couldn't catch it off a toilet seat.

He said he didn't believe anything anybody told him.

He said he'd even thought of doing it with his mother.

Tony's father and mother were interesting. His mother was tall and elegant, her face bony and beautiful. In some ways she was worse than my mother because she was extremely evangelical and used to request casual callers, the grocer's boy or the plumber, to kneel with her in prayer. She was earnest with strangers in buses and trains; she sang hymns a lot. It was Tony's opinion that she only had a few more years before they put her away for life. Tony's father was equally interesting. He was a rigid, trim, crisp man who had been a major in the war. He did not go to church at all and he drank and made Tony call him "Sir" and called me "old chap." He also actually used words like "tiffin" and "chotapeg"; I think I recognized him even then as a character from a novel. Whenever I thought of him the words "patent leather" came to mind. He called my father "padre," which I think secretly pleased my father considerably.

Tony's father had a .38 revolver and a box of bullets hidden in a dresser drawer under his shirts. One afternoon we shot Tony's toolshed in the garden twelve times. Tony had suggested that we shoot it just once, but we then decided with the strange logic of children that his father would be less likely to miss twelve bullets than one. We stained the fresh wood of the bullet holes with mud. We studied the illustrated instruction pamphlet in a box of his mother's Tampax; we stole two contraceptives from a big box full of them in his father's drawer and tried them on.

Tony was clever in all sorts of ways that I was not. He had rigged up an electrical device of wires under the stair carpeting which caused a red light to flash in his bedroom if anyone was approaching; invaluable, he explained, if one were smoking, wanking, or reading good stuff.

Tony stole more money than I did because his parents were richer, but we shared equally.

We bought brushes and tubes of oil paint and painted abstract pictures in his bedroom. In our painty jeans and reeking of turpentine, we sat about on Saturdays in coffee bars eyeing girls and hoping they'd think we were from the art school.

A girl we both knew at the church youth club had a penfriend in Yugoslavia who came that summer for a holiday. She was quite beautiful and her English was beautifully broken. We were both very attracted. One day we met her and she was wearing a kind of singlet thing that revealed her armpits. In these armpits were long tufts of brown hair. This aroused us immensely as it was the first time we'd seen such a thing. I was aroused and repelled. Tony said he'd like to put his mouth to her armpit, enclose all the hair, and suck it slowly, sweat and all. It was this wonderful quality of imagination in him I most admired.

Tony also introduced me to a new art form; he had a large collection of jazz records. He played for me Louis Armstrong, Bix, Muggsy Spanier, Kid Ory, Bunk Johnson, Johnny Dodds, Sidney Bechet, and Mezz Mezzrow. The music spoke to me immediately because its joy or sadness was easy to feel. I became a fervent convert. But the music had for us another great virtue; our parents detested it and churches and newspaper editorials thundered against it, invoking the Fall of Rome. And better still, it was played by Negroes, who were perfectly all right as long as they were in Africa suffering from leprosy and yaws, but otherwise not all right. And better than *that*, these were *wicked* Negroes who drank and whored, cut each other with razors, and died young.

We read *Shining Trumpets* by Rudi Blesh and *Mr. Jelly Roll* by Alan Lomax and countless other works of jazz hagiography. Our imaginations lived in New Orleans, Memphis, and

Chicago; they were our Jerusalem and we swore pilgrimage.

Tony favoured trumpet men: King Oliver, Punch Miller, George Mitchell, Celestine, Bix, Bunk, Ladnier, and the always wonderful Satchmo. The call sounded out over the privet hedges and rockeries into the decorous suburban streets until the telephones complained. I soon came to favour the pianists and bluesmen—Cripple Clarence Lofton, Jelly Roll, Speckled Red, Yancy, Meade Lux Lewis, and those massive women: Bessie Smith, Ma Rainey, and Bertha Chippie Hill.

To know anything of jazz in those days was like being part of an underground, a freemasonry, which led to immediate trust and friendship; more accurately, it was like being an early Christian. We listened to the radio at dead of night to pick up faint stations from France and Hamburg that played jazz records; we learned by heart the scanty details of the musicians' desperate lives; we studied the matrix numbers of defunct race labels.

We were ravished by the American language. Ten-shilling notes became "bills" and then "ten-spots"; we longed to taste black-eyed peas, chitlins, collard greens, and grits; we would have given years of our lives to smoke a reefer, meet a viper.

Neither of us could play an instrument or read a note but Tony, always a purist, bought a cornet and carried it on our Saturday expeditions to coffee bars.

(Years later, when I first came to Canada, I fulfilled the vow that Tony and I had taken. I drove to New Orleans through the increasing depression of the southern States, illusions, delusions lost each day with every human contact, until I reached the fabled Quarter, and sat, close to tears, listening to the Preservation Hall Jazz Band—a group of octogenarians which, as I entered, was trying to play "Oh, Didn't He Ramble"; the solos ran out of breath, the drummer was palsied, the bass player rheumy and vacant. The audience of young Germans and Frenchmen was hushed and respectful. Between tunes, a man with a wooden leg tap-danced. I knew that if they tackled

"High Society," and the clarinetist attempted Alphonse Picou's solo, he'd drop dead in cardiac arrest; the butcher had cut them down, and something shining in me, with them.)

Whenever I hear Freddie Keppard playing "Salty Dog," it brings to mind the party that Tony and I gave when we were fifteen. His parents had to go to a funeral in Scotland and had to be away for three days. Tony assured them that he wouldn't be frightened alone in the house and would be good and not make things dirty and be sure to turn off the gas taps before going to bed. He suggested that I come to stay for the weekend. It seemed to reassure his parents knowing that he would be with a nice boy and that my parents would not be too far away.

We called the party, of course, a Rent Party. Such a party as we envisaged needed drink. Lots of it. We'd tasted sherry, and Scotch once, and been pale drunk on beer, but neither of us knew much about the subject except that drunkenness was an ultimate good and inseparable from the artistic life.

The problem was that we were too young to buy the stuff; all we'd ever managed was a bottle of Bulmer's cider and six beers from an off-licence run by a benevolent old man, but his benevolence wouldn't stretch to what *we* had in mind. Tony had seven pounds and ten shillings; I didn't enquire where it had come from.

One of our older acquaintances from the El Toro Coffee Bar, one of the jazz fraternity, came to the rescue. He bought for us a large bottle of gin, six quarts of India Pale Ale, two bottles of Australian ruby port, six bottles of Newcastle Brown Ale, and a bottle of something from Cyprus.

Tony's father had recently bought a resplendent new radiogram—a large piece of furniture veneered in walnut which housed on one side a radio, speaker, and storage space for records, and on the other side a record player with a sprung turntable. Tony was strictly forbidden to even touch it.

We selected our records with care.

And there were girls. Tony, far more dashing than I with his amber cigarette-holder, good looks, and three-speed bike, had persuaded three girls he'd met at the municipal baths and the girl who worked after school and on Saturdays in the record shop. Other boys were bringing girlfriends.

As people arrived, more bottles were added to our stock.

My memory of the evening is not perfect.

Somehow, who knows how, miraculously, I ended up with the girl who worked in the record shop. She had blond hair in a ponytail and she was wearing a black felt skirt with a big red heart on it and a black sweater. She was beautiful. I have forgotten her name. She was wearing black shoes like slippers, like ballet shoes.

We were dancing. The radiogram was playing "Skip the Gutter." The label on the sherry bottle said: Commercial Sherry; it was sweet and I liked it but I stopped drinking it when another boy said it was a ladies' drink. The ruby port was all right but the gin made me shudder; the India Pale Ale was nicer than the Newcastle Brown.

In the upstairs lavatory, Tony and I were pissing together, a wavering aim into the bowl.

Tony said, "I tell you, man, she's hotter than a Saturday Night Special."

In the back garden, a boy we didn't know got stuck and wounded in the monkey-puzzle tree.

A girl passed out: a voice kept saying *Loosen her clothes*. It might have been mine.

Somebody took the jazz record off and put on some waltzes. The light was out. I felt strong but unsteady; she whispered in my ear,

My mother told me
She would scold me
If a boy I kissed

She licked the inside of my ear.

Behind the settee, she whispered,

"I like it."

My arm was around her; she made some contortionist move and I was holding a hot, naked breast.

I summed the situation up in my mind with perfect clarity.

I said: *I am sitting holding the naked breast of a beautiful girl. She is hotter than a Saturday Night Special.*

I knew that all was not well. It was worse when I turned towards her, better if I kept both feet on the floor and my head straight. "Salty Dog" was playing; I played the trumpet line in my head.

I let go of the breast.

I stumbled over another couple in the dark room. The only light was the green glow from the dials inside the radiogram. I knew the radiogram was near the door. I lurched towards that light and filled the glowing depth with noisy vomit.

* * *

BY THE END of my fifteenth year my conviction that I would never lose my virginity was becoming morbid. Tony by then had done it, or claimed to have done it, with a girl who worked at the confectionery counter in Marks and Spencers. By way of cheering me up, he said she was ugly; I said that you didn't look at the mantelpiece while stoking the fire.

I had attempted a couple of girls at the Methodist Youth Club and the girl who worked at MacFisheries. I had taken her to the cinema but every time I tried to touch her breast she had said "Cheeky!" until I'd become discouraged.

I brooded.

The idea of a prostitute grew in my mind. I knew myself to be the kind of person to whom women would always say, "Cheeky!" Mine was a hand which would always be slapped. I had no choice. My shyness, fear, and revulsion were overwhelmed by a kind of fatalism. I felt like a soldier in the trenches waiting for the officer to blow his whistle. The bombardment has stopped. A lark is singing. The whistle will blow and there will be nowhere to go but over the top and on in a steady walk towards whatever horror awaits.

Tony and I discussed the propriety of the services of a prostitute. He felt that it was all right so long as she was a personal friend. He instanced the cases of Toulouse-Lautrec and Van Gogh. Otherwise he felt that it was not all right. I asked him if he would, then, mind terribly introducing me to one of his prostitute friends in Croydon so that intimacy might blossom before I engaged her services. For two days we did not speak.

A remarkable chance came at the end of the school year. Three classes were to be marshalled into a trip to London to see Paul Scofield in a production of *Hamlet*.

The theatre was near Soho, where prostitutes jostled one on every pavement, where barkers called the attractions of unnatural acts from every doorway, where pimps physically dragged resisting passers-by into bordellos. I determined that, in the confusion of entering the theatre, I would slip away and hide until the coast was clear and then make my way to Soho, gratify myself, return to the station at the appointed time, and claim to have got lost on the underground.

Tony simplified this. He advised going into the theatre and then simply getting up to go to the lavatory and walking out.

Everything played into my hands. The master-in-charge was one of the younger teachers and more casual than most; school uniform was not obligatory.

Tony gave me ten shillings and sixpence and I closed my post office savings accounts, which gave me another two pounds, eleven shillings, and ninepence—the results of birthdays and the visits of uncles. I did not know how much it cost to do it but I'd decided to throw myself on her mercy and if I didn't have enough, to offer all I had just to have a look at it.

I did slip away and I did go to Soho. I spent an hour or more wandering about in Italian grocery shops looking at salami and strange smelling foods, browsing in a second-hand bookshop, looking at the menus in the windows of dingy restaurants, staring at the displays of the purveyors of rubber goods and artificial limbs. There were no prostitutes to be seen; I wondered if there were some custom governing harlotry unknown to me—like half-day closing on Thursday in shops.

I read the postcard advertisements in a newsagent's window; I'd heard about that. I phoned a likely sounding one ("The Service of Miss Roche—Stimulating, Healthy, Once Tried Never Forgotten") but it turned out to be a registered nurse who administered colonic irrigation.

I also phoned a Miss Ponce de Leon but a man's voice said,

"Piss off, sonny."

Finally, in Gerrard Street, a man in a doorway looked at me and I looked at him.

He said,

"You look like a fun-loving gentleman."

I said I was and he sold me membership in the White Monkey Club for seventeen shillings and sixpence. The White Monkey Club was at the top of a flight of uncarpeted stairs; it was about the same size as my former bedroom and had the same sort of smell. The barman, who wore lipstick and a grubby blouse, gave me a gin and orange; it came with membership. There were three other patrons, each with a gin and orange. A long time passed; the room was silent except for the barman filing his nails. Eventually a woman as old as my mother came in and danced about on the tiny stage to a record of "Pop Goes the Weasel." At the last, "Pop," she undid her bra and her tits fell down. And when I got back to the station there was hell to pay.

* * *

IRONICALLY ENOUGH, it is to Billy Graham that I owe my first brush with a girl's private parts.

But that came at the end of the affair, not the beginning.

After my failure in Soho I fell in love with a girl called Helen.

I had no alternative.

Squat in me somewhere sat that cold creature, my mother's gift, and the only possible resolution of my contradictory feelings was an extreme romanticism. Love elevated coupling, the beast with two backs, into the union of souls. As many a cynic has observed, romantic love is the result of unsatisfied desire and my romanticism was Provençal in its intensity.

Helen attended the local girls' grammar school and every day after school we sat on a corner on our bicycles, talking. I wrote poems to her. And although I saw her every day, I wrote her letters. One poem I wrote to her was modelled on a poem called "Helen" by H. D.

Hers ran something like:

All Greece hates
the still eyes in the white face,
the lustre as of olives
Something, something
and the white hands

or it might have been "pale hands." Such is fame that I've never been able to find the poem since.

My version, with a fine disregard of history, ran:

All Greece loves
the dark eyes
in the white face

"My eyes aren't dark," she said when I gave her the poem.

"I know," I said, "but I'm writing it as if you're Helen of Troy."

"Oh," she said.

Helen thought Tony was nice and handsome but wasn't he a bit wild? I agreed that he was. Didn't I think that smoking made people's breath smell? I agreed that it probably did. Wasn't beer rather a working class sort of drink and weren't Tony and I too young to go in the back parlour of the Quadrant? For two years I suffered indignities such as escorting her shopping on Saturday morning; for two years I trotted attendance on her like a small dog in the wake of a large bitch who is coming into heat but not yet ready and who encourages the entourage but snaps at too bold an advance.

Our sexual relationship had a curiously ritual quality; sexual favours were doled out in measured and mutually understood amounts, like a recipe.

On walks, endless walks, hands were held.

After the weekly meetings of the Methodist Youth Club when I'd walked her home, kissing was permitted for a few minutes.

During a party, if she were in a good mood, a breast might be fondled for a limited amount of time.

On three or four occasions I put my hand under her skirt some three inches above the knee, at which point she would say,

"We mustn't get carried away."

Her lips, to which I wrote poems, were thick and rather squashy, and she wore a lot of lipstick and perfume and powder so that kissing her was a sort of meal in itself.

Every Thursday after the youth club meeting, I walked her home along tree-lined streets, stopping in the shadows just before her house to kiss her for the statutory five or ten minutes. This always gave me an erection like an iron bar. Then she always said:

"Goodness! Just *look* at the time!"

And then my erection and I would limp homewards until we reached a front garden far enough away from a street light and, braced there on trembling legs, I would wank in an agony of relief onto laurel, lilac, or hydrangea.

The leader of the youth club, a man in his thirties called Ernest Langley, an enthusiast and ping-pong player of note, was mad keen to organize an expedition to London to hear Billy Graham, who was at that time saving England. I didn't want to go but Helen did, so we went.

The whole experience filled me with rage. Massed choirs in white and black sang soft hymns and a smooth man played meretricious trombone solos. Helen thought he was wonderful; I agreed that he was. I would have liked to grip him by the neck and shake him fiercely while forcing him to listen to Jack Teagarden playing "A Hundred Years from Today" or "Stars Fell on Alabama."

In spite of myself, I was quite looking forward to Billy Graham himself; I enjoyed a good speech or performance, whatever the subject. But even he was dismal. His timing was fair only, his gestures wooden, his brandishing of the Bible almost comic. He was too handsome; his suit too well cut. Evangelists need something of the maniac about them to be convincing. One could have imagined Billy Graham making hamburgers on the barbecue and feeding them to a gang of ill-mannered American kids who called him "Pop." One could not imagine Calvin, Wesley, Luther, Knox, or Savonarola being called "Pop," nor could one imagine them making hamburgers. Feeding *kids* onto a barbecue, yes; hamburgers, no.

Helen sang and prayed and cried a little; from time to time she gave my hand a tiny squeeze; at the end she went down to the front to be saved. I stayed where I was and waited for her; we agreed we had shared a wonderful experience. I agreed that the choir was indeed heavenly and that the trombone man was extraordinarily gifted. I secured the back seat in the coach. Ernest Langley led the coach in a few uplifting hymns as we rolled through London, but it was late and as we settled to the long drive back to Croydon the overhead lights in the coach, one after another, were dimmed.

Helen was amazingly ardent. She gave me open-mouthed kisses usually reserved for the most special occasions. Emboldened, I sought a breast. Two buttons were somehow undone; feast after famine. As we slowed down to roll through Penge, I put my hand under her skirt and reached the statutory point, when, unmistakably, her thighs relaxed, softened, opened.

My wrist was bent at a painful angle and my finger trapped beneath some unyielding elastic and then somehow—miraculously—I felt dampness and *pubic hair*.

My mouth and throat were dry. Over the top of her head I stared at my dim reflection in the window of the coach. "I will never forget this moment," I said to my hammering heart. "We are just out of Penge and are now on the road to Beckenham just passing the Beckenham Public Library and I am sitting in seat number forty-two of a Wondertour Coach *and I am touching pubic hair.*"

And then I realized that Helen was crying. In an immediate access of guilt I retrieved my hand. She was not sobbing; tears just rolled down her cheeks.

What was the matter? What had I done?

Nothing. Stop. Don't talk to me.

But as we approached Croydon all became brokenly clear. The beautiful service, and feeling so wonderful, she'd been carried away. She'd never done such a thing. I was the first. It was awful. Billy Graham, Jesus, sin, salvation.

I assured her with complete sincerity that I believed she'd never done such a thing before; I assured her that of course I would not think any the worse of her; I declared my love for her to be undying.

But when I awoke in the morning, stretched in sunlight, punched up the pillow and stared at the familiar dressing table and the thumbtack print of the *Yellow Chair*, I felt a giddy lightness inside me, a swelling, the bobbing of clustered balloons, a freedom I hadn't felt since I'd met her.

No hank of hair owned me. It was only with the slightest twinge of guilt that I realized Helen and I were finished. The spell was broken. For two years I'd been chained by a wisp of hair, two years of servitude and indignities.

I worked up an anger against myself to still the little nag of guilt.

I, who was destined for great things, I, whom the Muse had claimed, had squandered two years of my valuable life on a girl with fat lips, on a girl who probably thought Ezra Pound was a kind of cake, on a girl *who had been genuinely moved by Billy Graham's trombonist.*

By the time I got up I felt so good humoured that, instead of my usual coffee, I condescended to eat one of my mother's gargantuan breakfasts.

* * *

THE PHOTOGRAPHS left us largely silent. In most were two women and a man. One of the women was almost plump, with a crease of fat at the waist, the other was scrawny. The man had a very large organ. The photographs illustrated all the possible positions for sexual intercourse and the modes of oral stimulation. The pictures had a curiously formal quality as the three performers were wearing black domino masks.

Tony had borrowed the photographs from an older boy we'd met at the record shop.

We didn't say much to each other as we studied them; they were somehow not erotic. Their effect was deadening.

I kept returning to one particular picture; it disturbed me profoundly. A mattress lay on the floor. On the mattress, side by side, lay the two women. At the extreme edge of the picture was a toecap, a shoe belonging perhaps to the man holding the spotlight above the scene. One woman held in her hand a long animal's horn, the tip of which she was inserting into the other woman's vagina. The animal's horn was about two and a half feet long and spiral in form, the horn perhaps of some kind of antelope. The face of the woman into whom this was being inserted was partially obscured by the domino mask but she seemed to be smiling.

PART TWO

THE VISION of Bobby naked remained important long after those years of early childhood. I must confess that, during boyhood and youth, I suffered from what "sexologists" call feelings of "penile inadequacy."

I had seen Bobby's naked, shivering form, the repulsive whiteness of those parts of his body not covered with hair. Features, build, pelt, Bobby resembled one of those "artist's impressions" of prehistoric man. His scrotum was the size of half a large grapefruit and his member equine.

I've heard it said that the cretinous are always vastly endowed in compensation, as it were, for their lack of mental development. Whether this is an old wives' tale or not I do not know.

Cleland makes use of the belief in *Fanny Hill.*

Louise, desiring to substantiate or disprove the notion, seduces an idiot flower seller:

> A waistband that I unskewer'd, and a rag of shirt that I removed, and which could not have covered a quarter of it, revealed the whole of the idiot's standard of distinction, erect, in full pride and display: but such a one! it was positively of so tremendous a size, that prepared as we were to see something extraordinary, it still out of measure, surpass'd our expectation, and astonish'd even me, who had not been used to trade in trifles. In fine, it might have answered very well the making a show of; its enormous

head seemed, in hue and size, not unlike a common sheep's heart; then you might have troll'd dice securely along the broad back of it; the length of it too was prodigious . . .

Many men suffer from the secret fear that they are sexually inadequate, that other men's penises are bigger than theirs. I don't know where this belief comes from but it's a common anxiety. Possibly it stems from the child's impression of his father's organ—an instrument which compared to his own must seem impossibly vast. And the matter seems so important perhaps because of the early identification of "self" with penis.

Wash yourself.

Dry yourself.

That I chanced to see Bobby naked gave me a poor start in life and I suppose, on reflection, that anxiety has been the constant in my sexual career.

I had thought that particular anxiety stilled long ago, an anxiety of my boyhood and youth, an absurdity that marriage and fatherhood enabled me to smile over. But the other day my youngest daughter, who has the unpleasant habit of trailing me about the house from room to room, crept into the bathroom as I was urinating. She stood and watched. Then she said in a congratulatory tone,

"You can make it come out of your finger!"

I shared this latest cuteness with my wife and we laughed together over it. But later, I found myself, not brooding exactly, but *thinking* upon it.

Finger?

Finger!

I read of somewhere, or was told about, saw perhaps—or did I imagine this?—I am not being coherent. I believe there exists a monograph by Sir Richard Burton on the nature of penises. As frequently happens to me, I find I can't distinguish between real and imagined events. A story told me or a story

I've invented often becomes more real than an event I know to have occurred. And increasingly, I find myself doubting even those certainties.

You remember... says my wife. But I don't. And I say to her, *Didn't we...?* and she says, *We never have been there.*

I've always admired Sir Richard Burton, admired that hawk-like face in the portrait by Lord Leighton. Master of thirty-five languages and their dialects, poet, translator, soldier, diplomat, explorer—such a book would be typical of his mind and interests.

This book (I don't pretend to know its title) suggests that there are two basic and distinct kinds of penis—one which, when detumescent, is small but grows proportionately very large when erect, and one which, when detumescent, is relatively large and grows proportionately very little when erect. The first kind of organ is, according to Burton, typical of Caucasian peoples, the second typical of African, Semitic, and Hamitic peoples.

(The most interesting part of the research of Masters and Johnson was a confirmation of Burton's thesis, though their findings were not, I think, linked to race. They reported that *the longer the limp penis the less its length increases in erection.* They noted the case of a three and a half inch limp penis which in erection increased by one hundred and twenty percent!)

It would be a simple matter to discover whether the book exists or not, but I'm no longer curious. I am persuaded that it does. I can see it quite clearly. A folio bound in red morocco illustrated with page after page of steel engravings of penises drooping from left to right, root to tip, and then, in comparison, standing right to left. And a commentary in Burton's rather ponderous prose.

It was, of course, privately printed.

I've always taken a guilty pleasure in John Cleland. The following passage appeals to me.

Curious then, and eager to unfold so alarming a mystery, playing, as it were, with his buttons, which were bursting ripe from the active force within, those of his waistband and fore-flap flew open at a touch, when out IT started; and now, disengag'd from the shirt, I saw, with wonder and surprise, what? not the plaything of a boy, not the weapon of a man, but a maypole of so enormous a standard, that had proportions been observ'd, it must have belong'd to a young giant. Its prodigious size made me shrink again; yet I could not, without pleasure, behold, and even ventur'd to feel, such a length, such a breadth of animated ivory! perfectly well turn'd and fashion'd, the proud stiffness of which distended its skin, whose smooth polish and velvet softness might vie with that of the most delicate of our sex, and whose exquisite whiteness was not a little set off by a sprout of black curling hair round the root, through the jetty sprigs of which the fair skin shew'd as in a fine evening you may have remarked the clear light aether through the branchwork of distant trees over-topping the summit of a hill; then the broad and blueish-casted incarnate of the head, and blue serpentines of its veins, altogether compos'd the most striking assemblage of figures and colours in nature. In short, it stood an object of terror and delight.

My wife says she thinks they look silly.

Modern research and scientific method claim to have established beyond doubt that the average male organ, fully erect, is approximately six inches in length. (All measurements taken along the upperside of the penis from the pubic bone to tip.) It is further claimed that the average circumference is one and five-eighth inches. (All measurements taken one inch below the rim.)

I, personally, don't believe a word of this.

One of the first such studies was carried out in 1947 by the prominent sexologist Dr. Robert Latou Dickinson. He claimed the average size of the adult male penis, fully erect, to be within the range of five and one-half to six and one-half inches. He claimed the largest erect organ measured to date (i.e. 1947) to be thirteen and three-quarter inches in length and seven inches in circumference. He noted that many erect penises fell within the ten-to-twelve inch range.

The more recent studies of Dr. William H. Masters and Mrs. Virginia E. Johnson tend to confirm these findings.

Averages are, however, notorious.

Let us think logically.

Masters and Johnson measured "several hundred" penises; it is not enough. Let us imagine that they measured five hundred. Is it not possible that, by chance, they measured a majority of small ones? Or large ones? What would have happened to their average had they measured another two hundred, all of which, by chance, fell within the ten-to-twelve inch range? Or, by chance, in the two and one-half to four inch range?

These authorities are also disquietingly silent on the following point—were these all Caucasian organs?

And when they use the words "fully erect" can we, in fact, be sure that these penises were fully erect? Nervousness—indeed the very atmosphere of a clinic or hospital can produce profound physical reactions. Might not the very act of having one's penis *measured* inhibit full erection?

(This is no frivolous objection to the validity of the data. Doctors often find it necessary to test blood pressure two or three times because nervousness in patients produces inaccurate readings. I am reminded, also, of the time, during the first year of my marriage, when I had to undergo a fertility test. The instruction card stated that I must drink no liquids the night before, refrain from sexual expression, arise at 7 A.M. and produce a sperm sample that was to be delivered to the hospital no later than 8 A.M.

I arose at 7 A.M., still bleary with sleep, and stood in the bathroom trying to think of something erotic. All I could think of was breakfast. Eventually, however, I succeeded and stoppered the test tube I had been given. After a hasty cup of coffee, I rushed the sample to the Montreal General by taxi and handed it to the technician. He held the tube up to the light and said,

"Is this all?"

This suggests, I think, the point I'm trying to make.)

And then again, we might ask ourselves what, precisely, Dr. Robert Latou Dickinson means when he claims thirteen and three-quarter inches "as the largest erect organ measured to date." Surely, he can mean only "seen and measured by *him*." Why should we not assume organs in the nation greater in length and vaster in circumference *not* seen by Dr. Robert Latou Dickinson? How did he locate this specimen? Was an appeal made for the exceptionally endowed to come forward? And if so, where? Learned journals, after all, have a limited circulation.

Any logical examination of this evidence must also note that the data *in every study* are American. Conclusions should, logically, state that the average length, fully erect, of the adult male *American* penis is such and so. *American* circumference this and that.

It is not necessarily quibbling to suggest that the Canadian penis is a different penis. Not to mention the immigrant penis.

And while I have no particular wish to cast aspersions I do find myself wondering about the reliability and stability of these good doctors; devoting one's life to such measurement is a strange specialization to choose.

I cannot but regard this average of six inches as extremely suspect.

But whatever the truth may be—and does it really matter?—feelings of penile inadequacy are widespread. Even a casual glance through the correspondence columns of any sex magazine reveals the extent of this anxiety and its pathos. The following letter is not untypical.

> I am 26 years old. My penis is only three and one-half inches long when erect and about two inches long when flaccid. I have never masturbated—the one time I tried it didn't work. I tried intercourse once and think I reached orgasm. Sometimes when I have an erection it feels like I'm going to shoot out urine. I read in a magazine where a man took hormones every day and his penis increased in length. Would hormones help me?

"No, Mr. A.H. of Pennsylvania," was the curt reply, "you are too old."

The world over, men desire larger members. Certain African tribes suspend weights from their penises at puberty; others thrash their organs with bundles of nettle-like herbs in the hope the swelling will be permanent. The *Kama Sutra* recommends massage with a liquid made by boiling pomegranate seeds in oil. The Japanese, apparently more concerned with thickness than length, insert their penises into holes bored through heated bricks. Clinics in Switzerland give courses of treatment with vacuum developers; this treatment is used in conjunction with what is described as "double-handed milking massage" with theatrical cream "until the pain becomes unbearable."

Enlarging courses using the vacuum principle are marketed in the United States under the trade name *Megaphall.*

The Chinese are reported to do things with silver rings.

Style betrays me.

An easily written kind of humour, five-finger exercise.

My heart isn't in it.

"Truth," as my mother always used to say, "will out."

It doesn't matter that all those endearingly innocent American authorities state that an average-sized organ is preferable to one larger-than-average. *It doesn't matter* that women claim to prefer organs in the normal range. *It doesn't matter* that the average length of the vagina in a sexually aroused woman is only four and one-half inches. *It doesn't matter* that I'm married happily, the father of four children. I don't care what my wife and other women say, have said.

I have seen Bobby and I know what I know. I KNOW my thing is small. I know that hidden in all the trousers around me are huge organs. In every public convenience, happy extroverts stand back from the urinals, cosseting with justifiable pride members which, to me, seem to fall into the ten-to-twelve inch range while I fumble for it in my underpants, trying to find it, winkling it out.

I wish I had a big one.

How neatly the rhetoric of that confession is managed! How prettily worked its repetitions, its movements in and out of italic.

Lies. Mainly lies.

So much of my life is spent alone, in silence, creating illusions that, even when I set out to tell the truth, I cannot escape the professional gestures, the hands turned palms-and-backs to the audience, the cuffs pulled wide to illustrate emptiness—then the sudden string of flags.

I am not confessing here merely to "penile inadequacy" but to the continuing power of that disapproval of and distaste for "self"—for me—to the continuing power of those ghostly commands.

Wash yourself

Dry yourself

Why must in disappointment all I endeavour end?

* * *

WITHIN A VERY SHORT TIME of leaving home to go to university, I was relieved of my unlovely virginity by a kindly girl from Lancashire. She lanced the infection, cleansed, and healed. And with her laughter and affection flowed away the accumulation of tortured images, dogs strangely joined, dead hedgehogs, the lewd smile beneath the domino.

I did not love her nor she me; we liked each other. For some years after I came to Canada we exchanged Christmas cards and brief messages until time passed and one of us moved or forgot, or forgot to care.

From the loss of my virginity onwards, my sexual career was much as any other man's and of no particular interest to anyone but myself. Sex, thigh, and breast, which had seemed to shimmer and beckon like the gilded domes and minarets of an unattainable and mirage city were now, to my surprise, a fairly ordinary part of my life. Everything in the garden was lovely until anxiety intruded once again—this time in the form of a book.

I was about to say that the book was called—but its title, I find, is gone. And its author. Even its appearance. I *think* it had a yellow cover and was by Van de-Somebody. Dutch-sounding name. But what I do remember very clearly was its insistence that women derived no pleasure from intercourse unless they attained orgasm and this depended on the stimulation of the clitoris.

To a neophyte, as I was then, this insistence was disturbing. I didn't know if I had ever induced an orgasm, wasn't quite sure what one was. And the nature and location of the clitoris haunted me for years.

But the book was quite plain on the subject. It said:

"The shaft of the penis must at all times be kept in contact with the clitoris."

I thought about that sentence for a long time. The book was, after all, a manual, and it was written by a doctor. I tried to reconstruct the various anatomies which I'd felt under bedclothes and covers, and if the clitoris was where I thought it was supposed to be, and if vaginas were where *they* were supposed to be, I was left with only two possible solutions to the problem this sentence posed: either I was deformed, or I'd had the misfortune to have had sexual intercourse with four deformed girls.

I researched the clitoris: it was variously defined as "a miniature penis," "an external, erectile organ," and "a hooded member analogous to the male organ of generation." According to some authorities, it had erections and a kind of foreskin. Some authorities stated that it was the size of a pea, others the size of a large pea. Some just said it was "miniature." One authority stated that clitorises the size of the first joint of the thumb and which protruded through the outer lips were not uncommon.

When I first came to Canada, I bought a book in a United Cigar Store called *Clit Hunger*, published by Nightstand Books, but it was not illuminating.

The spontaneity of my sex life was ruined by my anxiety as I groped about trying to find this pea—or thumb-sized organ. It proved as elusive as a bird of paradise.

I never have actually *seen* one. I grudgingly admire direct men, those who milk their nursing wives into a cup of tea, or the explorers who take a flashlight to ladies' nether parts, but I am too shy, too unwilling to risk giving offence. My wife, too, is shy and sexually rather reserved—"modest," I suppose, would be the old-fashioned word, and I have come to approve of modesty.

(Though now, if I ever think about the subject at all, I *would* like to see a thumb-sized one, just once, just look.)

And then after the Clitoris Anxiety and the Shaft and Clitoris Anxiety, both before and after marriage, came new Anxieties as the fashions changed.

The Simultaneous Orgasm Anxiety.

The Clitoral versus the Vaginal Orgasm Anxiety.

The Multiple Orgasm Anxiety.

It was all mildly depressing.

Marriages were breaking up around us; women were leaving their husbands for electric toothbrushes.

Now, of course, things are different. Most nights we're both too tired or I go to bed early while Mary is out canvassing for the NDP, or I stay up writing while she goes to bed with a book. Saturdays are usually our day because of *Sunshine Saturday on ABC*. The two younger kids usually get up at about 6 A.M. and sit gazing at the blank TV screen waiting for the cartoons to start. Mary, who always wakes up before me, makes a jug of coffee and brings it into the bedroom. I always drink three cups. I am not sure whether or not she is aware that this pressure on my bladder stiffens my resolve.

We have no time for lengthy foreplay, by-play, toe-sucking, ice packs, orgasms simultaneous or multiple—we have exactly the amount of time that *Sunshine Saturday* allows before the next commercial and the demands for more toast or Wheaties and Jane trod on Peter's tractor and Peter took Jane's hockey cards and today *is* Saturday and if it's Saturday isn't Saturday allowance day?

* * *

LAST NIGHT the Waldmarks came to dinner. These dinners are a ritual, an observance ritually celebrated every two or three weeks—at their house or ours—and last night I cooked three wild ducks. Gerry was one of the first friends I made when I came to Canada; we were postgraduate students together, and for a year shared an apartment which was noted for its flow of girls, its spaghetti, and extraordinary gin-based drinks, which Gerry invented on Fridays. The friendship still endures. The evening had progressed, as it always does, with talk of old friends, old times, and Gerry insisting that early in the morning he'll be off skiing, taking a much-needed break from work and Alice and children and then, red-faced with exertion, Gerry always tries to stand on his head and Alice cries out, reminding him of his bad back, and his body wavers until he falls down. And then shouts of goodbye in the late street.

I woke early this morning, as I often do if I've had too much brandy to drink the night before. Drink used to render me unconscious, but now brandy seems to make my heart knock in my ears and I'm wakeful, drowsy, then stirred by sweating dreams and wake with unpleasant clarity. Mary was curled asleep, only her black hair visible on the pillow; I don't know how she doesn't suffocate. Her hair is touched now with grey which she used to dye but now does not; I asked her not to. The digital clock that I dislike clicked again and it was 6:03. I decided to get up and clean the dishes and the kitchen from the night before. It was still dark. I felt not too bad, slightly hung-over in spite of the aspirin, possibly still slightly drunk. It would get worse as the morning wore on. I eased out of bed, put on my bathrobe and closed the bedroom door behind me.

My knitted slippers still make me feel silly.

The sleep of others seems sacred. Perhaps, all too often, I can only express my love by washing dishes, shopping, saying it with flowers. I am no Heathcliff. In certain moods of self-loathing I feel I have become what my mother would have called "a good provider."

I went into the kitchen and closed the door to contain the noise and face the aftermath of duck.

I stared out across the sink into what would be the back garden, when the blackness paled, and looked at my reflection. I still felt odd—as though a few of the less-essential wires in my head were loosely connected. On mornings such as these my body forces itself on my attention in ways it never did before. I started on the roasting pan, scraping out dollops of congealed fat with a wooden spoon and plopping and smearing them onto an old newspaper. And something—wires disconnected, night thoughts, dreams perhaps—something about the duck fat, its opaqueness, its bland, dull surface, made me think of Gerry. Our friendship too was set, congealed. We all knew what must be avoided. We always talked about the past, things that happened twenty years and more ago, old wounds, old friends, old grievances, the two who were already dead, as though we could only be comfortable in mythology, in events upon which time had imposed some imaginable order. We seemed to live there more brightly than in our present, with more enthusiasm than we would in our imaginable future.

I drink too much, Gerry drinks too much, we all do.

I am more aware than I was of my heart and its mechanisms. I still felt uncomfortable, aware of its beating in my temples. And in my troubled sleep I had dreamed again the same dream, always the same, precise in every detail. I don't know what it means; it needn't so far as I can see, mean anything. Each part is as significant as any other.

The dream is a dream of journey.

It always starts on a railway station in England during the war. I am standing by a slot-machine which dispenses Nestlé chocolate bars but there are, of course, no chocolate bars because the war is on. The machine is dirty, its glass panel through which one might have seen the stacked bars is shattered, the brass handle you pull to get out the chocolate is tarnished almost black.

I am journeying to visit a friend. When I arrive in the town in which he lives I go to his house. My knock is not answered. The door is unlocked. I go in and find him hanging. The rope is brand new half-inch manila, almost yellow, stiff and varnished. His face is as I have always known it, calm, composed. There is no violence.

On the mantelpiece is an engraved invitation card with a deckle edge. It is an invitation to me from my younger brother to a civic reception in his honour.

I am in a taxi drawing up to the Town Hall. There is a red carpet, a footman. I am wearing evening dress. When I go in, I find porters in livery stacking chairs, stripping and folding linen tablecloths. They wear white, buttoned gloves. The reception, they tell me, ended an hour ago.

I am by a broken Nestlé chocolate-bar machine again. Again another journey. Again the door is unlocked. Another friend hangs from a length of manila rope. Again the invitation card stands on the mantelpiece and again I am too late and find the liveried porters dismantling the festive chamber.

Sometimes in the dream I seem to be angry with my brother, sometimes I feel nothing. I wonder why he figures in this dream? I have not seen him since I left England and we never write. I did not even see him when my father died. I was not at home when the telegram arrived—I was in Eugene, Oregon, teaching a summer-school session to afford whatever had to be afforded—repairs to the house, the car, the furnace, clothes for the children—and by the time phone calls from Mary traced me and airline schedules had been checked, it was too late. And my father was buried.

In a file under F, in a file marked Father, I have all the letters he ever wrote me. There are seven. They were never sent from home but always from somewhere on an infrequent holiday. They all start off with depressing ordinariness. They are addressed to My Dear Boy and signed Your Loving Father.

One starts:

The weather here is fine. We are, praise God, in good health.

Another:

The Lord has granted us good weather.

But then come his typical outbursts of eccentricity:

Here they pretend not to know how to boil eggs. I have given the strictest instructions—I could not have been

> more explicit. I can only conclude that this is done to aggravate me.
>
> Another said:
>
> Your mother constantly remarks upon the views. I have requested her NOT to remark upon views but to no avail. I am not blind. She desires me to take photographs of these views; this I have refused to do. God has given us memories and if we cannot remember what we have seen then it is not memorable. I have explained this to her.
>
> There are many Germans.

How I wish I had known him.

The bare branches of the lilac tree outside the window began to appear, stark in the blue blackness. I searched for the Brillo pads; Mary always puts things in different places. Scraps of the skin of the duck proved almost impossible to remove.

When my mother died, I did go back to England. It wasn't filial piety or respect. I think, secretly, I wanted to be sure. I wanted to see the coffin with my own eyes and hear the earth thudding onto the wood. What would her words have been? Laid to rest? Gone to her reward?

The minister of the church she'd attended, a Heepish creature, asked me if I would read from the Scriptures; I gravely declined and he hastened to understand my feelings. There were floral tributes and the singing of hymns. She had, an ancient uncle assured me, fought the good fight.

This time, ironically, my brother was away, somewhere in Greece on holiday, unreachable. It was left to me to dispose of immediate matters. She had been living in a small town in Kent. I wandered about that house for two days, touching, looking, feeling strange. It was all gone now, all finished.

The clothes neatly folded in all the drawers; the stink of lavender. Little silken bags of lavender. I gathered up all the little bags and burned them. The net gloves. Them too.

The same pictures from twenty-five years before when I'd left. The picture of Peter Pan she'd tried to keep hanging in my bedroom. *The Light of the World*—Christ with a lantern. Holman Hunt, was it? Anonymous landscapes. Few books—some volumes of popular devotion, the autobiography of a vet, a life of Wesley, Agatha Christie, and Dorothy L. Sayers.

In her bedroom, on the dressing table, still the remembered objects of childhood. The ebony hairbrush. A strange little ebony pot with a screw top with a hole in the top which was for putting hair into from a comb or brush before throwing it away. An amazing object—obviously common thirty or forty years ago, but now as oddly antique as a sand shaker for drying letters. Formidable hairpins and hatpins, brooches fussy with little coloured stones.

In a kitchen drawer, neat piles of *ironed* rags.

A bureau contained scissors, glue, and large scrapbooks in various stages of completion. They were haphazardly full of pictures of holly, mangers, Christmas trees, lanterns, candles, carol-singers, Pickwickian coaches and ostlers, etc. all cut from Christmas cards and intended for the missions in Africa. I was struck by some of the pictures that had taken her fancy—one in particular, I recall. A kitten sitting in a shoe. Harsh people are often sentimental.

I wondered what tiny Ibo or Luba children would make of these strange images from a different world. I burned them all.

A large cupboard in the kitchen was chock-full of patent medicines, strange bottles with nineteenth-century-looking labels. Most of them were laxatives and purgatives, infusions of strange bark and pods, extract of prune, and numerous bottles of something called Slippery Elm.

The only reminder in the house that my father had ever lived was a framed photograph of him, which stood on an occasional table in the sitting room. And that photograph, significantly, posed him with the mayor and alderman in their robes in the year he'd been mayor's chaplain. The mayor was wearing his golden chain of office.

All my father's books, the books he'd written, his occasional writings, his sermons, not a thing remained. She'd managed to restore the home of her last years to the spinsterish order and purity of her dreams. Her bed was a single with a new eiderdown.

Even with my mother dead and me a father in my forties, I still could not imagine them doing "that sort of thing." could not imagine her thighs loosening or that angular body softening or hear her cry out in the dark bedroom. They still were giant figures on a glaring stage, their lives the myth of my life. I believed when a boy and believe now they did it twice. Me and my brother. And duty done, she—what? Something must have driven him to his eccentricities and silence. How could he be explained? He collected, in his last years, first editions of Conrad. Of all writers, *Conrad*. He remains a mystery.

I can imagine her voice in their dark bedroom, a voice little more than a chill whisper.

Or perhaps stolid silence.

Silence.

Silence.

After I had given all her personal effects to Oxfam before my brother could return, after I'd signed tedious documents with a disapproving lawyer disinheriting myself in my brother's favour, I found myself bored, irritable, and thinking insistently about Croydon. I still had time on my excursion ticket, so I made the journey.

Croydon.

Though I've often been pissed by lunch and sometimes on champagne, I never did shave off half my moustache or take a lobster for a walk, live in brothels, or cut my ear off. I've never had syphilis either. But I did become a writer of sorts;

not the writer that I'd dreamed of becoming in my Croydon adolescence; the Muse hovers but does not ravish me. I write short stories, which are published in the little magazines and university journals. I have published two collections of these stories, one of which is still in print. Several stories have been anthologized. I wrote a novel about a boy's growing up. He was a rebel. It was remaindered in Classics' bookstores a year later for ninety-nine cents. Reviewers have described my work as "sensitive" and "finely tuned explorations of loneliness and self-discovery." I have some small reputation in a minor genre in the parochial world of Canadian letters. Like many Canadian writers, I support myself by teaching in a university.

In the calendar I am designated as:

T.D. Moore (Ph.D.): Modern British Poetry (2003)
Moore (Ph.D.): Contemporary Fiction (2001)

In Croydon I walked around familiar streets. I looked at the exterior of my father's old church. A notice outside stated the minister's name and the hours of services and white, plastic letters asserted beneath:

God So Loved The World That He Gave His Only Begotten Son.

I went to the park where Helen and I had walked and held hands.

I looked into the library.

I tried to find a shop I'd loved as a boy, a shop that sold antique arms and armour, but the whole area had been torn down and, in its place, stood a complex of office space, Odeon cinema, and bowling alley.

Tony and I had been smitten for a short time, perhaps between jazz and painting, with the idea of becoming diamond prospectors—pork-knockers they were called—in what was then British Guiana. We read Peter Fleming and *Green Hell* and all the books about Colonel Fawcett. We drew bold lines from Georgetown into the uncharted interior. Like Sir Richard Burton, we would write our names large on the map's white spaces.

I did not try to find Tony. I made no enquiries of his life.

I wanted to remember him for always and ever as the boy who imagined sucking the hair in Eliska's armpit.

In my hotel room that night, lying on the bed with indigestion after eating something the hotel menu called Gooseberry Fool and drinking their coffee—I found my mind full of pictures of that Yorkshire manse where I'd pinned worms to crosses, full of memories of Mrs. Henderson, the Scarlet Woman, and Mr. Montague.

Nothing held me now in England; she was dead. My life was wholly in Canada with Mary and the children in Montreal—in what my brother, an historian of medieval matters, still calls the New World.

He phoned me after our father's funeral—some legal matter—and I invited him to visit us in Canada; I can hear his hesitant voice declining—family responsibilities, money, pressure of work—and then, "I really feel that the New World offers little that could engage my interests..."

I was lonely in that hotel bedroom, unsettled, and those ghosts called me, beckoned to me across forty years. And so I struggled with the telephone system and British Railways—two institutions obdurately inefficient and unchanged since my youth, and arranged to journey to that northern town.

It's a common experience—all adults must remember particular school teachers and meet them after childhood to find them shrunken, mild-mannered, ordinary, ordinary. That huge manse where I'd hidden in alcoves and played on the vast expanse of polished landings, that mansion with its many rooms, turned out to be a seedy Victorian house, certainly not small, but not the monstrous pile that I remembered. I stood looking at it and thought of asking if I might go round into the back garden—to do what? Look at my crucifix plot? Open the coal-cellar door and peer down into the dark which had terrified me as a child? Little Pakistani children trundled up and down on their tricycles. I could not face the complexities of request or explanation.

I did find the Scarlet Woman. She must have been sixty-five or so, but looked older. I felt foolish. She turned out to be a lonely old woman who drank too much gin too early in the day.

"So you're the vicar's little boy!" she said, marvelling.

"I remember you. Yes, I do. Picked all my daffodils, you did, and put horse manure through my letter box!"

I confessed that it sounded like me.

"Of course, the neighbourhood's gone down," she said, "what with those Pakis and their customs."

On every surface in her living room stood framed photographs of her husband. Wedding pictures. The pair of them windswept on a seaside pier. A young man in uniform. A posed group of soldiers grinning like embarrassed boys.

He'd died in France, burned alive in his tank.

"Eh," she said, in that suddenly comfortable Yorkshire, "my Tom, he were a *lovely* lad."

We drank gin together all afternoon and I told her about a Canada I thought she might like to hear about, a Canada of skyscrapers, rivers wider than the eye could command, snow that buried cars in a single night, Red Indians, bears, and timber wolves.

She cried when I had to leave, and I hugged her and was glad I'd made the journey. And as I bent to kiss her goodbye, she said,

"Canada! Well, I never! Who'd a thowt it when tha was a little lad!"

I winced at the clatter of cutlery, held my breath and was silent in that silent kitchen, waiting to hear movement from the bedroom. It was beginning to get light. I could see the bulk of our neighbour's house, the whiteness of the white fence that

I'd have to paint again in the summer. The water in the sink was brown and greasy; horrid soft things nudged my hands in the water.

The glasses could go straight into the dishwasher.

Mary's life fascinates me; I love to observe all her drama and silliness. I often feel she's more *alive* than I am; sometimes I even feel I live *through* her. Her political rages and feuds amuse me though I try to disguise my amusement. Mary genuinely *believes* in justice and being fair and the dignity of man. She reminds me of Peter and Jane at bedtime when one or the other says it isn't *fair!* She accuses me of not caring about people and in the way she means it she's quite right. All that was long ago burned out of me.

"You're *cold*," she says. "You don't *care*."

And she's fiercely eccentric, too, in her own way, irrational, and I love that about her as well. She hasn't spoken to our neighbour in the back for six years. She's convinced he's a peeping Tom. The story, according to her, is that when she was about eight months pregnant with Peter, she was sitting on the lavatory one evening and the frosted bathroom window, which looks out onto the back garden, was open about an inch. She suddenly felt uncomfortable and looked up and there, watching her, she saw a pair of eyes.

How could she possibly identify our neighbour, I wanted to know.

"I'd know those eyes anywhere!" she declared.

The other week the poor man was up on his roof in the ice and snow mending one of the wire stays of his TV aerial.

"Just look at him!" she said indignantly. "He'll do anything to peer in."

Gerry had spilled wine on the tablecloth and I decided to take it and the napkins downstairs and put them in the washing machine. The basement is finished as a large room for the kids, but a part of it is partitioned off to enclose the furnace and the washer and dryer, and a part of that partition is closed off again to afford me a tiny, dark room where I grade papers, read, and write my stories. Mary calls it my "study" but the word "study" or "office" is rather grandiose for what is as narrow as a stall; I generally call it my "room." And there, with as much silence as I can get between the washing machine and kids and the rush of the bloody furnace, I write my stories of "loneliness and self-discovery."

I coiled the garden hose and hung it back on its rack; it's Peter's favourite toy, which he's been told numberless times not to touch. Someone had knocked over the plastic sack of Diamond Green Combination Lawn Fertilizer. I dragged it upright and propped it up against the wall again. The huge box of Tide was empty and I had to rip the top off a new one. I made a mental note to speak to Peter about the hose.

Truth to tell, I'm not all that interested in the kids. When they don't irritate me, they bore me. Angela is now fourteen and sulky, Billy thirteen and apathetic. I'd have been content enough to leave it there but Mary decided she'd like more so we had Peter and Jane. I study Billy covertly. I assume that he must be as I was, that he lusts after girls and women and wanks himself senseless. But sometimes I have my doubts. As far as I can tell, he spends most of his time watching TV and, when he isn't watching TV, he's reading *Mad Magazine*. Perhaps he wanks while he watches. Angela spends most of her life behind a slammed bedroom door; other than play rock music, I don't know what she does in there. They are both too interested in money and Billy deposits every cent he can get in his bank account. If he isn't reading *Mad Magazine* or *TV Guide*, he's reading his bank book. It is impossible to talk to Angela; she pouts, flaunts, and sulks. She is currently enraged that I have refused to have installed in her bedroom a Princess phone on a separate line. My considered desire is to flog the living daylights out of her but Mary says she's going through a difficult time.

They're children from another world, a world in which I'm alien; the New World.

I watch them sometimes on their bicycles, observe their play; Jane is almost fat. Sometimes I chauffeur Angela and even Billy to *dances* for God's sake! and I think them lotus-eaters, children lacking any drive or purpose, softlings.

And as for me, I come from the Pre-TV, the age which, in their ahistoric minds, followed the Bronze or Iron.

I am probably as remote from them as my father was from me.

Would I wish on them *my* history and *its* history?

Sometimes, yes.

On that trip to Yorkshire after I'd seen my mother buried, I made a sentimental excursion to Haworth Parsonage; my motivation wasn't literary. My father had taken me there once when I was a small child. I enquired about a taxi in town and the man said:

"Tha's not American. Bus is nobbut a shilling."

The gravestones, slate and shining in the rain, crowd right up the sides of the Parsonage. The children were buried there one by one; the remaining sisters wrote among the ghosts. Emily's fevered imagination, its mad intensity, reminds me of some quality in my own childhood; I read her book with recognition. It is the work of a virgin. Would she have written it, I wonder now, if she'd married, married and lived longer?

I walked among the gravestones, pausing now and then to trace weathered lettering with my fingertips and then out and up onto the moors. The heather was wet and springy and I shivered in my light raincoat. I stood for a few minutes by an outcrop of rock where so many years ago I'd stood with my father.

I, too, often feel I live my life among ghosts, that the stories I write are exorcisms. The dead are all around me. I am too much part of them.

Wash yourself
Dry yourself

It's as if I exhausted all my passion by the age of sixteen; nothing since has compared with the drama and intensity of that battle of wills, a titanic struggle fought against the backdrop of Hell.

And none of it now means anything I can understand; I no longer believe in the fire and ice of Hell and sex is what happens on Saturdays.

I watch Angela and her friends who lounge on our balcony and lawn in the summer. I observe the loveliness of their young bodies. Mary's breasts are fallen, disfigured with stretch-marks, her nipples like plugs. I wonder what is going to happen to Angela, how *her* story will unfold.

"Young girls with little tender tits."

Foals in an autumn field.

The wash was thumping about in the machine, water sloshing. My hangover was getting worse as I knew it would. Something vital in the washing-machine needed oiling. I groped through its rhythm and the pounding in my head for the rest of those lines, something I'd been teaching, "Young girls with little tender tits," teaching the term before, tried to remember the line that rhymed, remember . . .

Remember, imbeciles and wits
Sots and ascetics, fair and foul,
Young girls with little tender tits,
that Death is written over all

I sat and waited in my room.

A year or so ago I was wandering about near Craig Street in an unfamiliar part of Montreal searching for a stationer's that was reputed to carry a make of fountain pen I wished to buy. Down a side street, I found a store that was a cross between an army surplus and a chandler's. On some strange impulse, I bought a sextant. It was expensive and the moment

I'd paid for it I felt silly and went to some trouble to smuggle it into the house. I hide it under papers in a drawer in my room.

As the washing machine changed rhythm and the water drained away I took the sextant out. It sits in a mahogany box, the brass and glass nestled in green baize. I looked at it, at its telescope, index mirror, and horizon glass. I turned the clamp screw and the tangent screw, enjoying the feel of the milled edges. I'm not quite sure how it's supposed to work.

THE LADY WHO SOLD FURNITURE

PURPLE. Purpleness with a zigzag line of black. A zigzag line of black stitching. Peter pushed the bedspread down from his face and moved his head on the pillow. He expected for a second to see above his head the raftered darkness of the barn and to hear the clatter of sabots on the cobbles, the every-morning shout of *Monsieur Anglais!* But the only sounds were sparrows on the windowsill and the distant rattle of the milkman's van.

Sunlight lay over the floorboards and the worn carpet. His boots and rucksack lay where he'd dropped them the night before. The sole of one boot was grey with caked mud except where the tips of the steel cleats glinted in the sunshine.

Peter stretched and arched his back. He flexed the muscles in his shoulders and then eased himself over in the bed until the sunlight was across his face. The long weeks of labour in the Channel Islands, the hoeing, the tomato and potato picking, the clearing of vines and heaving of sheaves in the fields of the Maison Village de Philippe were finished, and three weeks of idleness remained.

The house was silent. It seemed strange to see the room empty, the other bed stripped down to the springs and piled with folded blankets. It seemed strange not to see Nick sprawled asleep across heaps of novels and crumpled paper and not to hear whistling, a typewriter, people shouting outside the bathroom door. He heard Anna stumping up the stairs, the chessmen rattling in their wooden box, and closed his eyes. She opened the door quietly and he sensed her approaching over the frayed carpet. He could hear the soft snuffle of her breathing, louder as she bent to peer at his face. When he felt her breath warm on his cheek, his eyelids fluttered.

Her voice barely above a breath, she said, "Are you asleep, Peter?"

"Yes," he whispered.

She squealed and pinched his nose and he grabbed her, swinging her up onto the bed. He held her struggling in the air and said in his gruff voice, "Anna! Are you still my girlfriend?"

"Do you want to play chess?" she said.

"Where's your mummy?"

"She said to tell her if you were awake."

Anna jumped down and ran out to the head of the stairs shouting, "Mummy! Mummy!" and then ran back and scrambled onto the bed. She opened the chessboard and said, "David and me are learning how to swim." She held out clenched fists and he tapped the hand that held the black pawn. "I start!" she yelled. "And do you know what? We have rubber waterwings and go on the bus." She tipped out the men onto the bedspread and slowly placed them on the board. "Peter? We go on the bus *alone*."

Jeanne came in carrying a cup of coffee. She was wearing a pink, quilted housecoat and was barefoot. As she sat down on the end of the bed, she said, "I'll make you some proper breakfast when you get up." Sipping the coffee, Peter watched her over Anna's head. Without make-up and in the morning light, her face was pale and gaunt.

"David and me go swimming now, eh Mummy?"

"David and *I*."

"David and *I*," said Anna.

"You certainly do," said Jeanne.

The lines seemed deeper drawn than he'd remembered, her eyes more shadowed. As she drew on her cigarette, her cheeks hollowed. He watched the jet of smoke falter, drift, wreathe up the path of sunlight.

"You're not paying attention," said Anna. "I said which way do they go?"

"Queen on her own colour."

She was sitting between Jeanne's feet. The toes were long and bony, knobbly with corns and calloused skin. He touched his fingers to his lips and lightly pressed her foot. She grinned at him.

"It's your turn, Peter," said Anna.

He advanced a pawn and said, "Does Jim know I'm here?"

"Yes. I told him before he left for work."

"And?"

"He urged me to collect rent in advance if you were staying for a week and otherwise to work out a per diem arrangement."

"*Per diem*, eh?"

"He's an educated man," said Jeanne.

"*Per ardua ad astra,*" said Peter.

"Do you want that move again?" said Anna.

Peter studied the board and said, "Why? What's wrong with it?"

"Oh, there's nothing *wrong* with it," said Anna. "You're sure you don't want it back?"

"Go on! Make your move."

"Got it!" shouted Anna, as she took his queen.

"Oh, that was stupid of me!" said Peter.

"I gave you a chance," crowed Anna.

"Oh, it's hopeless," said Peter.

"Give in?"

"Well, I'll have to, won't I?"

"I've won, I've won," she chanted as she knocked over all the men and started to scoop them into the box.

“Listen, poppet,” said Jeanne. “You can go and play with Marion for a while if you like. But you have to come home at twelve o’clock. All right?”

“Okay,” said Anna.

“Don’t say ‘okay,’” said Jeanne. “Speak properly.”

Anna scrambled off the bed and started for the door.

“Come back and take the chess game downstairs. Put it in the cupboard. And what are you going to ask Mrs. Williams?”

“When it’s twelve o’clock.”

They listened to the rattles and thuds as she ran and jumped her way down the three flights of stairs. There was a silence and then the massive slam of the front door. They heard the wire basket underneath the letterbox fall off and skitter across the tiles in the hall. Jeanne stood up and watched her from the window as she pushed open the Williams’ front gate and climbed the steps to the front door.

As she turned away, Jeanne unbuttoned the pink housecoat. Under it she was wearing a black nightdress. Peter moved over to the far side of the bed and pulled back the blankets. He felt her length slide down beside him.

“Your feet are cold,” he said.

“Give me some pillow,” she said.

He worked his arm under her shoulder.

“God! You stink,” she said.

“Take this thing off.”

“You don’t want to look at me,” said Jeanne.

“Yes. Yes, of course I do.”

* * *

JEANNE’S VOICE shouting something. Peter opened the bedroom door.

“What?”

“Hurry up! Your breakfast’s nearly ready!”

“Coming!” he called.

He put on his last clean shirt and started downstairs past the silent rooms. On the second floor a bedroom door was standing open and he stopped on the threshold looking in. Two iron bedsteads, one covered by a blue mattress. A black-painted chest of drawers. Under the window stood an old leather-topped table and a rush-bottom chair. The gas fire had gleaming new white mantles. On the bare white walls were tabs of yellowed Scotch tape.

He sat down on the edge of the bed and stared towards the window. Only a few weeks ago the walls had been covered with photographs and drawings of badgers. The tabletop had been littered with glazed pillboxes full of badger dung, glass-topped boxes of tiny bones, mounting pins, probes, scalpels, teeth, magnifying glasses, a badger skull, withered plants, and dried bluebell bulbs. And John Neil sitting oblivious of noise or intrusions, one hand playing in his beard, the other listing food types in an exercise book.

"Peter! Do I have to *beg* you!"

The sunshine through the dusty window was warm on his bare feet. He worked his toes into the green carpet and then got up and stood looking out. Most of the house across the road was hidden behind the leaves and branches of a sweet chestnut tree. He followed the slant of the purple slates up to the high point of the roof which was crowned by a golden weathervane. He remembered that afternoon of another summer when Jeanne had suddenly come into their room with an enamel bowl of ice and four bottles of Chablis and, as the wine went down, they had dragged his bed in front of the window and the three of them had fired at the weathervane all afternoon with Nick's air-rifle until the ice melted and the wine was gone and they had fallen asleep.

But he had enjoyed the winters more, lying on his bed for hours and days, reading, the counterpane grey with cigarette ash, feeding shillings into the meter for the gas fire, reading and reading until his head felt light and he resented the footsteps on the stairs, Nick and the rush of colder air as the door opened, and the sudden descent into the cluttered reality of the room.

And then dinner in the warm basement kitchen, often followed, when Jim was away, by wild darts tournaments which Jeanne organized to see who would do the washing-up, games which always seemed to swell and grow until they turned into events. The huge kitchen would become crowded with friends and acquaintances who brought beer and pork pies and chips and at ten thirty, when the pubs closed, the doorbell would ring to reveal old Fred Johnson from the Three Feathers with his entire darts team crowding up the front steps behind him, bottles clinking in the dark.

He stopped in the hall, the brown tiles cold on his bare feet, and fixed the wire basket under the letterbox again. He went down the stairs into the basement. As he walked into the kitchen, Jeanne was throwing darts into a new board. She was dressed now, wearing jeans, suede boots, and a sweater.

"Bloody *rude*," she said.

"I'm sorry."

"In the pan, there."

"When did you get the new board?"

"I got the new board two weeks ago in exchange for five hundred Red Dragon coupons."

Peter looked at her for a moment and then said, "You're still smoking *those* bloody things, are you?"

She shrugged and kept throwing for the double seven. Peter poured coffee from the pot on the stove and lit the gas under the frying pan to reheat the eggs and bacon. He slid onto the bench behind the long table.

The wall facing him was bright orange. The others were daubed with designs, foot and handprints, graffiti. They were the result of one of Jeanne's parties. Jim had complained at first but as the rawness of the colour had faded into the plaster nothing more had been said.

Jeanne's face was set, her lips a straight line. The darts thudded into the board. Peter watched her as he drank the coffee. He remembered the loud click of the key in her bedroom door; the white anger of her face the next morning as she ripped off the crumpled sheets.

There had been a barrel of beer in the sitting room on the ground floor and everyone brought draught port in milk bottles from the Excise Man. There had been dancing. Nick had been red-eyed and belligerent and had called a medical student a trainee plumber. The medical student had kept on saying he wasn't a plumber because he had to take an Oath. A very important Oath. Jeanne had ordered an art-school student thrown out for vomiting in a wardrobe. Then they'd thrown the medical student out for refusing to stop saying that he'd got to take an Oath. Jim beamed on everyone and reminisced about Biggin Hill and The Few and then cried and refused to go to bed until he'd made everyone promise to give their all if the call came.

The sitting room had emptied by about three thirty. A boy from the art school was asleep on the floor with a cushion from an armchair under his head. The ashtrays were heaped and spilling over. The air was frowsty. Bottles, glasses, and froth-ringed beer mugs stood on the sideboard, carpet, table, bureau, and mantelpiece. Drop after drop of beer from the leaking spigot plipped into an enamel bowl set underneath.

Jeanne and he had strolled through silent streets to Uplands Park. They had walked beyond the range of the glistening street lamps out onto the dark expanse of grass. Jeanne had picked an armful of lilac branches. As they were bending to catch the slight fragrance of the flowers, they had suddenly stopped, staring at the paleness of each other's face in the night.

She had given him the flowers to carry and he remembered the coldness of the drops of dew on his face and shirt. Then, holding hands, they had paddled in the icy grass until, holding onto his shoulder and hopping about on one leg, she'd said, "Hey, my feet have gone all white and crinkly."

When they returned, the house was dark and silent. He remembered they had giggled and said "Shsssh!" to each other as they had crossed the dark hall and tiptoed down into the kitchen.

He had been talking about Spain. She had made bacon sandwiches and coffee laced with brandy. He remembered pouring HP Sauce onto his sandwich; the gleam of the brown sauce as it curled out of the bottle.

He performed a dazzling *faena* of rhythmic *naturels*, *veronicas*, and audacious *mariposas*, using a tablecoth for a cape, until he tripped on it and hurt his leg on the ironing board.

He remembered her hands under his arms helping him up and the loud click of the key in her bedroom door.

When he awoke, she wasn't there. The curtains were drawn over the small window and the room was gloomy. He raised himself on his elbows and the blankets slid off onto the floor. As he bent out of the bed to pull them back, pain slopped through his head. He lay back and moved his head carefully on the pillow trying to find a cool place. He heard sounds from the kitchen; the clash of crockery, the kettle banging down on the stove. She had come in with two mugs of coffee.

"Why don't you make the bed properly?" he had said.

She had stood staring at him.

"All the blankets keep falling off."

"A gentleman's first words are usually, 'Thank you,' or at least, 'Good morning.'"

"Umm?"

"You arrogant, bad-mannered little snot! The bed isn't made because I happen to like it that way. And it happens to be *my* bed. And because you happen to be in it doesn't give you any rights over it. Or over *me*."

She banged the mugs down on the dressing table so hard that coffee slopped over the sides.

"Is that clear?"

"I'm sorry. I didn't...."

She grabbed at the blankets and jerked them onto the floor.

"Get up!"

She yanked off the crumpled sheets.

He'd stood naked and watched her as she made the bed. It seemed to take her only seconds. "Is this the sort of thing you mean?" she said as her hands twitched at the sheets, drawing them taut, binding them with hospital corners. "I did this every day," she said, banging and shaking the pillows until they lay plump and creaseless. "Every day for twelve months." She worked round the mattress, binding in the blankets. "And on every single one of those days I didn't get my breakfast until the nice lady had inspected my handiwork."

She snatched her purse from the dressing table and took out a half-crown.

"Look, Jeanne...."

"Don't speak to me," she said. "I don't want a conversation with you."

Facing him across the bed, she silently held the coin up to his eye level and then dropped it. It fell onto the centre of the bed. The blankets quivered.

"*She* always used to drop her whistle."

She glared at him, her housecoat hanging open.

"So now, my charming young friend, I have it the way *I* want it."

"Jeanne...."

"I am now going to have my breakfast."

"Really, Jeanne...."

"And another thing. I spent my days working in the laundry, so you needn't think you're going to get clean shirts out of this!"

The door had slammed and then bounced open again.

The monotonous thud of the darts in the board irritated him. There were muddy patches on the orange wall near the ceiling. The original paint seemed to be bleeding through. Possibly it was just dampness. He tried to remember what colour the wall had been before; whatever it had been, it was better than orange.

"Jeanne?" he said.

"What?"

"I'm sorry I was a long time."

"It's your breakfast, not mine."

"Well, I'm sorry if I was rude. I was in John's old room."

She planked a last dart into the board and then scooped out the eggs and bacon onto a plate. She put it in front of him and sat down.

"Have you heard from Nick yet?" she said.

"No, not yet."

"The rotten sod. Remember he said he'd write to tell us when he'd been in his first drugstore?"

"Jeanne?"

"Umm?"

"I was thinking."

"What?"

"I could tell Jim that he could give me a room to myself for the same price as a double one because I'm not a student now and so I'd be here—paying rent—while the others were on vacation."

"Don't make me laugh!" she said.

"Well, it's worth trying."

"It isn't. You ought to know him better by now—the nauseating little prick!"

"What's he done now?"

"Were you still here when he beat David for wetting the bed?"

"Yes, that was just before I left."

"It's a good job the poor kid's away from him for the rest of the summer. And, by the way, I learned that James has got his name down for some ghastly public school. But do you know what he said to me? 'It isn't manly for a boy of nine to wet his bed.'"

"Well, what's that got to do with asking about the room?"

"No. I was going to tell you about what happened last week. I was in bed reading—it was about eleven thirty—and there was a knock at the door.

Who is it?

It is I—Jim."

"He didn't *really* say that?"

"Don't interrupt. So I went to the door and there he was in his pyjamas—all buttons done up. Hair neatly brushed. Bulgy eyes."

She did her Jim-face.

"Did he have an RAF badge on his pyjamas?"

"*I think David's unwell* he says *and I wondered if I could prevail upon you to cast a motherly eye...?* So we went upstairs to David's room. You know, there were little wisps of pubicy hair sticking out of the collar of his pyjamas—he must have hair all over his back. Isn't that *disgusting!* Anyway, David was fine. Just a bit restless so I gave him an aspirin and puffed the pillows up. And while I was bending over the bed, he was bending over me. *You'll be all right, old chap. Right as rain. Just snuggle down and let Jeanne tuck you in.* And he was pressing himself against me so that I could feel his *thing*. Well, we went out on the landing and he said *It's extremely decent of you to be so kind with the little chap, Jeanne. Needs a woman's touch. Don't know how we'd get along without you.* Then his eyes started going bulgy again. *It's a lonely task for a widower* he says. *Lonely. Very lonely.* So I gabbled something about all of us being lonely at times and whipped off downstairs and locked the door."

"Poor old Jim," said Peter. "You know he's always fancied you. I don't know what you're going on about."

"Oh, *that* doesn't bother me," said Jeanne. "No. It's not that. It's what he says the next day—the snivelling little crapper. *Oh, Jeanne. I've been forced to give some consideration to the economics of the house and I'm going to find it necessary to make an adjustment to your allowance.* Pay, he means, of course. *Your duties are far less onerous while the students are on the long vac and I really think it not unreasonable.* Etcetera. Etcetera. What do you think of that?"

"*Did* he pay you less?"

"Don't be soft," she said. "But the nastiness of it, eh? Can't get his end away so he turns spiteful."

She stopped suddenly and pointed at the small window above the sink which was level with the grass of the front lawn. She mouthed something at him. She drew off one boot and suddenly hurled it through the open window.

"Tomcat," she said. "Always comes and pisses on the windowsill and taints the butter. No. It's the attitude, the spirit of the man that gets up *my* nose. And that's the man who's going to let you have a room cheap. Especially *you*."

The front door slammed and they heard Anna clattering down the basement stairs.

"Fancy being hairy all over!" said Jeanne. "He must look like King Kong when he's naked."

"King Kong! King Kong!" shouted Anna.

"You bad girl!" cried Jeanne. "You've been changing clothes with Marion again. You just go *straight* back and get your own dress and shoes."

"Oh, Mummy. . . ."

"This minute!"

They grinned at each other as they listened to her footsteps dragging up the stairs. Jeanne called after her, "And fetch my boot from the front lawn."

The boot dropped through the window into the sink. Anna's face appeared and said, "Can we go to the zoo this afternoon?"

"Why not?" said Jeanne. "Do you want to come, Peter? Anna found a rhinoceros that eats ice-cream."

"Well, I wouldn't mind but I've got to look at this school sometime, Jeanne, so I think I'll get that over with."

"It's nicer at the zoo."

"I know," said Peter.

* * *

HE STOOPED over the basin patting hot water onto his face to soften four days' bristle. He had run out of new razor blades but Jeanne had picked the lock on Jim's door and stolen one for him. He peered into the mirror, examining his face. Suntanned certainly, but the long weeks had left no lines or creases, no major changes. He pressed the button on Jim's aerosol can of shaving cream and watched the thick whorls rising in his palm.

Water gurgled into the hot water tank and the pipes whined into silence. *Three weeks* he said to his reflection. The house empty, the bed stripped down to its springs and piled with folded blankets, Nick now living in America.

Three weeks, but, if he didn't find out where the school was, check the bus numbers and time the route, it would only undermine the days he had left. And while he was out he must go down to the Valley to pay Mrs. Jenkins for cigarettes and Hilda at the newsagent's. There would be seven weeks of *Jazz Journal*, *The Listener*, and the *New Statesman*, and two copies of *Encounter*. He hoped she hadn't returned them. He smiled as he thought of Mrs. Jenkins searching through piles of old paper bags and the backs of cigarette packets to find the scrap on which she'd scrawled his account.

"Goodbye, Peter!" shouted Anna.

"Goodbye!"

"*The Zoo!*" shouted Anna to everyone.

"Back about six," called Jeanne.

"Bye!"

The front door slammed and their voices died away down the path.

His hands idle in the warm water, he pictured the vast Victorian houses all the way down the hill to the Valley where they gave way to grey Georgian tenements, divided and subdivided into flatlets and bedsitters. Windows here and there were broken or boarded over, and pink willow herb sprouted from roofs and guttering.

On the blackened walls of the United Methodist Chapel, gangs of grimy children had chalked a frieze of houses and trees and stick-people and airplanes. Behind the hoardings which masked the bomb sites, the older children threw rocks at the abandoned cars.

Behind the Chapel, in Canning Street, was the fish and chip shop run by a moody Chinese and, three doors up, the Three Feathers, where the Irishman showed everyone his scars. Next to the pub was a row of small houses. Over one door, painted into the brick, was a sign from 1945, *Welcome Home Our Bill.* Hilda in the newsagent's, shapeless in her floral apron, who gave him credit and urged him not to ruin his eyes with reading. The garage and then Ramsey Family Butcher, sawdust spilling out onto the pavement, where the ginger cat sat all day, so fat its tongue poked out of its mouth. Beyond the bomb site was the Universal Buy Sell Company with its window full of second-hand clothes and shoes, 78 records, *National Geographics*, chipped crockery, motor-bike parts, cutlery, old spectacles, and walking sticks.

On the other side of the road was Sam McAllister, chemist and barber, where he always had his hair cut. The window displayed a sun-faded board of ancient snapshots, which was propped against a jumble of fallen tins and boxes. At the top of the board were the words *We Develop*. Every surface was thick in grime and scattered with the husks of bluebottles. Mr. McAllister always fried his lunch, always sausages, on a gas ring in the middle of the floor.

At the end of the Valley, before the land rose again to the spire of the university, was the Post Office, regulated by the Misses Griffin, the younger sister well over seventy, who countered impatience by looking at the clock over her half-moons and remarking loudly, *Manners maketh man.*

He dried the razor and wiped the blade on a facecloth. He pulled out the plug and then squeezed a blob of Jim's foam into the water and watched it as it swirled lower and lower round the plughole. He studied his face again in the mirror.

Many of the houses were empty now, windows blind or boarded over, notices tacked on gates and doors. When the rest of the notices had been served, the wreckers would gut the houses, dropping roofs inside the shells and toppling walls, and the bulldozers would raze the Valley to an uneven field of rubble—broken brick and plaster, splintered lath.

* * *

THE BUS turned off the main road and lumbered up to the Gartree Hill Estate. The conductor had told Peter that the bus went as far as Gartree Square, where it turned around for the return journey; that Gartree Comprehensive School was a few minutes' walk beyond the square.

Peter looked out of the window at the parallel rows of streets. The concrete council houses marched along each road and out of sight as the bus passed. Hazel Row. Blackthorn Street. Honeysuckle Drive. Elderberry Avenue. Briar Street. There was not a tree in sight.

The bus stopped and he got out and looked around the square. There were shops on all four sides and, in the centre, a public lavatory.

He walked on up the hill, past the Clinic, Gartree Elementary School, the Gartree Community Centre, and the Parish Church of St. Michael and All the Angels, and turned down Beech Tree Way.

The school was glass and coloured panels, a deserted stretch of asphalt, ragged shrubs in a strip of garden by the front doors. It had taken him half an hour from the city centre. He stared through the railings.

On the padlocked gates was a metal shield—a blue ground on which was painted an oak tree. Underneath the roots of the tree were three black birds that looked like rooks. Underneath the rooks, a scroll. On the scroll were the words *Virtue and Knowledge.*

He turned back towards Gartree Square. He cut through Magnolia Street and passed a small public garden which was surrounded by a wire-mesh fence. An old man in a black overcoat was sitting on a concrete bench staring at the floral clock.

A hot wind blew grit and dust about the square and stirred the ice-cream wrappers. Five boys on bicycles without mud-guards rode round and round the public lavatory. He waited for the bus.

* * *

JEANNE was peeling potatoes when the bell rang.

"See who that is, Pete," she said.

He went upstairs and opened the front door. Two men stood there. The older one, who was wearing a tweed jacket and a yellow tie with red fox heads on it, stepped forward and said, "Good evening, sir. Sorry to inconvenience you. CID."

He held out his identification card. "I'm Sergeant Hope, sir, and this is Detective Constable Flynn." The younger man nodded.

"What's the problem?" said Peter.

"We'd like a word, if we may, with the lady of the house?"

"What lady?" said Peter.

"Mrs. Anderson?"

"There's no one of that name here."

"I see," said Sergeant Hope. He looked at Detective Constable Flynn.

"Are you the owner of the house, sir?"

"No. I'm just staying here. I have a room here."

"And the owner of the house is... ?"

"Mr. Rawley. James Rawley."

Constable Flynn wrote in his notebook.

"And Mr. Rawley lets rooms, does he?"

"Yes, that's right. University students."

"And I expect Mrs. Rawley does the housework—tidies the rooms and so on?"

"No. There's a housekeeper. Mr. Rawley's a widower."

"Ah! A housekeeper. And her name wouldn't be Anderson?"

"No. Mrs. Charleton."

"Would you happen to know Mrs. Charleton's first name, sir?"

"I believe it's Jeanne," said Peter.

"I see," said Sergeant Hope. "Jeanne."

"Why?" said Peter. "What's going on?"

"Oh, nothing to be alarmed about, sir. Just routine enquiries."

"Could we have a word with Mrs. Charleton?" said Constable Flynn.

"I'm afraid she's not in at the moment."

"This Mrs. Charleton, sir," said Sergeant Hope. "She wouldn't have a small female child, would she?"

"Yes, she has."

"Answers to the name of Anna?"

"Yes."

"Five years of age or thereabouts?"

"About that."

"And this Mrs. Charleton. About how old would you say she was?"

"About thirty-five or so. Maybe a bit older."

"Short? Tall?"

"I should think she's about five foot seven."

"I see," said Sergeant Hope.

"And she's not at home right now, you say?" said Constable Flynn.

"What awful crime has Mrs. Charleton committed?" said Peter.

"We just want to ask her a few routine questions in pursuance of enquiries, sir."

"When's she coming back?" said Constable Flynn.

"She's gone away for the weekend. To see her mother at Bridgeport, I believe she said."

"Get on all right with her, do you, sir?"

"Well, I don't see much of her. I'm usually down at the university and she's—well, she's just the housekeeper. I don't mean to sound...."

"Oh, quite, sir. Quite," said Sergeant Hope.

"It was just that she was leaving as I was on my way out."

"She didn't, by any chance, intimate when she'd be returning, sir?"

"Monday morning, I think. I think that's what she said."

"Is Mr. Rawley at home?"

"No. He's usually a lot later than this."

"Have there been any phone calls or letters here for a Mrs. Beazley?" said Constable Flynn.

"Not that I know of."

"I see," said Sergeant Hope. "Well, you've been most helpful, sir."

"Not at all," said Peter.

"Perhaps we can pop round on Monday and have a word with her. Sorry to have taken up so much of your time, sir."

Peter watched them turn out onto the pavement before he closed the door. "Jeanne!" he called as he hurried down the stairs and burst into the kitchen. "Jeanne, that was two policemen looking for you."

"What did you tell them?"
"I said you weren't here."
"What did they want?"
"They wouldn't say. They were asking for a Mrs. Anderson and Mrs. Beazley but they had a description of you and Anna."
"What did you tell them?"
"That you were away for the weekend and that you were coming back on Monday."
"Did they believe it?"
"I think so. It's hard to tell with them, though."
"CID?"
"Yes."
"Oh, *shit*!" she said.
"What's it about, Jeanne?"
She had turned her back and was staring out of the tiny window above the sink.
"Jeanne?"
"What?"
"What do they want you for?"
"How do I know! Maybe it's for drawing unemployment insurance."
"They don't send two detectives round for that."
"It's Friday today?"
"Yes. What's all this about Mrs. Anderson?"
"Friday."
She was staring through him, the cheese grater in her hand forgotten.
Just then, the front door slammed. They heard heavy footsteps in the tiled hall. Something thudded to the floor.
"Jeanne?" said Peter.
She chucked the cheese grater into the sink.
The footsteps crossed the hall again and Jim came down the stairs.
"Good evening, all and one!" he said. "Peter! *Delighted* to see you, old boy!"

He clasped Peter's hand and pumped. His pink moon-face beamed at them. Under his fair, thinning hair, his scalp glowed pink. He was wearing his usual navy-blue blazer with the RAF eagle on the breast pocket worked in gold wire. His tie was dark blue and dotted with golden airplanes.

"How's dinner, Jeanne? The inner man is crying out."

"Just waiting for the potatoes," she said.

"Jolly good!" said Jim.

"Peter, can you...." She pointed to the pile of cutlery on the table. He started to set the places.

"What an absolutely *putrid* day!" said Jim." Ah, salad. Jolly good. Traipsing around nasty little suburban boxes with difficult clients in *this* heat isn't my idea of jollies, *I* can tell you. And I'm going to have to give up Saturday to it as well."

"You're going to be working tomorrow?" said Jeanne.

"Crack of dawn, old thing. No rest for the wicked, eh?"

"Salt and pepper in the cupboard," said Jeanne.

"So, young Peter. Jeanne informs me you've been venturing off to forring parts."

"Not really very foreign, Jim."

"Cheap grog and ciggies, eh?"

"Yes, about a third of the price they are here."

"That's the ticket!" said Jim.

Jeanne started to mash the potatoes.

"Oodles of butter, old girl, mmmh?" said Jim.

She put plates in front of them and bowls of salad, grated cheese, hard-boiled eggs, and a platter of ham in the centre of the table.

"So, you've left the Alma Mater?" said Jim, helping himself to the ham. "The halcyon days are over. Out into the cold, harsh world. Nose to the grindstone, eh?"

"Would you...?"

"Ah, thank you."

"Jeanne?"

"If you could just.... Jolly good!"

"Salt?" said Peter.

"Still, I bet you're looking forward to it," said Jim.

"Well..." said Peter.

"How does it go?" said Jim. "'If all the year were playing holidays to work would.' No. That's not it. 'To play would... ' Something, something 'tedious.' Mmmm?"

"I expect you're right," said Peter.

A silence settled over them as they ate. Jeanne hardly touched the food in front of her. Peter kept on glancing at her. Jim ate heartily, frequently touching his napkin to his lips.

"Hal!" he said suddenly.

"Pardon?" said Peter.

"Prince Hal. That's the chappie. You can't beat the old Bard," he said.

"Jesus Christ!" said Jeanne and got up and walked out. Her bedroom door slammed shut.

"What on earth's wrong with her?" said Jim.

"I don't know," said Peter. "Maybe it's the heat."

"Probably *that time of month*," said Jim. "The monthlies, as we used to say in the service."

Peter nodded.

"A wonderful woman, though," said Jim. "A real character. Sterling qualities."

* * *

JEANNE was flipping through the dresses in her wardrobe. Peter was lying on her bed watching her. She was humming a waltz tune to herself. As she reached into the wardrobe, the short blue slip was lifted up her legs. She took out two dresses and held them up.

"Which do you like better?"

"The black one."

She stepped into the dress, pulling it up and shrugging her shoulders into it.

"Jeanne...?"

"No, Peter. Just shut up about it. I know you're worried and it's sweet of you but I've got everything under control."

"Sweet, my arse!" said Peter. "Stop trying to be so bloody patronizing."

She came around the bed and sat in front of him.

"What's all the mystery in aid of, anyway?" said Peter.

"Will you do me up at the back?"

"And for Christ's sake, stop humming!"

He lifted her hair away from the nape of her neck and hooked the collar of the dress.

"What if they come back before Monday?"

"Peter! I think you're deliberately trying to ruin my evening. I don't want to talk about it. I don't even want to think about it. So just leave it alone. We're both dressed up. We look respectable. We're going to have a fashionably late dinner. And we are going to behave *nicely*."

She lifted up her dress and pulled her slip into place. As she smoothed her stockings up her thighs, she looked at herself in the dressing-table mirror. She turned sideways, lifting her dress higher.

"I'm bony," she said, "and my mouth's too wide. And my tits are like empty hot-water bottles but I *have* got good legs."

"Where are we going?" said Peter.

"Chez Pierre."

"But you can't afford *that*!"

"You've got to admit I've got good legs."

"Let me pay for it."

"Learn to accept graciously," she said.

"But it'll cost...."

"Don't talk about money," she said. "It's vulgar."

She opened her purse and tossed a wad of notes onto the bed.

"You'd better take this now so you can pay for things. Go and call a taxi while I finish tarting myself up."

Chez Pierre was small and quiet. There were only eight tables. Thick orange curtains blocked out the night and the noises of the street. Peter lay back in the softness of the chair and looked at Jeanne as he sipped the martini. The pleasant rituals of the restaurant, the flash of the chef's knives, the smell of bruised herbs, the crisp linen, and the sparkle of wine glasses failed to soothe or lift his spirits. She was in the middle of a complicated story about smuggling watches through Folkestone customs just after the war. A piece of fat flared orange on the grill.

"Jeanne. Can you get sent up for this?"

"If you'd been caught."

"No. Not that. This afternoon. Whatever it is they want you for?"

"I thought we'd promised to drop that till tomorrow?"

He stirred the sludge of crushed ice in the bottom of the glass and drained the last drops of the martini.

The waiter brought the hors d'oeuvres and a bottle of Meursault. Peter tasted the wine and nodded. The waiter filled the glasses. As soon as he had gone, Peter said, "What *are* you going to do?"

"Did you really taste that wine?"

"Yes. No, I didn't. Stop trying to fob me off."

She half-emptied the glass, held the wine in her mouth, and swallowed.

"Good," she said. "*Very* good. It's a terrible mistake to *sip* things, I always say."

"Jeanne!"

"Look, Peter! You're becoming boring. I'm going to call someone in about half an hour and set everything up. And then tomorrow morning, after Jim's gone to work, we'll go away for a nice summer holiday."

"Oh, for Christ's sake, be serious!"

“Why?” she said. “More wine?”

“You’re in trouble.”

“Not yet. And I was being serious anyway.”

“Go where?”

“Hampshire.”

The waiter took away the plates and brought fresh wine glasses and the Beaujolais.

“My father’s got a cottage near the sea. He won’t be there now and I’ve got a key so we can all go down and have a holiday for three weeks before you start work.”

“Yes, but what about afterwards, Jeanne?”

She pulled a long face and stared at him.

“Good God!” she said. “What sort of question’s that? This doesn’t sound like my Peter. Not like the Peter I *used* to know.”

“I’m worried, Jeanne. That’s all.”

“Consider the lilies of the field, how they grow.”

“The lilies of the field weren’t wanted by the police.”

“Oh, dear!” she said. “This is serious. I think this teacher-training lark you’ve been doing’s rotted your mind.”

“Oh, don’t be daft.”

“What a *horrible* change,” she said. “It’s difficult to believe it’s the same person.”

She smiled at him and shook her head.

“What about afterwards, indeed! Can this be the Peter who once stole a parrot from the zoo?”

He smiled and said, “That was two years ago.”

“A man who steals parrots,” she said, “cannot change his spots.”

“For madam?” said the waiter.

“Tournedos Rossini.”

“And trout for you, sir.”

“Or the Peter, for example, who was arrested drunk and disorderly in the main fountain in the city centre. Sitting up to his armpits in water? Singing, ‘We Plough the Fields and Scatter’?”

He smiled as he remembered.

"Sir?" said the waiter.

"Fine. Thank you."

The waiter filled the glasses. Peter could feel the martini and wine expanding inside him.

"And do you remember that sergeant?" she said. "When I came down to get you out?"

Peter laughed out loud.

"*That's* more like it," said Jeanne. "That's more like the old Peter."

She smiled at him.

"And last year? When you were repatriated from Calais. And you bummed a ham sandwich from the British consul?"

"It's people like you," said Peter in a plummy voice, "who give England a bad name. Actually, he said, "People of your ilk." That was the first time I'd heard anyone *say* that."

Jeanne reached out and took his hand.

"Don't worry, little one. Don't ever worry. Because then you'll have to drink Milk of Magnesia and eat boiled cod."

He smiled at her and said, "Shsss!"

"Oh, am I becoming loud?" she said.

They ate silently for a few minutes.

"Where is this cottage?" said Peter.

"Pennyford. Right up on the cliffs. You'll like it."

He took out his cigarettes. The trout was a curve of fine bones. He pushed the plate to one side as he didn't want to look at the opaque discs of the trout's eyes. Brilliant yellow of a lemon slice. He sat back holding the wine glass against his lower lip.

"It's funny, isn't it?" said Jeanne. "I'd really intended staying at Jim's. For a while. . . ."

Peter passed her a cigarette. She lighted it from the candle in the middle of the table.

"Still, I suppose two and a half years is a long time . . ."

The woman at the next table laughed loudly at something the man had said. Peter looked across at her.

“What’s the time?” said Jeanne.

“About eleven thirty.”

“Well, I’d better make my phone call. I can’t manage any dessert. Just order me a coffee, will you?”

He leaned back and rolled the wine glass in his palms. The light danced on glasses and gleamed on cutlery. The conversation of the surrounding tables came to him as a muted buzz. The chair was warm and comfortable. He found himself rolling the glass and staring at a nylon calf. A yellow dress. He liked yellow. A froth of black lace on her slip bunching out where the dress pulled up.

Jeanne sat down again. He turned his head slowly to look at her, and smiled.

“You’re getting pissed,” she said.

“No, I’m not. What did you arrange?”

“Funds, little one. Funds.”

“How do you mean—funds?”

“I’m not going to tell you so don’t ask. You’ll find out tomorrow.”

She tasted the coffee.

“I feel awful,” she said.

“Pennyford, eh?” he said.

“Absolutely bloated.”

“Can we go fishing there?”

“Why not?”

“I like fishing,” he said.

“Good. Good.”

The waiter brought the bill.

“I’ve got to get some air and walk this food down,” she said.

He finished his coffee and pushed back his chair. He dropped his crumpled napkin on the table and counted out notes onto the sideplate covering the bill.

“That was a marvellous meal, Jeanne.”

“Don’t thank me,” she said. “Thank Jim.”

“What do you mean?”

"It was the next two weeks' housekeeping money."

After leaving the restaurant, they strolled down through the old part of town towards the river and the bridge. The night air was still warm. There was no traffic, and in the deserted streets their footsteps rang against the tall, curving façade of the Georgian crescent. Ornamental wrought-iron railings. Worn, hollow, paving stones. Yellow squares of lighted windows.

"Jeanne?"

"Umm?"

"This cottage. How do you know your father won't be there?"

"He works in the summer."

"What's he work at?"

"Did I never tell you about him? He's a captain."

"Of what?"

"Well, he was the captain of a tramp steamer in the Far East and the China Seas. About 1910, 1915."

"And he's still...?"

"God, no! The old bugger's about seventy-five now. He used to be a grocer in Liverpool. A squalid corner shop. Milk, cabbages, bread and tarts, bootlaces, the newspapers with the racing results. I can smell it now. Everything on tick. Most of the time he was selling sweets and pop to all the snotty kids—halfpenny bags of jelly babies. Then my mother looked after the shop and he sailed two or three trips as a steward. After she died, he suddenly became a captain. He gets it all out of Kipling and Conrad."

"Do you mean he's...?"

"Dotty? No. Although he sort of believes it himself now, I think. That's why he doesn't like seeing me. He wears white suits and carries a Malacca cane and complains all the time about being cold. Wears a fob chain with shark teeth and cowrie shells on it."

She laughed.

"He's really very charming."

“What does he do?”

“Lives in hotels in Bournemouth and Eastbourne—places like that—and gets money from rich old ladies. He’s still a handsome man, little white beard, tells them tales of pirates and coolies and typhoons and dusky maidens and being twelve days out of Bangkok with a cargo of burning teak and mutinous lascars running amuck. What the hell *are* lascars?”

“*I* don’t know.”

“Anyway, they get their money’s worth. You’d like him. Everybody does.”

The lime trees which lined the road leading to the bridge were bright acid green in the patches lit by the yellow globes of the streetlamps. They began to smell the river mud. They paid the toll-man and walked out to the centre span of the bridge. A light breeze was blowing off the water.

The river, tidal at this reach, was on the ebb. They leaned over an embrasure watching the white turbulence of the tide and listening to the river sounds. Jeanne was tracing her fingertips over the worn stone and staring down into the river’s flow.

She moved closer to him and he put his arm around her. The breeze stirred her hair against his face. Below them, the water was scouring down the central channel, riffling round the piles of the bridge and the tilted buoys, and sweeping out into a smooth curve where the river widened on a bend. The mudbanks were rising slowly, like sheets of pearl in the moonlight. A small lamp underneath the bridge cast a yellow wriggling light on the water. Far away, a train was rumbling through the silence.

“It’s better than being a grocer,” she said.

* * *

JEANNE was tapping a spoon in irritation on the top of the stove.

"Come on! Come on!" she said to the spice rack.

"Oh, for heaven's sake, shut up, Jeanne!" said Peter. "What's the hurry?"

She'd woken him at seven and had been emptying drawers and folding clothes ever since. She'd snapped at Anna, who'd gone out to play in the back garden. Peter felt slightly hung over. She went to the foot of the stairs and shouted, "Jim! Will you *hurry up*! Your eggs are going to be *solid*."

They heard a faint, "Right ho!" from the second-floor bathroom.

"Come *on*!" she said.

"There's bloody *hours* before the train," said Peter.

Jim's footsteps boomed down the basement stairs.

"Good morning, Jeanne. Good morning, Peter. What an absolutely glorious day!"

"Morning," said Peter.

Jim's face shone pink from soap and water. He gave off a strong scent of aftershave lotion. He hunched himself in the doorway and swung an imaginary golf club, following the flight of the ball up to the ceiling.

"Damn nuisance," he said. "I was really looking forward to brandishing the old clubs today." As he sat down, he said, "But one's duty calls one, eh?"

Jeanne put a plate of bread and butter and the boiled eggs in front of him.

"Oh, I say," he said. "Have we no Rice Krispies?"

"I ran out," said Jeanne.

He battered in the crowns of the eggs with a teaspoon and poured a mound of salt onto the plate.

"Ah, thank you, Jeanne," he said. "The cup that cheers."

She lit a cigarette and leaned against the sink, staring at him as he ate. He frequently patted his lips with a hankie which he always carried tucked in the cuff of his shirt.

"Absolutely glorious!" he said. "I really *am* tempted to go AWOL, you know."

“You can’t if there’s people waiting for you,” said Peter.

“Just once, eh?” said Jim. “Spit in the CO’s eye and damn the consequences.”

“You’re going to be late,” said Jeanne.

“Talk about the workers,” said Jim. “Very nice, too. Cushy jobs and strong unions. Nine-to-five and *goodnight*.”

“It’s ten minutes to nine,” said Jeanne.

“Downtrodden!” said Jim.” All my eye and Betty Martin, as they say.”

He poured another cup of tea and drank it standing up.

“Well, heigh-ho!” he said. “I’m going to have to cut along, I suppose.”

“When are you going to be back?” said Jeanne.

“Oh, afternoonish. Din-dins at about six?”

“Yes, the usual.”

“Bye,” said Peter.

A few minutes after he had gone the doorbell rang. Jeanne was in her bedroom lining a huge cabin trunk with fresh newspaper.

“Peter?” she called. “It’s probably for me.”

He went upstairs and opened the door, The man said, “Mrs. Carlyle?”

“Carlyle? No, I’m. . . . Oh! That wouldn’t be Mrs. Jeanne Carlyle, would it?”

“Ah,” said the man. “That’s the lady.”

“Jeanne!”

The man’s eyes swam behind glasses thick as bottle bottoms. Peter had to look away.

“Nice day,” said the man.

His jacket was filthy and burst under the armpits. Padding hung out. The pockets were torn and sagged under the weight of spanners, screwdrivers, and pliers. A grey woollen scarf was knotted at his throat like an ascot but did not cover the collarless flannel shirt and the brass stud. His few teeth were yellow stumps.

"A particularly nice day," he said.

"It certainly is," said Peter.

The man lifted his greasy cap and scratched his bald head with a pencil. His pate was pallid like lard.

Jeanne came up the stairs and cried, "Bill!" and kissed him on the cheek.

"Well now, Mrs. C.," he said. "Well now."

"Bill, I want you to meet Peter Hendricks. Peter, this is Mr. Arkle."

Mr. Arkle smiled and nodded in Peter's direction.

"Have you got Henry with you?" asked Jeanne.

"Ill, Henry is," said Mr. Arkle. "Done his back last week with a Welsh dresser."

"Oh, I *am* sorry," said Jeanne.

"Well, Mrs. C. How long we got?"

"An hour and a half?"

"Well, we'd better get them lads in," he said.

He went to the front door and beckoned. Peter saw a blue furniture van backing up to the front gate.

"All to go, is it?" said Mr. Arkle.

"Anything you can use," said Jeanne.

A boy of about seventeen wearing jeans and a tartan shirt came in.

"All right, Mr. Arkle?"

"Ah."

"Fetch Fred in, shall I?"

"Ah."

Mr. Arkle grasped the banisters and started to climb the stairs.

Peter said to Jeanne, "Do you mean you're going to sell...?"

"That's right."

"You're just going to...."

"Yes."

"And this is what Mrs. Anderson and Mrs. Beazley...?"

"And Mrs. Carlyle," said Jeanne.

"Good God!" said Peter. "But...?"

"What?"

"Won't the neighbours phone the police or something?"

"If you saw a furniture van next to your house, would you phone the police?"

"No, I suppose not, but...."

"Cheer up," said Jeanne. "He's got insurance."

As Peter walked into the first bedroom on the top floor, Mr. Arkle was bending forward, leaning on the chest of drawers, and massaging the small of his back. He peered round and said, "Ah, it's a bugger, isn't it? *He* claims it's in the urine but it's the bones what hurts. Just certain days, mind."

He straightened up and arched his back.

"Still they do say the Lord sends these things to try us."

"Perhaps it's arthritis," said Peter.

"Urine!" said Mr. Arkle. "That's what *he's* full of. Nothing but piss and wind. They sends them out these days no more than boys."

He took a packet of pink, gummed labels from his coat pocket. He peered around and then, sticking out his tongue, wiped the paper down it. He stuck the label on the headboard of the bed. He chuckled and said, "'Course, I shouldn't complain. You know what they wanted to do with the wife, don't you?"

"No?" said Peter.

Mr. Arkle stuck a label on the chest of drawers.

"They wanted to amputate *her*."

He stuck another on the table.

A boy came in and said, "Start here, Mr. Arkle?"

He was wearing tight black trousers and a pink, frilly shirt. His hair was long and elaborately combed. His shirt sleeves were rolled up and blue-and-red snakes writhed up his forearms.

"This here's Frederick," said Mr. Arkle. "A member of what they calls the Younger Generation."

Frederick got hold of the bed and started to drag it towards the door.

"You're going to have to undo the nuts and bolts, aren't you, Frederick?"

"Oh, ah," he said.

"No training, you see," said Mr. Arkle.

Jeanne came up the stairs.

"All right?" she said.

"It's a useful little lot," said Mr. Arkle.

The house shook with the traffic up and down the stairs, with the rumble and scrape of dragged furniture.

Anna came pounding upstairs shouting, "Mummy! Where are you? Mummy!"

"Hello, young lady," said Mr. Arkle. "Remember me?"

"Hello," said Anna. "We went in a big van."

"Ah, you're a bright one," said Mr. Arkle.

"We're going away on our summer holidays today, poppet," said Jeanne. "To the seaside."

Anna began jumping up and down on the spot chanting, *Going to the seaside. Going to the seaside.*

"This carpet's got a couple of years in it," said Mr. Arkle. "In my trade," he said, "carpets and mirrors. Can't get enough of 'em."

George!

Can you hear me?

The carpet from the room what we're in now!

Right, Mr. Arkle.

There was a tremendous crash and then the continuous clatter of angle iron sliding down the stairs.

"That'll be Frederick," said Mr. Arkle.

George!

The runner from the top landing!

Right, Mr. Arkle!

In the second-floor bathroom he stuck a pink label on the bathroom cabinet and then levered the brackets out of the wall with the bar of a screwdriver. Showers of plaster fell into the washbasin.

"'Ere, quick! Take this off me before I drops it."

Peter took the cabinet and Mr. Arkle called to Frederick, who was trudging up the stairs to the top floor.

"Take this down to the van, Frederick." Turning to Peter, he said, "Strong as an ox, that boy. Aren't you, Frederick?"

"I ain't weak," said Frederick as he started downstairs.

"Strong as an ox," said Mr. Arkle. He brought his face closer to Peter, whose eyes began to water in sympathy.

"Strong as an ox *and about as clever,*" he said. "*And about as clever.*"

He started to laugh but the laughter turned into a bronchial wheeze and then into a retching cough. His face grew purple and congested. Veins stood in his face. He clung to Peter's shoulder. Tears ran down from beneath the thick lenses. A final, open-mouthed, retching cough snatched him double. Bent over the bath, he started to make hawking noises. They got louder and louder until, with a final roar, he pushed himself upright and spat into the washbasin. Peter stared at the gob of yellow phlegm.

"Pick the bones out of that!" gasped Mr. Arkle.

He sat down on the edge of the bath and mopped his eyes with a grey handkerchief. A thread of saliva hung from his unshaven chin.

"Oh, Gawd!" he said. "That *were* a good one. Strong as an ox and about as clever, I said. Oh, dear Gawd! My sense of humour'll be the death of me yet. Going on like that. Be the death of me. Can't resist a joke, I can't."

He took his glasses off again and rubbed them up and down his jacket. He sniffed and sighed and wiped his nose on the edge of his hand.

They went into the bedroom next door. Peter helped Mr. Arkle take the door off the wardrobe.

"Too old fashioned, see," said Mr. Arkle. "But old Henry'll use the mirror for something."

Anna danced in, singing, *We're going on hol-i-day. We're going on hol-i-day,* and Peter caught her up into the air and said, "What's mummy doing?"

"Downstairs packing and we're going to have spades and buckets and I can take my waterwings."

"And we're going to go fishing, too," said Peter. "Do you think you'll like that?"

"Will you take *me* fishing?"

"Of *course* I'm going to take you."

Something heavy was being dragged across the floor in the room above and plaster was flaking off the ceiling.

George!

Can you hear me?

Yes, Mr. Arkle.

The carpets from the rooms with crosses on the doors.

And George?

Don't scratch up that little wardrobe.

As the house emptied, the noises sounded louder. The air swam with dust from the carpets the boys were dragging down the stairs. Wrinkled pennants of wallpaper marked the passage of bedsteads.

Mr. Arkle pushed open the door of the ground-floor sitting room and looked inside.

"Aha!" he said. "Now this is a different class of piece altogether."

He stuck pink labels on the bureau and the two armchairs. He lowered himself onto his hands and knees and felt along under the table.

"Lovely, that is. Come on. Get down here. Feel along under there."

"What?" said Peter.

"What can you feel?"

“Nothing.”

“Nothing,” repeated Mr. Arkle. He took hold of Peter’s arm and, pushing his face close, said, “*Exacly!*”

Peter stared into the swimmy, moist magnification of Mr. Arkle’s eyes.

“*Exacly!*”

They stared at each other.

“None of your glue. None of your nails. None of your screws.”

Peter nodded.

“*Joints* and *pegs*.”

“A bit of real craftmanship, that is. And do they care? They buy plyboard with plastic glued on it. The young ones now.”

He hauled himself up, breathing heavily, and slapped a label on the tabletop.

“It’s no use,” he said. “There just isn’t the honesty for it these days.”

Peter nodded slowly.

“Plyboard!”

Mr. Arkle slapped the tabletop even harder.

“This here’s *manogony*. Something you can *call* a wood. And none of your veneers neither.”

“It’s very nice,” said Peter.

“You remember,” said Mr. Arkle, prodding Peter in the chest, “you just keep it in mind. Your soft woods comes and goes but your manogony goes on for ever.”

Peter!

Hello!

I’ll put your suit and these books....

I’ll come down there.

A chest of drawers walked past the doorway. Anna was walking backwards alongside it.

Jeanne was in the kitchen buckling a strap around the trunk.

“I’ve put your suit and some other clothes and books in here and you can get them from Bill when you come back.”

“Fine,” said Peter. “He’s awful when he gets going, isn’t he?”

"Bill? He's been lecturing you, has he?"

Somewhere on the second floor there was a thunderous crash and the sound of rending wood.

"Jesus Christ!" said Peter.

Jeanne began to laugh.

They heard Mr. Arkle shout, *George*? and a faint voice calling *It's all right, Mr. Arkle. Fred went through the banisters.*

"The banisters!" said Peter.

Never mind Frederick. Just don't scratch no furniture.

His slow footsteps came down the basement stairs and he stood in the doorway rubbing his back.

"We don't get no younger, do we?"

"There's a double bed and a nice dressing table in my room across there," said Jeanne.

He took out his gummed labels.

Mummy!

Hello!

George says we can ride in the van. Can we?

Yes.

Mummy?

George can spit all the way across a room.

I don't want to hear about it.

"The hot-water heater," said Mr. Arkle, coming back into the kitchen. "Did you get it from the Gas Board or private?"

"A shop, I think," said Jeanne.

Frederick!

He peered at the name plate and checked the back for a serial number.

"Frederick. Use a spanner on that gas pipe and then have the heater off the wall. Then you can go back upstairs and help George."

"Right, Mr. Arkle."

"Frederick."

"Ah?"

"We usually turns the gas off *before* we undoes the pipe."

"Oh, ah," said Frederick.

"Oh!" said Peter. "What about the Hoover?"

"Right," said Mr. Arkle.

"Well?" said Jeanne. "What do you think?"

"What would you call fair?" said Mr. Arkle.

They sat down at the kitchen table and Mr. Arkle took off his cap and wiped his head with his handkerchief.

"A hundred and fifty?" said Jeanne.

He pursed his lips and whistled in.

"You've got to consider my overheads," he said.

"A hundred and twenty?"

"I'll tell you what. Seeing as how it's you, Mrs. C., we'll call it a hundred."

"Done," said Jeanne. "And you're getting a bargain."

"We all has to live, Mrs. C."

He reached into his pocket and brought out a pair of pliers, a pencil stub, a ball of string, a radio valve, screws, nails, a piece of fancy moulding, two spanners, and a cigarette end. Groping down into the lining, he brought out the fattest roll of money that Peter had ever seen. He slipped off the rubber band, and, wetting his finger and thumb, began to count. When he had counted out a hundred pounds, the wad looked no smaller.

George and Frederick came clattering down the stairs followed by Anna. They went into Jeanne's room and dismantled the bed.

"And there's a trunk and box in here to go," called Mr. Arkle, "and then we can get moving."

Peter took Jeanne's suitcase and his rucksack down to the van. He quickly dumped them inside. The van seemed just over half full. He glanced casually at the neighbouring houses but no one seemed to be taking any notice. The sides of the van were plain and there was no name on the front.

George and Frederick came down the path at a staggering run with the trunk between them. Jeanne, Anna, and Mr. Arkle followed.

"Finished?" said Peter.

"Ah," said Mr. Arkle, but then he turned and walked back up the path and onto the front lawn. He bent and peered at the small grey statue of a girl fighting down her skirts with one hand and holding onto her hat with the other.

"It's only an ornamental birdbath thing," said Jeanne. He poked at it with a screwdriver.

"Frederick! Come and put this in the van."

"What on earth do you want that for?" said Jeanne.

"Don't you think we'd better go!" said Peter.

"Solid lead, Mrs. C. Solid lead."

Anna and the two boys got into the back of the van. Mr. Arkle pulled himself up and struggled in behind the wheel. Jeanne sat in the other seat. Peter sat sideways, head bent, on the engine casing.

"All aboard, then?" said Mr. Arkle.

"Oh!" said Jeanne. "I've forgotten something. Won't be a minute."

She climbed down and hurried back into the empty house. Peter saw Mrs. Williams next door looking out of her sitting-room window. The floor of the cab was littered with peanut shells. A golliwog dangled from the mirror. The minutes lengthened.

"What's she *doing*!" said Peter.

"Strong as an ox," said Mr. Arkle suddenly, "*and about as clever.*"

A spasm of wheezy laughter took him and he accidentally sounded the horn. Peter hit his head on the roof.

"Oh, Gawd!" sighed Mr. Arkle. "That really *were* a good one."

A man further up the road washing his car seemed to be watching them. Peter listened to Mr. Arkle's breathing.

Then he heard the front door slam and, leaning forward, saw her running down the path. She waved to Mrs. Williams. Mr. Arkle started the engine. She climbed up into the cab and dumped a bundled towel into Peter's lap. The bundle slid down his knee and shilling pieces began to slide and pour out onto the floor.

"Well, bless my soul!" said Mr. Arkle, slapping the steering wheel.

"Yes," said Jeanne. "I nearly forgot to do the meters."

* * *

PETER AND ANNA strolled along the path through the dappled wood and out into the full sunshine of the clearing. In the centre of the clearing stood an old concrete pillbox and the remains of a prefabricated hut. Trees had been cleared through the wood to command a view over the estuary for the guns.

The top of the pillbox was grown over with grass and weeds and the angled stairwell was full of dead leaves. Speckled wood butterflies danced over the leaf mould.

The roof of the hut gaped open in places where the asbestos sheets had been smashed. What was left was moss-grown. Patches of moss were growing on the concrete floor, slowly covering over the shards of glass from the shattered windows.

Round the hut someone had planted lilac bushes which now grew wild, half masking the open doorway and pushing in at the window frames. The bushes were choked by convolvulus and honeysuckle.

Butterflies hung and battened on the tiny red and yellow flowers and basked on the sun-warmed concrete of the doorstep. Painted ladies, drab meadow browns, red admirals, and brimstone yellows, their wings winking shut and opening down into the full spread of their colours.

"What's that one?" whispered Anna.

"A red admiral," said Peter.

"I like the ones with eyes on them best," she said.

Anna squatted down to watch the caterpillar flowing over the bark. Its body was bright red and black, furry. As she reached out her fingers, Peter said, "Don't touch it. The bristles come out and make your hand swell up."

"Shall I squash it?" said Anna.

"Why? You should never do things like that."

"What's its name?"

"I don't know its real name," said Peter. "We always used to call them woolly bears."

"I want to touch it."

"I'll find you some you can take home, if you like," said Peter. "You can keep them in a box."

He looked about him for a ragwort plant and then said to Anna, "See that plant over there? The one with all the yellow flowers? See if there's any there."

She ran over and shouted, "Peter! Hundreds!"

The stem and leaves crawled with the yellow-and-black-banded caterpillars of the cinnabar moth, and Anna chose the fattest to put into his matchbox.

A breeze blew across the headland, swaying the harebells in the short turf. The river and the estuary lay like a model below them. Shadows raced over the slope.

"Where's *our* house?" said Anna.

"See those black houses right down there near the sea? That's Wildhaven where we came in the boat this morning. And Pennyford's about three miles further up the coast. You can't see it from here."

"What do you think Mummy's doing?"

"Making you something nice for tea."

Peter gazed out over the estuary. The far shore was lost in the shimmer of the heat haze. At the mouth of the estuary he could see the orange beach and the white surf line of the sea beyond; the black cottages of Wildhaven where the boatman had ferried them across the tide race. As the yachts heeled under the breeze, the white sails flashed in the sunlight.

Anna was laying out her shells on the grass, arranging them in order of size. She had been carrying them inside her blouse. Tiny yellow periwinkles, cockleshells, whelk shells with spiral horns, pairs of razor shells, mermaids' purses.

Peter lay back and closed his eyes. The sun swam red and yellow inside the blackness, lighter and darker, lighter and darker as the clouds passed. In his ears the heavy wash of the sea sounded; the scrunch of their feet on the shingle; a line of black rocks jumbling out to sea, the furthest rock splashed with birdlime where a brooding cormorant sat hunched over the surge and sway.

Beating out heavily over the pine trees, over the sedge, lumbering out into the sky over the estuary, the toiling black shape of an owl, mobbed by screaming starlings and thrushes.

"Peter! Peter! Look at me!"

He started up, blind for a second in the sudden light, and looked down the slope. Fifty yards or so below him, Anna was dancing about on a low, oval mound waving a bunch of flowers.

"Get down off that!"

"Why?"

"Come up here!"

She ran down the mound and came panting up the hill towards him. He sat up and watched her. She flopped down and said, "Why should I get down? It isn't high."

"Because somebody's buried inside it and it isn't nice to jump about on someone's grave."

"Whose grave is it?"

"I don't know who. One of the people who made that big dike we saw this morning. Thousands of years ago. It was so long ago that there weren't any towns or cities and there weren't even houses."

"What did they do here?"

"This was their fortress and they used to hunt here and catch fish in the river and the sea."

"Why weren't they buried in a churchyard?"

"Because there weren't any churches then and they liked to bury the people in high places where they could look out over where they used to live."

"Was I bad?" said Anna.

"No, sweetheart. Of course you weren't. Those little hills they're buried in are called long barrows and they sit inside them with all their favourite things with them. If you remember all that, you'll be able to tell Mummy about it when you get home, won't you?"

"Look!" shouted Peter. "Look, Anna!"

She looked along the direction of his arm.

"What?"

"See the yellow field, just over there. The stubble field? Look at the middle of it and then up into the sky. See?"

"What is it?"

"A hawk," said Peter. "You don't see them very often now. They're called kestrels. Windhovers."

The kestrel shifted its quarter and hovered lower over the field.

"If a mouse just twitches its whiskers they can see it," said Peter.

The hawk banked and hovered again.

"I'm *tired*, Peter."

"Just a minute. Watch. I think it's going to stoop."

The hawk climbed, slipped down the sky towards the middle of the field again, and hung motionless. Suddenly, as if a string had been cut, it plunged black down the air and dropped out of their sight behind the hedge.

"Can I have an ice-cream on the way home?"

"What?"

"Can I have an ice-cream cone on the way home?"

He looked down at her, her blouse stained and lumpy with seashells and her hair straggling out of the elastic band, and smiled.

"Of course you can, sweetheart. With chocolate in it, too."

Perched on Peter's shoulders and clutching his forehead, Anna shrieked with laughter as he gave her a jolting, running piggyback to the road and the bus stop.

* * *

PETER held up the top strand of barbed wire while Jeanne ducked through. Anna squirmed underneath on her back.

"Oh, no!" said Jeanne, fingering the triangular rip in her skirt. "I knew I should have worn slacks."

"I've gone in the mud," called Anna.

She was up to her ankles in the boggy ground where the stream spread into mallows and watercress.

"Well, don't just stand there!" shouted Jeanne.

Anna sloshed towards them, mud splashing up her legs.

"Oh, God!" said Jeanne. "That's her new sandals ruined."

She sat down near the bank and said, "This is far enough. Give me a cigarette. I've got a stitch and I still ache from all that walking yesterday."

The shallow stream which curved through the field was only four-feet wide. Its edges were lined by long rank grasses which trailed after the current. Polled willows marked the course of the stream into the fields beyond. A few yards downstream from where they were sitting, the cattle had churned the ground into a muddy bay with their sharp hoofs.

Jeanne burped loudly.

"Excuse *me*," she said. "I'm getting too old to eat cucumber at suppertime."

"Shall I take my shoes and socks off?" said Anna.

"Yes, and wash the mud off your legs, too."

Anna sat on the edge and dabbled her feet in the water. The sun was sinking but it was still warm. The oak trees in the far corner of the field were motionless under the blue sky.

Swallows starting their evening feed were flickering over the stream's surface.

"Peter?"

"What?"

"Shall we play skipping stones like yesterday?"

"The water's not wide enough."

"Play boats then."

"We haven't got any boats."

"I'll get some."

She clambered out of the stream and wandered about looking for twigs.

"Put your sandals on," said Jeanne, "or you'll tread in thistles or something."

"Go and look under the trees," said Peter.

"Can I have your jacket for a pillow?" said Jeanne.

He rolled it up and pushed it under her head.

"I've got a bellyache," she said. "I think it's indigestion."

When Anna came back, Peter broke the twigs into even lengths and they sailed them from the willow stump to the place where the bank was trampled down. Anna cheated by following her twigs down the stream and poking them free if they stuck in grass or lodged against the bank so Peter took off his shoes and socks and got into the water with her. They paddled down the length of the course, pushing their twigs and splashing them forwards with scooped hands to the winning post.

When all the twigs had sailed away, Peter sat on the bank to smoke a cigarette. Anna was crouched over the trampled part of the bank at the edge of the stream. Picking up a stone, she started to chip down the walls of the sun-hardened hoof pocks, letting water trickle in and fill them.

"Look at me, Peter. I'm making little pools."

"I can see."

"I'm going to make all these into little pools."

"You could dig a channel and let the water go from hole to hole," said Peter. "Or you could flood *all* this, right up to where I'm sitting."

"How do you do that?"

"You'd have to block the stream—build a dam."

"We're going to build a dam, Mummy," called Anna.

"It's getting close to your bedtime," said Jeanne.

"Oh, not yet! Just a *little* dam. All right?"

They wandered up and down stream searching for large stones and Peter lugged them back, one by one, to where Jeanne was lying, reading a paperback. When they had piled up fifteen or so, Peter got down into the water and started to place them across the stream just before it narrowed out of the little bay. He made a double row.

"We need two more big ones," he said. "Go and see if there are any under the oak trees."

Anna ran off and Peter hauled at the rocks, turning them, wedging them, changing their positions. The water was already showing a drift along their line and a heavier rush through the gap.

"One *huge* one, Peter!" shouted Anna.

He hurried over and knelt beside the big rock. He worked it backwards and forwards until he had loosened it in its bed. He pushed it forwards and forced his fingertips underneath.

"You bring that branch," he said to Anna.

His arms at full stretch, the rock bumping against his thighs at each step, he hurried back to the stream. He straddled the line of stones and dropped the big rock to close the gap.

Jeanne sat up at the noise and said, "You're going to rupture yourself if you're not careful."

As he straightened up and eased his back, he said "Feeling better now?"

"Yes, it's gone now. Where did you put the cigarettes?"

"Somewhere there. Near my jacket."

Anna arrived breathless, dragging the awkward branch behind her.

"Good girl!" said Peter. "We need small stones now to fill the holes underneath. Okay?"

She went off again and as she brought the stones, three or four at a time, Peter groped down into the deepening water, forcing them into holes and gaps. He saw his wrist coming out of the muddied stream and realized that he'd had his watch on all the time. He undid the soggy strap and held the watch to his ear. It had stopped.

"Hey, Jeanne. Catch this."

She put the paperback down on the grass and he tossed the watch up to her. He looked around the field. The light was just beginning to fade. The shapes of the trees looked darker against the sky.

"Lousy book!" said Jeanne. "My behind's *damp*."

She got up and plucked at her skirt.

"How's your dam coming along?"

"It's beginning to build," said Peter. "Look."

The water was rising, lapping at the sun-hardened mud of the trampled bank, flowing in a thin waterfall over the line of rocks.

He stripped the twigs off Anna's branch and jammed it from bank to bank behind the stones.

"Here's more little ones," said Anna.

"Put them in-between the rocks and the branch."

She stepped down into the water and cried, "Oh, Peter! It's up to my *knees*."

"What can we use for filling?" said Peter.

"How about turf?" said Jeanne.

"That's a good idea."

Peter started to tear up turfs and hand them down to Anna, who put them on top of the row of stones. The force of water curving over the top dislodged some of them and Jeanne said, "You'll have to press them in hard, Anna."

Another turf was washed forward and flopped down across the branch behind. The water surged over.

"Look at the way it flows," said Jeanne. "It looks like glass."

"Oh, *Mummy*," said Anna. "I don't know how to *do* it."

Jeanne took off her shoes and stepped down into the pool.

"Ooh, it's cold," she said.

"Soon get used to it," said Peter.

Jeanne began placing the turf, tamping the cracks, groping underwater to plug gaps. She looked behind her at the spreading pool. The water was more than halfway up the trampled slope. Slowly, the water flowing through the dam was being lessened to a steady trickle at the base.

"We'll have to build the top up fast," said Jeanne. "It's nearly over the edge now."

Peter worked his fingers forward under the turf, tearing and ripping at the matted roots.

"Hurry up!" said Jeanne. "It's beginning to go."

"I'm going as fast as I can," said Peter.

He passed the turfs down to Anna.

"Is it holding?" he said.

"Not for long. We've got to get higher."

"It's coming through the side!" shouted Anna.

"Here! Catch these!" said Peter as he tossed the sods to Jeanne.

"Get out of the *way*, Anna!" said Jeanne.

She slapped the turfs into position, stemming the burst through. The hem of her skirt was trailing in the water so she tucked it into her underpants.

"I've got to have something to work with!" said Peter.

"Anna, go and look for a piece of tin or something he can use to dig with."

Anna got up and wandered off across the field.

"Hurry up!" called Jeanne.

"I *am* hurrying!" shouted Anna.

"And fetch me some sticks as well."

Peter scrabbled at the turf as fast as he could. The cold water was nudging at the back of Jeanne's thighs. The pool stretched back from the dam, nearly level now with the field.

"Three more rows across the top'll hold it," said Jeanne.

Anna trailed back with a rusty tin can, which Peter stamped flat. He sliced and hacked at the turf, peeling back long strips. Jeanne was wedging the turfs in, driving sticks through the layers to skewer them together, forcing props into the banks, laying the turfs higher and higher. Anna sat on the bank, plunking pebbles into the water.

"I'm cold, Mummy."

"There's a hell of a pressure," said Jeanne. "I can feel it pushing against my legs."

"Reinforce the sides," said Peter. "Where it got through before."

"Mummy, I said I was cold."

"Put Peter's jacket on."

Dusk was falling. The trees were black shapes against the flushed sky. A cool breeze was beginning to blow.

Jeanne piled and shaped the turfs until the dam was slightly higher than the level of the field. Her blouse was splashed and mud-stained.

Peter dropped the flattened tin can and, sitting back on his heels, wiped his hands on his thighs.

"Just look at that!" he said.

Jeanne waded out and stood beside him. The water lay wide and sullen in front of them.

"How long do you think it'll hold?" she said.

Peter shrugged.

They looked down on the pool, watching a thick swirl where the current moved in.

"Are we going home now?" said Anna.

"It's holding up pretty well," said Jeanne. "Don't you think?"

Peter realized that his hand was smarting. He had a cut in his palm and had torn a fingernail.

“You look funny with your skirt in your knickers,” he said.

“Give me your handkerchief,” she said. “I want to dry my legs. And don’t use the word *knickers*. It sounds disgusting.”

“Are we going home now, Mummy?”

“Yes, poppet.”

“Can I have cocoa?”

“I should think so.”

“Can Peter tell me a story?”

“You’ll have to ask him when you’re in bed.”

At the fence, they stopped and looked back. The place where Peter had torn up the turf was black. In front of the black patch there was a glimmer in the grass. The rising water was overflowing, seeping and trickling forward between the roots, glinting in the twilight.

They took it in turns to carry Anna home. Jeanne undressed her in the kitchen and gave her a quick wash at the sink before taking her up to bed. She was so tired she forgot to ask for cocoa and a story. Peter took off his damp trousers and dropped them on the kitchen floor with Anna’s clothes. He went into the sitting room and plugged in the electric fire.

He stood in front of it warming his behind and legs. The sitting room was small and square, crowded by the chintz-covered settee and the two armchairs. On the wall facing him was a large painting of a windjammer under full canvas. On an occasional table under the chintz curtains was a basket made from the shell of an armadillo, its tail curving round into its mouth to form a handle. It was lined with red silk and full of wax fruit.

He knelt in the armchair and looked over the back, glancing along the shelves of the small bookcase. Most of the books were sea stories, Edwardian travel books, memoirs. He heard Jeanne’s voice upstairs and her footsteps going into her own room. He took out a book called *Travels on the Upper Yangtze* by a Major K. Frazer and flipped through the pages. He felt too tired to read. He looked at a sepia photograph of a Chinese peasant with a pack on his shoulder. The caption read: A Typical Son of the East.

Jeanne came down the narrow stairs, tying the cord of her housecoat. She gathered the cushions together on the settee and plumped them into a comfortable heap at one end. Then, she took a cardboard box from the top of the bookcase and settled herself into the cushions. She opened the box and took out bundles of Parker's Red Dragon coupons, her albums, and the Free Gift Catalogue.

She smoothed back the cover of a new album and slipped the elastic band off a bundle of coupons. She separated them into two piles, those worth five units and those worth ten. Then she started licking the top edges of the coupons and fixing them into the book. Peter sat in the armchair watching her. He could hear the wind strengthening, stirring the brass flap of the letterbox in the front door.

"Jeanne?"

She did not look up.

"Umm?"

"Do you know if there are any Band-Aids or a tin of Elastoplast or anything? I want to cover this cut."

She shrugged.

"Have a look in the bathroom."

He went upstairs and washed the cut again. The cabinet in the bathroom was empty except for rusted razor blades. When he went downstairs, she had started on a second album.

As she pressed the coupons into place, she was humming. He wandered over to the table and ran his fingers over the armadillo's bristly plates. He pressed his thumbnail into a wax pear. He walked back and stood at the end of the settee watching her.

"Hmmph."

"What?"

"I was just thinking. I nearly killed myself humping that suitcase all the way from the bus. Blistered my hands, probably slipped a disc, and half of it was full of your bloody old coupons."

"Well, I wasn't going to leave them behind. You don't get things for free very often in this life."

Peter tucked himself into the armchair again.

"They're not *really* free," he said. "You pay for all that with the price of the cigarettes."

"Well, they *seem* free, then. Just as important. And anyway, I enjoy sticking them in the books."

"Those cigarettes taste so bloody awful though. Nobody'd smoke them if they didn't have gifts."

"I hadn't noticed you refusing them," said Jeanne.

She took the elastic band off another bundle of coupons and began to sort them.

"And the things you get for them are very good anyway," she said.

"Such as?"

"That dartboard I had. Solid cork. It was a good one."

"What other sort of things?"

She picked up the catalogue and turned the pages.

"Steam irons, power drills, ironing boards, spice racks, bathroom scales, Hoovers, tricycles, Ronson table lighters—oh, here's one for you—document case. Genuine All-Leather Document Case. Best Quality Hide. All-Brass Mercury Zipper. Measures 30" by 15". Executive Styling."

She looked across at him.

"You could use it to carry all your little papers in. Your register and so on."

"Very nice," said Peter.

"Just the thing," said Jeanne. "Executive styling, too. You could put all your little report cards in it."

"It'd be very handy," said Peter.

She laughed and said, "Peter has not worked hard enough this term. He has often been a naughty boy. He lacks team spirit and must try harder and cooperate with others."

"Extremely comical," said Peter.

"Yes, this case is just the thing for you. Cheap, too. Only two-and-a-half albums."

"Pack it in, will you, Jeanne. Whatever you say, I still think that teaching's an important job."

"Of course it is."

"Well, it *is*."

"I know. I agree with you."

"Oh, stop trying to take the piss. You're not subtle enough."

"I'm *agreeing* with you, for Christ's sake!"

"Oh, up yours!"

"Tut! Tut!" said Jeanne. "I don't think that's the way *teachers* speak, is it?"

Peter opened *Travels on the Upper Yangtze.*

One of the older porters was a particularly sullen sort of chap. We suspected him of creating trouble for the very "Foreign Devils" who were supplying his daily food! All the efforts of Captain Frisby, who often quizzed him in his own lingo, failed to draw him out. Sullen he remained.

"What's the heavy silence for?" said Jeanne.

"I'm *trying* to read."

"Oh, pardon me. Interesting book?"

"Yes."

"Educational?"

Peter got up, dropped the book into the armchair, and went upstairs to his room. He put the light out and got into bed. He smoked a couple of cigarettes, using the packet as an ashtray. He had not drawn the curtains and he could see clouds scudding across the moon. His hands behind his head, he lay staring out into the night.

About an hour later, there was a knock at his door.

"Who is it?" he said.

"That's a stupid question," said Jeanne as she came into the room and closed the door behind her.

"Who did you think it was? Jack the Ripper?"

She sat on the edge of the bed.

"Peter?"

"What?"

"I'm sorry I was bitchy."

"That's all right."

"I just felt . . . Oh, I don't know. Just a bitchy mood. Forgive me?"

"Yes. I said, yes."

"Oh, come on, Pete. Don't be cold to me. Really, I'm sorry."

She stretched out on the blankets and nuzzled his ear.

"Say you forgive me," she whispered.

He put his arm around her and kissed her.

"Pete?"

"What?"

"I haven't got any knickers on."

"You rude thing!" he said.

"Let's go to my room. The bed's bigger."

They made love to each other in the Captain's double bed. The bed was brass, brass rails and knobs and curlicues, arabesques of brass which rattled and jangled with their every move. Their bodies were pale in the moonlight.

Peter pulled the sheet and blankets up over them and they lay quietly in the warm bed. Peter's breathing slowed and deepened and his head turned on the pillow. He felt Jeanne's hip nudging him.

"What's the matter?"

"Don't go to sleep here, Pete."

He grunted.

"I don't want Anna coming in. In the morning. Pete."

"All right," he said.

He rolled over and kissed her and then heaved himself out of the rattling bed.

Jeanne giggled.

"What?"

"Your little bum. It looks lovely in the moonlight."

* * *

"I'LL CALL YOU," said Jeanne." A couple of weeks or so."

"Gartree Comprehensive School," said Peter.

"I put Bill Arkle's number in your wallet so you can get your suit. Don't forget."

"Take care."

He swung the rucksack up in front of him and climbed the steps into the bus.

"I'll phone you," called Jeanne.

"Gartree Comprehensive," he shouted.

* * *

THE GLASS DOORS of the foyer sighed shut behind him, cutting off the surge and babble of the playground. On the wall facing him was a reproduction of some dim pastoral scene and flanking him two broad-leaved plants in wooden tubs.

He followed the arrow which pointed to *Enquiries*. The woman sitting at the desk looked up at his knock and raised her eyebrows.

"Mr. Stine's office, please?"

"And the nature of your business...?"

Peter handed her his letter of appointment from the Education Authority. Rimless spectacles. A frizzy perm. A white blouse secured at the throat by a spray of enamel flowers. She looked up from the letter over her glasses and said, "Welcome to Gartree Comprehensive, Mr. Hendricks."

"Thank you," said Peter.

She pointed to the name plaque on her desk.

"I am Miss Brice. The School Secretary."

Peter smiled and nodded.

"Now before you see Mr. Stine there are a couple of items...."

She opened desk drawers and folders.

"This is your G. 34, the Ministry Form for use as a temporary register. And these are your School Dinner Numbers Returns."

"Thank you," said Peter.

"Both these are due in no later than ten-thirty this morning."

"Ten-thirty," said Peter.

"On the dot," said Miss Brice.

"Right," said Peter.

"And if I may suggest?" said Miss Brice. "That you fill in the G. 34 in pencil first and ink it in after you've rechecked."

Peter nodded.

"Pencil first," he said.

She smiled at him.

"We don't want a lot of unsightly erasures, do we?"

Peter nodded again.

"You'll notice *here*," said Miss Brice, "that the children are asked to state their age in years and months *as on June thirtieth of this year.*"

"Yes," he said.

"Many of them," said Miss Brice, "will not do this." She looked up at him over her spectacles and said, "It is your responsibility to check this information."

"I see," said Peter. "June thirtieth this year."

"Now, Mr. Hendricks. I believe that Mr. Stine is free to see you, if you'd care to...."

"Yes, thank you."

"The second door along, on your right," she said.

"Thank you very much," he said.

He stood outside the door and glanced up and down the corridor. He straightened his tie and tried to smooth down his hair at the back. He knocked on the door just above the words: *N. Stine. Headmaster.*

Nothing happened. He knocked again.

"Come in, child!" said a voice. "Come in!"

Mr. Stine, a toy watering can in his hand, was looking out of the window. He turned round slowly, his head back and to one side. Then he made a strange noise. It sounded like the creak of a door opening. He seemed to make it through his nose.

"Good morning, Mr. . . . ah. . . ."

"Hendricks," said Peter.

"Ah, yes. Mr. Hendricks. Of course. Good morning. As you see, I am watering my plant."

Peter smiled and nodded.

Mr. Stine put the small red watering can down on the window ledge and moved to stand behind his desk. On the wall above his head hung a photograph of the 1962 Junior Football Team. He made the creaking noise again. His nose was prominent, a high ridge of bone pulling the skin white.

"Ah . . . yes."

He squared a few papers on his desk and moved the calendar backwards until it was in line with his In/Out tray. Then, rearing up to his full, gaunt height, and, forcing his head even further back until he seemed to be sighting along the blade of his nose, he clasped the bands of his gown and said, "Well . . . ah . . . welcome to Gartree Comprehensive School. I hope you will be very happy here."

"Thank you very much," said Peter.

"Very happy."

Mr. Stine seemed to be gazing at something above Peter's head.

"It is, I believe, a Happy School."

He turned and walked across to the green filing cabinet. With his back turned, he said,

"It is not," and turned again to pace towards the window and the plant,

"An Easy School. But it is," and he stopped to gaze at the photograph of the 1962 Junior Football Team.

"And therefore, I want you to feel free to come to me at any time."

The room was stuffy. Peter could feel his shirt sticking to his back. Both bars of the electric fire glowed red.

"Thank you," he said to Mr. Stine's back.

Mr. Stine seemed to be regarding his plant. The silence deepened. The papers in Peter's hand were wilting and sticky. He tried to think of something to say. He noticed that Mr. Stine's trousers ended six or seven inches above his ankles. On the desk was a green tin box that looked as if it contained sandwiches. The electric fire was making slight fizzing noises.

"Discipline!" said Mr. Stine suddenly. He turned round and stared at Peter.

"Send any Troublemakers to me."

Interlocking his fingers and turning his palms outwards, he cracked his knuckles.

"Oh, yes. There *are* Troublemakers in this school. I know them. I know their families."

His eyes searched Peter's face.

"I have met them before and I expect to meet them again."

Peter nodded, unable to look away.

Mr. Stine walked over to the window and stood looking out for a moment. Then, picking up the red watering can, he pointed it at the filing cabinet.

"It is all noted down," he said. "Records are kept."

He walked back to his desk and placed the watering can in the centre. Then, wrapping his gown tightly about him, he lowered himself into his chair.

"There's really no need to stand, Mr. . . . . ah. . . ."

"Hendricks," said Peter.

"Do sit down."

"Thank you," said Peter.

"Ah . . . white shirts, Mr. Hendricks."

"Pardon?" said Peter.

Mr. Stine made his creaking noise very loudly and started to stroke his thinning grey hair with the flat of his hand. Peter looked at the watering can. On the side was a yellow triangle. Inside the triangle were the words: *Triang Toys*.

"Some people have strange ideas, Mr. Hendricks."

He reached inside the folds of his gown and brought out a silver propelling pencil. He held it up in front of his face and stared at it.

"There are those who think. . . ."

His words trailed away and he twiddled with the end of the pencil, extending and retracting the lead.

". . . ah . . . progressive thinkers. But it is essential that we remain at all times In Control."

He looked up suddenly from the end of the pencil, as if startled. The lead toppled out and broke into three pieces on his desktop.

"Ah . . . so there you are, you see."

He placed the pencil on the desk beside the watering can.

"Now, Mr. Hendricks. You'll find the staff room along the corridor, up the stairs, and on your right."

"Thank you very much, Mr. Stine," said Peter.

Mr. Stine remained bent over the desk, staring at the broken pencil lead. Peter got up, hesitated, and went out, closing the door quietly behind him. The air in the corridor was much cooler.

The door to Miss Brice's office was now closed and he could hear the clacking of her typewriter. He walked along the corridor towards the stairs. Allan's alarm clock had lost twenty minutes during the night and he'd had no time to get any breakfast. His stomach was achingly empty. He hadn't even had time for coffee or tea.

His back and neck were stiff from sleeping on Allan's spring-smashed settee and his eyes felt hot and gritty. Three more weeks before he got his first pay cheque. After they had drunk beer at the Three Feathers until closing time and then eaten fish and chips at the Chinaman's, they'd stayed up until two thirty chatting about Allan's thesis.

When he had got into his sleeping bag and stretched out on the settee, Allan was still padding about the littered room, unearthing still more books and pamphlets, mumbling, laughing, reading out choice pieces of Whig scurrility.

The room was piled and stacked with books and folders. Eighteenth-century pamphlets, newspapers, prints, and broadsheets formed dumps under the window and by Allan's bed. His table was heaped with litter except for a small writing space. Foolscap, covered in his large handwriting, lay on books which balanced on ashtrays. Old milk bottles stood on dictionaries; antiquarian book dealers' catalogues covered bits of rock-hard sandwiches and mould-filled coffee cups; notes and references clung to sticky teaspoons.

The floorboards creaking, Allan's voice, the eventual thud of his shoes on the floor. Peter did not remember the light going out.

There was a strong smell of wax polish in the corridor. Another reproduction of a pastoral scene. Sheep. A lady in a straw hat. A clock on the wall by the stairs said eight thirty. He turned to the right at the top of the stairs and went into the staff room. A few people glanced at him and then turned back to their conversations. There were no empty chairs. He stood against the wall holding the official form Miss Brice had given him to use as a temporary register.

... not a bad lad, but he can't concentrate. Just like his sister ... so I wasn't going to stand for that sort of insolence, so I said ... lovely handwriting.

On the opposite wall was a letter rack. Peter wandered across and looked at the names under the pigeon holes to see if his was there. Most of the holes were empty. From one hung a stiff football sock. His name was not there.

Near him, a large man in a blue suit and a maroon tie was talking to a nervous-looking man in a black suit.

You know the turning for the bypass!

Yes.

Don't take it. You need the left turn before.

Where is that!

You know Needler's? The chocolate factory?

Needler's, yes.

Well, you don't go quite that far. You box clever, you see, and miss the lights.

On a table under the window stood a large copper urn. Some of the teachers were drawing cups of tea from it but Peter couldn't see where the cups were coming from. They seemed to bring the cups with them.

On the counter below the letter rack was a heap of papers and books—publishers' catalogues, old exam papers, under them a collapsed rugby football, a few grimy playing cards, and three textbooks, spines ripped off and covers ink-stained. Peter picked up one of the texts, a first-year Latin grammar. It opened at an illustration of a Roman orator. In a balloon from his mouth were the words, "What do you think of that?" and emerging from the centre of his toga, a large drooping penis.

A tall young man, a college scarf draped round his neck, came into the room letting out a rebel yell.

Hey, it's Bunny! shouted another voice. *Ready for battle, boyo?*

Raring to go! bawled the man. *Just wheel the little buggers in.*

More and more teachers were crowding into the room. Peter looked at the notice board which was empty except for a piece of paper which said: *Tea Money. Still Unpaid—Mr. B. Williams, Miss C. "Curves" Jones, Mrs. C. Bagshaw.*

A young man with ginger hair came up to him and said, "Good morning. Are you a new boy?"

"Yes, that's right. Peter Hendricks."

"Tony Rogers. PE and junior history."

"I'm going to be teaching English," said Peter.

"You're welcome to that. Too much marking for my taste."

"I wonder," said Peter, "if it's possible to get a cup of tea?"

"Surely. I'll see if I can pinch a mug for you . . . Be right back."

Peter watched his ginger hair moving through the crowd towards the cloakroom.

Wait a minute said the nervous man. *So now you're going along Canal Street?*

Right! said the man with the maroon tie. *Now on the corner there's the Odeon cinema? With me?*

"Here you are," said the young man with ginger hair. "One mug teachers for the use of."

"Thanks very much," said Peter.

They moved through the crowd to stand in the line behind the urn.

"Have you met your head of department yet? Jim Curtis?"

"No, not yet."

The tea was black and stewed. A faint slick of oil floated on the surface. He poured in a lot of milk.

Tony Rogers peered round and then said, "No. Can't see him. He's a brilliant chap. Built a large-scale model of the Globe Theatre last year with the fourth forms. About twenty-feet long. Papier mâché, you know. Earned himself a lot of kudos."

"No," said Peter. "The only person I've met so far is Mr. Stine."

"Oh, there's Jim just coming in."

Peter looked round and saw a tall, blond man going into the cloakroom.

"Is Mr. Stine always . . . well, sort of absent-minded?"

"Stiny? Oh, he has a few odd—what's the word?"

"Eccentricities?"

"No. You know. *Mannerisms*. A few odd mannerisms. Some of them complain about him—that he keeps himself to himself too much. But he's a good egg really. After all, he *is* headmaster."

"It was just that he seemed a little. . . ."

"The best thing about him is that he'll always back you up if you have discipline problems. He'll bring the cane in and sort a whole class out."

The young man glanced at his watch.

"Well, I'll see you around," he said. "I've got to boot some kids out of the gym before assembly."

"Thanks for the mug," said Peter.

Painted on the side of the mug was the name *Owen Thomas*. Peter sipped the tea and looked down into the playground.

A girl was back-combing another's hair. Two boys just outside the gate were straddling the crossbars of their bikes and passing a cigarette between them. A huddle of small girls were reading a comic. Some of the older boys were snatching caps from the heads of new first-formers and chucking them over the railings into the road. A football game surged up and down the asphalt. Each side seemed to have about thirty players. When they barged too close to the matronly girls in the fourth and fifth forms, the girls beat at them with their wicker baskets of domestic science supplies. Some younger girls were dancing to a transistor radio, absorbed, solemn. Peter watched the goalie crouching between two piles of satchels. The mob charged closer, hacking and blocking, trying to clear the green plastic football out to runners on the wings. The goalie hunched himself. His eyes following the ball as they charged nearer, he tensed down like a spring.

His pose suddenly reminded Peter of the blue Turf cigarette cards he used to collect when he was nine or ten. *Stars of Association Football*. There had been one he'd never found.

A complete set except for that one card. Stanley Mathews? It was the only name that came to him from the past. Now they collected cornflakes cards, bubble-gum cards.

He remembered, too, suddenly, vividly, a story in a comic. He could smell the smell of the paper and the cheap print; feel the paper's coarse texture in his fingers. *The Hotspur? The Rover*? A serial, and he'd never found out what happened; how they did it. It had been set in Canada. Engineers were going to flood a valley but they received a series of fatal telephone calls. When they answered the phone, they suddenly dropped dead, their faces contorted in agony. He could even see the illustrations; a man with a safety helmet on, his eyes bulging, falling to the ground, the telephone swinging on its cord.

He couldn't remember why he'd stopped reading; why he hadn't followed the serial to the end. He stared through the glass into the playground.

A man in a blue tracksuit came out of the side door and stood in the middle of the playground blowing a whistle. The football game slowed, stopped; the boys gathered up their satchels. The children drifted into lines. The boys on the bicycles rushed to put them into the concrete slots. A small man came out with sheets of paper. All movement stopped.

Gradually, Peter became aware of someone standing beside him. He turned and looked at an old man with grizzly eyebrows who was glaring at him.

"That's my mug," said the old man.

"Oh, I'm terribly sorry. I'm new here and someone gave it to me."

"I want my mug," said the old man.

The bell burst into its deafening clangour. Peter followed the others out of the door and down the stairs. The big man in the maroon tie was saying, *Vine Street'll often save you two or three minutes.*

Outside the assembly hall, the classes were waiting, boys in one line, girls in another. Teachers were patrolling the length of the lines, which stretched all the way along the bottom corridor and out into the playground. At the head of them a small, fierce man, the man who had been in the playground with the papers, was trotting up and down, shouting.

"Keep against the wall. DON'T talk. Are you chewing, boy? Yes. You know who I mean. You. The boy in the red sweater. Go and stand outside the headmaster's office."

The children stared at him with blank faces. On the wall above their heads hung a reproduction of a Dufy painting, brilliant white sails cavorting on the blue water of a bay.

"What did I say? Didn't I say NO talking?"

Upon command, the lines began to shuffle forward. Peter followed the other teachers to the back of the hall. The fifth and fourth forms sat on chairs at the back. The few sixth-formers sat on chairs along the sides of the hall. The rest of the school, the third, the second, and the new first-formers, filed in endlessly, class by class, and sat on the floor in rows. The fierce little man mounted the steps to the stage and stood behind the lectern.

There was a grand piano on the stage at the right and a table and lectern in the centre at the front. The music master appeared from the wings and propped open the lid of the piano. There was an immediate buzz of conversation. The little man started forward and stood gripping the edges of the lectern, darting fierce glances.

The music master began to play. The air was becoming stuffy. The shuffling, the whispering, the coughing, and the hollow plap of dropped hymn books was growing louder. Some of the teachers got up and joined the prefects in the aisles. They glared, snapped their fingers, threatened. The piano played on and on.

The gym teacher who had been blowing the whistle in the playground started to open windows. All eyes watched the wavering end of the long pole as it tried to hook onto the window catches. "Face the front!" shouted the little man.

Suddenly the piano stopped playing. Mr. Stine appeared through the curtains at the back of the stage. Those sitting on chairs scraped them back and stood up. The rest scrambled to their feet. Mr. Stine advanced towards the lectern. He moved stiffly, head back and to one side. He waited until there was absolute silence and then surveyed the ranks down the length of his nose. Into the silence, he made his creaking noise.

"Good morning, boys and girls."

There was a vast answering roar.

"Good morning, sir."

"Ah..."

"Ah..." and the noise died away.

"Open your hymn books at page seventy-one. Hymn number one hundred and thirty-four. This is a Joyous hymn and we are singing it to celebrate the beginning of a new school year. It was written by Josiah Wentworth, born 1737 died 1803.

"We have all had an enjoyable... ah... holiday but now we must Buckle Down. And so, I want the fifth and sixth forms to sing verse one, and the third and fourth forms verse two. Now the third verse...."

There was a long silence.

"The third verse will be sung by the second forms. Girls will sing the last two lines, and the boys will sing the first three."

Mr. Stine stopped and stared down into the first few rows. They sat very still.

"A special word to the new boys and girls in the first form. I like to Hear when people sing. You must remember that this is a Secondary School."

He looked down at the lectern.

"We will omit verse four and the whole school will sing the last verse."

The music master gave an introductory pound on the piano and the hymn got under way. In the middle of the thin singing of verse three Mr. Stine shouted, "Louder! Louder!"

When the hymn was finished, he nodded and everyone sat down. Chairs scraped and there was a start of whispering. Shuffling. He gripped the lectern and stared.

"Some boys and girls," he said quietly, as if amazed, "don't seem to remember how to Behave."

The assembly hall grew still. A breath of air was stirring one of the long curtains. The brass knob on the end of the curtain cord was clicking against the glass.

"STAND UP."

Peter jerked in his chair.

The children got silently to their feet, silently stood and waited.

"Now!" said Mr. Stine. "We will sit down again. We will sit down like little Ladies and Gentlemen."

The children eased themselves into their places. They looked straight ahead. Someone coughed. Head bent back, Mr. Stine stared. After what seemed minutes, he opened the Bible on the lectern. With no introduction, he started to read.

Then Solomon assembled the elders of Israel, and all the heads of the tribes, the chief of the fathers of Israel, unto King Solomon in Jerusalem, that they might bring up the ark of the covenant of the Lord out of the city of David, which is Zion. And all the men of Israel. . . .

Peter soon heard only the steady drone of Mr. Stine's voice. The air was hot, heavy with the smell of polish, sweat, dust. He remembered mornings like this, the same smell, a voice reading, the rows of boys in their blazers with the white flower badges, the tall prefects lining the sides of the hall; mornings when he had sat with Tony and Dell Latter playing noughts and crosses over the pages of hymn books, telling jokes, trying to make them laugh out loud during prayers .

... There was nothing in the ark save the two tables of stone, which Moses put there at Horeb, when the Lord made a covenant with the children of Israel, when they came out of the land of Egypt.

The voice stopped. Mr. Stine was closing the Bible.

"May God add His ... ah ... to this reading of His Holy Word."

Stepping forward to the very edge of the stage, he lowered his head and raised his arms so that his gown hung like giant wings.

"All heads bowed. Eyes closed. The Lord's Prayer."

Mr. Stine delivered the prayer with strange pauses and inflections. After *Lead us not into temptation*, he stopped for so long that heads popped up here and there in the hall and looked round. He finished the prayer at a gallop and there was a rustle and murmur as the school sat up.

He clasped the bands of his gown and surveyed the silent rows.

"Apparently," he said, "there are Some among you ... they know who they are. There are Some...."

His words trailed away. He clasped his hands behind his back and stared down at his shoes. He began to sway slightly.

"The majority of you are Decent boys and girls. You behave Decently."

He moved the Bible into the centre of the lectern.

"I have no wish to start this term in an atmosphere of unpleasantness but the condition of the ... ah ... Boys' Lavatories this morning was deplorable."

He looked slowly round the hall. He turned to stare at the music master.

"Quite deplorable."

From where Peter was sitting, he could see heads bending together, whispering.

"Disgusting would not be too strong a word."

The children sat rigid and stared straight ahead.

"There was paper."

Silence.

"Paper everywhere. And Filth. Deliberate dirty Filth!"

Somewhere in the middle of the hall, someone with a runny cold sniffed.

"Would you do this in your Own Homes?" shouted Mr. Stine.

He glared around the hall. His face was mottled.

"No! You would not! Your parents would not allow it! Nor will I allow it. Filth! Deliberate, Nasty, Filthy Dirtiness. If I catch any children being Filthy...."

He stopped. Holding to the lectern, he lowered his head. In a quiet voice he said, "I cannot express.... It is beyond words ... even on the walls...."

His silence seemed endless. Finally, raising his head, he said, "During the holidays, the, and we must congratulate them, the ... ah ... First Eleven won through to the finals of the County Championship.

Dismiss."

* * *

THE ROOM was heavy with breathing, creaks, the rustling and flick of turned pages as the class worked on the comprehension exercise. Peter drifted further down the side aisle and stopped to study the Centurion. The Centurion, *Living History* Number Seven, was exhorting his men, pointing his sword towards a lot of hairy ancient Britons who were jumping up and down on the opposite side of the stream. His face was a nasty salmon colour.

Peter turned away and surveyed the whispering heads and scribbling pens and then turned back again to the display board. Beside the Centurion picture was a *National Geographic* map of the world. In the middle of England someone had drawn a black dot. From the dot, a line shot out into the Atlantic. At the end of the line were the words: *My House*.

He wandered down to the back of the room and leaned against the wall behind the pretty girl, Jennifer, Jennifer Something, and gazed at the auburn down on the nape of her neck. The low bookshelves, which stretched the length of the back wall, were pressing against his thighs. Copies of the blue book, the title stamped in gold, marched all the way along every shelf. He used the book for all his literature classes, first, second, and third forms. An administrative mistake, Curtis had explained, but the money had been spent. Yet another set of the books was stacked on top of the shelves under *Living History* Number Eight—a Viking standing in the prow of his ship pointing his sword towards the beach.

He picked up a copy of the book. *The Realm of Gold*. Essays by Addison, Steele, Lamb, Hazlitt, Arnold, Belloc, and Chesterton. Milton's *Lycidas*. Odd chunks of Shakespeare. The author, in his introduction, hoped that his selections would open magic casements.

Peter walked back up the aisle, glancing at exercise books as he went. Most of them would be finished in about five minutes. He sat down at his desk. He glanced at the clock.

On the desk in front of him was a stack of exercise books belonging to 2E. They had been lying there for nine days. *My Atobagifry. Autobiogriphy. Attobagioph. The Story of My Autobiography*. He took his red pencil out of the centre drawer.

> *I will learn JUDO and KRATE and beat them all and then nobody will beat me up but will look up to me and my statue in the park and they will all love me and I will be great great great and great.*

He opened another book. The brief paragraph stared up at him. The first sentence read:

Last night I went to the flims with a gril.

He dropped the books back on the pile. The red second hand was sweeping round the face of the clock. Thirteen minutes to go before the end of the lesson. Thirteen minutes before dinner time. Today it was Irish Stew. He had smelled it all morning. With the Irish Stew there would be Boiled Potatoes. The vegetable would be either Diced Carrots or Diced Turnips. Irish Stew was always followed by Steamed Pudding and Custard.

Eleven minutes to dinner time; to the roar and clatter of the assembly hall and the sticky, lino-topped tables, the green plastic beakers, the aluminum cutlery.

Mr. Hottle would chew with his mouth open and say that for two shillings and sixpence a week, the food was really much better than one could expect, and then he would say: *I happened to be watching TV last night and there was a most interesting program—not that I watch just anything, mind you. I suppose I'm what my wife calls a selective viewer. I was going to switch it off but it really was quite informative. About Patagonia.* And while he talked about Patagonia, about juvenile gangs in Glasgow, about skin diving, about neo-Nazi movements in the New Germany, about faith healing, Mr. Carlton, the metal work teacher, would say: *It's not what I'd call fair—the present scale. What about experience? The School of Hard Knocks was where I got my degree.* And then, between the stew and the pudding, he would clean his nails with a scriber. Mr. Owen Thomas would sit staring across at the next table, his eyes fixed on the two or three inches of thigh exposed by Miss C. Jones. Mr. Hottle would say: *Well, if you're quite sure you really don't want it . . . it does seem a pity to waste. . . .*

There was a knock on the door and the office monitor came in.

“Please sir, Miss Brice says you're to go to the office urgent.”

“Thank you,” said Peter. “Just carry on with your work and get the exercise finished. I'll be back in a couple of minutes.”

He walked along the top corridor, past the art room where a fourth form was drawing a Chianti bottle, a plaster-of-Paris foot, and a bunch of leeks, past Mr. Hughes chanting French conjugations in a strong Welsh accent, Miss Jones, Mrs. Chetwynd, past two refugees from Owen Thomas' backward class who ducked back into the girls' lavatory, past the caretaker who was covering a splatter of vomit with sawdust, and down the stairs by the staff room. In the bottom corridor, the smell of Irish Stew was much stronger. He saw Miss Brice standing in her office doorway. She hurried towards him.

“I'm so sorry, Mr. Hendricks. It's your mother.”

“What? What's wrong? She isn't…?”

“Oh, no! She's not….”

“What is it?”

“It's her arm. She caught her arm in a machine.”

They turned into the office and she pointed at the phone lying on the desk.

“Long distance,” she said.” A neighbour.”

She went over to the window and stood looking out.

“Hello?”

“Mr. Hendricks?”

“Yes, speaking.”

“Sweetie pie!” said Jeanne. “Can you talk?”

“No.”

“Well, listen. I'm in town now at a new place—I just went a few miles out to make this long distance and get the operator into the act. Call me at about three this afternoon at 337914. Got that?”

“Wait a minute.”

Peter gestured at Miss Brice and made a scribbling motion. She came over to the desk and gave him a pad and pencil. She stood watching him as he wrote down the number. She raised her eyebrows when he looked up and Peter shook his head.

"And you're at the hospital now, are you?" he said.

"I've missed you," said Jeanne. "I'm feeling *very* randy."

"Good," said Peter.

"Shall I tell you what I feel like doing?"

A desk diary. Calendar. Half-empty pot of glue.

"No. That won't be necessary."

"Who's there with you?"

"How long do you think it will be?"

"It's hot in this box," said Jeanne, "and I feel extremely—what's the word you always use? You know."

"Horny," said Peter. "Dr. Leopold Horny."

He crushed his ear with the phone to contain her laughter.

"I'm going to have a massive party," said Jeanne. "Probably this coming Friday—I think they'll be away—but I'll tell you all about that this afternoon."

"Yes, I see."

"Oh, Peter!"

"Yes?"

"When you call. It's Mrs. Abercrombie."

"Who is?"

"I am."

"Oh, right."

"About three, then."

"Yes."

"Well, keep a stiff upper thingy," said Jeanne, and rang off.

"And they're still giving transfusions?"

"Yes, I see."

"The artery."

"Yes. Yes, I suppose so."

"Oh, look, there's no need to meet me."

"Well, it's very kind of you. Yes. Yes. Thank you. About six o'clock then. Goodbye."

Peter put the receiver down and stood resting his hand on the phone. He stared at the Glue pot. Slowly he raised his head and looked at Miss Brice.

"They're still operating," he said.

* * *

HE SAT at a window table in the Old Gartree so that he could see when the bus came into Gartree Square. The bar was empty except for two old men who were sitting in silence one table away. Two glasses stood in front of him, a double Scotch and a pint of bitter. He raised the Scotch to the fake hunting prints, the fake post horn, the rows of fake Dutch pewter mugs, and swallowed it in one, shuddering gulp .

... our sympathy. It is a most distressing and ... ah ... melancholy ... ah. ... And so. ... He smiled into the frothy, golden beer. He had only just avoided a lift to the railway station.

The rest of the week was free; he counted. The rest of the afternoon and then all day Wednesday, Thursday, Friday, Saturday, and Sunday. Five and a half days. He traced his name in spilled beer on the Formica tabletop. Today was his day for School Dinner Supervision. He'd have to phone Stine on Friday—and he'd have to make it long distance—to say he was travelling back on Sunday. He tried to recall the form he'd filled in for the Education Authority, tried to remember whether they had his home address and telephone number. But there really wasn't much danger. Their hopes for a speedy recovery had gone with him. He finished the beer and went up to the bar for another pint.

The landlord was stacking side plates by the cash register and sprinkling sprigs of parsley over the ham sandwiches in preparation for the lunch-time trade. A green silk ascot, sporty shirt.

"Similar, sir?"

Behind the bar were picture postcards from the regulars, poker-work plaques.

Old Golfers Never Die—They Only Lose Their Balls.

Shakespeare's Dead, Nelson's Dead, And I Don't Feel So Good Myself.

An old woman came in.

He took the beer back to his table. The two old men had started talking. As he passed them, one was saying, ". . . and they've come on wonderful."

The other said, "Course, if I hadn't been bad last week, I'd have planted 'em out then."

"Ah. They do well in frames, mind."

Peter moved the curtains aside and looked out for the bus. He'd have plenty of time to change at Allan's, get out of his suit, and then potter about in the Western Book Shop for an hour before calling Jeanne. Before calling Mrs. Abercrombie. He smiled at the smoke rising from his cigarette. The beer and Scotch were moving inside him.

"There's no justice to it," said one of the old men.

Peter considered eating a ham sandwich. The bus was nowhere in sight and it always stopped in the Square for seven or eight minutes before making the return journey. He took another mouthful of beer and thought about Mr. Hottle. About Mr. Hottle eating a ham sandwich.

"Nobody!"—the old man slapped his hand on the table—"Nobody can manage on that. You just can't do it."

The other old man nodded.

"If I didn't have my war pension, where would I be? Eh? Eh?"

The old man who was leading the conversation was wearing a dark blue suit which was frayed at the cuffs and shiny. He leaned forward to speak, his hands one on top of the other on his stick. The skin was loose, big with blue veins. A few strands of hair were plastered across his pate.

"And you'd think these glasses would be free, wouldn't you? But I had to pay a pound. A pound!"

The other man who seemed quieter, nervous, said. "Well, take me now, and my leg. One of the straps broke so I went down the Labour to see about it. They don't *do* the straps down the Labour, but you have to go there first, see, for the papers. They *mend* 'em up in the Rehabilitation, where I was. And this young fellow said it'd cost ten shillings. Ten shillings, he said. So I said, 'Now look here, young fellow, I want to see the manager.'"

"Quite right!" said the forceful man. "Quite right. These young men just don't understand."

"So I said to him, 'Although I lives with my daughter,' I said, 'ten shillings is a big part of my week's money.'"

"Exactly," said the other. "Quite right. I've lived carefully all my life—I'm not a spendthrift like some—been a member of the Mutual for, let me see, nigh on fifty-seven year. Shilling a week regular as clockwork. Joined 'em when I was twenty."

The nervous man kept running his tongue over his top lip and making a sticky clicking noise with his mouth.

"Where did you get that?" said the forceful man suddenly. "Hope you don't mind me asking?"

The nervous man reached down with both hands and pulled the braced leg closer under the table. Peter heard the leather creak.

"The war, that was. The Great War. I was one of the lucky ones. Yes, the Battle of the Somme, that was. Sent home."

"And me," said the other, touching his spectacles. Underneath one lens was a pad of lint.

"Wipers that was. Remember that? The officers used to call it 'Epree.' Wipers was what we called it."

"Ah," said the nervous man.

"Epree," said the other. "French, that is."

"Parlez-vous?" said the nervous man. "That's what they used to say. Eh? Parlez-vous."

Peter lit a cigarette. The match rasped in the silence. The forceful man's legs were crossed and the top leg was jiggling up and down. His black boots were highly polished.

"Do you remember," said the nervous man, "how they collected all the horses from the farms? For the gun carriages, they were. You don't see many now. Horses, I mean. You don't see many horses now."

"I remember," said the forceful man, "when I was a little fellow—five or six years old I must have been at the time. No, perhaps a little older. Every Sunday my father took me, morning and evening. He was what they call a God-fearing man. Nineteen-thirty *he* died. A regular churchgoing man he was. Morning and night, regular. Baptist. He said to me," and he leaned forward to tap the other on the knee, "he said to me, 'The Land of Canaan. That's where I'm going when I'm dead, my boy. I shall be with the Lord in Canaan. A land flowing with milk and honey,' that's what he said. My father. It was in nineteen-thirty, if I remember it right, when he died."

"Ah!" said the other. "That's it. That's right. You don't see many now. For pulling the gun carriages they were."

Peter saw the bus pulling into the square. Standing up, he drained the last of the beer. As he went past their table, he nodded and said, "Afternoon!"

The forceful man stared up at him and did not speak but the nervous man nodded and said, "Goodnight, boy, goodnight."

A sharp triangle of sunlight lay across the green Rexine of the front seat of the bus. He sat so that the sunlight fell on his face. The bus was empty. The driver nicked out his cigarette and swung himself up into the cab. The conductor chucked his clipboard and satchel into the rack and rapped on the glass partition with his ring finger. The bus juddered into life and slowly pulled out of Gartree Square, turning down the hill, gathering speed past Briar Street, past Elderberry Avenue, past Honeysuckle Drive, past Blackthorn Street and Hazel

Row, and out into the traffic on the main road. Peter rested his head against the vibrating glass feeling mildly drunk.

* * *

PETER set his wine glass down on the edge of the table in the hall but it fell off and shattered.

"Oh, dear!" said Allan.

"Did I?" said Carol.

"Did you what?" said Jeanne.

"Have a handbag with me."

"Oh, I shouldn't think so," said Peter.

"Who can say?" said Allan.

"Peter, leave that alone. You'll cut yourself," said Jeanne.

"Well, thank you very much, Jeanne," said Allan. "Really enjoyed it."

"We'll walk down with you," she said.

They started down the gravelled drive to the front gate. The wind was cold after the stuffiness of the drawing room. The garden was black and mysterious, surrounded by a high black wall of holly trees.

"Listen to our feet crunching," said Carol.

At the gate, they drew together.

On the other side of the road, the globe of a street lamp among the branches. The wind seemed to splinter the light, blowing it deeper into the layers and rifts of leaves. The tall, wrought-iron gates clanged to and vibrated. Footsteps on the pavement. Their voices calling again,

"Goodnight."

"Goodnight."

Rafts of leaves, layers of leaves, leaves lime green as the wind lifted.

"What?" said Peter.

"I said, 'I'm freezing.'"

They turned back towards the black bulk of the house. The open front door spilled light into the porch, onto the gravel and the edge of the ornamental lily pond. Something black lay on the gravel. A sports jacket.

"Is that Allan's?" said Jeanne.

"He was wearing a jacket, wasn't he?"

"I wonder whose it is?"

"Somebody's, I expect," said Peter.

She tossed the jacket onto a chair in the hall and pushed the heavy door shut.

"Boom!" echoed Peter.

"I think you need some coffee," she said.

"No. I feel fine. I feel great."

"You know what *I* need?"

"What?"

"Bed."

"A truer word," he said, "was never spoken."

"It was nice seeing everybody," she said, "but I'm glad they've gone."

She went into the drawing room and started switching off the lights.

"See the lights are off downstairs in the billiard room, Pete. The bedroom's upstairs. On your right."

As he went into the billiard room, he trod on a cube of French chalk which powdered under his heel. He stood looking at the pool of yellow light and the green baize. Near the far corner pocket, a wine glass stood on the baize shining. In the cue rack, there seemed to be an umbrella. He switched off the light.

The hall was dark and silent. He stood there for a few moments listening to the tick of the grandfather clock.

He went up the wide staircase and turned to the right. He opened a door but it was a linen closet. There were doors all along the landing. Pampas grass in a huge Chinese vase rustled against his sleeve.

“Jeanne?”

He opened the next door and found himself in a vast bedroom. A small table lamp by the bedside glowed pink, but Jeanne was not there.

“Jeanne?” he called. “Jeanne, where are you?”

“In here.”

The voice seemed to come out of the wall.

“Where’s here?”

“*Here!*”

A door he hadn’t noticed opened and Jeanne stuck her head round.

“It’s a bathroom.”

“Oh.”

“There’s one for you on the other side.”

“A bathroom all for me?”

“A master bathroom and a mistress bathroom.”

“Isn’t that *nice!*” said Peter.

He went into the small bathroom and closed the door behind him. The back of the door was a full-length mirror. He sat on the lavatory with the lid down and took off his shoes.

Then he opened the door again and called across the bedroom,

“Has yours got a lavatory?”

“Yes.”

“So’s mine.”

He switched on a lamp over the washbasin. The spouts of the taps were fashioned in the form of curving, silver dolphins. He turned both taps full on and watched the water gushing from the dolphins’ mouths. He jammed his finger over one so that the water squirted from the side of the mouth. He washed his hands and dried them on a gigantic blue towel.

He opened the mirrored medicine cabinet and examined the bottles.

Hearts of Oak Deodorant. Hearts of Oak Cologne.

The Tablets: To be taken: *One Twice Daily.* Capt. Compton-Smythe.

Hearts of Oak After-Shave: An Invigorating Lotion.

He took off his shirt and sprayed his armpits.

On the shelf beneath the bottle-shelf was a pair of silver-and-tortoiseshell hairbrushes. He brushed his hair different ways, studying the effects in the mirror.

A round, flat tin. Dr. Blackly's Renowned and Efficacious Tooth Powder. There was even a new toothbrush in a little cellophane box. He took it out and dripped water into the tin of tooth powder, stirring it about until he'd mixed a smooth paste.

"Efficacious," he said to the right-hand dolphin.

He dropped his cigarette end, which he'd wedged in a dolphin tail, into the lavatory, and then hounded it with a fierce jet all round the bowl until the paper split and the shreds of tobacco blossomed over the water.

The bedroom was in darkness. The pile of the carpet was squashy under his feet. He made his way towards the shape of the bed.

"Where are you?"

His hands felt over the surface of the bed.

"You're inside," he said. "Come out."

"No. It's cold."

"'Course it isn't. Come on. Come out."

He pulled back the sheets and blankets and lay beside her, scooping his arm under her, pulling her close. He kissed her throat and breasts.

"I wish they were bigger and not all collapsed," she said.

"Silly."

"You should have seen them when I was pregnant. Like grapefruit."

"Don't like grapefruit," he mumbled.

"Perhaps I should get pregnant again," she said.

“Mmm.”

He pushed the sheets and blankets down further with his feet.

Afterwards, he hung still above her, breathing hard.

“Oh, Peter! It was lovely. It was. . . .”

He gave a sudden grunt and shot one leg out rigid.

“Oh!” she said. “Don’t go!”

“Aahh!” screamed Peter, collapsing and rolling off her. “Cramp! Oh, God! My toes are stuck!”

He clasped his foot with both hands, working it desperately as she laughed; then he fell back on the pillows.

She snuggled closer and put her arm over his chest. She kissed his chin, his cheek, his mouth, his closed eyes.

“Warm,” he said.

“Mmmm,” he sighed.

She nibbled his ear and whispered, “Go to sleep. Go to sleep, you drunken old wreck.”

“Mmmm.”

He could feel her breath, moist against his neck. He wanted to kiss her goodnight but his head was too heavy to move. The blackness was spinning. The lights, the grey flashes in the darkness, were growing fainter and fainter.

Peter stirred in his sleep. A noise, a movement, something. Something wrong. He started up on one elbow and lay in the strained darkness, his heart thudding. The bed seemed to be quivering.

“Jeanne?”

He heard her sob, heard the harsh catch of her breath.

“Jeanne, what is it?”

He sat up and tried to turn her towards him, pulling at her rigid shoulder.

“Jeanne! What’s the matter?”

Leaning over her, he tried to see her face but she turned into the pillow. Her shoulders shook with crying. He worked his arms around her, forcibly turning her, pulling her towards him. Her body was stiff. She pushed her face into his arm. He kissed the line of her jaw, stroking her hair, stroking her hair.

"Don't cry. There's nothing to cry about, Jeanne."

"Everything's all right. You'll see," he said.

He could feel her hot tears on his arm. He bent and nuzzled at her, lifting her face, mumbling up her tears with his lips, kissing her wet eyelids.

Her sobbing quieted, dying away into shuddering breaths. Her voice muffled, she said, "You've got smelling stuff on your armpits."

Slowly, the stiffness melted, he felt her legs relaxing against his. She gave a runny sniff and turned her head on his arm. He pulled the blankets up to cover her shoulders.

"Disgusting *nose*," she said.

Somewhere in the bedroom a clock was ticking. They lay together silently, from time to time her breath still catching.

"Feeling better?"

"Yes. I'm all right."

"What is it, Jeanne? What's wrong?"

"It's nothing."

"Why don't you tell me?"

"No, it's nothing."

The breath caught again in her throat.

"Umm?"

"I was just being silly. Really. There's nothing wrong."

"You can tell me," he said.

"It's *nothing*, Peter. Just too much to drink."

"You weren't crying before," he said.

She didn't answer. She tightened her arms around him.

"Jeanne?"

"Oh, leave me alone!"

He sighed and then cleared his throat. Her hair was tickling his lip and he moved his head away. She tightened her arm, her fingers digging into his back. She moved her leg against him. He could feel that she was wet.

"Do you want to?"

Sliding her leg across his, she lay over him. He could just see the paleness of her face above him. Her eyes seemed shut. As the headboard of the bed tipped, tipped against the wall, she was grunting. She stiffened suddenly, slowing, and let her weight down on him. He held her tight, stroked her hair.

She rolled down beside him and lay on her stomach. She turned her head away on the pillow. Peter lay listening to the tick of the clock, the sounds of her breathing. After a few minutes, he moved his leg carefully, trying not to shake her in the bed.

"It's all right," she said. "I'm awake."

He stretched and eased his arm free.

"Are you feeling any better?"

"Yes. Yes, I'm all right."

"How about a cigarette?"

"Yes," she said. "I'll get them, though. I've got to go to the lavatory anyway."

She sat up and pulled the blankets aside. Sitting on the edge of the bed, her back to him, she said, "Peter?"

"Umm?"

"I'm sorry."

"Don't be silly. There's nothing to be sorry about."

"I feel so stupid."

"There's no reason to."

"I'm behaving like a silly bitch," she said. "It's been so good tonight and then I had to cry and make a fool of myself and spoil things."

"You didn't spoil anything. Get some cigarettes."

"It's been the nicest present you could have given me," she said.

She reached behind her and patted his leg.

"What do you mean, 'present'?"

She switched on the light in the bathroom.

"Forty-three candles on my cake today," she said, as she closed the door.

He lay watching the line of light. The taps were running. He heard the click of the medicine cabinet opening and then she was quiet for a long time.

The lavatory flushed. Suddenly she started to make herald trumpet noises, fanfares. The door opened and she stood in the light wearing a low-cut blue nightdress and carrying a blue silk robe. The hollows below her sharp collarbones stood out.

"Ter-TUM!" she said.

"Oh, *look* at you!" he said.

"Thank you. Thank you."

She curtsied to left and right.

"Jeanne by Jeanne," she said, "and gowns by Madam Compton-Smythe."

"And many happy returns!" said Peter.

"I don't know about you," she said, "but *I'm* bloody hungry."

"I think I feel puky," he said.

"Eating's just what you need. And a nice glass of milk."

She switched on the main light and draped the silk gown about her shoulders. As he got out of bed, she said. "You can't go wandering round the house bollock-naked. It's rude."

She rummaged through the drawers in the dressing table and tossed him a pair of yellow silk pyjamas. On the breast pocket was a large black "s" superimposed on a smaller "c".

"Won't he find out?"

"He's got hundreds of pairs."

"Posh, eh?" said Peter.

The trousers were too long and flopped over his feet.

"Posh isn't the word," said Jeanne. "When I answer the phone—honestly—I have to say, 'The Compton-Smythe residence.' And Anna isn't allowed in the front garden because it wouldn't be suitable."

As they went down the stairs, she said in a loud, fluting voice, "Oh, Mrs. Abercrombie! The ashtrays."

They sat in the fluorescent kitchen eating ham sandwiches. The counter was crowded with empty bottles, littered with bottle caps and the dry crusts from the sandwiches she had made for the party.

"Smells funny in here," said Peter.

"Sort of sour," she said.

He got up and looked along the counter. He stared into a carved walnut salad bowl near the refrigerator.

"Oh, Jesus Christ!" he said.

"What?"

"No. Don't look. Some dirty bastard puked in a salad bowl. Filled it."

"Oh, leave it," she said. "We can clear up tomorrow."

"When are they coming back?"

"Sunday afternoon."

"What if they come back earlier?"

"Well, even if they come back tomorrow there isn't a train before three-thirty. I checked. Don't worry about it."

He put the bowl in the sink and turned the hot tap on.

"Did you bring the cigarettes?" she said.

"No."

"See if there's any left in the drawing room."

He went along the passage and groped for the light switch in the hall. He went across into the drawing room.

"Holy shit!"

"What's the matter?" she called.

"*Look* at it!"

Her slippers slapped across the hall.

"Just *look* at it!"

Glasses and mugs everywhere. Bottles. The rug heaped back towards the window. The hearth and fireplace littered with cigarette ends; the mantelpiece, a deep charred groove, ash, sticky yellow.

"It's only mess," said Jeanne. "No need to worry about it."

The shards of a smashed plate on the floor by the radiogram. The tablecloth pinkstained with wine, curling sandwiches, wilting celery hanging out of a cut-glass jug. An egg sandwich with a cigarette stuck in it.

"I'm sure I saw a packet in here somewhere," she said.

"What about this chair?"

He pointed to the long, splintering crack, the sprung inlay.

"A *blue* packet," she said.

He bent over the piano and blew cigarette ash away from between the keys. He watched her as she lifted cushions and moved plates and bottles; his fingertips explored a raw wound in the patina of the dark wood of the piano lid.

"You won't be able to fix this," he said.

"What?"

"This."

"In the morning," she said. "Ah! I *knew* I'd seen some."

"It's spoiled," he said.

He stirred the heaped carpet so that one end flopped down. Trodden into it was a sardine sandwich.

"What's that humming noise?" she said.

"What?"

"Oh, we left the radiogram on."

He knelt and started picking bits of greasy sardine from the pile of the carpet. The music made him jump.

"Turn it *down*, for God's sake!"

Violins. A large orchestra. Waltz music.

She was lounging on the settee, her arm along the back tapping the rhythm. She rearranged the folds of the silk gown over her knees.

"I'd better get some hot water," said Peter.

"How romantic of you," she said.

"What?"

"On my birthday, too."

He stood up and looked at her. She raised her eyebrows. He wiped the grease and gritty fibres from his hands with a paper napkin. Bowing low, he said, "May I have the honour of the last waltz?"

She stood and bobbed a curtsy; they moved together. They danced through the medley of waltzes on the LP. Peter stumbled once or twice on Compton-Smythe's flapping pyjama legs, and Jeanne's swirling robe caught and pulled over the jug of celery. Holding each other lightly, formally, they danced without talking, silently about and about the square of cleared floor. They danced, turning and lilting, danced until, with a loud *click*, the record ended.

Still holding each other, they stood for a moment listening to the silence before letting their arms fall.

Jeanne walked over and switched off the radiogram. Light gleamed off the facets of the celery jug; the spilled water was soaking down the tablecloth. He stood looking down at the dark patch on the carpet.

"Well," she said, pulling the sash of her robe tight, "I suppose we'd better go to bed."

He nodded.

"I'm going to sleep downstairs," she said. "Because of Anna."

"All right," he said. He went out into the hall and switched off the light.

"Goodnight, Jeanne."

"Goodnight."

He started up the wide staircase.

"Goodnight," she called again.

A voice was shouting in Peter's sleep.

"Come on! More!"

He turned over and dragged the blankets up over the hump of his shoulders.

"Left hand down a bit!" shouted the voice.

Underneath the voice, there was a deep throbbing sound.

"Come on!"

He sat up, looking towards the curtains. It was morning. The throbbing was an engine coming closer, wheels crunching the gravel. He scrambled out of bed and ran to the window, lifting aside the curtains. A furniture van, directed by Frederick, was backing up to the front door.

"Come on!"

Just scraping past the low wall of the ornamental lily pond.

"Yes! You're all right!"

With a grating crash and jangling of chains, the lowered ramp struck one of the stone pillars of the porch.

Peter hurried across into the bathroom and got dressed. His mouth tasted foul. Dr. Blackly's Renowned and Efficacious Tooth Powder had hardened into an unworkable lump.

As he went down the stairs, he saw Jeanne and Mr. Arkle and a small man in blue overalls and a bowler hat.

"You should try heat rays," she was saying.

Looking up, she said, "Oh, good morning, Peter."

"Morning."

"I don't believe you've met Henry, have you?"

"How do you do?" said Peter, nodding.

Henry raised the brim of his bowler.

"It's turned out a nice day," said Mr. Arkle.

"You've got a very nice place here," said Henry loudly.

"He works more down the shop now," said Mr. Arkle. "More on the restoring side."

"*Very* nice," said Henry. "Spacious."

Mr. Arkle tapped the bib of Henry's overalls. Henry groped inside and brought out a large black hearing aid. He twiddled with the knobs on the side until it whined and crackled. He twisted the pink plastic bulb into his ear and looked at Mr. Arkle expectantly.

"Him," bellowed Mr. Arkle, "him there—Mr. Hendricks—he was the one as was with me when I said it."

"Said what?"

"About Frederick!"

"What about Frederick?"

"Go on! You remember! Strong as an ox! Eh? Eh?"

Henry smiled and looked round at their faces.

"It's getting worse, isn't it?" said Jeanne.

"They should write 'em down in a book—the things he says," said Henry.

"I takes him around now and then just for the ride," said Mr. Arkle. "He enjoys getting out a bit, going in houses."

"Bill's a proper card, all right," said Henry.

They all looked at him.

"Poor old bugger," said Mr. Arkle.

"Yes, he is," said Henry.

"Who?" bellowed Mr. Arkle.

"That Frederick. Often rude to me, he is. Rude young bugger. Hair like a girl's."

"Well," said Peter, "if you'll. . . ."

"Needs a taste of the stick," said Henry.

"If you'll excuse me," said Peter, "I think I'll get some coffee."

"Ah," said Mr. Arkle. "Don't let us disturb you. We'll be taking a look around."

"Across his bare behind," said Henry.

Peter stood waiting in the kitchen. The refrigerator was making odd clicking noises. They were still in the hall, talking. He heard her laugh.

Get started, lads! Carpets and mirrors.

Her footsteps sounded down the passage.

"Well?" he said. "What sort of a game do you think *you're* playing?"

"I'm not playing games," she said.

"You knew," he said. "Last night."

"There's some coffee already made," she said.

"You'd planned this."

"Obviously," she said. "Sit down and I'll put some toast in."

"Well, why didn't you tell me?"

"What difference does it make? Dark or light toast?"

"Well, Jesus Christ! You might have said."

She put the coffee in front of him.

"I mean, it's not as if I'm a stranger, exactly. Why didn't you?"

"Well, you know now, don't you?"

"Thank you very much," he said.

"I didn't want to spoil our evening, Peter. I'm going away."

Move it over to the side!

No! Your side! Your side!

"Why would it have spoiled it?"

"Because I'm going away."

"All right. You're going away. I still don't see. . . ."

"As far away as I can get."

"What do you mean?"

"And I'm not coming back."

He spooned sugar into his coffee and stirred it. The toaster made twinging noises and the toast clanged up.

"You've planned this for weeks," he said.

"Marmalade?" she said.

He stared across the table at her.

"Just like that, eh?" he said.

"I think there's some of that lime sort you like," she said. She got up and looked in one of the cupboards above the counter.

Hey! Mrs. C!

Are you finished in this big bedroom?

"Did you leave anything there?" she said.

"No."

"Yes, you carry on!" she shouted from the doorway.

"Just like that!" Peter said again.

She put the jar in front of him.

"For *weeks*," he said. "You've known for weeks."

She sat down again.

"Jesus Christ!" he said.

"Oh, don't be childish, Peter."

"I wasn't aware that I was."

Footsteps pounded on the stairs. In the bedroom overhead, dragged furniture was rumbling and screeching on the bare boards. Peter looked up again and stared at her.

"Jeanne —"

She dropped her cigarette end into a half-finished bowl of cornflakes.

"What?"

"No. Nothing."

He buttered the slice of toast.

"Swim! Swim!" said Anna's voice. "Swim! Swim!"

She came through the door. "Swim!" she shouted.

"Hello, sweetheart," said Peter.

"Where are your shoes?" said Jeanne.

"I don't know. I've got a fish. Look."

She held out a large brass dolphin.

"Isn't that nice!" said Peter. "Where did you get it?"

"George gave it me. Off the front door."

Making a humming noise, she pushed the brass dolphin round the table, round the marmalade pot, round Peter's plate and the toaster.

"We're going on holiday," she said.

"Peter and I are talking," said Jeanne. "Go and see what Mr. Arkle's doing."

The dolphin made a wide curve and landed on the counter. Still humming, she pushed it along the counter and went out of the door.

Peter spread marmalade on the toast and then cut the slice in half.

Frederick! Bring the little trolley in!

And some rope!

He licked butter off his fingers.

"I *did* come back," she said.

The refrigerator started its clicking sounds again.

"Don't you realize how long they'd send me up for?" she said.

He filled his coffee cup again.

"How do you think they found me before?"

The trolley wheels rattled on the tiles in the hall. He reached over for the sugar.

"They've got old photographs. They've got a description. They'll be doing the rounds—grocers, laundries, employment agencies, doctors—maybe they even phone people who advertise for housekeepers. How long do you think I've got here?"

He looked at her as he took the second slice of toast from the toaster.

"Oh, Jesus Christ!" she said, and getting up, slammed her chair back against the table.

Mrs. C!

Can we have a word with you?

"Coming!" she shouted from the doorway.

Peter spread marmalade on the second slice of toast.

"This isn't the best time for having tantrums," she said.

He did not turn round.

"You've known for weeks," he said.

Mrs. C!

"You knew this even when we went to the cottage."

She did not reply.

George and Frederick were trundling something through the hall.

Now! Get it under!

One end of the piano crashed onto the tiles; the strings vibrated.

"Didn't you, Jeanne? Even at the cottage?"

The reflection of his hand. Rose's Lime Marmalade. The reflection of his hand in the chrome toaster, distorted by the curving side.

"I'm very fond of you, Peter."

He pulled his fingers in towards his palm so that his knuckles rose like pink lumpy mountains in the shiny chrome. He heard her move from the lino in the kitchen doorway onto the loud tiles in the passage leading to the hall.

"But I'm not ironing five years of shirts for you."

When he had finished the toast and coffee, he put the cup and plate in the sink. The walnut salad bowl was still there. He turned away and stood gazing out over the garden, over the white-painted herb boxes, over the rusted lawn roller, the compost heap, the bundles of canes, towards the wall of holly trees.

The shouts, the bump-bumping down the stairs aroused him. He turned from the window and looked around the kitchen. He looked at the table and along the littered counter. A frying pan on the stove, congealed fat and the lace of a fried egg. He looked down at the cigarette end floating in the cornflakes bowl.

He went over to the sink, fitted in the plug, and turned on the hot tap. He squirted in liquid soap and swished the water about with the mop. He washed the salad bowl, the plates and cups, the cutlery. He swept the counter down, clearing away the hardened crusts from the sandwiches, the bottles. He let water out and scoured the sink.

Upstairs, someone was hammering something. He read the laundry instructions on a packet of Tide. He switched on the radio. The noise grated on him. He switched it off. He wandered out into the hall.

The hall was empty. The three carved chairs, the piecrust table were gone. Only the grandfather clock still stood against the wall. Two red tiles in the middle of the hall were broken.

Footsteps boomed on the hollow stairs. He turned and looked up. Frederick was struggling with a Jacobean dower chest which had stood on the landing. The front of the chest was carved in a design of interlocking circles. As it went past, he saw the pink sticker, the blue-and-red snakes on Frederick's arm.

Standing in the open doorway, he looked into the drawing room. The carpet, the piano, the radiogram, the table, the settee and armchairs were gone.

Bottles, paper, bits of sandwiches, celery, and dust-covered olives littered the bare boards. In the middle of the room, the chair with the broken back.

He wandered back down the passage and into the kitchen again. He opened one of the cupboards above the counter. Pyrex dishes. A cast-iron casserole. A chipped gravy boat. He clicked the cupboard shut. Fixed to the wall at the end of the counter was a large can opener. He spun the handle. The electric kettle had dried coffee grounds sticking to it. As he reached for the sponge to wipe it clean, footsteps sounded down the tiles.

Henry appeared in the doorway and stood there, nodding.

"This is a nice room," he said. "What with the window, it's nice and bright, eh?"

He made his way over to the table and lowered himself into a chair. A sigh escaped him as he sat back.

"Making a cup of tea, are you?" he said. "That'd be nice. A cup of tea'd go down nicely."

Peter filled the kettle and plugged it in.

"I've been upstairs," said Henry. "Having a wander round up there."

Grunting with the effort, he bent down and unlaced his boots. Peter looked at the black dome of his bowler hat.

"What did you say?" said Henry.

Peter shook his head and smiled.

"I'm a bit hard of hearing, you see."

Peter opened cupboards, searching for the tea caddy.

"There's some nice pieces up there," said Henry. "A few as'll fetch a pretty penny. You don't find so many now with the right brasswork on 'em."

Peter filled a milk jug and put it on the table.

"You know what I saw up there? On the landing? One of those big Chinese vases. Put me in mind of my old auntie."

"Why's that?" shouted Peter.

"Why's what?"

"Your auntie!"

"Ah, that's right," he said.

"*Chinozzery*," he went on, "that's what they call 'em. Collectors' items now, those things. Pictures of 'em in books. All that kind of Chinese item. *Chinozzery*."

He nodded.

"Sixty years ago, seventy years ago, you couldn't *give* 'em away. Nobody wanted 'em. You know what they called 'em? Dust-gatherers. Ah! Dust-gatherers."

Peter filled the teapot and put it on the table. Henry nodded slowly.

"It's a different story today though, eh? My word, yes! They pay a pretty penny for 'em now. Hardly a sale goes by but what there's one *and* the bidding's sharpish."

He pulled the teacup and saucer in front of him.

"My old auntie, now she had one. Lived in Brighton. She had one in her hall full of walking sticks and umbrellas. That one upstairs put me in mind of it. My Auntie Clara. 'Course, *she's* been dead and gone these many years."

He supped at the tea.

"Warm and wet, eh?"

Peter smiled and nodded.

"It's all right so long as it's warm and wet, eh?"

He wiped his loose lower lip with the back of his hand.

"Ah, in the hall it was. Nobody wanted 'em, you see. Same sort of colours but bigger than that upstairs. Handles made like lions with big, snarly faces. Quite took my fancy they did, when I was a little 'un. Orange heads with big black eyes. Square eyes, as I recall."

He smacked his lips.

"Drop more sugar, have you?"

He took off his bowler hat and put it on the table. The fringe of white hair at the sides of his head was fine and fluffy, soft like the down of a dandelion clock.

He stirred the tea.

"Oh, ah. Marvellous took with 'em, *I* was. Though you'd never see a lion with square eyes. Marvellous took. Now, Henry, she'd say, don't you go breaking my vase, she'd say. I'm *stroking* 'em, I'd say. Stroking 'em. Oh, a house-proud woman, that one. A proper Bessie! Up at six polishing the doorknob, whitening the step. Don't you go trailing dirt through *my* house. Don't you go breaking that vase, Henry, she'd say."

George! You're getting cloths over all that stuff?

Yes, Mr. Arkle!

I don't want nothing scratched!

"Ah, it isn't that easy, Mrs. C," said Mr. Arkle's voice.

They came into the kitchen.

"Oh, *there's* Henry. We was wondering where he'd hid himself."

"Why can't you give me a price?" said Jeanne.

"Don't you go breaking that vase, Henry, she'd say."

"What?" shouted Mr. Arkle.

"Why can't you?" said Jeanne.

"Is there another wet in the pot?" said Henry.

Mr. Arkle unhooked his glasses. His naked eyes squinted towards the window. He pulled the front of his shirt out of his trousers and rubbed the thick lenses.

"It's the class of piece, you see," he said.

He hooked the glasses back on.

"Most of the stuff what we've got here is antiques. And Henry says it's right. He may wander a bit but Henry knows *wood*. And if he says it's right. . . ."

"So?" said Jeanne.

"I can't handle that class of stuff." He shook his head. "I wouldn't dare, Mrs. C."

“What do you mean?” said Jeanne.

Mr. Arkle leaned over and tapped the bib of Henry’s overalls. Henry took out his hearing aid and screwed the pink bulb into his ear.

“What’s that table and the six chairs?” bellowed Mr. Arkle.

“Chippendale,” said Henry.

“Is it right?”

“Ah.”

“How much is it worth?”

“Couple of thousand quid,” said Henry.

“Two thousand!” said Jeanne.

“No repairs? Nobody been antiquing on it?” bellowed Mr. Arkle.

Henry shook his head.

Turning back to Jeanne, Mr. Arkle said, “Perfect, see? Now how many places round here—within fifty *mile* of here, if you like—how many’s got perfect Chippendale? Eh? You get my meaning? Eh?”

Jeanne nodded.

“Ah,” said Mr. Arkle. “The bogues’d have us in no time. No trouble at all. They’d be onto this quick as a flash of duckshit. I *do* beg your pardon, Mrs. C!”

“So what do we do?” said Jeanne.

Mr. Arkle chuckled. He groped in his torn pocket and pulled out a block of pink stickers. He stuck one on the fridge.

“Ere!” he bellowed. “She wants to know what we’re going to do!”

“We’ll be going up to see Sammy in Sheffield,” said Henry.

“Ah,” said Mr. Arkle. “There’s your answer, Mrs. C.”

“And you’ll pay me. . . .”

“That’s it. When I’ve seen Sammy.”

He stuck a label on the electric mixer and stood it on top of the fridge.

“Make a nice little nest egg, this lot will,” he said.

Mr. Arkle!

Right here, George!

George came in carrying two leather suitcases and a cardboard carton.

"That's about it, Mr. Arkle," he said. "Frederick's roping the load up now."

"Where's Anna?" said Jeanne.

"Helping him, Mrs. Carlyle."

"And what's this?" said Mr. Arkle.

"They're my new suitcases," said Jeanne. "Smart, aren't they? I expect these initials'll come off."

"And this box was in a cupboard upstairs," said George.

Mr. Arkle ripped it open and pulled out a silver trophy. The cup was about ten inches high. He took out four more and peered at them.

"Sporting things," he said. "Not enough weight to 'em."

Peter picked up one of the cups and tried to make out the inscription. The silver was badly tarnished. *Presented to Lt. Compton-Smythe by the Officers Mess*. The only other word he could make out was *Hussars*.

"Well, there's just this fridge left, then," said Mr. Arkle.

"I'll get the trolley," said George.

"Ah, and take them cases out to the front door."

Mr. Arkle opened the fridge and started chucking vegetables and fruit and foil-wrapped packages onto the counter and into the sink.

"Oh!" said Jeanne. "I'd forgotten about it! There's a bottle of champagne in there. In the vegetable thing underneath."

She gathered up four of the silver cups and swilled them under the tap. She took the dark green bottle from Mr. Arkle, twisted off the seal and wire, and popped the cork. She dashed the spuming bottle over the cups and handed them round.

"Gentlemen!" she said. "I give you, *Captain Compton-Smythe!*"

"I've had this before," said Henry. "At a wedding."

George, Frederick, and Anna came in. Frederick tipped the fridge and then they tried to juggle it forward onto the metal trolley.

"Push!" shouted Anna.

"Here's to a successful end to our business!" said Mr. Arkle.

"How about unplugging it?" said George.

"Oh, ah," said Frederick.

"Ah!" said Henry loudly, beaming at them all, raising his cup.

"Happy days!"

"What about you, Mr. Hendricks?" said Mr. Arkle. "You're the scholar here. Give us a good one."

Peter looked down into the silver cup.

"Well," he said. "Here's. . . ."

He moved back against the counter as the fridge rumbled past. He waited until they were out of the door.

"Here's to all of us!"

"Happy days!" said Henry.

"And here's to Sheffield!" said Jeanne.

Mr. Arkle plonked his cup on the table.

"Very nice," he said. He belched. "Very nice. Well, Mrs. C! We'd better go and have a look at that load." Peter followed them out into the hall.

"What about that?" said Jeanne, pointing to the grandfather clock.

"That's no good to *us*," said Mr. Arkle.

"We're ready! We're ready!" shouted Anna from outside.

"Why not?" said Jeanne. "They fetch hundreds."

"It's engraved, Mrs. C. On the face, on the dial. The maker's name and date."

"Mummy!"

"We're coming!" called Jeanne.

"We'll just check them ropes," said Mr. Arkle.

Henry and he went out of the front door. Jeanne lifted one of the suitcases and dumped it on the window seat. She unsnapped the locks and lifted the lid. She took something out.

"Peter?"

He walked over to her.

"I've got something for you."

She held out a flat cardboard box.

"Take it."

"What is it?"

"Open it."

He undid the flap and slid out a leather document case.

"Two and a half albums," she said.

He looked down at the glossy leather. He unzipped the case. It was stuffed with tissue paper. He zipped it up again.

"It's executive styling," she said.

She turned away and closed the lid of the suitcase. She snapped the locks shut. She picked the suitcases up and walked to the door.

"Jeanne?"

She turned and looked at him.

Fastened to the tab of the zipper by a loop of thread was a gold-foil disc. He held it out towards her.

"It's best quality hide," he said.

She smiled and went out.

He stood in the empty hall, light gleaming on the scratched tiles, holding the document case. He heard the chains rattle as the ramp was closed, the pins banged into place. Footsteps. The slam of the cab door. He heard the motor turn and catch and then the sounds of the van crunching down the drive.

GIRL IN GINGHAM

FOLLOWING his divorce, frequent dinners with the Norths had become habit for Peter Thornton. Nancy fussed over him and stitched on lost buttons; Alan plied him with beer and had distracted him in the early months with ferocious games of chess. Now, two and a half years later, his family relationship was declared by their daughter, Amanda, to be that of Uncle the Best.

"I'm ready!" she yelled from upstairs.

"No, don't go up yet, Peter. Have some more coffee," said Nancy. "She still hasn't brushed her teeth."

"TEETH!" bellowed Alan.

"She's getting so bitchy and *cunning*," said Nancy. "She runs the tap, eats some toothpaste, smears it round the basin, but *now* the little swine's learned to wet the brush."

"They *all* seem to hate it, don't they?" said Peter. "Same thing with Jeremy."

"By the way," said Alan, "nothing new with the woman situation, is there?"

"No. Not particularly. Why?"

"Well, don't be too long up there. Might have something to interest you."

"What?"

"This wine," said Alan, emptying the bottle into his glass, "confirms one's prejudices against Hungarians."

"What might interest me?"

Alan shook his head and wagged a solemn finger.

"What are you being so mysterious for?" said Peter. "Oh, *no!* You haven't got someone coming over?"

He glanced at Nancy who shrugged.

"Our wife," said Alan, "privy though she is to our councils and most trusted to our ear..."

"READY!"

"Before you get *completely* pissed, dear husband," said Nancy, "you can help me with these dishes."

"Your merest whim, my petal," cried Alan, "is my command."

"Oh, Christ!" said Nancy.

As Peter went upstairs, Alan in the kitchen was demanding his apron with the rabbits on it; Nancy's voice; and then he heard the sounds of laughter.

"The woman situation."

Whom, he wondered, had Alan in mind for him?

The woman situation had started again for him some eight months or so after his wife had left him. The woman situation had started at the same time he'd stopped seeing Dr. Trevore, when he'd realized that he was boring himself; when he'd realized that his erstwhile wife, his son, and he had been reduced to characters in a soap opera which was broadcast every two weeks from Trevore's soundproofed studio.

And which character was he?

He was the man whom ladies helped in laundromats. He was the man who dined on frozen pies. Whose sink was full of dishes. He was the man in the raincoat who wept in late-night bars.

That office, and he in it, that psychiatrist's office with its scuffed medical magazines and pieces of varnished driftwood on the waiting room's occasional tables, was the stuff of comic novels, skits, the weekly fodder of stand-up comedians.

In the centre of Trevore's desk sat a large, misshapen thing. The rim was squashed in four places, indicating that it was probably an ashtray. On its side, Trevore's name was spelled out in spastic white slip. Peter had imagined it a grateful gift from the therapy ward of a loony bin.

It presided over their conversation.

How about exercise? Are you exercising?

No, not much.

How about squash?

I don't know how to play.

I play myself Squash. I play on Mondays, Wednesdays, and Fridays. In the evenings.

Following one such session he had gone home, opened the bathroom cabinet, regarded the pill bottles that had accumulated over the months. He had taken them all out and stood them on the tank above the toilet. He arranged them into four rows. In the first row he placed the Valium. In the second, the Stelazine. In the third, the Tofranil. In the fourth, the Mareline.

Uncapping the bottles, he tipped the tablets rank by rank into the toilet bowl. Red fell upon yellow, blue fell on red, tranquillizing, antidepressant psychotherapeutic agents fell, swirled, and sifted onto agents for the relief of anxiety, emotional disorders, and nausea.

The results had suggested to him the droppings of a Walt Disney rabbit.

Following this, he had twice attempted suicide.

In spite of Montreal's entrenched and burgeoning underworld, the only weapon he had been able to procure, and that in a junk shop, was an ancient .45. Bullets had proved impossible to obtain without a permit.

He shrank from the *mechanics* of a shotgun—bare feet and the cold, oily taste of gun metal filling his mouth, and the absurd fear that in the second of death the kick of the barrels would smash his teeth.

His second attempt was with prescription sleeping pills, blue gelatine capsules. He had written to his mother and father, swallowed twenty-five, and lain wakefully on his bed clutching the plastic bracelet that had been secured round Jeremy's wrist at his birth. His stomach felt distended and, after belching repeatedly, the taste of the gelatine had made him vomit.

Subsequently, with a large weariness and a settled habit of sadness, he had become active in the world of those whose world was broken. First it was the single women of his married friends' acquaintance, awkward dinners where he had learned the meaning of "intelligent," "interesting," "creative," and "kind." Later, he had encountered childless women, women married but embittered, divorced women with single, maladjusted children who demanded to know if he was to be their new uncle. He had even met a twenty-eight-year-old virgin who one night confessed that she hated men because when they became excited their things came out of their bodies, red like dogs.

He had acquired an almost encyclopedic knowledge of Montreal's restaurants.

He had become an authority on films.

He had learned to avoid women who took pottery courses and had come to recognize, as danger signs, indoor plants, Alice in Wonderland posters, health food, stuffed toys, parents, menstrual cramps, and more than one cat.

Amanda was trying to whistle.

He whistled a few notes of the tune she was hissing.

"Come *on*," she called.

Her bed was littered with books; she had chosen *Paddington Bear* and *The Sleeping Beauty*. The Bear book was one he had recently given her. When he bought books for his son, who now lived in distant Vancouver, he always bought Mandy duplicates. He mailed off a book and a letter weekly into the void from which few answers returned. Mandy snuggled against him as he read.

... mounted the Prince's white charger ...

"What's a charger?"

"A big, white horse."

... mounted the Prince's white charger and rode away to his kingdom in a far country.

"Look at all the flowers in the picture," she said.

"The end," said Peter, getting up and kissing her goodnight.

"Peter? How many flowers are there in the world?"

"THE END."

"More than people? More than cars? Not more than ANTS?"

"I don't know. Get to sleep."

"Will Nanny die?"

"*Good night.*"

As he went along the landing, he heard her half-singing, "Nanny'll die and Grampy, Mummy, and Daddy, Uncle Drew *and* the mailman and Mary and the Volkswagen *and* Nanny and Grampy ..."

He stood silently in the bathroom for a few moments, resting his hands on the edges of the washbasin, staring down. He saw, unbidden, like a succession of frozen movie frames, that other bathroom in a silent apartment where dirt and empty beer cans had accumulated until the lease expired.

In the cabinet, the daily reminder of the blue plastic diaper pin, the sticky bottle of Extract of Wild Strawberries, Gravol, the smiling tin of Johnson's Baby Powder.

The room that had been his son's he had not been able to enter. The frieze of animals sagging from its thumbtacks, a deflated elephant on the dusty carpet, scattered blocks.

He washed his face and then remembered to flush the toilet.

"No trouble?" said Nancy as he came into the living room.

"She'll be off in a few minutes."

"A suggestion of cognac?" said Alan. "You'll have to use a tumbler because I broke the last snifter."

Peter sank into his usual armchair.

Nancy was lying on the couch staring into the fire.

Alan rolled the glass in his palms.

"Well?" said Peter.

"Well, what? Oh! Oh, yes."

Alan produced from the inner pocket of his jacket an envelope. He straightened a bent corner. He leaned forward and passed the envelope to Peter. He sat back. Peter opened the envelope and glanced at the contents.

"Funny," he said. "Witty. Exquisitely comical."

"I thought you'd react that way."

Peter tossed the letter over to Nancy.

"Oh, Alan!" she said. "That's not very funny."

"It wasn't intended to be," he said.

"'A Scientific Date with CompuMate,'" read Nancy.

"An unfortunate name, agreed," said Alan.

"Sounds like 'copulate,'" said Nancy.

"'Consummate,'" said Peter.

"Shut up!" said Alan. "Listen, I'm being serious. Okay? We've listened to you talking about the situation for hours on end so you can just sit there and hear me out. Now, I want to look at this rationally. The first fact is that you claim you want to get married again. God knows why, but that's *your* funeral. So what's stopping you? It isn't that you're not attractive to women because over the last couple of years there's been a veritable *parade* of the creatures..."

Peter sipped the cognac, martinis before dinner, wine with, conscious of becoming floatingly, pleasantly, drunk, watching the play of expression on Alan's face rather than paying attention to his words, feeling a great affection for him. It was soothing to be with friends in this room with a fire in the fireplace, in this room which was part of a house, part of a household; soothing to be, however briefly, in some sort of context.

"...so it's not lack of opportunity. Montreal's bulging with women..."

A log in the fire slipped and sparks sailed up. When the fire had burned down and the talk had finished, he would have to go out into the snow. He thought of his apartment. In a closet in his apartment there still sat a carton not unpacked—a "barrel" the moving men had called it. For two years he had reached over it to take out his coat. He did not know what it contained.

"...and just think of the bunch of... of Dulcineas you've brought round here," Alan was saying, "eating us out of house and home. And I expect they were the pick of the crop. Now what I'm getting at..."

Nancy's hand patted the carpet for the packet of cigarettes. Watching the oily curves of the cognac on the glass the word "meniscus" came into his mind but he knew it wasn't the right word. Bulky as the still-packed carton, sadness sat inside him.

"Well, *I* think the whole idea's *silly*," said Nancy, "Any woman who'd sign up for that'd be crazy."

"Why don't you *listen!*" exclaimed Alan with a drunken earnestness. "Of *course!* That's just what I've been saying. The women he's found on his *own* were mostly crazy. Right? What about that blonde one? Eh? You know."

"Marion," said Nancy.

"Right. All *that* nonsense. And that other woman with the adhesive tape over it. If you didn't know Peter, you wouldn't believe they were walking around, would you? Of *course* ninety per cent of these'd be mad as hatters, but what if there was *one* woman just like him. The same reasons, I mean. Why not? What's he got to lose?"

"Peter wouldn't like a woman who'd sign up for that sort of thing."

"How do you know?"

"Because I know Peter."

"And what do you mean 'that sort of thing?'"

“You know very well what I mean.”

“Peter!” said Alan. “What do you think?”

“The other day,” said Peter, sitting up, “I went into Dominion to get some apples and I was wandering around sort of glazed with the music and everything and I'd come to a halt in front of a shelf and I found myself staring at a box of toothpicks.”

“Fascinating,” said Alan.

“And do you know what it said on the box? It said: ‘Stim-UDent: Inter-Dental Stimulators.’”

“Do you want to give it a try or not?”

“I had a hamburger last week,” said Peter, “that was served on a paper plate embossed with the word ‘Chi-Net.’ And I've sipped my milk through straws manufactured by the ‘Golden Age Scientific Company.’”

“Stop babbling,” said Alan. “It's only fifteen dollars for a month's trial.”

Peter laughed.

“Okay?” said Alan. “Or not?”

Peter shrugged.

“Good!” said Alan. “ So we can fill in the form. I *love* forms. I'll just get something to rest it on.”

He took a large book that was on the side table and near the couch.

“What the fuck's this!”

“It's that book club,” said Nancy. “I keep forgetting to send the don't want cards back.”

“*Fish Cookery of Southeast Asia*.”

“They bury them until they rot,” said Nancy.

“What?”

“Fish.”

“Who?”

“Southeast Asians.”

Alan stared at her.

“And you,” he said, turning to Peter, “want to get married again.”

Spreading out the form, he started to read.

Many of us have come to realize that we need the love and companionship of a compatible Mate with whom we can share our deepest beliefs, our gravest sorrows, our wildest joys. CompuMate promotes harmonious relationships between mature individuals and encourages personal growth through deep and meaningful long-term, male-female interaction. Any single or legally unattached person who is serious minded and of sound character and who meets the computer's acceptance standards is eligible to become a CompuMember.

"Just who does that computer think it is?" said Nancy.

"Haughtyputer," said Peter.

"Now the first thing, then . . ." said Alan.

"Wait," said Peter. "How's all this nonsense supposed to work?"

"You answer all these questions and then it matches you with someone who's given the same kind of answers. And then you end up with a Computer Compatible."

"A 'Computer Compatible?'"

"Now don't start being awkward. Are you ready? Okay?"

Mark the Character Traits which are YOU: Popular, Well-to-do, Artistic, Puritan, Sexually Experienced, Bohemian, Diplomatic, Free Spirit, Romantic, Shy, Well-Groomed, Sensual, Sporty, Sensitive, Smoker (non, moderate, heavy), Drinker (non, social, heavy).

"So?" said Alan. "What would you like to be?"

"Artistic," said Nancy.

"Romantic, do you think?" said Alan.

"Of course," said Nancy. "And Sensitive. And Shy."

"Can't I be Sexually Experienced?"

"No," said Alan, "it might put her off."

He marked crosses in the appropriate boxes.

"And for smoking and drinking," he said, "I'm putting 'Moderate' and 'social.' Or we won't get any Compatibles at all."

Can Premarital Sex Be justified?

"What choice do I have?"

Never. After Engagement. If in Love. Between Mature Individuals. Always.

"Do people still *get* engaged?" said Nancy.

"*I* was engaged," said Peter.

"Yes, but you're as old as we are."

"Not only was I officially engaged, I purchased an engagement ring complete with diamond."

"You're an antique," said Nancy. "Just like us."

Alan cleared his throat.

Which of the following interests would you like to share with your CompuMatch: Dancing, Athletics, Skiing, Winter Sports, Spectator Sports . . .

"Hate *all* of them," said Peter .

. . . Politics, Photography, Music, Animals . . .

"Animals?"

. . . Animals, Fine Arts, Natural Sciences, Parties, Psychology, and Sociology.

"I don't like any of them."

"Well you've got to."

"What do you mean, *animals?*"

"How the fuck should I know?" said Alan. "Take her to the zoo."

"It's not open in the winter."

"Oh, stop being difficult!" said Alan. "I'm putting you down for Music, Animals, and Fine Arts."

"And what's more," Peter said to Nancy, "the engagement was announced in the paper with, believe it or not, a photograph of the charming young couple. So how about that?"

"What are your age requirements?" said Alan.

"What?"

"How young and old are you prepared to go? There's a note here that says the wider the range the more choice the computer can provide."

"Remember her father, Nancy?" said Peter. "I even asked him for her hand in marriage."

"*Peter!* Come on! You're not paying attention."

"Sorry, sorry. What was it? How young, you said?"

There flashed through his mind a vision of an evening he had spent some eighteen months earlier. He had met her at a party. She was young and beautiful, her eyes dark and entrancing. At three thirty in the morning he had escorted her back to her apartment on Sherbrooke West. Her apartment was furnished with plants, posters, and a pinball machine.

It was summer; she gave him a large glass of Kool-Aid. She went into her bedroom.

One of the posters was electric blue.

In the centre was a red circle.

Under the circle was the word NOW.

She reappeared in a long, white nightgown. Her bare feet were brown. Across the road from her apartment was the Montreal Association for the Blind. Yellow floodlights lit the front of the buildings. She insisted they go out into the night because she wanted to share with him something rare, something mysterious.

She flitted across to the island in the middle of the road, her legs dark through the white gown against the light of the approaching cars. She smiled and beckoned to him. On the lawn in front of the building she urged him to take off his shoes and socks to walk in the dew. His feet looked pale and silly in the dark grass. She took him by the hand and led him to one of the floodlights. Her hand was cool on his. She made him kneel and gaze into the glare of one of the yellow bars of light while she counted aloud to a hundred.

"See!" she cried, when they stood up. "Everything looks purple."

Peter drained the last drops of cognac.

"I'll put the maximum as your age," said Alan, "so how about twenty-five as minimum? That's ten years."

“Make it thirty.”
“Why thirty?”
“The heart,” said Peter, “has its reasons.”
Alan crossed something out and turned the form over.
“How about race?” he said. “Of your CompuMatch, that is.”
“Peter?” said Nancy.
White. Coloured. Oriental. Any.
“Apart from all *this*,” she said, “do you know what sort of girl you really want? You know, if you could... Or is the whole idea just silly?”
“What *sort* of girl?” said Peter.
Protestant. Catholic. Jewish. Unaffiliated. Other.
He held up the empty glass to look through it at the fire.
“Yes,” he said. “I know *just* the sort.”
He tilted the glass creating changing shapes.
“I want a girl in gingham.”

* * *

PETER SIPPED the coffee, watching the waitress, watching other diners, half-listening to scraps of conversation near him, extending as long as was decent the minutes until he would have to pay the bill. He ate at Chez Jean-Guy two or three times a week. It was not exactly cheap but he liked the linen, wine, flowers on the table. The food was respectable. As he was a regular, they rarely hurried him and he often sat over coffee, sometimes cognac, glancing through trade journals and the catalogues.

Above the background sound of voices, cutlery, crockery, he heard a sharp click and *Jesus Christ!* from a man at the next table. He hadn't looked at the two men when they'd come in, as he'd been watching his waitress stretching to clear off a vacated table. Both men were in their forties and wearing expensively tailored versions of teenage clothing. One wore a necklace and medallion. On the near man a heavy gold bracelet.

“What a jeezely looking thing!”

"Couldn't tell, eh?" said the necklace man. "Swear it was a Parker pen. I came through three international airports with that in my suit pocket."

Peter couldn't see what it was because of the flowers on their table.

"Where in hell did you *find* a thing like that?"

"This one?" said the necklace man. "Tokyo, this one. Never," he said, "never underestimate your Japanese."

"A very ingenious people," said the bracelet man.

"The Jews of the East," said the necklace man.

"Let bygones be bygones," said the bracelet man.

"Of course," said the necklace man, "in the travel business you're always on the move. Locating. Different countries all the time. The personal touch. And it's become—well, I suppose you'd have to call it a hobby of mine."

"Well," said the bracelet man, "it sure is different!"

There was another click.

"Refill all round?" said the bracelet man.

Beckoning to Peter's waitress, the necklace man said to the bracelet man, "Two more vodkatinis, are we?"

Peter felt a surge of irritation. They were ten years older than he was. Why couldn't they accept with dignity what faced them in the morning mirror? Slackening. Caries. The intimation of jowls.

He wondered what they thought about when locked alone in the burnished steel and strip-lighting of a jet plane's toilet.

"Yes," continued the necklace man, "every different place I go I buy their kind of switchblade. As I say, I suppose you'd call it a hobby."

The waitresses wore blue tunics with white blouses. Peter watched the changing blue planes across her thighs as she placed the martinis in front of them.

"But it's in the south," continued the necklace man, "the southern countries where I've found what I'd call my best pieces. The time before last in Mexico, for example, I bought a crucifix. Crown of thorns. Loincloth. Little nailheads in the hands and feet. Enamelled. Brown beard. But press his navel and you've got yourself five and a half inches."

The waitress smiled at Peter from her buffet and raised the coffee pot. Nodding, he smiled back.

He always tried to get a table at her station. The other girls were French-Canadian but she, he had discovered, was German. It was not the length of leg nor the strange severity of her haircut that attracted him but rather the way she spoke. There was something about her speech; it was nothing as definite as, say, a lisp; if it was an impediment at all it was so slight, so elusive, as to be indefinable. But he was not comfortable with the idea of "impediment"; it did not quite capture what he seemed to hear. That something, he had almost decided, must be the suggestion of a long-ago-lost accent. He found it charming.

He did not know her name.

Sometimes it was Eva. Sometimes Ilse.

She wore no rings.

The austere tunics reminded him of girls' gym slips, stirred idle thoughts of Victorian pornography, the backs of hairbrushes, correction, discipline.

Miss Flaybum's Academy. Sexual pleasures he'd never been able to even vaguely understand.

Necklace and Bracelet had exhausted compact cars and the prime lending rate and were now fairly launched into the virtues of aluminum siding.

He watched her deft movements, her smile, the formal inclination of her head as she jotted down each order. The elusive something about her speech was, he decided, like a faint presence of perfume in an empty room.

He found himself wishing that he wasn't wishing that she wasn't German.

He embroidered upon the possible permutations of Alsace-Lorraine.

Recalled a poster he'd seen outside the Beaver for a movie called *Hitler's Hellcats*. A Nordic beauty aiming a Sten gun, her blouse severely strained. He had come to consider most psychological solemnities, such as the gun-penis thing, as dubious as Dr. Trevore and his lumpy ashtray. Yet the poster had stayed in his mind for months. And then, too, he remembered the security guard at Man and his World.

Last year with Jeremy. The mechanical delights of LaRonde, ice-creams, Orange Crush. The rites of summer. And while Jeremy had been riding out his minutes on the merry-go-round, the paunchy guard *stroking* the revolver butt.

Peter cradled the globe of cognac.

Snapshots of Jeremy.

Half-frightened laughter into the sky as the chains of the swing groaned in the park. Magic Markers. Counting his popsicle-stick collection. Fear of spiderwebs. Tiny feet swinging under the kitchen table, the flannelette pyjamas, the pyjamas with elephants. Snapshots already fading, fading like the yellowed snapshots found in albums gathering dust in a thousand junk shops, the last unwanted effects of auctioned families.

Clinging to his refrigerator door were Jeremy's magnetic letters. He had saved them from that other apartment.

Reliques.

He used them to hold notes to himself, shopping lists, bills. Sometimes late at night, taking out another beer, he used the letters to compose messages.

Four of them presently held a sheet of paper from CompuMate which bore five names. The evening at Alan's had ended like so many evenings, vague memories the next day of snow, a taxi, swallowing down four aspirins with milk from the carton against the morning. He had been surprised and irritated with Alan when the list arrived.

He had ignored it for several days. The very idea was ludicrous. He knew himself to be incapable of phoning strange women.

Marjorie Kirkland
Stella Bluth
Nadja Chayefski
Elspeth McLeod
Anna Stevens

As the days had gone by he found the names wandering his mind. He wondered if Marjorie was once Margery; what nationality Bluth might be; if Nadja's hair was of raven lustre; if Elspeth were elfin and wandered lonely as a cloud, mist, rock, and heather.

But even more vividly he had imagined the conversations, the receiver glistening with sweat, silences, fingers clenched, armpits wet. That, most likely that, or fevered Woody Allen performances, fumbling blather ending with his accidentally garrotting himself with the telephone cord.

How, he had wondered, did one open? And, possibly worse, how did one close? And what could conceivably come between?

Marjorie Kirkland.

Marjorie Kirkland had been quite understanding. Marjorie it turned out, had been married for two years. She had reserved her asperity for CompuMate which, despite several registered letters, had not removed her name from the active list.

Stella Bluth.

Six generous cognacs followed by three Molson Export to prevent dehydration, he had phoned Stella Bluth. After he had diffidently presented his credentials, Stella Bluth had assumed command. It was best, she always found, for each to describe each other to the other and then, if they liked the sound of each other, he could call her again.

It's a good thing you can't see over the phone.

Why?

Because.

Because what?

just because.

Silence.

Well, if you must know, my hair's all wet and I'm not completely dressed.

Stella Bluth was sobering; it took Peter only a few moments to form the impression that she was possibly unhinged. He would have liked to close the conversation at its start but was incapable of replacing the receiver.

She frankly held out little hope; she was a Cancer and he was an Aries and she was sure he knew what *that* meant.

Upon command, he described himself. He was thirty-five and six feet tall. He was divorced. He was of medium build. His hair was brownish. He worked as an appraiser for a firm of auctioneers. Appraiser meant he had to estimate the value of antiques and *objets d'art*. No, it wasn't a French company. He was interested in music and animals.

Are you sure you're not coloured?

Quite.

You sound like you're coloured. Because I'm Catholic.

Stella was twenty-seven years old. Why lie about it? It was nothing to be ashamed of. She wasn't married and she hadn't been. She wasn't fat and she wasn't thin. They said she had a good figure. Her hair was brunette. She was at Alcan and did seventy-three a minute. She wasn't in the pool; she usually worked personally for Mr. Edwards. Who was quite nice though she didn't want him to get the wrong impression and sometimes he took her to the Golden Hinde in the Queen Elizabeth where they gave you triple martinis. Did he know the Golden Hinde? But she was only a social drinker. That and if she went to a party. She liked hockey and animals.

In the silence, Peter had heard the magnified sound of his breathing.

And she was interested in the environment.

The advent of the two middle-aged ladies caused an eddy in the flow of restaurant movement as they were seated, the table pulled out, lifted back, chairs settled. They spoke loudly in American voices; one asked Ilse in English if she spoke English. They were a parody of affluent American middle-aged womanhood; white and rinsed hair tended, fingers bedizened with diamond rings. They were explaining to Ilse that they were on a Winter Tour; that the other girls were eating in the hotel; but they had read about Chez Jean-Guy in Gourmet magazine. And what did the menu mean?

Rejecting with increasing amazement kidney, cod, sausage blood and sausage garlic, quail and rabbit, they settled on poached salmon.

Peter signalled for his bill.

Three or four people were standing near the door waiting for a table.

Two full weeks had passed before curiosity and imaginings had nudged him into calling Nadja Chayefski. She had seemed abrupt and said she couldn't talk to him but had asked for his address.

A few days later in the mail he received an envelope from Sun Life.

It contained a poem on Sun Life letterhead.

Hey You!

I love you—please, it's not "dirty"!
I love trees and grass and plants and anything that lives.
Do you believe me?

It's not an intended, on-purpose thing,
it's just here, in me,
and I want you to know it.
Please, it's not "dirty."

Quite likely you won't need it
or want it.

But that's O.K.

I just wanted you to know.

"The flavour's very different from canned," said one of the American ladies.

Peter smiled as he scanned his bill.

One of the ladies clattered her fork on the plate.

"Your joints swell up," she said, looking at the back of her hand.

They were silent.

"One of the girls was taken sick last night," said the other, the one who had spoken first, the one who was wearing tinted spectacles.

Peter regarded her.

"Carrie told me. The Director had a doctor come," she went on.

She paused.

"It was in the middle of the night."

They were silent again.

The other said suddenly, "It's all different since Herb's gone."

* * *

PETER HAD FORTIFIED himself for the encounter by drinking a severe vodka during his bath and another while dressing. He had then re-cleaned his teeth with Close-up: Super-Whitening Toothpaste and Mouthwash in One. Elspeth Mcleod lived in a recent apartment building called the Michelangelo, which boasted a commissionaire and live foliage in the foyer. On the fence surrounding the hole next door, a large sign proclaimed the imminent construction of the El Greco.

The yellow light tacked its way up the indicator panel above which was a plaque that said Otis Elevator. He imagined Otis as the given name of the company's owner, a fat, cigar-smoking, Midwestern American; rotund Otis; Rotarian; orotund.

He realized that he was not entirely sober.

"Peter Thornton!" she said, opening wide the door.

His impression was of colour. Her hair was blond, her dress white, but her face was tanned a stark and startling bronze. She ushered him into a white, Danish living room, angles, glass tables, teak wall unit, striped grey couch.

"First things first," she said. "What can I get you to drink?"

"Well, whatever . . ."

"I've made some martinis if you'd . . ."

She went away. In the brighter light of the living room the tan was even more unlikely. It looked as if she'd been enthusiastically made-up for some theatricals; the Chief's Daughter who falls in love with the Captured White Scout. Obviously, she'd been a little naughty on her CompuSheet. She was, he guessed, about forty. A year or two older possibly. Attractive in a carefully arranged kind of way. On the glass table in front of the couch lay a gigantic soapstone seal with a bulbous Eskimo trying to do something to it. He stared. Kitchen sounds, glasses, the slam of the fridge door. He wondered what he was doing here.

"Well," she said, raising her glass, "what's the new word that they're trying to make the Canadian word for 'Cheers!?'"

"Ookpic?" said Peter.

"Or 'Inuit' or something?" she said. "Is that how you say it?"

"Well," said Peter, "cheers!"

The martini stopped his breath and hit his empty stomach like a well-aimed brick.

"So," she said, nodding her head and smiling, "*you're* Peter Thornton."

He smiled.

With her every movement the massive silver charm-bracelet jingled.

"Your tan . . ."

"Florida. I've just come back. Three glorious weeks in the sun."

"So you missed the big storm," he said. "An eleven-inch fall, I think they said."

They made faces.

"Are you starving?"

"No, no, not at all."

"Because if you don't mind I'll start dinner now and it'll be ready in about an hour, if you'll excuse me."

The skirt was one of those skirts with lots of pleats in it. Fine legs. Her shoes were white too. He wondered if her legs, under the brownness of the stockings, were as intensely brown as her face and wrists.

He wandered over and looked at the things in the compartments of the wall unit. A stereo set. A photograph of a girl. A photograph of a boy. A few recent bestsellers held upright by the polished halves of a geode—Yoga, Possession, Diet, Herbal Secrets, Yogurt. Some miniature bottles of liquor and a clustering of tiny animals in pink glass. The bowl caught his professional eye. Flower decoration, vigorous in the Kakiemon style. Opaque glaze. It felt right. He checked the hunting-horn mark. The Chantilly factory before 1750. He wondered what it was doing there, where it had come from, if she knew what it was. It contained a squashy peach.

He followed the sounds to the kitchen.

"Can I do anything to help?"

"Would you like another?" she said, setting down her glass. "This one's cook's privilege."

The kitchen gleamed. Appliances. The table was littered with chrome bar implements; salt and pepper were contained in two large wooden blocks, each four inches square. He hefted one.

"Teak," she said, as she filled his glass.

"There's really nothing to do," she continued. "I bought a gorgeous cut of salmon."

As Peter watched, she enclosed the fish in two layers of aluminum foil, pinching and securing the seams. She then opened the dishwasher, placed the foil package on the upper rack, slammed and locked the door, and switched it on.

Peter stared.

She looked up and caught something of his expression.

"I calculate by weight, you see," she said.

"By weight," repeated Peter.

"That'll need two full cycles," she said.

Peter nodded.

"Anything heavier," she said, "and I'd add two Rinse Holds."

"Ah," said Peter.

He carried the pitcher of martinis and a chrome ice-bucket thing and she brought the glasses, closing the kitchen door behind them to muffle the throb of the dishwasher. She put on some kind of Latin-Americany music and joined him on the grey-striped couch.

"Well," she said, "you must tell me all about appraising. What does an antique appraiser do?"

"Well," said Peter, "furniture's the bread-and-butter side of ..."

"That's a dip I make myself," she said, lifting a white limp leather handbag from the floor by the end of the couch and rummaging.

"But porcelain and silver," said Peter, "are my ..."

"And I'm sorry about the chips—I was rushed and picked up those awful ones that taste of vinegar by mistake—but the dip's very good. It's very easy in a blender—sour cream and Danish Blue, chives, and a teaspoon of lemon juice."

She found cigarettes at the bottom of the bag.

"Delicious," said Peter. "Absolutely delicious."

And listened to himself crunching.

"Tell me," she said, snapping and snapping the mechanism of the slim gold lighter, "we didn't seem to talk about this, did we? Or did we? I was rather flustered—well, *you* know, and my memory's awful but did you say you *weren't* married? My memory! Sometimes I can't even seem ..."

"No," said Peter, leaning across and lighting her cigarette with a match. "No, I'm not."

"You're lucky," she said.

He smiled and then sipped.

"Peter," she said, "you listen to me. You pay attention. You're a very lucky man."

"I don't know if I'd agree with that," he said with a smile.

She turned towards him.

"And just how," she said, "did an attractive man like you escape so long?"

"I'm divorced," he said.

"Aha!" she said.

"What about you?"

"I will be soon," she said. "Divorced. It's on the rolls for March."

He nodded.

"And it can't be soon enough," she said. "Let me tell you."

"It's a strange business," he said.

She filled her glass, holding the pitcher with both hands.

"Peter," she said. "Do you know what I'm going to do? I'm going to phone my friend."

"Your friend?"

"We girls have to stick together," she said. "Right? So I'll tell her *not* to come at nine. Because you're not *ughy* and—you know what they say?"

"What?"

"Three's a crowd."

She got up and smoothed her dress, straightening pleats with her fingertips, running them down the pleats at her thigh.

"And I don't think you're likely to molest me," she said. She smiled down at him. "Are you?"

She started from the room.

"You have some more dip," she called back.

He was beginning to feel satisfactorily sloshed. He leaned back on the uncomfortable Danish couch and looked at his watch. He felt relaxed and the pitcher of martinis was still half-full. He sucked his olive. He then initiated some exploratory dental work with the cocktail-stick thing.

He had phoned Elspeth McLeod a week earlier on his return from dinner at Chez Jean-Guy. When he had entered his apartment, he had taken off his rubbers and put them on the sheet of newspaper inside the front door. The paper was scratchy with grit and sand; he had been meaning to change it for weeks.

He had tried to read but the conversation of the American ladies had echoed in his mind. Doors slammed. The TV in the next apartment was switched off. In the deepening silence, the refrigerator started and stopped.

Magnetic letters on the fridge door still held his CompuSheet. As he had stood over the toilet, he had seen into the empty room he maintained for Jeremy. Light from the bathroom glinted on the rims and spokes of the two-wheeler propped against the bedroom wall, last summer's birthday present. The bicycle had come in a large cardboard carton and he had skinned his knuckles working with an unaccustomed wrench to attach handlebars and pedals. Jeremy had been frightened of the bicycle and had hysterically resisted Peter's efforts, but had loved the carton, playing with it every day until it was forgotten overnight on the balcony and the rain rendered it limp and soggy.

Peter struggled to sit upright on the sloping couch. He dropped the olive into the crystal ashtray.

The toilet flushed and he heard water running.

The bicycle and the carton seemed as if they ought to be symbolic of something but of what, exactly, he was unable to grasp.

"Hello, again!" she said.

"I've been admiring your bowl," he said.

"Bowl? Oh. That belonged to my Drex. Well, he isn't but he *will* be. I've got a red ring around it."

"Pardon?"

"Oh, don't mind me," she said, "it's just my way, the way I am. It's what my girlfriend calls *hers*. She's a riot. My Drex did this, my Drex did that, she says. It stands for Dreadful Ex."

"What," said Peter, "have you got a red ring around?"

"March 17th," she said. "I was looking at it when I was on the phone. On the calendar," she added, in answer to his puzzled look. "Of course, I should have done it years ago. Everyone says so. So in a way I blame myself."

She fumbled at the lighter again.

She gestured encompassing the living room.

"We used to live in the Town of Mount Royal. Do you know the Town? We lived in a very big house in the most expensive part, the most exclusive part. And we had three cars."

She eased off her shoes and let them fall on the carpet.

"Good old TMR!" she said.

She raised her glass.

"And what else," she said, "what else did we have?"

She started to tally.

"A large garden. And an Italian gardener who came twice a week. And a swimming pool. Fieldstone fireplaces. A woman came four times a week to clean and . . ."

"Sounds very pleasant," said Peter.

"Oh, yes. Very pleasant. Very, very pleasant. I can assure you it was certainly very pleasant."

She laughed.

"Boog," she said, "will not set foot in that house. I've just come back from Florida visiting him. Did I mention that?"

"Boog?"

"My son. He's working there now. In a hotel until he finds himself."

Peter looked at the white shoes, one of them standing, one lying on its side. He'd always felt absurdly moved by women's shoes. Such frail shells. Compared with men's shoes, like toys. Glass slippers. He'd never been quite sure, though, what he felt, sexually, about feet.

"Boog'll be up for the trial," she said. "It's physical and mental cruelty."

"Trial?"

"*Thing*."

"I thought physical was supposed to be the hardest to prove?"

"Oh, I've got grounds," she said. "He's admitted it. I've got grounds all right. You just don't know."

"I hope it just goes…"

"You just don't know," she said. "I could tell you all sorts of things."

Peter knew she would.

He recognized and remembered the condition. He remembered the need to tell friends and acquaintances, the compulsion to inform even strangers of his anguish. He remembered the long drunken nights in patient apartments, words said, actions described, the paralysing replay of words. He said. She said. Words becoming meaningless sounds which were the echo of the pain that would not go away.

He remembered standing in Dominion, the Muzak and bright light enveloping, standing in front of the freezer section, glass, chrome, gazing with unseeing eyes at the carcasses of Butterball turkeys, tears running unheeded.

"He used to lock me in the bedroom," she said.

"Oh, yes!" she said in answer to Peter's raised eyebrow.

"He didn't even like me to leave the house. Always wanted to know where I was. There's nothing wrong with bridge, is there? Just a group of girls. It wasn't as if it was men. Because that isn't true. I mean, you understand these things. You've been married. I know he works very hard. You have to give him that. But he wouldn't for night after night and then sometimes when he did he couldn't, you know, couldn't manage. And then he used to shout at me and say it was my fault and beat me up. He used to hit me with a shoe tree."

"Good God!" said Peter.

"And if I even spoke to another man at a party he'd beat me up when we got home. That's why Boog left. Boog hates him."

"Boog."

"My son."

"Yes, I know. You said. But I mean *Boog*."

"In Florida," she said.

Peter stared down into the diminished ice cubes in his glass.

"There isn't any harm in discotheques, is there? I've always been a good girl. Nineteen years. Nineteen years and I've always been a good girl. But that's not what *he's* saying. And after I told him I was leaving, well, he wanted to do things."

She nodded.

"You mean...?"

"*You* know," she said. "After I told him, after I'd seen the lawyer, he changed, couldn't get enough of me. Pestered me all the time wanting to do things in chairs and from behind and in the afternoon. I was a good wife to him. I bore him two children. I was always a good girl. He used to listen on the extension phone."

Peter shook his head.

"I shouldn't be telling you these things," she said.

Peter nibbled around the olive.

"He stopped going to the bathroom," she said.

"What?"

"Four or five months," she said, "he stopped going to the bathroom. Before, I mean. Before I left. That isn't normal, is it? You can't tell me that's the action of a normal person."

"What do you mean, 'He stopped going to the bathroom?'"

"Last Christmas," she said, "I bought him a winemaking kit that was just part of his present—not *last*, Christmas *before* last—and there was a shiny thing in it like soda-water things, you know, the things that make soda water, the bubbles, but it was for putting corks in bottles. He had a funnel from the office in the upstairs bathroom and another in the powder room—I did mention he was a doctor, didn't I?—the office's in the house, you see, and he did it in bottles and then he used the thing to put corks in."

"When I was a little boy," said Peter, "my mother used to make jam and she stuck on little labels with the name of what it was on it. They were white with a blue border. I remember that. Sticky on the back."

"Rows and rows and rows of bottles," she said. "It isn't very nice, is it? He kept them in the den."

"Perhaps," said Peter, "he was an oenophile."

"You're quite right," she said. "It's filthy. Nobody could call that normal."

She sighed and patted his arm.

"But the past's the past," she said. "Aren't I right?"

"Right," said Peter.

"So let's drink," she said, "to the future! To our futures!"

They drank.

He followed directions to the bathroom.

The dishwasher seemed to be mounting to some sort of climax.

It was nice in the bathroom. There were big mirrors and on the floor a furry carpet. And net curtains looped back on either side of the bath. And a coloured plastic box to put a box of Kleenex in. And a cut-glass jar of bath salts with a pink ribbon round the neck. He weighed himself. Trying not to make a noise, he eased back the mirrored cabinet doors and examined the pills, salves, tubes, pots, and potions. Here there were *two* jars of Vaseline; all women had jars of Vaseline; it was puzzling. He could think of only two bathroom uses for the stuff—to smear on infants or to facilitate the commission of unnatural acts. Neither seemed likely here, he hoped. Vaseline, he decided, was one of the mysteries of the female life.

He weighed himself again but it was difficult to see the wavering arrow. The toilet seat had a furry cover too and he suddenly wanted to know what it would feel like. He lowered his trousers and sat. It was nice.

He thought of the fallen white shoes, one standing, one lying on its side.

Sad he; sad she.

Children's feet, though, were a different matter. Children's feet were pink, diminutive, not deformed by shoes, veins, calluses, not hardened at the heels by yellowing skin.

Poor sad Peter Thornton he whispered to the furry floor *what are you doing in this sad lady's house?*

He would have liked to have stayed in the bathroom, read, gone to sleep on the carpet. Leaning forward was making him dizzy. He consulted his watch. Sitting on the furry seat was like what sitting on a St Bernard would be like. Which would rescue him and take him home and give him aspirins and milk. He stared at the tiled wall. Home, he thought, for no good reason, is the sailor home from sea, and the hunter home from the hill.

As he passed the kitchen door he saw Elspeth McLeod standing to one side of the open dishwasher throwing handfuls of green stuff into the billowing steam. The steam was making her hair wilt.

"What are you doing?" he said.

A strand of hair hung across her puzzled face.

"Parsley," she said.

"Parsley?"

"Forgot the garnish," she said.

She locked the dishwasher and started the cycle again.

"Did you know," said Peter, "there's a kind of wine called *Pisse Dru?*"

“You always forget something,” she said.

She linked her arm with his and they went back into the living room.

“I shouldn’t really have told you the things I told you,” she said, “but some faces you can tell about. I can see from your face that you’ve been through a lot of suffering. There are two kinds of people in this world—there are faces that have suffered and there are faces that haven’t suffered.”

She drew away from him and touched his brow, traced the corners of his mouth. Nodding, she snuggled closer again, drawing her legs up onto the couch. Her skirt was rucked. Peter looked at her thigh.

“Your face is nice,” she said. “Very strong but very gentle. It’s a masculine face.”

He regretted the advent of pantyhose. A nasty garment; peculiarly asexual. Before, when he was younger, there had been brownness, sheen, then, shockingly, the stark contrast of white thigh. Always an incredibly intimate whiteness.

“You’re a very cautious person, aren’t you, Peter?”

“‘Am I?” he said.

He stared at the Eskimo carving. The larger they got the less artistic they became; great nasty lumpy thing.

“You don’t have to be cautious with me,” she said.

There was a silence.

The silence extended.

“Well,” she said, “I’ve been telling you all about me. What about you?”

“There isn’t much to tell. It all happened three years or more ago.”

“But what happened?”

“She seemed to feel there was more in life or something. Or ought to be. And she met another man and . . . well, she just left.”

“Does she love him?”

"She seems to, yes."

"And you were unhappy?"

He nodded.

"Yes."

He lighted another cigarette.

But she had said *what happened?*

It was a question he couldn't answer. Even after three long years he did not know what had happened. With the passage of time, it had all become, if anything, even more senseless. One day, it seemed to him now, he had been a father who brought home flowers and did the shopping on Saturdays, the next, the occupant of a dismantled apartment.

Of course it could not have happened in quite that way. There had been talk, a lot of talk. Words. "Growth," "Fulfilment," "Freedom," "Human something-or-other." He suspected now that, for all the mornings he had awoken crying, he was merely victim of the clichés of *Cosmopolitan* and *Ms.*

And Jeremy?

What he felt, he did not know. He did not know.

"You're very quiet," she said. "Did I say something?"

"No, no. Sorry. Just thinking."

She sighed and squeezed his arm.

He stared at the Eskimo thing.

"How about another drink?" she said. "Do you think we should?"

They drank. She sighed again.

"You don't find me unattractive, do you? I'm not unattractive, am I?"

"You're *very* attractive."

"I'm not ugly or anything," she said. "I bore him two children."

"Certainly not," said Peter.

"I've got Hester," she said. "He needn't think he can kick me out without a penny."

“Certainly not,” said Peter.

“There are some things,” she said, “that people shouldn’t say to other people. There are some things you just don’t say.”

“I think I’d agree with that,” said Peter.

“My lawyer says it constitutes mental cruelty.”

“What does?”

“When he’d done it—you know—*when* he did it, which wasn’t very often *I* can tell you and, it’s not as if I’m unattractive, he’d stand up on the bed and shout at me—would you believe that? And I worried he’d wake the children because it isn’t the sort of thing . . .”

“Shouting about what? What do you mean shouting?”

“Well, that’s the point. That’s mental cruelty.”

“What is?”

“Because do you know what *I* had to say?”

“No.”

“I had to say, ‘You are, Robert.’ Standing on the bed,” she said, “shouting.”

“You are what?”

“Not a thought for the children.”

“You are what?” said Peter.

“What do you mean?” she said.

“What did he shout when you had to say you are?”

“You mean, what did he shout?” she said.

Drawing away from him, she straightened her back, turned.

“WHO’S YOUR MASTER?”

“Shsss!”

“WHO’S YOUR MASTER?”

“Shsss! They’ll hear next door.”

“Was I speaking loudly?”

“Just a bit.”

“I’m sorry.”

“It’s just . . .”

“If I was speaking loudly,” she said, “I’m sorry.”

“That’s terrible.”

"I apologize," she said.

She peered into the empty cigarette packet and then dropped it on the glass table. She groped for the white handbag and rummaged again.

"Oh!" she said. "Look what I've found! I knew they were somewhere."

She opened a fat paper wallet of colour snaps.

"These were all taken in Florida," she said. "Did I mention that?"

Leaning heavily against him, giving his thigh a quick squeeze, she started to pass him the photographs one by one. Dutifully, one after another, he stared at beaches, palm trees, hotel façades, swimming pools, swim-suited groups, reclining people in reclining chairs.

That's me.

And with dismissive gestures, *You don't know these other people.*

That's the ocean.

He stared at two lounging young men who were grinning at him. They held tall drinks. They were tanned and muscled. One wore red trunks, the other white. There was a palm tree. The pool was blue. To the side of the picture stood a waiter in a white jacket.

"There's not an ounce of fat on their bodies," she said.

She tapped the photo with a be-ringed finger.

"They're famous," she said. "There's one—here it is—of me with them in a group. Here. You don't know these other people."

He stared at the captured smiles.

"They're very famous junior league hockey players," she said.

* * *

SITTING in the Happy Wanderer finishing his dinner and gazing at the travel posters of ruined castles, bare-knee bands, and Rhinemaids with steins, Peter realized that he had arrived at a decision.

Three weeks or more had passed since Elspeth McLeod. He had not been out much—a movie with Alan and Nancy North, a farewell evening with one of the young assistants who was going to London for a course at the V & A, bridge with Hugh and Noreen. He had allowed the coming March sale to take up most of his time; afternoons and evenings spent examining the furniture and bric-à-brac of lives, suggesting reserve prices, met always with incredulity that cherished objects would fetch but a fraction of what had been paid for them, bread-and-butter work usually left to the younger men.

Peter realized that the decision that had been growing in him during these days and weeks was probably an inevitable one. It was, he told himself, a decision towards which the course of his life had inevitably and inexorably brought him. He examined the decision, tried out forms of words in his head, declarations. Declarations which began: *The die is cast . . . From now on . . . From this time forth . . .*

His quest, he had decided, was ludicrous. What had he to do with Stella Bluth, Elspeth McLeod, and stretching fore and after, all that sad sisterhood? His life was in need of rationalization and restructuring. All, he told himself, was not lost. He was not exactly young—middle age approached—but neither was he old; not handsome but not unattractive. He had friends, a comfortable income, wide interests. He would embrace the single life, honourably discharge his duties as a parent so far as that was possible, live to himself.

As a sign of this decision, he would make his apartment habitable, invest in it time and care. He would, after two years of camping in it, *move into* his apartment. With growing excitement, he saw that he would paint, polish, scour, and burnish, re-arrange the lighting, buy new furniture. He would cook. He would buy supplies, utensils, Copco enamel pots.

He finished his coffee.

His waitress was the large woman. He watched her making out the bill. He was pleased he'd got her and not the small, Heidi-like one. He pocketed his cigarettes and matches. The large woman's handsome face had reminded him of some other face and the likeness had troubled him for months until he'd recognized it as the impassive gaze of the woman in Giorgione's *Tempesta*. The resemblance was striking. She frowned as she figured the tax from the table on the back of her pad. He imagined her as in the painting, naked, babe at breast. He left a large tip. Past the smelly, damp overcoats and striding towards his local A & P, he saw himself the painting's other character, that enigmatic youth against the violent sky.

In the foyer of the apartment building he checked his mailbox; it contained yet another letter from the Victorian Order of Nurses addressed to Mary Chan.

In his living room, he took his purchases from the shopping bag and stood them one by one on the coffee table. Cling-Fast Dust Remover, Mr. Clean, J-Cloths, lemon-scented liquid furniture polish, Ajax, Windex.

He wondered where to start. He moved a sticky brandy snifter and picked up a sweater. He opened the closet to throw the sweater in and saw the carton, still secured by glossy tape, the barrel. He hesitated and then, with sudden resolution, reached in to grasp its far corners. To unpack the carton was a kind of declaration, he decided, a laying of ghosts, a line ruled beneath the column. He wrestled the box out into the living room and then sat on the couch to look at it. Someone had scrawled on the side "Bedroom."

He remembered the two moving men, white patches on the walls, echoes, the rooms becoming hollow. At nine in the morning they had been drinking beer. One, he remembered, called the other "Kangaroo."

He hunted for a clean knife in the kitchen and slit the glossy tape. Inside the carton:

three blankets
newspaper-wrapped things
a wooden train (Jeremy's)
bundles of catalogues from Sotheby's and Parke Bernet (his)
an electric appliance which made yogurt (hers)
a scarlet winter coat and her fur hat

He smoothed the fur and spoke her name in the silence. "Patricia." And immediately wondered why he had. He had never called her Patricia, always either Pat or a private name he would not now say.

Snowflakes drifting from the darkness into the light of the street lamp, glistening, settling, melting on the fur that framed her face. He tried to see her face within that frame but all he could recall was her face as it was in the few photographs he had kept.

The blankets, too. He touched the topmost blanket; it often must have covered them. He tried to remember her body, tried to remember making love, but she, his wife, Pat, dissolved, faded, assumed the postures of models in *Penthouse* and *Cavalier.*

He wondered why he felt so sad, her real face gone, her real body. The moving men remained more vivid, past drama more acute than present feelings. He wondered if perhaps he was deliberately inducing a sense of desolation. He tried the word "desolation" in his mind to see if he felt "desolated," but all the word conjured was the memory of a photograph of Ypres.

He felt, he decided, as if he'd suffered amputation. He was no longer whole. And the pain he felt, the sadness, was part real and perhaps part pain in a phantom limb. This formulation struck him as penetrating and clever, and he sat on the couch staring at the carton. The carton was just a cardboard box full of things he once had used and now did not. He sat on the couch feeling sad and holding the wooden train.

The telephone in the bedroom shrilled. Rushing to answer it, he stumbled over a chair in the kitchen. The voice wanted George. The number was right? Then how come no George? Did George *use* to live there?

Peter sat on the edge of his bed and switched on the light that stood on the chest of drawers. The cat woman was on the next door balcony calling kitty—kitty. He could grow herbs in the summer on the balcony in a box—basil and oregano to flavour salads and egg dishes he would cook for friends. He could hang up strings of onions in the kitchen.

Kitty-kitty called the cat woman. *Kitty-kitty*.

He sat on the edge of the bed staring at the chest of drawers. In the chest of drawers, under his shirts, was the list from CompuMate. There remained Anna Stevens. Anna Stevens held for him no interest; the die was cast. But the sheet of paper was a presence. Taking out a daily shirt, he was aware that the list was there, grit and oyster, irritating. To throw the list away was to leave loose ends; to throw the list away was to leave unread, as it were, the final chapter. To throw the list away was, it might be argued, a refusal to test his position. To not phone her could be seen even as a weakness. To phone her was, in a way, part of cleaning up, unpacking, settling in.

He thought of a piece of Battersea enamel that had been through his hands the previous week, a 1780ish patch-box. The plaque had read:

Happy the Man who Void of Care and Strife
In Ease and Friendship lives the Social Life

Exactly so.

Who loves you the most in the world? called the cat woman.

He opened the drawer and took out the paper. It was rather late to phone but on the other hand he didn't much care what her reaction was. He wished to deal with the matter in a summary way. He felt about it, he decided, as he did when he stayed up late to finish a detective story. The action and the minor characters intrigued him, but towards the end of the book exhaustion dragged him down and all that remained was the tedium of the explanation—a scene always contrived, the villain revealing all before pulling the trigger, the cast assembled in the library. Tedious, often silly, but essential before he could brush his teeth and go to bed.

He listened to the ringing, twice . . . three times . . . four.

"Oh . . . Miss Stevens, please."

"Speaking."

"I hope I'm not disturbing you calling at this hour?"

In the background Bach or Vivaldi.

"No."

"My name is Thornton. Peter Thornton. I was given your name by CompuMate."

"Oh, God!" she said.

He listened to the breathing silence for a few seconds.

"Hello?"

"I'm sorry," she said. "I didn't mean . . ."

"Is there something wrong?" he said.

"Look!" she said. "This is all a mistake. One of the men I work with filled out a form in my name and he's caused me a great deal of—"

"But that's exactly what happened to me!" said Peter. "A friend thought—"

"Then you know how distasteful—"

"But what a strange coincidence!" said Peter.

"Yes," she said. "It is."

"What do you mean? Don't you believe me?"

"Why shouldn't I?" she said.

"I'm sorry—just your tone."

There was silence.

"Mr. . . . Thornton, did you say? Let's agree that it *is* a strange coincidence and leave it at that. I really don't want to seem rude but it *is* late—"

"I wonder . . ." said Peter.

"What?"

"No. I'm sorry. I'm sorry to have troubled you."

He replaced the receiver. His hand was sweaty.

Later, lying in bed, drifting towards sleep, his thoughts wandered around the conversation. It was not the sort of ending he'd imagined. In the morning, first thing, he'd throw the list away. He had said, "I wonder . . ." and she had said, "What?" and then he'd said, "No." Had said, "No. I'm sorry." Vivaldi in the background. It was not what he'd imagined; not an ending he'd foreseen.

He wondered if, somewhere in the city, she too was lying in bed awake, wondering what he might have said when he said, "I wonder. . . ," curious, less determined than she'd sounded, provoked perhaps by a coincidence so strange.

But mainly he thought about her voice. Ever since his adolescence he'd been oddly excited by women with a certain kind of voice, and she had it. "Husky" did not describe it; that was the property of torchsingers and the like. "Deep" or "low" did not do it justice. For some reason he had come to associate the timbre with coolness, the coolness of moss, of ancient masonry, and over the years had imagined a scene that was somehow the equivalent of the voice.

At a cocktail party, he was introduced to a beautiful woman. They talked. He was holding her glass while she searched her purse for matches. Before taking the glass back, she placed her forefinger across the inside of his wrist for a second. Her finger was slim and cool. The touch was almost solemn yet shockingly erotic because proprietorial. A cool finger across the heat of his pulse, a sophisticated "yes."

And that was the sound of the voice.

During the next two days, Peter frequently caught himself thinking of the voice, the telephone conversation, that music, the strange coincidence of their situation. The coincidence was so strange that it might even be considered a sign, or portent. While not at all superstitious or neurotic, Peter often made minor decisions, this restaurant or that, to go out, to stay in, by whether ten cars or more had passed while he counted fifty, by whether a bird flew across the portion of sky visible from his bedroom, by whether, in ten dealt cards, he drew an ace. On days when he forgot his nail clippers on the night table he felt oddly uncomfortable. This business of Anna Stevens deserved thought. He kept remembering something that Alan had said when he filled in the form—something about the possibility of there being one, the same sort of reasons, one like him.

Her existence in no way altered his earlier decision, of course, but he was forced to admit that he was intrigued. Although he entirely agreed with and approved of her attitude on the phone, her cool rejection had irritated him. An admittedly irrational part of him even felt hurt. On the other hand, had she not taken that position, had she accepted or welcomed his approach, he would probably have let her talk and, whatever might have been said, would have tended to consider the matter closed, brushed teeth and so to bed. Just like, who was it—Groucho Marx?—whoever said that any club that would accept him as member was not the sort of club to which he wished to belong.

Silly.

He acknowledged his perversity.

She, of course, probably *did* consider the matter closed.

That was a problem.

The coincidence so tantalizing, the effect of her voice, her obvious intelligence and self-possession—she had deprived him of anything he could consider a fitting conclusion to this dismal adventure. This was not the way that stories ended. Before embracing his decision, he wanted to feel that his past—he sought an image—burning of boats, clearing a campsite before shouldering a pack and moving on, yes, that was it precisely. Litter buried, fireplace stones dispersed, the fire kicked out.

To phone her again was impossible; he was not a man who importuned strange women. The most sensible course of action was to write. This would obviate any embarrassment on either side and allow them both their dignity. He would include in the letter sufficient information about himself for her to make a reasoned response. If she chose not to reply; then he would accept that refusal as a considered refusal—the circumstances being completely different from an unexpected phone call. If she chose not to reply, he could accept that refusal as a fitting conclusion to what had been a silly business from the start.

If she *did* reply, if she did reply, then, simply, he would see what happened.

On his return from work on the third day, he sat down at the desk in his bedroom to construct the letter. He had determined on a light and civilized approach. The letter's stated intention was to apologize for his gauche intrusion upon her privacy. He presented himself as a victim of Alan's misplaced sense of humour who—but why had he co-operated, why phoned these dreadful women in the first place? *Pitfall.* Lightheartedly? Presumably he'd have phoned them in the same spirit he'd phoned her. *Pitfall.* He used up endless sheets of his office scratch pad.

He wove all necessary information about himself into the fabric of his chronicle of misadventure. All references to his past, marital status, occupation, income, and interests were oblique and present only to make clear word and action. He did not request a meeting or any further contact—the fact of writing implied enough.

He wrote and rewrote, shading an emphasis here, burnishing a highlight, lengthening there, excising. Humour with a dash of pathos dealt with Stella Bluth and Nadia Chayefski. Elspeth McLeod he played as comedy degenerating into farce. He himself emerged as a slightly bruised idealist, rueful, the Philip Marlowe of the antique trade, a man unafraid to admit to loneliness, a man, who, in these untender times, was not ashamed to admit to the possibility of love.

Love, which, strip away our sterile sophistication, our bright brittleness, was perhaps ... *etc.*

Difficult, this part. Such rhetoric clashed with the letter's general tone. He struggled to bring it under control.

The letter was five pages long. Looking at his watch, he saw with surprise that he'd been working on it for more than three hours. He realized suddenly that he was hungry and exhausted. He felt lightheaded, oddly disconnected from his bedroom with its familiar furniture, as if he'd been living for those hours in a different world where a part of him still lingered. He poured himself a large Scotch and read the letter through, smiling still at certain turns of phrase. The letter pleased him; it was a fine blend of humour, self-deprecation, and manly emotion. In a quiet way, it was moving.

He decided that he must eat before writing out a fair copy. He investigated the kitchen. He had bought supplies, tins, meat in the fridge, the *Penguin Book of French Provincial Cookery*. The haricot beans he had been soaking with the intention of using in a simplified version of cassoulet seemed to have gone funny. There was a grey scum on the water and they smelled. As he had further work to do on the letter and felt tired, he decided to eat, for the sake of convenience, at Chez Jean-Guy.

He took the Scotch and the letter into the living room and sat down to read it again. It *was* moving. He sipped the Scotch. And what was more, he realized, it was true.

He mailed the letter the next morning and immediately began to brood about the anarchy of the Montreal postal situation. It was not unheard of for letters to take eight days to cross the city. Letters were sorted ten times, redirected, trundled to Ottawa and back, burned even by union goon squads. Burned, dropped down drains, stabbed through and through by separatist postmen.

His mail was usually delivered at about 10 A.M. and, on the third possible day for a reply, he drove home at lunchtime to check his mailbox. It contained advertising matter from Simpson's and a Hydro bill.

The weekend intervened.

On Monday, however, the whiteness inside the mail slot was an envelope addressed in an unfamiliar hand.

The letter read:

Dear Mr. Thornton,

Thank you for your charming and humorous letter. There was no need to apologize. If apologies are needed, then I should apologize for being so abrupt. How were you to know that I'd been made the object of someone's spite? Strange as it may seem, passions in libraries do exist—it must be something to do with being so enclosed—I was about to say cloistered! Please don't feel guilty and excuse my curtness—I'm sure with your experiences, you'll understand it.

Yours sincerely,
Anna Stevens

Peter studied the letter.

The most important point, of course, was that she had written it at all. Any kind of reply was a clear indication of interest. That she had gone further and unnecessarily revealed the nature of her occupation ... He wondered about the words "cloistered" and "passions"—words possibly full of obscure promise.

He imagined her voice saying those words.

On the phone she had said, "one of the men I work with," and the plural was interesting. In most public libraries, the staff was mainly women—one man, perhaps. But "men"? Possible in the main branch of a large city, but Montreal had no large public English-language library. And the private or semi-private libraries—Fraser Hickson, Atwater, Westmount—were definitely female preserves. Could it be that, better and better, she worked in a university? And he wondered about "one of the men"—why he'd done that, filled in the form. A discontented underling? A rejected suitor, perhaps, spurred by bitterness.

The letter was written in ink, not ballpoint—much in her favour. The paper was a heavy bond, pleasant to handle, the handwriting graceful and firm. The emphasis of "do" and "cloistered," and "your" and the excessive exclamation mark were possibly a little feminine but the letter was not hideous with green or purple ink and circles instead of dots over the i's—characteristics with which he had become familiar over the last three years, infallible indicators of mental or emotional unbalance.

What should be his response? To phone, even now, would be injudicious. Another letter was required, a letter simple and to the point. A letter that explained how he was haunted by how strangely they were yoked by coincidence, which proposed they meet entirely outside the sordid context of CompuMate, perhaps for dinner. Solitary dining uncheering and bad for the digestion. Something along those lines. He would gamble everything on one throw of the dice.

It was as he was labouring over the composition of this letter that the phone rang. He reached over from his desk.

"So what's new?" said Alan.

"Nothing much. You?"

"Just been invited to give a paper in England at a Shakespeare orgy. Expenses paid."

"Will Nancy let you go?"

"I'll have to try being nice to her for a bit," said Alan.

"I'll tell you what *did* happen," said Peter. "I've just met a most interesting new lady."

"What sort of lady?"

"A librarian lady. Very bright. Very good-looking. It all looks very promising."

"Large personalities, has she?" said Alan.

"Really, North!" said Peter. "Must you sully everything you touch?"

"Sully my ass," said Alan. "I'd rather have a pair of first-rate knockers than all those old Chinese pots and pans you moon over."

"You have a point, I suppose," said Peter.

"So have they," said Alan. "But listen. Enough of this Pat and Mike stuff. You want to come to dinner? Nancy's doing something disgusting from a new cookbook and I want you to eat some before I try it. Half an hour or so? Dress informal."

"I'll pick up some wine," said Peter.

"If you want," said Alan, "bring this librarian creature."

The next morning, after the alarm had gone off, dozing, Peter dreamed a most vivid dream, which was part dream and part memory. It was the last day of his summer holiday at his uncle's farm. He was saying goodbye to the girl who lived at the next farm. He was thirteen and loved her achingly. Marjorie was twelve.

He was standing in the lane looking up at her where she sat on her pony. Their conversation was stilted. Suddenly he blurted out:

"Can I kiss you goodbye?"

A deep blush suffused her and she bent to pat the horse's neck.

After a silence she said:

"I'd like to but I can't."

They seemed held there then in the still sunshine, the shade of the hazel trees almost black, the buzz of insects in the roadside flowers. He stared at a place in the rein where the leather was cracked and blackened.

And then she said:

"You can have this to keep."

And she thrust at him her handkerchief, a large, man's handkerchief, white with a green-and-brown border. And later in the bedroom with the black oak beams where he always slept, he moved aside the basin and ewer and smoothed and folded the handkerchief on the washstand and put it in the brown plastic wallet his Auntie Anne had given him for a going-away present.

On his way to work, to his pots and pans as Alan called them, he drove down to the main post office and mailed the letter. He had thought of driving to a post office in Outremont, where she lived, and posting the letter there, but realized that all mail probably went first to the main branch for sorting.

He did not doubt that she would reply.

He was working now on the catalogue, his desk covered with numbered file cards bearing descriptions of each item—dates, hallmarks, troy weights, factory marks, furniture labels, repairs noted, flaws and defects noted, provenance.

Pots and pans.

Thoughts of Anna Stevens possessed his mind.

A bedroom in Madrid full of sunlight, a red-tile-floor. Breakfast late, and then, in the afternoon, beer and *tapas* at a sidewalk café, she in a blue-and-white cotton frock, sunbrown legs. And, at five in the afternoon, the black bulls in the bull ring, the yellow-and-magenta capes. And then, through the warm and quickening streets, strolling towards dinner at eleven.

He would take her to his favourite places, the farmlands of his childhood, Madrid, Angoûlème, to the rows of dealers in Amsterdam in their ancient, leaning buildings, to the Hebrides, to his student rooms in the rue de Vaugirard.

Yes.

They would walk in the Jardin du Luxembourg eating lemon water-ice.

He thought again of Paco Camino, slim in a silver suit of lights, and counted the years in shock. He had seen the boy take his *alternativa*, followed him in those sun-filled student days through San Sebastian, Bilbao, Huesca, Pamplona, down through the orange groves to Seville, watched him work the bulls with mad and terrifying grace.

So many years ago like yesterday. What had become of that nobility? Dead now, perhaps, or fat, or fighting bulls with shaved horns like the rest.

Was he too old, Peter wondered, too old to start again?

File cards. Pots and pans.

The day bore on.

On the way home from work he bought the *Montreal Star*. His mailbox contained a mangled *New Yorker* and a letter from an insurance company informing him that he had been chosen from thousands to receive a prize. He poured himself a drink and sat in his living room. He got up and put on a record he'd bought in a Greek store on Park Avenue, bouzouki music and a man singing, very sad-sounding and Eastern, but after a couple of minutes he took the record off.

The apartment, cleaned and now quite neat, was somehow oppressive. He stroked the intricate surface of the cloisonné vase that stood on the bookcase. Pots and pans. He stood at the window looking out and feeling restless. He wanted to be a part of the life out there but if he went out he had nowhere he wanted to go. The glass of the window was cold. He went into his bedroom and called Alan, but there was no answer. Ray, too, was not back from work.

He sat looking through his address book. So many names crossed out, friends of Pat's, acquaintances fallen by the wayside since his divorce. He stared at her familiar handwriting, numbers from their old locality—grocers, beer, laundry, dry-cleaners, diaper service.

He thought of Jeremy last summer and the summer before, of those desert hours in the sandbox in the park, the suspicious stares of the suburban mothers and their huddled conversations, the sun crawling towards the hot tears of bedtime.

He saw himself in the living room at night, stupefied with exhaustion, listening to the child's breathing, waiting for a sigh or a cry, drinking Scotch too fast, too tired to eat.

He was unable to concentrate on the news in the *Star* and he found himself doing something that he never did, working his way through the classified section, through the columns of houses for sale. Outremont, lower Westmount, Montreal West.

He pictured them together, a family again. Anna and Jeremy, on picnics, at the seaside, in fields full of flowers.

After the third day of waiting, Anna's reply arrived. He had known that it would be there, had dawdled deliberately on the way home doing some unnecessary shopping. He did not open the letter in the elevator. In his apartment, he hung up his coat. He took a beer from the fridge and poured it into a pewter tankard he rarely used. He took the beer into the living room and set it down on the table by his chair. He hunted for the brass letter-opener, which he never used, a gift from someone once, its handle the three monkeys. He slit open the envelope and drew out the letter.

He read the note quickly, then read it through again. He could feel the smile stretching his face. He raised the tankard and said aloud, "Your health sir! Your very good health."

He felt so happy it was as if he'd breathed in as much as possible, then a bit more—he felt full. He blew a kiss to the drawing that hung near the door—gorgeous grainy charcoal, a backview of a nude brushing her hair.

"An army," he said sternly to her back, "marches on its stomach."

He took the dog-eared copy of *Where to Dine in Montreal* from the bookcase and started to thumb through it. He felt he could compile a better guide himself, one which named names, which exposed corruption in high places, which advised of the venerable patisserie, the Bisto sauces, the crêpes manufactured from Aunt Jemima at $6.50. It was mildly depressing to think of the procession of women he had squired to most of Montreal's many restaurants. He wished he could think of some other socially acceptable way of meeting her, of meeting Anna, something less *used.*

He needed a meal that would be lengthy with no pressure from waiters seeking to seat the starving hordes. He considered the St. Amable—tables too close together. Chez Bardet? Too oppressive, too much conscious good taste, everyone on his or her best behaviour. His own favourite going-out place was the Symposium, but it was not a restaurant for intimate occasions—at nine o'clock it filled with rattletrap drummers, amplified bouzoukis, and men who danced intensely and alone.

He needed, then, an unhurried restaurant with a relaxed atmosphere, but not *too* festive, with tables decently separated, and, as he was dealing with unknown tastes, a cuisine not aggressively ethnic. The idea came to him of the Port and Starboard; if she didn't like seafood, the meat dishes were more than passable, salads good, wine list reasonable, the whole place nautically silly with portholes and pleasant and comfortable.

He felt that, even now, it would be safer to write again with day, place, and time but he knew that he could not stand more writing, more waiting, more hours, days, mailmen and letterboxes.

The conversation was brief, the most convenient arrangement made, and even the part he'd been dreading was carried off with the minimum of awkwardness.

"This is rather ridiculous," he said, "like spy stories—but how will I recognize you?"

"I'll be the one," she said, "carrying a copy of *Pravda* and a saxophone and wearing a red coat."

He laughed deliberately and gratefully.

"Red coat it is," he said. "Until tomorrow, then."

Peter sat the next night, half an hour before the appointed time, in the Crow's Nest drinking a nasty drink called a Capstan. The Crow's Nest was a small bar just outside the main dining room of the Port and Starboard, which gave a view of the staircase, the cash desk, and the cloakroom. The tables in the Crow's Nest were made of barrels and the seats were fashioned from kegs. Special low prices were being offered on drinks called the Capstan, Bluenose, and Blow the Man Down.

Since his last visit, to his horror, the restaurant had fallen prey to a prodigal decorator. The overall effect was of an end-of-lease sale at the premises of an unsuccessful chandler. Every nook, recess, and area of wall had been jammed, plastered, and festooned with nets, buoys, bollards, binnacles, belaying pins, barnacle-encrusted brass bells, anchors, cutlasses, hawsers, harpoons, lanterns, strings of bunting, and lengths of rusted chain.

Peter imagined the whole restaurant as a bad stage set for a musical. At the entrance to the Crow's Nest, facing the wide staircase, stood a ship's figurehead in the form of a mermaid. The sequence formed before his eyes—a muscular matelot in striped jersey and canvas bellbottom pants dancing down the staircase, leaning forward from the waist, arms akimbo, to plant a chaste kiss upon the mermaid's carmine lips, and then, whirling away into the restaurant proper to dance on tables for Annabelle, the Admiral's lovely daughter.

Peter felt nervous and looked frequently at his watch.

His drink was becoming nastier and *thicker* as he neared the maraschino cherry.

He felt constrained in his newly pressed suit and the white shirt he had bought that morning, dressed up, costumed. He fiddled with the knot of his tie. He fiddled with his silver cigarette lighter.

And then, on the stairs, a flash of red movement, legs, red coat, a girl standing on the bottom step looking about her.

He got up from the table and moved towards her. She was tall and had long black hair tied at the nape with a red wool ribbon like the ones that Nancy bought for Amanda. Her eyes were large and dark. She was beautiful.

She turned again and saw him coming towards her.

He raised his eyebrows.

She smiled.

"Anna?"

"Sorry I'm late," she said. "There's a blizzard starting out there—cars abandoned all over the road."

"I have a table through here," he said. "Thought you might like a drink while we're waiting."

"Lovely," she said.

"Shall I check your coat."

"No, thanks. I'm still freezing."

As she manoeuvred round the barrel and kegs to sit down, the hood of her coat caught on the fluke of an anchor and he had to disentangle her.

"I'm sorry," he said, gesturing at the walls. "It wasn't like this the last time I was here."

"I *like* silly places once in a while," she said. "What's that?"

"I've been wondering," said Peter. "I think it's a donkey engine."

She undid the wooden pegs of her coat, slipped her arms out of it, and then settled it back over her shoulders. In the bar's half-gloom, pretending not to be watching, Peter saw that she was wearing a black turtleneck sweater with some kind of large silver pendant over her breasts.

"Drinks!" said Peter. "What would you like? I'll wade through the lobster traps to the bar."

"Sherry, please. A *fino*. *Tio Pepe*, if they have it."

"This," said Peter, "is a Capstan, as advertised, and it is unbelievably vile and I'm going to get a Scotch to take the taste away."

When he came back from the bar, he raised his glass and said,

"Well, Yo-ho-ho!"

"It does all crowd in on you a bit, doesn't it?" she said.

"I hope the food's still as good," said Peter. "If the decor's anything to go by we might be eating hardtack and tapping out the weevils."

"With lashings of putrid salt pork," she said.

"And dumplings sewn up in canvas," said Peter.

She sipped the sherry and smiled at him.

"I like dry sherry," she said, "but I don't like it as much as martinis but if I drink *them* before I eat I get tiddly and can't taste the food."

"Half-seas over, as it were," said Peter.

"Three sheets to the wind," she said.

"In irons on a lee shore," said Peter.

"You made that up," she said.

"I swear," said Peter, "by all that's nautical. I got it from a Hornblower book."

"What does it mean, then?"

"I don't know," he said, making a severe face, "but it's *not good*."

She giggled.

"You're silly," she said.

"Far from it," said Peter. "You behold one who is Captain of his Fate."

"Men who play," she said, "are more to be trusted than men who do not play."

"Is that one of your Laws?"

"The Third," she said. "And I don't feel so nervous now. Can I have a cigarette?"

"Me neither," said Peter.

They occupied themselves with cigarettes and his lighter and the ashtray.

"Can I ask you something I shouldn't?" said Peter.

"What?"

"Why did you come tonight?"

She shrugged.

"I don't know," she said. "It was against my better judgement but—well, I wasn't doing anything else. And your letter, I liked your letter. Curiosity. Who knows?"

"Meeting people is sort of sordid, isn't it?" said Peter. "I'm sorry."

She laughed.

"I didn't mean to be funny."

"I know you didn't," she said. "You just are."

They looked at each other, smiling.

"When that wretched little man in the library sent in my name to that *thing*..."

"Why did he do that?"

"I think he thought it was funny," she said. "Men who work in libraries tend to be strange—not all of them, of course—but quite a few are eccentric or homosexual or just childish—I suppose like men who choose to teach elementary school or become nurses. The way things are, it's a strange occupation to choose. Shouldn't be, but it is. But you wouldn't *believe* some of the things I went through. Breathers and panters and abuse and men asking me how much I charged—"

"Good God!" said Peter.

"Someone kept sending religious tracts and one man kept sending me postcards—always the same one. On the writing side it always said I MEAN TO HAVE YOU and the picture-side was always a reproduction of a sort of scroll that had a chant or a prayer by Aleister Crowley on it."

She looked enquiry at him and he nodded.

"Always the same thing," she went on, "one of those 'Do What You Want Shall Be All Of The Law' Crowley things—gibberish, horrible—murder being good if you feel like doing it, you know? I was getting really frightened."

"I've always thought it was funny," said Peter, "that the Great Beast was cremated at Brighton. He should at least have disappeared in a clap of thunder and forked lightning."

"I didn't think *any* of this was very funny," she said.

"True," said Peter. "I was just thinking about Brighton."

"One man," she said, "even sent me a sheet of paper—foolscap—with some obscene doggerel at the bottom and with a drawing of his—his apparatus on the rest."

Peter laughed out loud.

"Really," she said. "And there was an asterisk by the, well, the *tip* of it and beside the asterisk it said 'Actual size.'"

She joined in his laughter.

"Did he *need* foolscap?" said Peter.

"But what was funnier than *that*," she said, "if you stop to think about it, I mean, and sad too, it was a Gestetner stencil."

The maître d' appeared at the doorway of the Craw's Nest, menus cradled in his arm, and inclined his head in stately summons. They followed his measured pace and majestic bulk towards the dining room. In the more brightly lighted foyer and corridor, Peter was violently aware of the swing of Anna's skirt, the trimness and tension of her body beside him.

The dining room itself was less ravaged; the prints of Ships of the Line remained and the decorator had confined himself to blocks and tackle and a few flurries of swords. They quickly settled the details of the meal; Anna decided on crepes stuffed with shrimp, clams, mussels, and oysters and baked in cream and cheese; Peter on a dish of herring and roe. Anna traded in an hors d'oeuvre for a dry martini and Peter ordered another Scotch. Much ado was made with a wine cooler, napery, and the solemnities of label-inspection.

"I was meaning to ask you," said Peter. "Which library do you work in?"

"McGill," she said. "In the Rare Book and Special Collections."

"Aha!" said Peter. "I've had dealings with them. We once took some medieval manuscripts there we'd had in an estate sale—sort of contracts or leases—bits of parchment with wavy edges?"

He made scissors with his fingers.

"They're called foot of fine," she said, nodding.

"We wanted them dated," he said, "and not a soul in that place had even a clue."

"You aren't surprising me," she said.

"What's more than one of them? *Feet* of fine? Foot of *fines?*"

"Lovely," she said, putting her hand over his for a second. "You don't know how lovely it is to be talking to someone who you *know* won't say, 'What's the point of first editions when you can buy it in paperback?' Or, 'Is it fair to students to buy things they can't read?'"

"*They*," said Peter, "are always with us."

"I try," she said, "but I don't like *they*."

"Isn't it *nice*," he said, raising his Scotch in salute, "you with your squiggly old manuscripts and me with my old pots and pans, isn't it nice to have two *us's* together instead of an *us* and a *them*?"

"Yes," she said, "it really is nice."

A busboy arrived with wine glasses, a water pitcher, bread basket and butter dish and they drew apart as he busied himself.

"So tell me," said Peter, "what *are* the Special Collections?"

She laughed.

"The two main ones," she said, "are Winston Churchill and books and pamphlets relating to the Boy Scout movement."

"How depressingly Canadian," he said.

"And of course," she said, "even those were a bequest."

The cork was pulled, wine tasted, glasses filled.

Salads arrived.

"So it's not entirely fascinating?" said Peter.

"I often wish I'd stayed in London," she said.

"What were you doing?"

"Well, after university and library school here, I went there to King's College—I was taking the diploma course in palaeography."

"And then?"

"I *did* stay for a year but then I fled the country and here I am back with Winston Churchill and the Boy Scouts."

"Fled?"

She laughed.

"Yes, I really did flee—all very dramatic and intense. Possessions abandoned and dishes left on the table. It all seems very *young* and silly now."

"Don't be tantalizing."

"Oh, well, I was living with a very agonized Englishman who was trying to decide if he was or wasn't homosexual, and one day I knew I just couldn't take it any more. I didn't know what to do. So I ran away. He was a Marxist, too, and that's a bad combination because they *talk* a lot."

She traced the rim of the wine glass with her fingertip.

"Perhaps it was the talking," she said, "more than anything else."

Peter nodded.

"Bad talk," he said, "is not good."

"That's a profound remark," she said. "*You're* not a Marxist, are you?"

"No," said Peter, "nor homosexual."

"That's a relief," she said. "Most nice men are."

The waitress arrived. Dinner was served from casserole and platter onto plates, wine glasses were replenished. When the waitress had withdrawn, Peter said,

"Okay. If we're asking intimate questions, let me ask you one."

She looked up.

"Have *you* got a cat?"

"A cat?"

"A cat."

"Can I take the Fifth?"

"Not allowed."

"Well," she said, "no. I hate them."

He nodded slowly, as if weighing her reply.

She made a mocking little-girl face at him.

"Did I pass?"

"We're not allowed to say," he said, preparing to dissect a herring.

She gestured at the seafood crêpes with her fork.

"*Delicious*, Peter. Like to try some?"

He shook his head.

"All that heaving brown cheese—it looks like a thing a friend of mine makes—he calls it 'Disgusting Potatoes.' You'll like Alan."

As they ate, they chatted of other foods and restaurants, other cities, until the talk turned, inevitably, to the drama of families. Anna's mother was a martyr whose sufferings were inflicted on the entire cast. She ironed underwear and saved paper bags. She rearranged Anna's books in Anna's apartment according to colour. Anna's father was a mining engineer who, unable to stand the provocation of ironed underwear and paper bags, now lived in Edmonton. This desertion was a matter of profound satisfaction to his estranged wife. The script demanded from Anna guilt that she lived in her own apartment.

Peter related the saga of how his much-loved grandfather, in an inebriated state, had introduced a horse into his grandmother's teetotal kitchen. This event with its conflicting values was, he explained, the archetype of all relationships in his family. It explained, he said, why his mother had a brooding fear of firearms, why his father had built a second bathroom, and why his brother had gone to Australia.

Anna was smiling and stemming with Kleenex after Kleenex the explosive sneezes and sniffles that had overtaken her.

Plates were pushed away and cigarettes lighted.

Talk turned to Peter's job, the shop he had opened and which had folded, the general duplicity of the antique trade. Anna was fascinated by the fakes, the frauds, the piracy of buying and selling. He explained to her that, contrary to appearances, provenance, or apparent age, *all* antiques were made in the closing years of the nineteenth century.

She kept making faces of apology for her fits of coughing and urged him to go on, to pay no attention.

He told her of the workshops and factories that turned out Luristan Bronze-Age artifacts, Solingen sword blades, Delftware, and eighteenth-century English silver with genuine eighteenth-century hallmarks; of the intricacies of the aging process in the faking of early Quebec pine, how pieces were usually buried first for six to eight weeks in a manure pile; of the vast Chinese industry and the Chinese copies of European copies of Chinese originals.

Her coughing seemed to be getting more rasping and uncontrollable. He suggested ice cream in the hope it would soothe her throat. Her face was startlingly red and she kept mopping at her eyes. He suggested that they leave, that the night air might make her feel better, but she made a pantomime of refusal, of swallowing something followed by immense relief

They sat waiting for the ice cream to arrive. It had become impossible to talk. She was restlessly plucking at the neck of her sweater, pulling it away from her throat. The coughing tore at her and between bouts her breathing was audible, harsh, and wheezing.

"I've got an idea," said Peter. "I'll go and get some of those after dinner mints from the bowl at the desk. The sweetness might do something for it."

He had to wait behind a noisy crowd of people arguing about whose privilege it was to pay the bill and then for an old man doddering over the choice of a cigar and then the bowl was found to be nearly empty and the girl insisted on refilling it from an enormous bag she had to fetch from a cupboard in the cloakroom. She then searched through drawers and cupboards for an envelope to put the mints in.

As he made his way back to the table, he saw standing there a waitress and the maître d'. They were looking down at Anna. As he came up to them, the maître d' said,

"It is too much to drink."

"She was doing that," said the waitress.

Anna was making movements with her hands as if unaware of what she was doing, rubbing the bunched sweater under and between her breasts. The red ribbon had come undone and her hair hung about her face. The chain of her pendant had snapped and it lay snaked on the table in front of her. There was something disturbing, almost frightening, about the movements of her hands; it was a movement that reminded him of the violence of a sleeping baby.

"Anna?"

Peter knelt beside her chair and lifted back her hair, smoothing it away from her face. Her eyes seemed to see him. Her skin looked coarse and grainy and sweat glistened under her eyes.

"Can you tell me what's wrong? Anna?"

He pried her fingers loose from the sweater and pulled it down to cover her. Her body was slippery with sweat.

"She would like to go to the ladies' room," said the maître d'.

Peter put his arm around her and prepared to lift her up but her head lolled.

"I don't think she can move," he said to the maître d'.

"She didn't say anything when I brought that order of ice cream," said the waitress. "She was just doing that."

They looked at her. Her breathing scraped at their silence.

“Well,” said Peter, straightening up and turning to the maître d’, “I don’t think she can walk.”

“It is wine,” said the maître d’.

There was a crash of broken glass and cutlery falling as she collapsed across the table. Her shoulders were working and she was making noises. Vomit spread out around her face.

Her eyes were closed. Heads were turned; some people were standing up. Peter gathered her hair and lifted it from the path of the vomit. The hair was heavy and alive in his hands. Water dripped onto the floor. The maître d’ started to pile the shards of glass at the corner of the table.

“Anna?” said Peter. “Can you sit up? If I help you?”

“Excuse me,” said a voice behind them. “Thought I’d better pop over and take a look.”

The dapper middle-aged man bent over her. His tie trailed in the spilled water.

“Are you a doctor?” said Peter.

“She has fainted,” said the maître d’.

“Sneezing, coughing, and so forth,” said the doctor. “How long’s it been going on?”

“About half an hour,” said Peter. “Maybe more. What is it? What’s wrong?”

“Do you have oxygen?” said the doctor to the maître’d. “Canister sort of affair with a mask? Well, you should have.”

“What’s wrong with her?” said Peter.

“Shock,” said the doctor. “Anaphylaxis.”

“When I brought that ice cream …” said the waitress.

“I need a room,” said the doctor, “and blankets.”

“By the side of the cloakroom,” said the maître d’, “is the wine cellar.”

“That sounds just the job,” said the doctor. “And now phone for an ambulance—as fast as you like. You,” he said to Peter, “take her other arm. Right? Better this way in case she vomits again.”

As they lifted her, there was the sudden stench of diarrhea. Urine trickling down her leg.

"Never mind that," said the doctor. "They usually let it all go. Thank God for pantyhose, eh?"

In the long, narrow room which served as a wine cellar, they lowered her to the carpet. It was cold there and silent with the door closed. Her breath laboured on, harsh, rasping in the quietness. The sour smell of vomit and the sweeter stench of excrement hung on the chilly air. The doctor turned her head to one side. She was unconscious.

The doctor was breathing heavily from his exertion.

"Not getting any younger," he said.

"But what *is* this anaphylactic shock?"

"It's the devil of a thing," said the doctor, looking at his watch. "Like an extreme allergy reaction. Food can do it, insect bites."

There was a knock at the door and a waiter came in.

"The lady's shoe, sir."

"But I don't understand," said Peter. "She was all right. I was only away a few minutes ..."

"Can be as short as two minutes," said the doctor.

"Is it ... serious?"

"Well," said the doctor, scratching at his moustache with his thumbnail, "yes. I'm afraid it is."

"But I don't understand," said Peter.

"Results in a massive fluid imbalance, you see. The, ah, serum in the body engorges the tissue—can't breathe as a result of that. Throat closes. Lungs fill with liquid. That's what all the coughing and sputtering was in aid of. The whole thing—well, it's rather like drowning, you might say, but drowning from the inside."

There was another knock and the maître d' came in with two blankets.

"Any sign of that ambulance?"

The maître d' shrugged and shook his head.

"Phone again. Immediately. We haven't much time. And send us two brandies—none of your wretched bar stuff. You don't want two poisonings in one night. I don't like that fellow," said the doctor to the closing door. "He seated me in a draught."

He covered her with the blankets and knelt, taking her pulse.

"No sense of humour these Italians," he said. "They hadn't got one in the war and they haven't developed one since."

Peter stared at her face.

"But what happens?" he said.

"Happens? Oh. Well, the heartbeat becomes more rapid and eventually so fast that the heart isn't circulating at all. No crossover of blood between the, ah, whatnames. Everything demanding oxygen, you see, and the heart doing its best to push round what there is—works harder and harder with less and less—a losing game, you might say. And death results from cardiac arrest."

"Death?"

"No, *no*," said the doctor. "Clap on an oxygen mask—takes care of the breathing. And an injection of what you'd call adrenalin or cortisone steadies the heart—right as rain in no time."

He glanced at his watch and then felt the pulse in her neck.

"Boccaccio was a good chap," he said thoughtfully, "but I haven't a lot of time for them since."

The waiter entered with two snifters of brandy on a tray. He stared at Anna as they took the glasses. The doctor swirled the brandy, inhaled, swallowed. Peter drank from his gratefully. The smell of the room was beginning to make him feel queasy.

"Forbes," said the doctor.

"Pardon?"

"Forbes," he said. "I'm Forbes."

"Oh, I'm sorry. Peter Thornton."

"Wife?" said Forbes, gesturing with his glass.

"No. I've just met her."

Anna was stirring under the blankets.

"You just hang on, old girl," said Forbes.

"Do they have oxygen and adrenalin and things in the ambulance?"

"Standard equipment, old chap," said Forbes. "Not to worry. We can set her to rights down here."

Forbes checked her pulse again. Peter stared at Forbes' forefinger as it lay across the inside of Anna's wrist. The finger was bright yellow with nicotine. He tried to read the expression on the man's face. The face told him nothing.

They sat waiting. Peter began to count the wine bottles in the racks. The rasp of Anna's breath filled the silence. He counted all the bottles up to the first partition. There were one hundred and sixty-one bottles.

"They put me in one of their silly prisons, you know," said Forbes.

"Pardon?"

"The Italians. And a damned inefficient place it was."

They were silent.

"Come *on*," said Forbes suddenly.

"Is she all right?"

Forbes knelt by Anna's side again taking her pulse. He considered his watch.

"Is she?"

"Look!" said Forbes. "Scurry up there above-decks, would you, and investigate that bloody ambulance."

Peter hurried out past the mermaid with the carmine lips and up the wide staircase. He pushed open the heavy, padded door and stared out into the blizzard. It was difficult to see much further than the width of the road. Sidewalk and kerb were obliterated, cars were white mounds. The wind nearly wrenched the heavy door from his grasp. From St. Catherine Street came the muffled sound of horns.

He stood shivering there, trying to peer through the flying snow, straining for the sound of a siren.

As he opened the door to the wine cellar, he saw Forbes kneeling over Anna, the blankets thrown back, her sweater pulled up.

"Nothing?" said Forbes.

"You can't even see," said Peter. "Everywhere's blocked."

"Heart's moving into fibrillation," said Forbes, taking off his jacket. "We're going to have to get some oxygen in there."

"But there isn't any."

Forbes held out his wrists.

"Can you manage these damn cufflinks? Wife usually does it."

"What do you mean—oxygen?"

"Tracheotomy, old chap. Bit of a long shot, but ..."

He pulled the blanket off again.

"Sweater?" he said.

They worked her limp arms out of it and pulled it over her head.

From his trouser pocket, Forbes produced a fat red knife.

"Swiss Army job," he said. "Ingenious thing. Use it in the garden. It's got a pair of scissors and a saw."

"But won't she bleed? I mean ..."

"Can't make an omelette, old chap," said Forbes, rolling up his sleeves. "Simple enough. Not to worry."

Peter stared down at her. A small blue-and-white cotton tab stuck out from the edge of the left cup of her bra. It said: *St. Michael. Registered Trade Mark.*

"Get all that hair out of the way," said Forbes.

Then,

"*Bloody* HELL."

"What? What is it?"

Forbes crouched across her.

He remained like that for long moments.

Then, slowly, he raised himself up, sat back on his heels.

Then Peter, too, became aware of the difference, the change in the room. The room was silent. The sound had stopped.

Forbes took the tip of the blade between forefinger and thumb and eased the blade inwards to the half-closed position. He then pushed the back of the blade with the flat of his hand and the knife closed with a loud click.

Peter stared at her body. Just above her navel and to one side there was a faint, brown birthmark. He stared across her at Forbes.

"But she was all right," said Peter. "I only went to the desk. I was only away a few minutes."

"I'm sorry," said Forbes. "Without oxygen, without drugs ..."

He stood up and started to roll down his sleeves.

"It doesn't make sense," said Peter.

"It's all right," said Forbes. "Not your fault."

"But she was all right," said Peter.

"Look, old chap ..."

"We were talking. She was all right."

"You need a drink," said Forbes. "Do you a world of good. I'll take care of details here. Phone and suchlike—have a word with Chummy out there. Then I'll join you. Right?"

Forbes led him to the door.

"Get yourself a drink. Doctor's orders."

Peter went out into the restaurant. It was noisy and warm. Her red coat was still draped over the back of her chair. The table had been cleaned and reset. The carpet was dark where the water had spilled. Someone had sprayed the area with a lemon-scented air freshener. He sat down. He picked up a fork and sat staring at the flash of light on the tines.

A voice said something.

"Pardon?"

A waitress stood there with an order pad.

"Are you the party that was at this table before?"

He nodded.

"The other girl, she's finished her shift. She's gone off now."

He stared at her.

She was middle-aged with frizzy, yellowed hair and glasses. She looked tired. Like the other waitresses, she was wearing baggy red pirate trousers and a blouse with puffed sleeves fastened at the breast with black thongs. Round her waist was a wide leather belt with a brass buckle. Stuck in the belt was a plastic flintlock pistol. She was wearing the sort of boots that are illustrated in children's stories, *Dick Whittington*, *The Brave Little Tailor*, *Puss-in-Boots*.

"Anything else?" he repeated.

"Yes," she said. "Something nice for dessert?"

POLLY ONGLE

PAUL DENTON'S morning erection was thrusting the sheet into a comic tent. He regarded this sheeted protuberance with resigned pleasure. In one of those manuals which he somehow always found himself ashamedly scanning in bookstores, it had stated that REM sleep was accompanied by erections in males and by engorgement of the labia in females. He thought about that; he thought about engorged labia. He felt generally engorged most of the time but summers were more engorged than winters. He had thought when younger that sexual desire would diminish with age but now, his forty-sixth birthday approaching, he found it was getting worse.

The day's heat was already building.

He felt swept as if on tides of sap, febrile, almost deranged.

Visible in the corner of the window, a great, still spread of maple leaves. In front of the window, the hanging plant's soft tendrils were already brushing the Victorian balloon-back chair. At the back of the house, the small garden plot was teeming with a matto grosso of zucchini and cucumber, stiff, hairy stems and open-mouthed flowers. The tomato plants were heavy with green clusters. The tight skin of the green tomatoes, their chaste shine, the hints of white and yellow beneath the green as though they were somehow lighted from within, promising a warmth and swelling, made him think of firm, girlish breasts …

Beneath the sheet, he worked his ankle. The pain was quite severe. His laboured jogging along the canal would be impossible for a few days until the shin splints abated, which was probably just as well because it would spare him the torture of having to observe the bob of breasts, cotton shorts wedged in buttock clefts, nipples standing against sweaty T-shirts.

Though the word "bob" hardly summed the matter up. Some, simultaneously with the "bob," seemed to *shimmy*, a tremor of flesh which suggested, regardless of size, such confined amplitude, such richness, that it made him want to whimper.

He cranked his ankle harder to see if the pain would dispel, or at least control, the summer riot in his mind of breast, thigh, cleavage, pubic mounds etched by cotton shorts or wind-tautened skirts.

From three floors below rose the voices of Martha and Jennifer.

But what's so bad about goldfish?

Because white cords come out of them and it makes me sick and who has to flush them down the toilet?

What white cords? What are white cords? What …

The front door closed on the voices.

He regretted, daily, having been swayed by the mad enthusiasms of the renovator; he regretted, daily, the very idea of open-plan architecture. The restless night-turnings of his children, the blurts of sleep talking, the coughs, the soft padding of bare feet on cushioned carpet, the rubber seal on the refrigerator door meeting rubber seal with a *plup*—from his bedroom eyrie in what had been the attic, he could have heard a mouse break wind.

It was open-plan design which he blamed, in part, for the impoverishment of his sex life. Martha felt uncomfortable, unable to relax if the children were still awake or restless. They used the word "children" to refer to Alan and Jennifer, who were eleven and eight. Peter at fifteen had passed beyond being thought a child by either of them, and especially so by Paul.

It seemed to Paul that whenever he was gripped by sexual desire, which was very often, his desires were thwarted by Martha's worrying that the children would hear, would interrupt, that Peter, who was inevitably out, would come in, that the phone might ring, a phone that could not be taken off the hook because Peter, who was out, might have been run over by a truck or fallen into the river or been entrapped by white slavers. Experience had taught him the futility of attempting to counter these anxieties with reasoned argument; it was futile to point out that Peter had been crossing roads unaided for ten years, that there were no open bodies of water within miles of the movie theatre in which he was seated, that only the most desperate of Arab potentates could lust after a boy with an obnoxious mouth and purple hair.

Nor were the prospects any brighter if Peter *were* in, the family door secured against the legions of burglars and perverts. If he *were* in, he refused, flatly, to go to bed. This meant that lubricity in any form was impossible because he was awake, probably listening, possibly *recording*, and almost certainly drinking the last of the milk and eating the fruit for the children's lunches.

Outsitting him was not feasible strategy. Exhausted by her daily labours at the Ministry of Energy, Mines, and Resources and then further exhausted by cooking, homework consultations, and the general wear and tear of motherhood, Martha was red-eyed with fatigue by nine thirty. Any sexual activity past that hour bordered on necrophilia.

Mornings were an impossible alternative. The differences in their circadian rhythms were such that Martha's eyes sprang open with the dawn chorus while his were blear and his mood surly until eleven thirty, at which time Martha was beginning to droop.

Weekends were no better and were not exactly weekends. Saturday was his busiest day in the gallery and on Mondays, the traditional closing day for galleries, Martha was, of course, at work in the Ministry of Energy, Mines, and Resources. This left Sundays. The logistics of organizing the absence of all three children at the same time and ensuring that absence for at least an hour were next to impossible, and if he attempted to hustle her upstairs for a rushed sortie she complained that it didn't seem very "romantic," a charge that left him stunned.

He had learned not to count his chickens even when Martha and he, by some miracle, lay naked and entwined; open-plan coughing would erupt, open-plan allergies would strike, so that nights that began with tumescent promise ended with the dispensing of Chlor-Tripolon and Benedryl.

When she or he returned from these errands of mercy—usually she because of his monstrous and adamantine visibility—she would always say:

I'm sorry, Paul. Do you mind if we don't tonight? It's just that, well, you know....

He did not, in fact, know *really* what it was that she presumed he knew because *he* would have been capable of enjoying intercourse had the house been under frontal assault by urban guerillas, but he always made polite noises before going into the bathroom and getting his mouth round the gritty-sweet neck of the Benedryl bottle in the hope that the side effects of two disgusting swallows would assist him towards unconsciousness.

Paul had endured these frustrations for years and as far as he could see they could only get worse, because when the other two were a little older they, too, like Peter, would stay up past nine thirty and would wish to go out and come in.

In his more despondent moments, it seemed likely to Paul that he would not be able to make love to his wife again for ten more years—and that figure was based on the assumption that

Jennifer would leave home at eighteen, which was probably being optimistic. At which time, and over his most violent objections, Peter, who would then be twenty-five, and who would have contracted a disastrous marriage, would doubtless be returning to offload on them damned babies which would be subject every night to croup, grippe, projectile vomiting, and open-plan convulsions.

In ten more years he would be fifty-six.

In ten years after that, if he lived, sixty-six.

He thought about being old; about being him and being old; about being married and being old. He thought of a funny line from a forgotten thriller, an aging lecher who had said that intercourse in the twilight years was all too often like trying to force a piece of Turkish Delight into a piggy bank. Paul was perfectly prepared to accept that this might be so; what depressed him was the almost certain knowledge that he'd still ache to try.

Since his heart attack, or what he persisted in thinking of as his heart attack, he often found himself considering the form and shape of his life. He lived with a great restlessness and longing, as if the frustrations of his semi-celibacy had spread like a malignancy. He did not know what it was he longed for. His life, he felt, was like a man labouring to take a deep breath but being unable to fill out his lungs. Everything, he felt, seemed somehow to be slipping away, fading. He daydreamed constantly, daydreamed of robbing banks, of doing sweaty things with Bianca Jagger, of fighting heroically against BOSS to free Nelson Mandela from Robben Island ... Kalashnikov rifles, the pungent reek of cordite ...

This restlessness had expressed itself the night before, in Montreal, in his impulsive purchase at Pinney's Fine Art Auction of a stuffed grizzly bear. Driving back to Ottawa on Highway 17 with the grizzly's torso and snarling head sticking out of the window, he had felt pleased and superior to all the cars that lacked a bear.

Now, he did not wish to think about it.

He lay on his side of the bed listening to the throaty pigeons fluttering and treading behind the fretwork gingerbread which framed the dormer window and rose to one of the twin turrets which were the real reason for his having bought the house.

On the bedside table lay the packet of Nikoban gum.

"Effective as a Smoking Deterrent," he said into the silence of the bedroom, "since 1931."

The other turret rose above the curved end of the bathtub; during the night more granular insulation had sifted down. He had run out of renovation money eighteen months before. Only the ground floor was finished; the rest of the house looked as if it were in the early stages of demolition. The turret above the bathtub, the renovator had said, could be opened up and finished inside, painted white, lighted possibly, so that when one was lying in the tub it would be rather like looking up the inside of a "wizard's hat." Paul remembered his exact words; he remembered the turn of the renovator's wrist and fingers as he conjured this whimsy from the air. All that could be seen through the smashed hole in the ceiling was a dangling sheet of tin or zinc, pieces of two-by-four, and deepening blackness punctured by a point of light. Lying in the tub and gazing up always made Paul think not of the inside of a wizard's hat but of being trapped at the bottom of a caved-in mineshaft.

He bent to examine the wavering arrow. It returned obstinately to 168 lbs.; this meant that, despite not eating bread at lunch and despite passing up potatoes at dinner he had, in the face of the laws of nature, gained three pounds overnight.

He teased the four white hairs on his chest.

Treat this as a warning, Mr. Denton.

Staring unseeing into the mirror, he pictured himself jogging along the side of the canal, felt the flab over his kidneys jounce. His route unreeled in his mind like the Stations of the

Cross: Patterson Avenue, past First, Second, Third, and Fourth Avenues, the stand of pine trees, then the Lansdowne Stadium stretch, and then, rounding the curve, the first sight of the Bank Street bridge. In the final stretch between the Bank Street bridge and the bridge at Bronson, the canal narrowed, the trees overhanging and the bushes crowding in to suggest a sombre tunnel. It was here that he always saw the carp, great silent shapes rising to the scummed surface to suck down floating weed, their lips, thick and horny, gaping into orange circles.

And then, rubbery legs, breath distressed, almost staggering, into the shadows of the Bronson bridge and out, out to the canal widening into the blue expanse of Dow's Lake sparkling, the open sky, the gentle slopes of the Arboretum on the far shore, white sails standing on the water.

Treat this as a warning, Mr. Denton.

He had known when the intense pains came that he was dying and so had done nothing. But Martha had detected it, something in his face or posture perhaps, and had badgered him until he'd admitted to some slight discomfort. It was she who had phoned their doctor and she who had secured him an emergency appointment. Constriction of the blood vessels and the muscles of the chest wall caused by tension was the diagnosis.

Overweight, under-exercised, a pack of cigarettes a day, tension ... *treat this as a warning.*

"You would be wise to avoid," the pompous little fart had said, "life-situations which generate anxiety and stress."

Paul shook the can of shaving foam, tested the heat of the water in the basin.

He pulled flesh tight over the angle of his jaw.

How would *you* avoid, he would have liked to ask, how would *you* avoid being consumed with unsatisfied sexual desire? *Unsatisfiable* desire, given the combination of Martha's anxieties and the interior construction of the house. Answer me that, smug little physician. Go on! What do you suggest? Castration? Investing in a sound-proofed house? Trading in the present wife for something a touch more feral? Snuffing the kids?

And *how*, you scrawny little processor of Ontario Health Insurance Plan cards, how would *you* avoid just the faintest twinge of anxiety about a business that's barely paying the rent? A business, furthermore, of which the proprietor is ashamed.

Two aspirins and retire to bed?

Keep warm?

And while we're on the subject of tension, stress, anxiety, surges of adrenalin, and so on and so forth, here's a life situation over which you might care to make a couple of magic passes with your little caduceus. What advice do you have to offer about the best way to avoid one's son?

Yes, son.

S-O-N.

He had noticed the blue-sprayed markings on neighbourhood walls weeks earlier. The script was cramped, busy, fussy squiggles and dots; he had thought it might represent slogans in a foreign language, possibly a very demotic Arabic or Farsi. Given the high concentration of Lebanese in his area, he had thought that these bright blue writings might possibly be charms against the Evil Eye. It had taken weeks of glancing before he'd suddenly recognized them as being in English.

Two of the more decipherable of these mysterious blue messages said:

Check out!

and

(something) *Zod!*

Coming home late one night from a local estate auction at the Ukrainian Hall, which had advertised "primitive African carvings" that had turned out to be two slick pieces of Makonde junk and a pair of salad servers from Nairobi, he had let himself into the silent house to find in the vestibule a can of blue spray-paint fizzling indelibly onto the newly installed quarry tile.

He had stood there long moments, staring.

Paul no longer attempted to deny to himself or to Martha that the presence of his son snagged on his nerves and curdled the food in his stomach. He did not understand the boy; he no longer *wanted* to understand him. It was not unusual for Paul immediately after dinner to be stricken with nervous diarrhea.

Even *thinking* of Peter constricted Paul with rage, made his pulse pound in his neck, throb in the roof of his mouth. He knew that the words "burst with rage" were no cliché. During these rages, he always found the word "aneurism" swelling in his mind, pictured a section of artery in his neck or near his heart distending like a red balloon to the very palest of terrifying pinks.

Paul was enraged by his son's appearance, manners, attitudes, reflex hostility, hobbies, and habits. He was reduced to incoherent anger by the boy's having mutilated all his clothes by inserting zippers in legs and sleeves, zippers which were secured by bicycle padlocks, so that he looked like an emaciated scarecrow constructed by a sexual deviant, by his smelly old draped jackets which he purchased from what he called "vintage clothes stores," by his bleached hair which he coloured at weekends with purple food dye, by his ruminant of a girlfriend whose mousy hair was bleached in two stripes intersecting at right angles so that she looked like a hot cross bun, by his wearing loathsome plastic shoes because he didn't want to be party to the death of an animal, by his advocacy of the execution of all "oppressors," which seemed to mean, roughly, everyone over twenty-five who could read, by his intense ignorance of everything that had happened prior to 1970, by his inexplicable and seemingly inexhaustible supply of ready cash, by his recent espousal of self-righteous vegetarianism, which was pure and total except for a dispensation in the case of pepperoni red-hots, by his abandoning in the fridge plastic containers of degenerating tofu, by his rotten music, by his membership in an alleged band called The Virgin Exterminators, by his loutish buddies, by the *names* of his loutish buddies, names which reminded Paul of science fiction about the primitive descendants of those who'd survived the final nuclear holocaust, names like Deet, Wiggo, Munchy, etc., by his diamanté nose-clip and trilby hat, which accessories, in combination with his dark zippered trousers and draped zippered jacket, gave him the appearance of an Hasidic pervert, by his endless readiness to chip in with his mindless two bits concerning: the Baha'i faith, conspiracies, environmental pollution, the injustice of wealth, fibre-rich food, the computer revolution, the oppressive nature of parental authority—*Jesus Christ! Oh, God, was there no end?*—by his festering bedroom, by his pissing on the toilet seat, by his coming into his, Paul's, bathroom and removing his, Paul's, box of Kleenex, by his pallor, his spots, his zits, his dirty long fingernails, his encyclopedic knowledge of carcinogens, his pretentious sipping of Earl Grey tea, his habit of strumming and chording during dinner on an imaginary guitar, of bursting into sudden ape noises, of referring to him, Paul, as "an older person," by ... *Dear Christ! How he hated that malignant cat with its obnoxiously pink arsehole!* Misguidedly saved, but days ago, from the SPCA without his, Paul's, permission. Not for *his* bloody son a kitten but a mangy, baleful presence which was missing one ear and had *things* in the other.

It would, inevitably, shed some of what hair it had left. The hair would, inevitably, stimulate a new range of allergies in Jennifer and Alan. The allergy attacks would strike, inevitably, just as the stars stood in rare and fruitful conjunction leading, inevitably, to yet more nights of throttled rage and Benedryl.

Paul completed the series of faces indicative of amazed contempt, loathing, rage, and resignation, all of which were slightly invalidated by the blobs of shaving foam under his ears and on his Adam's apple, and washed off the razor under the hot tap. Only a friend, he thought with sudden honesty, could describe his pectoral muscles as "muscles." And even such minor movement as brushing his teeth set jiggling what once had been triceps.

Sunlight bathed the hanging plant and lay warm across his bare feet. His feet were sweaty on the cool tiles. The plant always received Martha's special attentions. It hung down in ropes of leaves shaped like miniature bunches of bananas. Peculiar-looking thing. He chomped with sudden savagery on the two pieces of Nikoban gum in the hope that this would release into his bloodstream increased surges of the active ingredient, lobeline sulphate, effective as a smoking deterrent since 1931.

He deliberately thought of breakfast as an antidote to thoughts of a Rothman's King Size. He could have one egg, medium, boiled, and one slice of toast, dry, with black coffee for a calorie count of (140) or a small bowl of Shredded Wheat with no sugar for (150) or a piece of melon, cantaloupe, medium, one half for (60). And then, if at lunch he stuffed his face with alfalfa sprouts or handfuls of grass, he'd be able to splurge at dinner with a nice bit of tasteless chicken with the skin removed.

He could feel bad temper tighten and coil.

The bunches-of-bananas plant made him think with exasperation and affection of Martha and of the generally peculiar and incomprehensible nature of life. Martha would soon be picking off green tomatoes to make chutney, filling the house with the smell of vats of the evil stuff, onions, vinegar. She did it every year. No one ever ate the chutney. Not even Martha. In their various moves, the vintages of preceding years had accompanied them. The basement was full of the stuff. She put little labels on the jars. It seemed to be some blind, seasonal activity like spring-stirred badgers lugging out the old bedding or bowerbirds dashing about in the undergrowth collecting shiny stones, though the chutney-making had, so far as he could see, absolutely no sexual motivation overt or otherwise. It only made her more tired than usual.

Over the shower rail hung a damp and dwarfish pair of pantyhose.

The edge of the washbasin and the countertop were freckled, as they were every day, with some dark orange powder she brushed on her face. He wiped it off with a Kleenex as he did every day. When he put on his bathrobe after his shower, her plastic shower cap, always lodged on top of his bathrobe on the back of the door, would plop onto the floor.

He stood staring at the array of her bottles, unguents and lotions, creams. With its scarlet cap, there stood the bottle, the red label: *Dissolvant de polis d'ongles.*

Norma, the girl he'd come to think of as Polly Ongle, would soon be in the gallery, would soon be busying herself shining up bits of Ethiopian silver, necklaces, pendants, Coptic crosses hammered from Maria Theresa thalers. He could picture her working over the glass top of the display case, the curtain of black hair, the incredibly slim waist cinched by the wide, antique Turcoman belt studded with cornelians, her long fingers sorting and stringing old trade beads and copal amber, following the designs in colour photos in *African Arts* magazine.

Since Christmas Eve, he had tried to stop himself thinking about her hands, those slender fingers.

He sighed as he settled himself on the toilet seat.

He enjoyed the emptiness of the house in the mornings, Martha off to work, the deepening silence left behind by the children after the fights about who'd taken this, touched that, *his* lunch had grapes, well *yours* had an orange, the penetrating *shushings* rising to shouts of *Be quiet! Daddy's sleeping!*

This morning hour seemed the only period of complete peace in the entire day.

He reached round behind him for his copy of *The Penguin Book of Modern Quotations*. He placed the box of Kleenex at his feet. Recently, bowel movements had been accompanied by a stream of clear liquid running from his nose. He had thought at first that this was probably the symptom of some terminal disease, but as nothing had happened further and he felt relatively healthy, he had accepted it as possibly being natural. Though it had never happened to him before and he'd never heard of it happening to anyone else. But, on the other hand, it wasn't the kind of thing likely to crop up in normal conversation.

The bear was worrying him.

He was pleased that he'd had the sense to stow it away in the gallery stockroom before coming home. He could not have stood a morning conversation with Martha about stuffed bears, the questions leading to denunciations and accusations of fecklessness and immaturity, the whole entirely justified harangue shrilling off into the price of sneakers, orthodontistry, day camps, the mounting fines at the Ottawa Public Library because he was so bloody lazy, the price of meat.

"Ha!" he said aloud.

His eye had fallen on an apposite quotation from Frances Cornford concerning Rupert Brooke:

Magnificently unprepared / for the long littleness of life.

He wondered what would have happened to Rupert Brooke if he'd lived long enough to have had a slight paunch, stuff running out of his nose every time he had a crap, and a kid with purple hair. No one was prepared for that. Who could imagine it?

Who in *hell* could he sell a very large bear to?

He wondered what Polly had thought when she'd opened the stockroom and seen six feet three of reared grizzly.

He thought about the Turcoman belt studded with cornelians; he thought about the belt clasping her waist; he tried to stop himself thinking about navels. Shirts or blouses knotted above the waist exposing midriffs, in strong sunshine a down of fine hair glinting...

He had given her the belt for Christmas. He had not told Martha that he had given it to her. He felt vaguely guilty about having given it to her. He felt uncomfortable both about the gift and about keeping it from Martha.

On Christmas Eve, after the flurry of last small sales, he had taken Polly for a Christmas drink. Nothing had happened. They were sitting in a booth at the back of the dimly lit bar. On the wall just above the table was a lamp with a yellowed shade. It cast an almost amber light. She'd been drinking Pernod. She didn't usually speak much; she'd been saying something about the ambassador from Togo who'd been in that morning and who'd been offensively imperious, as he always was.

Her hands were within the pool of amber light. He'd been tranced by the light glinting on the clear nail polish, hinting as she gestured. That was all. Light, glancing. That was all that had happened.

Paul stiffened and stared at the back of the closed bathroom door.

From below, a doorknob, footsteps.

He gripped the book.

A stream of urine drilling into the toilet bowl.

PETER!

Must have persuaded Martha he was sick.

Probably had an exam.

Or gym.

A loud, moist fart.

Orangutan noises.

Bam BAM ba-ba Bam

Bam BAM ba-ba Bam

Burn DOWN the fuck'n town.

A drawer opening, slamming.

"Dad-ee?"

Creakings up the stairs.

"Oh, Dad-deee!"

Probably peering through the open-plan banisters like something from a zoo.

Only feet away.

Outburst of ape-gibbering.

Pyjama bottoms wrinkled round his ankles, breathing carefully through his open mouth, silently, Paul sat tense on the toilet.

* * *

PAUL FOLLOWED what Dr. Leeson called his "auxiliary" into what Dr. Leeson called, always, "the inner sanctum."

"How!" said Dr. Leeson, raising a palm.

Paul smiled.

Dr. Leeson had started greeting Paul in this way some four years earlier after he'd chanced to see, in the Ottawa *Citizen*, a review of an exhibition of Indian *pichwais* in Paul's gallery. Despite references in the review to India and to Krishna, Ganesh, and Shiva, Dr. Leeson had somehow understood the show to concern Indians from North America. Paul thought the greeting was probably a fair sample of dental humour.

"No more gum trouble? Bleeding?"

Paul shook his head.

"No more looseness in the front here?"

"No, just fine."

"That looseness," said Dr. Leeson, "that can be a sign of adult diabetes but periodontal infection's the—that's it, your head here towards me ... *hmm hmmmm—hmm hmmmm* ..."

Warm, peppermint breath.

"... *and broke it apart, Suzanne, Oh my Suzanne!*"

Paul, his eyes pulled open wide, stared over the back of Dr. Leeson's immense hand at the setting sun, an orb in yellow majesty against a wild red deepening to a foreground black. Printed on the blackness of the poster in white were the words:

The goal for my practice is simply to help my patients retain their teeth all of their lives if possible—in maximum comfort, function, health, and aesthetics—and to accomplish this appropriately.

Dr. Leeson settled the small rubber nose mask and pulled the tubes high up onto Paul's cheeks. Paul breathed in the thick, slightly sweet gas waiting for the tingling in his hands and feet to start. The mask quickly became slimy, a rubbery smell mixing with the smell of the gas. His mouth was dry. He closed his eyes.

"... up to the lake?" said the auxiliary.

Sounds of instruments on the plastic tray.

"How you doing?"

Paul grunted.

In the coloured darkness, his mind raced. He made a mental note to speak to the kids about picking at the plaster on the second floor. And about not leaving their skateboards in the hall. After this, the bank. Capital Plastics, another phone call that had to be made.

"Relax," said Dr. Leeson, "we're doing good."

As always when the noise started, he felt panicky, felt he must be insane to trust a man younger than himself who wore plaid trousers, felt he *must* check the man's credentials, actually *read* those framed certificates. He felt that no really responsible doctor would wear cowboy boots to work; there was something about the man, something about his large red face and blond eyelashes, which suggested the Ontario Beef Marketing Board; this Leeson, he realized, in whose hands he was, frequented roadhouses and rode mechanical bulls.

The steel was in his mouth.

They were talking at a dark remove from him; he had a sudden conviction their relationship was more than dental.

He concentrated on picturing the silent kitchen where for breakfast he'd eaten half a cantaloupe; he conjured up the Boston fern in its earthenware pot, the sleek chrome-and-black-plastic design of the Italian espresso machine Martha had bought him for Christmas, the dark aroma of the coffee beans in the waxed-paper Van Houte bag, cluttering the fridge door the invitations to birthday parties, the shopping lists, medical appointment cards, crayonings of intergalactic battle, all held by Happy Face magnets.

Until he'd heard Peter slamming out of the house, Paul had remained hidden in the bathroom.

On the kitchen counter, beside a glass that had contained orange juice, Peter had left a library book. The book was in French. Judging from his report cards and the comments of Mrs. Addison on the last parent-teacher evening, he'd be entirely incapable of reading it. The book was entitled *C'est Bon la sexualité* and contained diagrams of wombs.

Sitting there in the whiteness of the kitchen, the sunshine, the silence, Paul had been moved by a surge of pity and compassion.

He was swallowing water; could feel wetness on his cheek.

He tried to think, deliberately, of what was to be done that day.

Letters to go out, bulk mailing, for the exhibition of Shona stone carving. The photocopy place. Capital Plastics to price lucite bases for the Mossi flutes. Rosenfeld in Washington to deal with over the crate of pre-Columbian pots; Customs. A new rubber ring-thing—what *was* the word?—rubber *belt* for the carpet part of the vacuum cleaner.

The carpet in the gallery was coir matting, suitably simple and primitive, hard on the vacuum cleaner's wheels and brushes.

The word "coir" made him think of "copra," "coitus," "copulation."

Nearly everything did.

The current exhibition at the Uhuru Gallery of Primitive Arts was a collection, on consignment, of modern Makonde carvings, every single one of which he loathed. Preceding them had been exhibitions of contemporary "temple" carvings from India, shadow puppets from Indonesia, *papier-mâché* anthropomorphic frogs from Suriname, garish clay airplanes from Mexico, and drawings from the remote highlands of New Guinea executed in Magic Marker.

Soon it would be twenty years since his life had taken the turn that had led him to where he was now. Okoro Training College. Port Harcourt. Sometimes when he looked through the old snapshots in the chocolate box he felt he was looking at preposterous strangers: Martha with long black hair tied back with a ribbon; he wearing ridiculous British khaki shorts and knee socks; Martha standing with Joséph, the houseboy, in his shabby gown, with his long, splayed toes; Mr. Oko Enwo in his academic gown; he and Joséph posing on either side of a dead snake slung over the compound clothesline.

Strangers.

Sun-bleached strangers.

At first, the gallery had done well; he had sold, cheaply, many of the good carvings he'd collected in Nigeria. But then what small supply there was dried up. The young men were drifting from the ceremonies of the dance to the beer-hall bands and city discos. The world he'd been privileged to glimpse on holiday expeditions to those Igbo villages upcountry all those years ago had been even then a world close to extinction, a world about to be swept away on a tide of plastic sandals, cheap stainless-steel watches from Russia, Polaroid cameras, calculators.

The Uhuru Gallery, which had opened with passion and vision, had become little more than an emporium of Third-World tourist junk. The only genuine carving on his walls was a stern Bambara mask whose austerity was a daily rebuke.

He dreamed, sometimes still, of the journeys upcountry jammed in the back of the rackety Bedford lorries that served as buses, journeys of dust and shimmering heat which ended in the packed excitement of the village commons surrounded by the mud walls and thatch of the compounds.

Often he had been offered a seat of honour among the elders in the shade, while Martha had been packed in with the women and the glistening children, the sun splintering through the leaves and fronds of the trees beyond the compounds.

And then the tranced hours of the festival, glasses of palm wine cloudy green, the sun beating down and the air pulsing with the rhythms of the four drummers, quivering with the notes of the gongs and the village xylophone, shush-shuffle of seed rattles. Muzzle-loaders exploding into the blue signalled the approach of the procession from the Men's House of the cloth-and raffia-clad masks—*beke, igri, mma ji, mkpe, umurumu*—individual dancers breaking from the chorus to raise the red dust until their feet were lost in the haze.

Then the slow unfolding of the story-songs, the high call-and-response of the two leaders, the great wave of sound from behind the painted masks. And between the stories, the masked dancers burrowing into the crowd to demand "dashes," the lines of *akparakpa* dancers in parody of female dancing, each man wearing thick rolls of women's plastic waist-beads, buttocks stuck out, greeted by the women with shrieks of *aiy aiy aiy aiy aiy*. Until there seemed no end, the drums sounding inside one's head, the notes of the xylophone vibrating, gong and slit drum, dust, sun, the praise-sayers, the singing.

"Mr. Denton?"

"Umm?"

The chair rising to an upright position.

"Mr. Denton! You're all finished now. I'm going to leave you just on the oxygen for a couple of minutes, okay? Like we usually do? Okay?"

He opened his eyes.

Yellow. Red. Black patterned with white marks.

"Fine. Sorry. Yes, sure."

He lay staring at the poster of the setting sun against the wild red sky.

* * *

THE FRAGRANCE from a tangle of wild roses in front of a house on Gilmour Street lay heavily on the humid air. Paul stopped to breathe it in; it was almost indecent. His teeth felt foreign. Exploring them with his tongue, he turned onto Elgin Street. After the darkness of the gas, after the strange shapes of chairs, carpets, counters, the buttons in the elevator, had once again assumed their form and function and steadied into place, he always felt almost resurrected when he walked out into the world.

Sunlight glittering on spokes and rims. Back straight, fingertips of one hand on top of the handlebars, a girl on a ten-speed bike coasting in towards the red light. White top, blue linen skirt, she jutted like a ship's figurehead. Just before she drew level, she swooped to apply her brakes. Staring into an abyss of pristine cleavage, Paul stumbled over an Airedale terrier and, babbling apologies, shot through the doorway into Mike's Milk.

After prolonged dental torture, nerves stretched to breaking point, *one* cigarette, he reasoned, was understandable and forgivable; he was not really letting himself down; he would probably throw away the rest of the package. Or perhaps ration them judiciously, using them in conjunction with the Nikoban gum to effect a more *rational* withdrawal; it was, he thought, an unrealistic and possibly injurious strain on the system to diet, jog, and stop smoking all at the same time.

With some five minutes in hand before the bank opened, he strolled down Elgin Street. The cigarette tasted so wonderful that he felt he ought to be smoking it through a long onyx holder. His trousers seemed definitely looser at the waist. He crossed against red lights.

Standing in the line-up idly watching the top halves of tellers, he thought about the girl with the huge hoop earrings, wisps of hair escaping from her collapsing bun, the absent eyes. Unless she was in the vault, she wasn't on duty. Oddly *Victorian*-looking girl. As one might imagine the daughter of an impoverished rural vicar in an old novel. He suspected she was profoundly crazy and was attracted by the idea of whatever mayhem or enforced redistribution of wealth she might be capable of. Once when he hadn't seen her in the bank for some weeks, he'd asked her if she'd been sick.

Oh, no, she'd said, *I'm a floater.*

He still wondered what she'd meant and why he kept on thinking about it.

Despite the air conditioning, the cheques were wilting in his hand. Beside him, a rack containing deposit slips, brochures about Registered Retirement Savings Plans, copies of that month's Royal Bank Letter entitled: *Regarder la mort en face*. The next shuffle forward brought him round the curve of the furry blue rope and closer to the counter; he stood watching the outline of panties beneath the slacks of the teller who was waiting at the central cage for cash.

He walked on up Elgin past the National Gallery and the National Arts Centre. Before crossing towards the Château Laurier, he paused to glance in the window of the Snow Goose at the latest display of native Canadian arts, alleged Haida masks, horrible great green lumps of Eskimo soapstone. Not, he thought, with sudden heaviness of spirit, that he could afford to feel superior; they were no worse than Indonesian frogs with hats on. He decided to phone the Snow Goose later to see if they'd like a nice grizzly bear; just the thing to pull in tourists and their kids. Stick it out on the sidewalk opposite the London double-decker tour bus.

He had promised Jennifer and Alan to bring home those plastic things from the bank for saving a dollar's worth of pennies and had forgotten; he had promised Jennifer bubblegum with Star Wars cards inside. If he could have raised ten thousand dollars, he'd have bid the night before in Montreal on all the Sepik River lots, bid against Mendelson, and against Lang, Klein, too. What a delight it would have been to have mounted a genuine exhibition, authentic tribal art, masks, and boards made long before the luxury boats started pulling into the river-bank villages to disgorge the corruption of tourists. But the whole game was climbing beyond his reach. He thought of the dinner he'd had on rue St. Denis before the auction, a street completely changed since his day. And walking along Sussex Drive towards the Uhuru, he found himself thinking for some reason or other of a rented room in a house on rue Jeanne Mance.

Strange that after all those years he could still see the room so clearly after he'd been in it only once; strange, too, that he had only the vaguest memory of the girl. He could see the frayed central hole in the threadbare carpet, the paperbacks on the mantelpiece between two white-painted bricks, empty Chianti bottles strung above, the mobile, tarot cards, Braque poster of white dove, vast glass carboy containing moulting bulrushes, the brass incense-burner in the shape of a Chinese lion . . .

He remembered how intensely excited he'd been returning with her to her room after an afternoon drinking Québerac—*that* was what he remembered so clearly. The intensity of it. It wasn't simply sexual anticipation but something more complicated, more difficult to think about, mysterious. A room—bed, hotplate, washbasin—was so much more private than a house. Being in a stranger's room, a room that contained the bed in which she slept, a room which was furnished with the things that were hers, entering into that privacy was somehow at that moment more intimate, more exciting than nakedness. There had been a pink facecloth, he remembered, draped over the edge of the basin.

It was the revealing, the unfolding, the unfurling, the opening up of what had been closed that excited him, the sense that this intimacy—difficult to put this into words, difficult to think of the feeling—the sense that this intimacy could draw him into a new . . . well, *current* suggested the sort of thing, a current that would carry him out from the mundane shores, sweep him into the violent invigoration of white water.

So far as he could remember, the intimacy had dissipated in suddenly awkward talk. Of what, he wondered?

Some comically pretentious nonsense.

The wisdom of the Upanishads, perhaps.

In those now-distant undergraduate days at Sir George Williams University, he'd spent much of his time with the arty crowd in the various cafés on Stanley Street, the Riviera, Carmen's, The Pam-Pam, The Seven Steps, Marvin's Kitchen. Sitting for hours over a single cup of coffee, he'd yearned after the arty girls, the girls who sat with guys who'd published poems. Arty girls then had all looked much the same. Hair very long and straight with bangs, faces mask-like with makeup, eyes rimmed with black. Black turtlenecks, black skirts, black mesh stockings. The way they all looked, it all had something to do with Paris, Sartre, existentialism, and a movie starring Juliette Greco. He wondered if Sartre was still alive and hoped not.

And the artiest ones of all, he remembered, wore green nail polish and white lipstick. How had he forgotten that? That lipstick. And ballet slippers. And handmade silver earrings. And carried huge handmade leather bags. And they'd all looked anorexic and temptingly *unwholesome*, as though they'd lend themselves, impassively, to amazing sexual practices. Not that Polly Ongle was at all like those girls. But there was something of all that about her. Something of that sort of stance. She was, he suspected, the same *sort* of girl.

* * *

“*Tabarouette*!” said the waitress, depositing on their table a bowl of potato chips. “Me, I’m scared of lightning!”

Turning the glass vase-thing upside down, she lighted the candle inside.

“Cider?” she repeated.

“No?” said Paul.

“Oh, well,” said Norma, “I’ll have what-do-you-call-it that goes cloudy.”

“Pernod,” said Paul. “And a Scotch, please.”

“Ice?”

“They feel squishy,” said Norma, stretching out her leg.

“Umm?”

“My sandals.”

He looked down at her foot.

It was Happy Hour in the bar on the main floor of the Château Laurier. People drifting in were pantomiming distress and amazement as they eased out of sodden raincoats or used the edge of their hands to wipe rain from eyebrows and foreheads. Men were seating themselves gingerly and loosening from their knees the cling of damp cloth; women were being casually dangerous with umbrellas. Necks were being mopped with handkerchiefs; spectacles were being polished with bar napkins.

“Well,” said Paul, raising his glass, “home and dry. Cheers! Thank God for that old umbrella of yours.”

She smiled and made a small gesture with her glass.

“What’s this obsession you seem to have with cider?” said Paul.

“It’s not an obsession. It’s just that it doesn’t have chemicals in it, that’s all. It’s just straight juice.”

“Well, not *quite* straight,” said Paul.

She shrugged.

“But I don’t use alcohol much at all usually.”

“Not like this stuff,” said Paul, tapping his glass. “It’s supposed to be full of some sort of stuff—estrogen?—no, a word something like that. *Esters*, is it? Some sort of *oils*. Begins with 'e,' I think. Anyway, supposed to be *very* bad for you."

"You shouldn't do things that are bad for you."

"Well, that sounds a bit boring," said Paul, smiling. "Now and again, things that are bad for you are fun."

Norma stirred her ice cubes with the plastic paddle.

"No?" said Paul.

"Maybe," she said.

Small talk, chat, flirtation, all were uphill work with Polly. Silence didn't seem to bother her one bit. She was usually rather taciturn and—not grumpy exactly—but perhaps "contained" was the word. Or "detached." She gave the impression of being always an observer. She reminded him uncomfortably at times of Jennifer. Once, when Jennifer had been four or five, he'd taken her to a zoo where she'd considered the llama over which he was enthusing and had said,

"What's it for?"

He was painfully aware that he seemed unable to strike the right tone, that his chatter sounded less flirtatious than avuncular. The whole situation made him feel like an actor in a hopeless play, plot implausible, dialogue stilted.

He glanced again at the dangling sandal. They were rather elegant. They were what he thought were called buffalo thongs, just a sort of leather ring which held the sandal on the foot by fitting round the big toe. Her toes were long and distinctly spaced, nor cramped together, the little toes not at all deformed by shoes. He wondered how that was possible. They were almost like fingers. He felt an urge to trace their length with his fingertip.

"Pardon?"

"I said, 'Do you know where the washroom is?'"

He watched her threading her way through the tables. The black harem pants were loose and baggy but in places, as she moved, very much *not* loose and baggy. All through the hot, close afternoon he'd been disturbingly aware of them. Her slimness, the tautness of her body, her carriage, she moved like a dancer; the silk scarf knotted round her waist as a belt added to the suggestion. In the patches of spotlighting, the white cotton top glowed blue and purple.

It was irritating him that he couldn't remember the name of the carcinogens that, according to Peter, Scotch was supposed to contain. He had, God knew, heard it often enough. And Polly's saying that she didn't "use alcohol much" also reminded him of Peter; it was an expression always used by Peter in some such formula as, "Older people use alcohol but young people prefer soft drugs"; the expression irritated him on a variety of fronts.

At the next table, the two ghastly government women were still trading acronyms. The older, dykey woman's voice was husky. In front of her was a large, round tin of tobacco and a packet of Zig-Zag cigarette papers. Her lipstick was thickly applied and shiny; when her face was in the light from the candle, he could see a faint smear of lipstick on her front teeth. Her bechained spectacles hung down the front of her beige linen suit. She kept relighting the cigarettes with a flaring Zippo lighter. As she talked, she was scattering ashes. Paul thought that, in some way he didn't understand, she was being cruel; there was something in the conversation of cat and mouse. The younger, softer-looking woman had fluffy hair and was wearing a blazer; the brass buttons glinted.

Oh, I do so agree! said the older, rapacious one. *David's a heaven guy. Just a heaven guy! But there's the problem of Beth, baby girl.*

But Beth's just not a mainstream person.

Well, yes, darling, agreed—and therewith you win the coconut.

Paul signalled to the waitress for another round.

What Beth needs, baby girl, is a vote of confidence from life.

But I thought there was consensus . . .

Darling, said the other, sticking out the tip of her tongue and picking off a shred of tobacco and then leaning forward and placing her hands over the younger woman's hand, *let's approach what one might call the nub.*

He saw Polly coming back through the tables and stood up.

"Look, I'll just be a minute," he said. "Got to go myself."

Once out of the bar, he wandered into the hotel lobby in search of a public phone. He was directed past a florist's and a showcase exhibiting portraits by Karsh. He found that he'd travelled more or less in a circle and had ended up at the rear entrance to the bar. The phones were between the two washrooms. As he was looking for a quarter, a woman in an elaborate bridal outfit came out of the washroom. Two other brides followed her. Pinned on the bosoms of the brides were buttons the size of saucers which said: Happy Occasions Inc.

"Honey?" an American man was saying. "Yeah. I'm in Ottawa. It's the capital of Canada. We're coming into Kennedy tomorrow in the morning."

Paul listened to the ringing.

"Martha? Everything okay?

"I'm in the Château Laurier having a drink.

"No, just a bit damp. I managed to get in here before it really got started. And you? Did you get a cab?

"What? Can't hear you. It's all crackly and your voice keeps fading.

"Well, that's what I'm phoning for. I'm not sure exactly when. I've arranged to meet a guy here to look at some photographs of carvings he wants to sell. If he ever shows up in all this. So I don't really know.

"No, no. You go ahead. Eat with the kids and if I get back I'll get a sandwich or something. And if I'm going to be late, I'll probably get something out somewhere. Okay? So don't worry about it."

“No. There’s no reason why I should be. But if I am, don’t wait up for me. But I won’t be.

“Don’t forget tomorrow’s *what*?

“*Garbage* day! Thought you said ‘Harbour.’ Yes, I’ll put it out when I get back.

“The meat tray in the fridge—I got that bit.

“Salami. Good.

“What do you mean?

“How *can* I be careful? Please, for God’s sake, don’t start one of these. If lightning is going to strike me, Martha, what can I do to prevent it?

“Yes, okay. I promise not to go near metal street lights.

“No. I’m not just saying it.

“Love you, too. Bye.

“What?

“Alan lost his *what*?

“I’ll speak to him tomorrow.

“Bye.

“Yes.

“Bye.’”

He wandered back into the hotel lobby and pushed out through the revolving doors. The wind was chilly. He stood under the noisy canvas awning. The rain was still lashing down with a violence that reminded him of the rains in Africa; it was as if the asphalt of Wellington Street had quickened into a broad river. He stood watching the rain pock the surface of the sheets and rills of water flooding down towards Rideau Street.

Just off the main lobby near the entrance to the bar were the windows of an art gallery. He stood there. It had recently changed hands. The stock, however, looked much the same. He stood staring at all the landscapes, the still lifes, the flowers in vases, the paintings of decrepit barns and split-rail fences, the paintings involving horses, maple syrup, logs.

He could have told her he was sitting out the storm with Norma without bothering her in the slightest. There was no reason not to have told her. Amazingly, she seemed to think of Norma as a pleasant-enough girl who was useful in the gallery; she'd once said that Norma would look so much more presentable if only she'd do something about her hair.

He stared at a large, gilt-framed picture, which was exhibited on an easel; lumpy purple mountains, the central lake, the maple trees. It could as easily have been the other view: lumpy mountains, central lake, foreground rock, jack pines. It was all the same, the same sort of thing as Eskimo carvings and frogs from Suriname with hats on.

After the Makonde, the Shona stone.

As he walked through the archway and into the bar, he saw that the two government women had left, and felt an odd sense of relief.

"It's still absolutely pouring out there," he said, sitting down and hitching the chair closer. "And the sky's still black with it. Hasn't that waitress come yet?"

"Paul?"

"What?"

"You know, Paul," she said, leaning forward to rest her arms on the table, "I've been thinking."

"What about?"

"You really *ought* to take better care of yourself."

"Pardon?"

"Well, you can't just ignore it."

"Ignore what?"

"The trouble you had with your . . . your chest. Those pains."

"You're losing me. How did we get onto *this*?"

"What we were saying before. About cider. About drinking things that can damage your body."

"Oh! I see. Well, what are you trying to suggest? That I drink too much?"

"No, of course not. But . . ."

"Sound," said Paul, opening his jacket and tapping himself over the heart, "as a bell. Lively as a two-year-old. Chirpy as a cricket. Fit as the proverbial fiddle."

"Don't *joke* about it!"

He stared at her across the table, at her eyes, the long eyelashes somehow accentuated by the glow from the candle below. The candlelight was picking up auburn tints in the sweep of her black hair.

"What's all this great seriousness in aid of, Norma?"

"You don't have to treat me as if I'm a child!"

"I wasn't aware that I was. I don't. But what I mean is, what brought all this on? I mean, so suddenly?"

"No reason."

"Well, what are you so annoyed about?"

She shrugged.

"Norma?"

She concentrated on stirring about the remains of her ice cubes.

"Hello?"

"It shouldn't take a genius," she said, "to work it out."

The waitress placed the Pernod and Scotch on the brown napkins, glanced through the checks on her tray, propped their check between the bowl of chips and a triangular cardboard sign advertising a specialty of the house, a drink involving rye whisky, piña colada mix, orange juice, egg whites, and a maraschino cherry.

It was called Sunset Flamenco.

He couldn't think of anything to say.

Norma was sitting back in her chair, head bent, plying the plastic paddle. He stared at the white line of the part in her hair.

He felt—he wasn't sure *what* he felt. It was many, many years since he'd played verbal footsie with girls in bars. If she'd meant what he *thought* she'd meant, the situation seemed to be opening up possibilities he'd tried to stop himself thinking about for months. But it was entirely possible that she hadn't meant to imply what he thought she'd meant to imply, that the inferences he'd drawn were influenced by desire, by watching all afternoon the folds and furrows of the matte-black material of those harem pants . . . but it certainly *felt* as if the inference he'd drawn was what had been intended.

He drained his glass of Scotch.

"Ah . . ." he said, "you know what I think would be a good idea? If it's all right with you, I mean. If you haven't got anything planned. Norma?"

"What?"

"Well, as it's still pouring, if we had dinner here together. What do you think?"

"No, I haven't got anything planned."

"So would you like to?"

"Why not?" she said. "Sure."

"Good!" he said. 'I'd like that."

He glanced at his watch.

"It's a bit early yet," he said, "so if you think our bodies could stand the strain, we'll sit for a bit over another drink. Okay?"

She nodded.

He wished he hadn't used the word "bodies."

He lighted a cigarette.

"I thought you'd quit," she said.

He blew out a long, deep jet of smoke.

"I am in the process of quitting."

"Is it—" she said.

"I think—" he said. "Sorry. What were you . . ."

"No," she said.

"I was just going to say that I think there's supposed to be a band."

"Where?"

"In the restaurant."

“What sort of band?”

“I don’t know. A dance band, I suppose. It’s supposed to be quite good. The restaurant, I mean.”

“Do you like dancing?” she said.

“Not much, I’m afraid. Do you?”

“It depends.”

“You *look* like a dancer.”

“What do you mean?”

“A professional dancer.”

She smiled.

“What’s funny?”

“I was thinking about you dancing.”

“So what’s funny about that?”

“I couldn’t imagine it.”

“Why not.?”

She shrugged.

“Well, in the gallery you always seem so . . . oh, I don’t know.”

“Seem so what?”

“Well . . . *dignified*.”

“What do you mean, exactly, by ‘dignified?’”

“I mean . . . I couldn’t imagine you dancing.”

“Let me tell you,” he said, “that in the days of my youth . . .”

“You’re not old,” she said.

“Well, of course I’m not *old* but . . .”

“You’re *not*,” she said. “You shouldn’t say that.”

She was staring at him with uncomfortable intensity.

He decided it would be a very good idea to go to the washroom again.

It was empty and echoey in the washroom and smelled of the cakes of cloying air-freshener stuff in the urinals, a smell that he was rather ashamed of not disliking. He examined himself in the mirrors and combed his hair. All he’d had for lunch had been a container of yogurt. He was beginning to feel the effects of the Scotch.

He thought of Polly's eyelashes.

Like Bambi.

What else *could* she have meant?

To the blank tile wall facing him, he said in a deliberately boomy voice,

"Bum like a plum."

In the farthest cubicle, someone stirred, shoes grating on tiled floor.

Paul coughed.

Facing them just inside the entrance of the Canadian Grill as they waited for the maître d' stood a sort of Islamic tent.

It was octagonal. It was large enough to have slept two. But higher. It rose to an ornate finial. Or rather, it was *tent-like*. Gauzy, chiffony stuff was stretched over the eight ribs. The shape suggested something of the dome of a mosque or a Mogul helmet. On a platform inside stood a huge basket of artificial flowers.

Paul stared at this amazing thing wondering who could have imagined such a folly in a Canadian National Railways Hotel in a room whose decor seemed otherwise baronial.

Or it might have been intended to suggest a miniature bandstand.

Or a gazebo.

"I don't think I'm dressed for this," whispered Norma.

"Nonsense," he said. "You look beautiful."

He smiled at her.

"As a matter of fact," he said, "you *always* look beautiful."

He followed her down the acres of tartan carpet, the khaki army-surplus bag bumping on her hip. Sticking out of it towards him was the shiny, black handle of a hairbrush. The maître d' was a short, gorilla-shaped man in a bulging tuxedo. He kept hitching at his white gloves. His face was battered and, as he walked, he moved his head and shoulders as if shadow-boxing.

At a table at the edge of the dance floor, the maître d' heaved out Norma's chair with his left hand and, raising his right, with his gloved fingers fumbled a silent snap. They sat and were overwhelmed by waiters. Waiters seemed to outnumber customers. The waiters wore tuxedos but the servers and their servitors wore brown outfits with orange lapels; the width of the lapels seemed to indicate gradations of rank. Narrow lapels poured glasses of water. Wide lapels placed baskets of bread. Tuxedos inquired if they desired an apéritif.

"Scotch," said Paul.

"What a weird man!" said Norma.

"Which?"

"That head waiter."

"He's a retired boxer," said Paul.

"How do you know?"

"Undefeated CN/CP Bantam Champion."

"Really?"

"They use him for thumping temperamental chefs."

"Oh, he isn't!"

"Customer complaints a specialty."

"I've never been in a place like this," said Norma.

It was as if the decorator had attempted to marry vague notions of a baronial Great Hall with the effects of an old movie theatre. Diners formed islands in the room's vast emptiness.

"Wine?" said Paul to the waiter. "Oh, I would think so but we haven't decided yet what we want to eat."

They opened the padded leatherette menus.

"*L'omble de l'Arctique*," said Paul.

"Oh, look!" said Norma. "Behind you, look!"

"What *is* an Arctic omble?"

"Paul, look!"

Waiters were converging.

A party of nine, all of whom seemed to have ordered roast beef.

Narrow lapels were hurrying in bearing aloft silver-coloured covered dishes; servers were pushing up to the table wheeled heating grills; servitors were lighting the gas. Wide lapels were taking the dishes from the narrow lapels and were handing them to the tuxedos, who plucked off the domed lids and slid the dishes onto the flames, poking artistically at the contents with spoon and fork until the gravy was boiling briskly.

An atmosphere of muted hysteria gripped the drama. There was much tense French-Canadian cursing. Chafing-dish lids were left with an edge in the flames so that narrow lapels burned their fingers removing them; a Yorkshire pudding fell on the floor; lapel bumped into lapel; dishes forgotten on the flames sent up fatty smoke as the gravy burned onto them.

"Tell him!" said Norma.

"Monsieur?"

"Your napkin thing," said Paul, pointing. "On your arm. Appears to be on fire."

Norma was hidden behind her menu giggling.

"Value for money, eh?" he said.

He was beginning to feel merrily sloshed.

The smouldering napkin was rushed from the room in a covered dish.

The acrid smell lingered.

One of the waiters was touring the table with a gravy boat; his progress was sacerdotal. Each time he stooped to dispense horseradish, his abbreviated jacket rose, revealing under his rucked shirt the elasticized top of his underwear.

"You know what it's all like?" said Paul. "It's like a Fernandel movie or Jacques Tati. That film he made about a restaurant. What was that called? The one that came before *Traffic*?"

"Are they French?"

"The reason *is*," said Paul, "the reason it's all a bit off-centre, is because it's a railway hotel. All these Bowery Boys aren't real waiters. They're all guys off *trains*—the guys that put the hotdogs in the microwave ovens at the take-out counter place. The guys that are grumpy about serving you once you've passed Kingston because it takes them two hundred miles with their lips moving to fill in the sheets about how many sandwiches they've sold. Which are full of ice crystals anyway. And after years of loyal service on the Montreal-Toronto run, they're all rewarded with a job here on land. Which is why there's so many of them. And look! Here he is. He's coming again."

They watched the bobbing and weaving of the maître d' as he led a couple to a nearby table.

"The Caboose Kid," said Paul.

"What?"

"That's the name he used to fight under. No. That's not quite right, is it? *Kid Caboose*! That's it. That's better."

"Honestly!" said Norma. "You're so *silly*."

Head on one side, she was considering him.

"You really get into it, don't you?"

"What do I 'get into'?"

"All this stuff you make up."

He shrugged and smiled at her.

"Do I?"

He was beginning to find it difficult to keep his mind on what his lips were saying. For some moments, he'd been aware of her leg touching his beneath the table; this contact was generating a most marvellous warmth. The play of the matte-black material filled his mind, furling, fitting plump, furrowed. Through his lower body and down his thighs seeped a different kind of warmth—luxurious, languorous—as if he were bleeding heavily from the hot centre of a painless wound.

He knew that he ought to be saying something.

He glanced across at her.

"Oh! Are those new?"

"What?"

"Those earrings. Hadn't noticed them."

With the back of her hand, she lifted and steered away the weight of her hair. This movement and the cocking of her head, tensed the tendon down the side of her neck and raised her left breast towards him.

What he had intended as an *mmmm*! of appreciation broke from him as something closer to a groan.

"It's lovely," he said.

"Vous avez choisi?"

Startled, Paul glanced up.

"Pardon? Oh, I don't know. Ah, Norma?"

"Oh," she said, and opened the menu again.

"Oh, I don't know. I'd like a steak, I think."

"L'entrecôte, madame?"

"I guess so."

"Monsieur?"

"*L'omble de l'Arctique à l'infusion d'anis*," said Paul. "What is it?"

"L'omble de l'Arctique," said the waiter, "it is a fish."

"What kind of fish?"

"That's a pink fish."

"Pink," repeated Paul.

"Inside the fish," said the waiter, gesturing with pad and ballpoint, "is pink."

An arm removed the ashtray and replaced it with a clean one; cutlery was set; the *sommelier* performed upon foil and cork. Paul duly tasted the grotesquely overpriced Mouton Cadet, remembering when it had been available for the present price of a pack of cigarettes and not much of a bargain even then.

She raised her glass and touched it to his.

Bambi.

Light danced off the polished tops of the salt-and-pepper shakers, flashed off cutlery. He watched the wink of light inside his glass, the play of pinks cast on the tablecloth. He was aware of light and shadow above him. He was, he realized, more inebriated than he'd thought. He tried the word "inebriated" inside his head. It seemed to work perfectly.

The brown sleeve placed under him a shrimp cocktail.

He stared down into it.

"Et pour madame, les hors d'oeuvres variés."

The shrimps were minuscule, grayish, and frayed. He speared one. It was limp and didn't taste of anything at all. He would have sworn under oath that the sauce was a combination of ketchup and Miracle Whip.

"It's not good?" said Norma.

"Try it," said Paul. "Here. I'll put some on your plate."

"No," she said. "Just give me some on your fork."

Holding the fork poised, she said,

"Paul?"

"What?"

"You didn't really think I'd mind, did you?"

"Mind what?"

"Using your fork," she said. "I don't."

He watched her lips close over the tines.

From behind the stage curtains with their flounced valance, a tuning "A" sounded three times on a piano. It was approximated by a guitar.

She wrinkled her nose.

"It's not special, is it?" she said, handing back the fork.

Three ascending trumpet notes sounded.

The last one cracked.

The curtains drew back to reveal the resident band. They all wore baby-blue blazers and blue shirts with blue ruffles. They looked dispirited. The trumpet player spoke too close to the microphone so that the only words Paul caught were what sounded like "block and tackle" and "for your dining pleasure" and then they launched into "The Tennessee Waltz."

After they'd worked it through, there was scattered applause.

"Oh, groan," said Norma. "Groan. Groan."

"This place," said Paul, "is beginning to make me feel about ready for my pension."

"You know what we ought to do?"

"What?"

"Well, if you feel like it, I mean."

"Like what?"

She paused.

"I think," she said, "that you're beginning to get spliffed."

"Spliffed? Oh! Certainly not," he said. "Here, in an amazing exhibition of total clarity, is precisely what you said. You said that you'd like to do something if I felt like it but you didn't say what. You see?"

"Go somewhere where there's some non-plastic music."

"Where's that?"

"I know somewhere. Would you like to?"

"A magical mystery tour?"

Accented with rattles, woodblocks, and a cowbell, the band started hacking at something vaguely Latin-American.

"Well," said Paul, "nothing could be much worse than this."

"Oh, look!" she said. "I think this is us."

A wheeled grill was advancing on their table; domed dishes held on high were heading in their direction; servitors were congregating.

The mummery commenced.

When bits of this and clumps of that had been arranged and rearranged, the plates were set before them.

"Et, voilà!" said the waiter.

Beside the chunk of fish was a plump greyish thing whose outer layers were almost translucent; these translucent leaves were heavily veined; they looked like veined membranes, like folded wings; whatever it was resembled the cooked torso of a giant insect.

They studied it.

"Could it be one of those things you get in salads?"

"Oh!" said Paul. 'An endive? I suppose it *could* be. Braised?"

It reminded him of the nightmare things he'd batted down with a tennis racquet in their bedroom in Port Harcourt. He pressed it with his fork and yellow liquid issued.

He pushed the plate away.

He summoned a waiter.

He studied the brandy's oily curve on the side of the glass. Changing with the angle of the glass, the brandy's colours reminded him of stain and varnish, of the small chest of drawers he'd promised to strip and refinish. He tipped and tilted the glass; oak, amber, the colours in the centre exactly the colours of the patina on rubbed and handled carvings.

After the Makonde carvings, the Shona stone.

And after the Shona stone, Rosenfeld's pre-Columbian pots, and after Rosenfeld's pots . . . he looked down a dreary vista of crafts elevated to the status of art wondering if the honest thing wouldn't be a return to teaching.

He thought of the years after his return from Nigeria, years no longer cushioned by a salary from CIDA and a government house, the years he'd spent languishing at Lisgar Collegiate. What with the compelling arguments of Martha, the baby, the mortgage payments, he'd tried to persuade himself that he cared about teaching and the minutiae of school life, but the future had yawned before him, mountains of exercise books in which, until the age of sixty-five, he'd be distinguishing with a red pencil between "their" and "there."

Uhuru!

He grunted.

And after Rosenfeld's pots . . .

He was startled by the applause.

A girl had come out onto the stage. She was blonde and pretty. She was wearing a long green dress, the sort of dress that Paul thought of as a "party dress." Her voice was small but sweet.

He found that he was humming along audibly with the melody of "These Foolish Things." And then began to find his phrasing diverging from hers. He was so used to Ella Fitzgerald's version of the song that he was anticipating adornment and shading which this girl could never reach. Pretty but somehow asexual, she was a crunchy-granola girl, an advertisement girl, impossibly wholesome, a toothpaste girl, under her party dress and white immaculate undies as waxen and undifferentiated as a doll.

He breathed in the brandy's rising bouquet. Opening the pack of Rothman's King Size, his fingers fumbled to discover that there were only two left. He somehow had smoked twenty-three cigarettes since ten o'clock in the morning.

The girl was singing "Ev'ry Time We Say Goodbye."

When, he wondered, could he have smoked them?

Tried to recall; tried to count.

He was moved and moving with the melody, could feel his head swaying.

He closed his eyes .

. . . how strange the change
from major to minor
ev'ry time we say goodbye.

Behind the girl's voice, he seemed to hear Ella's voice, dark and brooding.

He'd always liked the song, thought it the best of Cole Porter's, the least offensively clever, one of the few where intelligence and emotion seemed to marry.

He gazed into the snifter, amber light fragmenting, sipped.

The song was drawing to its close .

. . . from major to minor
ev'ry time we say goodbye.

He thought about that. Admired the subtlety, the poetry, admired the line's *movement*. Was "elegance" the word he was looking for? Partly. It was partly that. But it was also *true*. Things *did* move from major to minor. Though in *his* case it was more minor to major, more a question of hello—the long day in the Uhuru and then the anticipation on the homeward journey, *the seeing her*. But major to minor, minor to major—that didn't, so far as he could see, change the *point*. Change the point of what the song *said*.

He suddenly found himself groping.

What?

Said?

Said what?

He considered the possibility of his being drunk. His thoughts seemed to be moving slowly, thickly, as if viscous, somehow like the brandy in the glass. Which added up to roughly (200) calories. He patted his pockets, listening for the rattle of the Nikoban gum. He attempted the painful mental arithmetic of computing the number of calories he'd drunk; it was hard; large numbers were involved; it seemed to total somewhere in the region of (2,000).

Not taking into account two bowls of potato chips.

And shrimps slathered in mayonnaise.

The girl was singing "Misty."

He closed his eyes again.

I get misty,

she sang,

just holding your hand . . .

Suddenly, he felt like crying.

It was true.

Yes, it was true.

Even after all these years, he *did*, he *did* get misty. Not that there weren't other parts of her he'd like to hold, and much more frequently. But sometimes still—after dinner, say, when the kids were in bed, and they strolled up in the twilight towards the yellow bloom of the corner-store window for an ice cream or an Oh Henry bar, along the sidewalks, black where the sprinklers were arcing, under the deepening green mounds of the maples, past the squall and chirping of sparrows roosting behind the Virginia creeper on the side of St. Andrew's Church—sometimes still he'd hold her hand, shy and happy as a boy.

He shifted his chair further from the table, crossed his legs. Banged his knee.

Straightened the rucked tablecloth.

The girl was singing.

the way you sip your . . . the memory of all that . . .

Nothing *could* take away from him the things they'd shared, the way they'd become. The way she worried he'd be struck by lightning via metal street lights, the way she unpacked grocery boxes on the front porch to prevent the entry of mythical cockroaches, the way she poked with a broom handle because of miners' lung disease, parrots, psi-something, whatever it was called, poking with a broom handle attempting to dislodge nesting pigeons from the upper windows' gingerbread—the list was endless, part of life's fabric, a ballad without end. And this morning? What had been this morning's contribution? Goldfish!

White strings.

In which case, that being so, which it unarguably *was*, what, just *what* was he doing in this ridiculous restaurant with this—*ordinary*. With this very *ordinary* girl? What was he doing with a girl who was nearly young enough to be his daughter? *Was* young enough to be his daughter. With a girl who was only—he calculated—was only—good God!—*five years older than Peter!*

What was he doing with a girl whose silences were abrasive, whose conversation was boring? Who spoke of "getting into" things? What was he doing with a girl who'd never heard of Jacques Tati? With a girl in whose hands he'd once seen an historical romance, tartan and claymores, entitled *The Master of Stong*? What was he doing with a girl who transported her toiletries in an army-surplus bag?

He stared at it where it hung from the back of her chair.

The writing in gilt on the hairbrush handle glinted.

Pinned to the front of the bag was a black-and-white button that said:

GRAVITY SUCKS

Behind her head, the movement of figures on the dance floor.

The brightly lit stage.

Knife and fork.

She looked up and smiled.

With sudden and startling clarity, the realization came to him that she wasn't her at all. *She simply wasn't her.* Polly, he realized, was Polly but Norma wasn't.

But Polly...

What of Polly? What was she?

He sat thinking about that.

* * *

THE WAITRESS was mouthing something. Leaning forward and peering up at her face from about eighteen inches away, he watched her lips moving.

He pointed at his ear and shrugged.

He traced on the low tabletop a figure 5 and a zero. Her lips seemed to shape: 50?

She disappeared into the gloom.

The noise was hurting his eyes.

Beside him on the banquette sat a pair of lovelies whose hair was shaved off to a line an inch or so above the ears; above that, it was cut the same length all the way round so that it sat on their heads like caps. They reminded him of the mushrooms in *Fantasia*. Of collaborators. Of a boy called Gregory who'd had ringworm. Light glanced off the skulls, off the shiny, pallid skin. The girl was drenched in obnoxiously cheap perfume which was beginning to make him feel nauseated. Under the shiny skin, a vein crawled. Her escort was naked to the waist save for red-and-white suspenders.

From behind the amplified drummer, lights like lightning flick-flickered flick-flickered. He began to fear induced epilepsy. On the dance floor in front of the stage, shapes heaved and cavorted in the stuttering light. Some were running on the spot. Some seemed to be miming log-rolling. Others were leaping erratically as though to avoid bowling balls being launched at their ankles.

One of the guitarists was wearing ear-mufflers of the kind worn by ground crews at airports.

The Iron Guard looked much like all the other sneering degenerates who adorned the record albums littering Peter's room—sexually ambivalent, grubby, *used*.

The banquette itself was vibrating. The amplified white-plastic violin which had started up was making his teeth ache. Its sound was demented. He could feel vibration deep inside his body; his very organs were being shaken loose.

Norma had described The Iron Guard as being "mainstream"; he could not imagine the sound of something she'd consider avant-garde. The word "mainstream" made him think of "midstream," of the tests he'd undergone after his heart-thing, of his kidneys vibrating.

The waitress planked down two bottles of Labatt's Fifty Ale and two wet glasses, took his proffered ten-dollar bill, and disappeared into the fug. He felt Norma's breath on the side of his face as she shouted something. He smiled back then stopped because smiling seemed to intensify the pain in his teeth.

Now and again, he caught a few words bellowed by the lead degenerate...

MIS-ER-*RY*
AS YOU ALL CAN *SEE*...

A large pink bubble was swelling from the mushroom girl's blank face. She and her mushroom consort looked, he thought, as if they'd been used for medical experiments.

He wondered if they found each other sexually attractive; he wondered if they would breed.

He was feeling very tired and very old.

He wished, more than anything, that he was at home in the silent kitchen with a peanut-butter sandwich, a glass of milk, three aspirins, and a new issue of *African Arts*, the only sound the occasional scrabble of the basement mouse.

Outside the Château Laurier, and before the taxi, he had not been able to think of any kind and plausible way of excusing himself but now, oppressed by guilt and toothache, he decided that he would leave—the advancing hour—as soon as the beer was finished and the band had executed another number. If this monstrous and outrageous noise was indeed divided into "numbers."

It seemed more than possible that it just went on.

Despite his severe pangs of guilt, despite his realization that Polly wasn't Norma, or, more clearly, that Norma wasn't Polly, and despite his welling love for Martha, it was, at the same time, undeniably flattering that Norma felt attracted to a man with drooping pectorals and four white hairs on his chest. But flattering as it *was*, he almost winced as he thought of the way the evening *could* have turned out. He dwelt for a few moments on the compounding horror of an embroilment with a child-woman and employee. He blessed his blind and stupid luck that had preserved him from laying hot hands on her essentials.

Surveying his behaviour over the course of the evening, he could not recall having responded in any way, verbally or physically, that had in any sense committed him. His responses had, he believed, been sufficiently ambiguous. It was she, amazingly enough, who had made all the running. He had not really stepped over the line. Legs under tables could, he decided, be looked on merely as friendly contiguity. Bridges intact, retreat was possible.

Caught in an extraordinary storm, a pleasant evening with a charming young employee of whom he was fond. A few comments tomorrow about how pleasant it had been, up past his bedtime, a matter of taste, of course, but this sweating hell-hole perhaps better suited to the younger generation ...

Harrumph!

Major Hoople.

That was the stance.

Avuncular.

The harem pants stretched over her long thighs, she was leaning back on the banquette with her feet up on the ledge beneath the table. He looked at her pale toes.

She *was* attractive, of course, impossible to deny, but he saw that it was the attractiveness of a kitten or a puppy, the charm of a filly in a summer field. A matter of sentiment and aesthetics. He appreciated her, he decided, much in the way that he appreciated a painting or a carvmg.

No.

That had some truth in it but it was not *strictly* true.

He thought of the glycerine-drenched inner parts of ladies which greeted him in the corner-store every time he went to buy a quart of milk.

Fantasy.

That seemed the essential point to hold onto.

Surreptitiously, he tried to lick off the back of his hand the blue heart and arrow the doorkeeper had stamped him with.

A change in the noise was taking place. To the continuous-car-crash effect was being added a noise which sounded like the whingeing of giant metal mosquitoes. The mushroom girl was gawping, a bubblegum bubble deflated on her lower lip. And then the white-plastic violin capered into high gear and the lead degenerate, bent double for some reason, started moaning and bellowing again and Paul realized that the whole thing was still the

MIS-ER-*RY*
AS YOU ALL CAN *SEE*...

recitative *still* going on but possibly, he dared to hope, ending.

There was a long-drawn-out crescendo of appalling noises—noises of things under dreadful tension snapping and shearing, of tortured metal screeching, of things being smashed flat, crushed, ripped apart, ricocheting—and then, suddenly, silence.

The crowd's applause, wild whistles, and rebel yells sounded by comparison soft and muted as the shush of waves on distant shore.

He could scarcely believe it had stopped.

He extended his wrist and watch towards Norma and tapped the watch-face.

He mouthed: Let's go.

"What?"

"Sorry."

"Go?" she said.

"It's late. I need my beauty sleep."

"But we've only just got here."

He stood up.

He wanted to be on the other side of the padded doors before The Iron Guard grated again into gear. Sound was coming to him oddly as it sometimes did during the descent into an airport; the inside of his head felt as though it had been somehow *scoured*.

The set of Norma's body suggested disgruntlement.

They threaded their way through the hairstyles and vintage clothing and he heaved open one side of the heavy doors. It was immediately easier to breathe. The tiny foyer was ill-lighted and tiled white like a public washroom. The concrete stairs rose steeply to the door that led out onto the sidewalk.

He was still trying to think of something to say that would be suitably old-dufferish, avuncular, and affable and which would set the tone for their parting, and, more to the point, for their meeting again in the morning, when the street door above them banged back against the wall and the narrow doorway was jammed by three struggling figures in black. The two outer figures were manoeuvring a central, drooping figure.

As Paul and Norma stared up at these noisy shapes looming over them, the nearest stumbled on the first step. He let go of the central figure to save himself. The central figure slumped to one side, pulling the other supporting figure off balance and then, as if in slow motion, fell forward. A yell was echoing. Rubbery, more or less on his feet, gaining momentum, his body hit the handrail, caromed off to hit the wall, bounced off the wall turning somehow so that he was tumbling backwards, windmill arms, hit the rail again. Reflex pushed Paul forward and the figure landed against his chest and arm. He staggered back under the impact.

"Fuckin*ankle*!" screamed a voice on the stairs.

Paul was staring down at the face of his son.

"Peter!

"Peter! Are you hurt? *Peter*!"

His face was white and his eyes were closed.

"Who is it?" said Norma.

"Come on! Peter!"

Someone belched.

"What *happened* to him?"

"Oh, good evening, Mr. Denton."

It was the one in his twenties who wore things suspiciously like blouses.

"What happened to him?"

"Do you mean," said Norma, "it's *your* Peter?"

Paul lowered the body to the tiled floor and knelt beside him. He quickly checked arms and legs. Felt round the back of his head. Nothing was obviously broken.

"For Christ's sake, what *happened* to him?"

"Is it?" said Norma. "Peter?"

"Well, I lost my balance, Mr. Denton, and he . . ."

"I *know* you lost your balance, you fucking dimwit. I want to know what happened to him *before*."

Peter groaned and opened his eyes.

His head rolled.

He seemed to be staring at Norma.

"Peter? Hey, Peter!"

He was trying to say something.

Bent over him, trying to peer at his pupils in the uncertain light, Paul could scarcely believe the obvious: it was not concussion; it was not hypoglycemia; it was not cerebral edema; it was booze. The boy reeked of booze. He felt suddenly weak and shaky; he could still hear the terrifying sound the boy's head would have made as it hit the tiled floor.

He stared up at—Deet, was it? Wiggo? Or was this the one that sounded like something from *Sesame Street*?

He was regarding Paul and Peter owlishly.

As Paul stared at him, he wrinkled his upper lip and nose and sniffed moistly. He wiped his nose on his sleeve.

Paul shook his head slowly.

"Jesus Christ!" he said. "*Je-sus Christ!*"

"Paul?" said Norma. "Is he okay?"

Paul got slowly to his feet.

With both hands, he smoothed back his hair.

He lowered his head and massaged the muscles in his neck.

"Norma," he said, looking up, "I'm sorry, but I'm going to have to ask you to excuse me. I think it'd be better if you left me to deal with this."

"Oh," she said. "You mean . . ."

"I'd like to talk privately to these . . ."

He gestured at Wiggo and at the other character who was sitting on the steps.

"Well," she said. "Umm . . . okay."

"I'll talk to you in the morning."

She hitched up the strap of the army-surplus bag.

"I'm sorry," said Paul.

"Well," she said, "thank you for dinner."

Paul nodded.

Her sandals slapped up the echoing stairs.

At the top of the stairs, she looked down and said,

"Well, goodnight, Paul."

The push-bar door clanged shut behind her.

"*Now*," said Paul. "Let's start again. Wiggo, isn't it?"

"It's Munchy, Mr. Denton."

The one who worked in the speculative-fiction bookstore, the one Peter had said was into Tolstoy.

"Munchy, then. Listen carefully, Munchy. I am going to ask you a question. Where has Peter been and what happened to him?"

"We were in my apartment, Mr. Denton."

"*And*?"

"Listening to tapes."

"You were in your apartment and you were listening to tapes—I haven't got all night, Munchy."

He could feel the pounding of his heart, the dryness in his mouth. It would have been a release and a pleasure to have thumped this pair until stretchers were necessary. He felt pressure at his temples and behind his eyes, thought of tubes contracting, pictured pink things swelling. He took a deep breath and held it.

Munchy was groping about in his pockets.

"Pay attention! I'm *talking* to you!"

"I'm sorry, Mr. Denton. Have you got a Kleenex?"

Peter was stirring on the floor, groaning. Paul glanced down at him. Then stared. He was drawing his knees up to his body. His exhalations were becoming harsh and noisy. Red-tinged saliva was drooling and spindling from the corner of his mouth. It was beginning to pool and glisten on the white tiles.

Quickly, Paul knelt beside him.

"Did he fall before? Was he hit or something? A car?"

Munchy shook his head.

"Did he hurt himself *before* he fell downstairs?"

Munchy shook his head.

"*Answer me!*" shouted Paul. "Can't you see he's bleeding? What kind of friends are you? He's bleeding and he's bleeding *internally. What happened to him?*"

They stared at him.

"He didn't," said Munchy.

"Jesus Christ!" said Paul. "Go! Just go! Go and phone for an ambulance."

"*No, no, no,*" said the other creature, shaking his head emphatically.

"What do you mean, *no?*"

Pointing at Peter, he said,

"Issribena."

Paul stared at him. The hair was bleached to a hideous chemical yellow and he was wearing a combination false-nose-and-spectacles. His T-shirt was imprinted with the word: Snout.

"It *is*, Mr. Denton," said Munchy. "That's what it is."

"Is *what?*"

"*Issribena*!" said the one on the steps.

"What," said Paul, "is *it?*"

"Ribena," said Munchy.

Paul wondered if The Iron Guard had done something permanent to his head.

He said:

"Say that again."

"Ribena?" said Munchy.

"Yes. What do you mean, 'Ribena'?"

"It's black-currant juice."

"Ribenasafruit," added the creature with the chemical hair.

Paul knelt again and smeared his finger through the slimy, red-tinged spittle. He smelled it. It immediately made him feel queasy.

He got slowly to his feet.

The Iron Guard sounded through the padded doors like the throb of industrial machinery.

Brushing the dust off his pants, he said,

"Ribena, eh?"

"It isn't bleeding, Mr. Denton."

"No," said Paul. "And Ribena did this to him, did it, Munchy?"

Munchy shook his head.

"It didn't?"

"Grover put rum in it."

Paul nodded slowly.

"*That* is Grover?"

There didn't seem much point in trying to talk to Grover. He was engrossed in trailing his fingertips backwards and forwards along the concrete step.

"But *you* didn't drink much of it."

"Well, I don't use it, Mr. Denton. I'm not really into alcohol."

Paul closed his eyes.

He breathed, consciously.

After a few moments, he said,

"Do you know how old Peter is?"

Munchy nodded.

"Speak to me, Munchy."

"Pardon?"

"Tell me. In words."

"Peter?"

Paul nodded.

"Fifteen?"

Paul nodded.

"Well?" he said. "Do you have anything to say?"

Grover was making automobile noises.

Munchy snuffled.

Paul stared at Munchy.

Staring at Munchy, at his eczema, at his safari shirt over which he wore a broad belt in the manner of Russian peasants, at his tux pants and what looked like army boots, the words "diminished responsibility" came into Paul's mind. Munchy was the sort of character who'd be sentenced to months of community service for drug possession and who'd genuinely find emptying bedpans a deeply meaningful learning experience; interrogating him was like wantonly tormenting the Easter Bunny.

Munchy wiped his nose on his sleeve again.

Paul looked down at Peter and sighed.

He felt immensely weary.

Above the door that led out onto the sidewalk the EXIT sign flushed the white tiles red.

"It's the pollen," said Munchy.

"What?"

"In the season, I always suffer with it."

He pointed at the tip of his nose with his forefinger.

"Or sometimes," he added, "just with environmental dust."

"Munchy," said Paul, "SHUT. UP. Do you understand?"

Munchy nodded.

"Right. Good. Now get hold of his other arm."

Munchy pushed his glasses higher on the bridge of his nose and stooped.

"And Munchy?"

The glasses flashed.

"*Don't speak to me!*"

Munchy nodded.

"*Just don't speak to me!*"

It was drizzling, a thin mist of rain. There were few people on the streets. Paul had hoped that the torrential storm would have cooled and rinsed the air but it was still close and muggy. Peter's head hung. His legs wambled from sidewalk to gutter; his legs buckled; his legs strayed. Most of the passing couples averted their eyes. Supporting him was like wrestling with an unstrung puppet.

Back wet with sweat, Paul propped him against a hydro pole. It was not when he was moving but when he stopped that he felt the pounding of his heart, that his hot clothes clung, that the sweat seemed to start from every pore. The boy felt so thin, his chest like the carcass of a chicken; it amazed Paul that such frailty could weigh so much.

Leaning against Peter to jam him against the pole, Paul stared across the road unseeing, his clumsy tongue touching the dry corrugations of his palate. The muscles in his shoulders ached. Pain stitched his side. He did not seem able to breathe deeply enough.

A lot of girls in a passing car yelled cheerful obscenities.

His eyes followed the ruby shimmer of their rear lights in the road's wet surface.

Stapled to the hydro pole above Peter's head was a small poster advertising a rock group. The band's name seemed to be:

BUGS HARVEY OSWALD

He changed his grip on the boy's wrist and stooped again to take the weight.

Lurching on, he began to set himself goals: as far as the gilt sign proclaiming Larsson Associates: Consultants in Building Design and Research; as far as the light washing the sidewalk outside the windows of the Colonnade Pizzeria; as far as the traffic lights; as far as the next hydro pole.

And the next.

When he reached Elgin Street, he stood propping Peter at the curb waiting for the traffic lights to change. Further up the street, someone in a white apron was carrying in the buckets of cut flowers from outside Boushey's Fruit Market; knots of people were saying noisy goodnights outside Al's Steak House; a couple with ice-cream cones wandered past; he realized that although it felt much later it must just be approaching midnight. He stood staring across Elgin into Minto Park, into its deepening shadows beyond the reach of the street lights.

It was quiet in the deserted park; the surrounding maple trees seemed to soak up the noise of the traffic. The wet green benches glistened. The houses along the sides of the square looked onto the park with blank windows. Paul felt somehow secluded, embowered, as though he were in an invisible, airy, green marquee. Just before the shadowed centre of the park with its circular flowerbed, the path widened and there stood the large bronze bust. The bust sat on top of a tall concrete slab which served as a pedestal. Before lowering Peter to a sitting position on its plinth, Paul glanced up at the massive head, the epaulettes, the frogging on the military jacket. Against the bank of moonlit cloud behind, the head stared, black and dramatic.

Peter sat slumped with his back against the slab.

Paul rearranged the boy's limbs.

The drizzle had stopped; the sky was breaking up. He began to hear the short screech of nighthawks.

He worked his shoulders about and stretched. His legs felt trembly. He thought of quenching his thirst with a quart of Boushey's fresh-squeezed orange juice but imagined Peter's body being discovered in his absence by a dog-walker, imagined sitting in the back of the summoned police car giving chapter and embarrassing verse.

The cuffs of his shirt were sticking to his wrists.

Beyond the central flowerbed was a drinking fountain.

Two of the four lamps had burned out, their white globes dull and ghostly.

Zinnias. Zinnias and taller pink flowers whose name he didn't know.

His footsteps echoed.

He drank deeply at the fountain and splashed water on his face.

He walked back slowly to the bust. Around at the front of it Peter was invisible but audible, groaning exhalations. Paul bent forward and peered at the bronze plaque bolted into the back of the pedestal.

April 19, 1973

The Embassy of Argentina presents this bronze to the City
of Ottawa as a symbol of Canadian-Argentine Friendship
Mayor of Ottawa
Pierre Benoit
Ambassador of Argentina
Pablo Gonzalez Bergez

Paul walked around the plinth. Peter had not moved. He leaned close to the pedestal to read the plaque above the boy's head. It was darker on this side, the bulk of the bust and pedestal blocking most of the light from the two lamps, and he had to angle his head to make out the words.

GENERAL JOSÉ DE SAN MARTIN

Hero of the South-American Independence
Born in Argentina on Feb. 25, 1778
Died in France on Aug. 17, 1850
He ensured Argentine Independence, crossed the Andes and liberated Chile and Peru

Sirens.

Sirens on Elgin Street.

Ambulance.

Silence sifting down again.

Crunching up two tablets of Nikoban gum, Paul stood looking down at Peter. The drizzle had wet his hair and purple food dye had coloured his forehead and run in streaks down his face. Pallor and purple, he looked as if he'd been exhumed.

Paul sat down beside him on the plinth.

"Peter?

"How are you feeling now? Feel a bit better?

"Peter! Listen! Are you listening? I'll tell you what we're going to do. We'll stay and rest here for a while and let you get sobered up a bit. If your mother saw you like this neither of us'd ever hear the end of it. Come on, now! Sit up! You'll feel a bit better soon.

"Okay? Peter?"

Peter mumbled.

"What? What was that? *You're* tired! And what? You don't feel very well. No. I can imagine. You're a lucky boy, you know. Do you realize that? It was an amazing coincidence I happened to be in that place tonight. It was the first time I'd ever been there and I can assure you that it was also the last. That *violin!* Christ! It was like root-canal work. If that's the kind of place you hang out in, it's a wonder to me you aren't stone deaf. But you're lucky, Peter. It could have turned out differently. You could have hurt yourself badly on those stairs. You might have been in the hospital right now with your skull smashed. You think about that."

"*ohhhhhhhh,*" said Peter.

"Yes," said Paul, "you think about it."

He cleared his throat.

"Norma and I—you saw Norma, didn't you? Norma who works for me? You met her once, I think. It was pure chance that I—that we—were there. As I said before. We'd been having dinner after work with a guy who's got some masks for sale and after dinner he wanted to go on and listen to some music—you know, visiting fireman sort of stuff—tedious really—and Norma'd heard of that place so that's where we ended up."

Paul again glanced at Peter.

"Fellow from Edmonton."

Peter seemed to be studying his kneecap.

"And it was your good luck we did. End up there.

"Even if you hadn't hurt yourself on the stairs, the police would have picked you up. Imagine that? And Munchy and that other creep wouldn't have been much use to you either. Christ! What a pair! One pissed and the other congenital. You ought to have a think about those beauties, Peter. *Real* friends wouldn't have let you get like this. But can you imagine it? You know how she gets. Your mother down at the police station? In the middle of the night? In full flow?

"Anyway, you're safe. That's the main thing. I don't intend to go harping on about this. I just want you to think about it. That's all. Think about what might have happened. Okay?"

"*ohhhhhhhh*," said Peter.

"Yes," said Paul, "well, that's what happens when you drink Ribena."

He leaned back against the pedestal listening to the screech of the invisible nighthawks. The cries grew louder and then diminished, fading, grew harsher again as the birds swept and quartered the sky above.

"It's strange, really," he said. "I was just thinking about it. About that club and that abominable bloody music. Know what I was thinking about? It hadn't really occurred to me before. And perhaps it should have. But when *I* was your age I used to drive *my* parents mad with the stuff *I* listened to. Of course, with me it was jazz records. To hear my mother on the subject—well, you know what your grandmother's like—you'd have thought it was Sodom and Gomorrah and the papacy rolled into one. And it didn't help, of course, that most of them were black.

"Oh, I've had some memorable fights with her in my time. She was sort of a female Archie Bunker, your grandmother. Backbone of the Ladies' Orange Benevolent Association. A merciless church-goer. She refused to listen to the radio on Sundays till she was about sixty-five. Yes, in the days I'm talking about your grandmother was a woman of truly *vile* rectitude.

"I remember one time up at the cottage—one summer—I hated it up there when I was about your age. Every day—every single day—she used to bake bread on that old wood stove. Can you imagine? In that heat? It was all just part of her summer campaign to make life unbearable and martyr herself. And piss my father off. But when I was about your age, that summer . . .

"I'd only got a few records. I can see them now. 78s, of course. And an old wind-up gramophone. Benny Goodman and Artie Shaw and Ellington and Count Basie. Buddy de Franco.

"I used to sit out there on the porch—it wasn't screened in those days—I used to sit out there playing them over and over again. 'Take the A Train' and 'Flying Home.' And she could have *killed* me. When *she* listened to music—and she didn't really *like* music—she used to listen to a dreadful unaccompanied woman called Kathleen Ferrier singing some damn thing called 'Blow the Wind Southerly.' A very horrible experience, my boy. And if it wasn't that, it was the other side. 'We'll Lay the Keel Row.' Which was, if possible, worse. You don't know what suffering *is*.

"But the stuff *I* played was like waving a red flag. Getting up late and not eating a proper breakfast and then refusing to swim and just sitting, sitting listening to that . . . to that . . . And off she'd go about vulgarity and nigger minstrels and why couldn't I listen to something decent like John McCormack, and then *I'd* say that Benny Goodman was not only white but a respected classical musician and then it'd get worse and her face red with rage and it'd swell into all decency fled from modern life and girls flaunting themselves shamelessly and listening to that concatenation of black booby-faces . . . well, you can imagine what it was like. You know how easy it is to get her started. Though she's mellow now compared with the way she used to be. All that business over Jennifer's shorts last year. About their indecency? Remember that?

"Anyway. What I'm getting at is that maybe when you get a bit older you forget—I don't mean *you*—you, Peter—I mean *one*. One forgets what one was like oneself. *That's* what I'm trying to say. Understand? And I'm trying to say that I don't want to be towards you the way your grandmother was to me.

"What?"

"*nerrrrrrrr*," said Peter again.

"No? No you don't want me to be?"

"*nrrrrrrrr*," said Peter.

"Now," said Paul, "I'm not saying I could ever *like* the music you like because, in all honesty, I couldn't. And I don't want to lie to you. But certainly I ought to be able to tolerate it. Because I don't want something like taste in music to come between us. There'd be something . . . well . . . so *petty* about that, wouldn't there?"

Peter said nothing.

His head was back against the pedestal and he seemed to be staring up into a maple tree. Paul got to his feet and stood looking down at him.

"Wouldn't there, Peter? Be something petty about that? And that's something that, well . . . you know, as we *are* talking, it's something we ought to talk about. I know it isn't *just* the music. It's everything the music *stands for*. I realize that. And whatever you might *think*, I *do* understand, Peter, because that's what jazz used to stand for. For me, I mean. When I was fighting with *my* father and mother. It meant the same kind of thing that punk or new wave or whatever you call it means now. But I'll tell you what I resent. What I resent is this being cast in the role of *automatic* enemy. *I'm* not Society. *I'm* not The Middle Class. I'm *me.* A person. Just like you're a person.

"And *I've* got feelings, too.

"Okay?"

Paul stood looking down at Peter's bowed head.

"Look!" he said, beginning to pace. "We've been having a pretty hard time lately, haven't we? Always arguing and squabbling about one thing or another. Getting on each other's nerves. And it's been making me very unhappy, Peter. But you know, for my part, I only criticize you because I want you to grow up decently and become a kind and considerate person. I don't *enjoy* fighting with you. Believe me. But think of it this way. If I *didn't* care about you and love you—care about what you're going to become—and care very deeply—I wouldn't bother with you, would I? It'd be much easier just to ignore you, let you go to hell in a handcart. It'd be a lot easier for me just to shrug my shoulders, wouldn't it?

"But I don't do that, Peter.

"And I think, really, that you *know* why I don't.

"Don't you?"

Paul sat down on the plinth again and turned to face Peter. Peter had not moved. Paul looked at him and then looked down at his shoes. A breath of wind shuddered the leaves in the maple trees and drops of rainwater pattered down on the concrete path.

"I don't know, old son. It's a funny business—the way things work out—and I don't make much claim to understand it. I suppose we all just blunder along doing the best we can, just hoping for the best but . . . *this* thing—you and me, I mean—it's all so *ridiculous.*

"Peter?"

Paul put his hand on Peter's arm and then shook him gently.

"What? Yes, *I know* you're tired. What? Yes, soon. We'll go home soon. But listen! Let's get this thing thrashed out. I was saying how ridiculous it was, this constant squabbling about things. I mean, it wasn't so long ago that you went everywhere with me. I couldn't even go to the store for a packet of cigarettes without you tagging along. And remember how we used to go fishing every weekend? Just you and me? Remember that? All those sunfish you used to catch? Remember that day a racoon ran off with our package of hotdogs? And those water snakes you used to catch? Revolting damned things! I used to be quite scared of them. You didn't know that, did you? You thought I was just pretending. And remember that day you made me hold one and it vented all that stuff on my hands and shirt? And how it stank? You thought that was very funny.

"Remember, Petey?

"So what I'm getting at is that, although we've been getting on each other's nerves a bit lately, you can't just wipe out the past. You can't just ignore . . . well, what it amounts to, most of your life. I guess we're just stuck with it, aren't we? Wretched thing that I am, I'm your father. And you're my *son*, Petey. So I guess . . ."

"*nrrrnnnnnnnn*."

"What?"

Peter leaned forward and, without apparent effort, gushed vomit.

Paul jumped up and out of range.

Peter sat staring ahead, his mouth slightly open.

Threads of drool glistened from his lips.

"Peter?"

Paul passed his hand in front of the boy's face. He did not blink; he did not stir.

"*Peter!*"

Paul stared down at him, astounded.

"You ungrateful little *shit!* You're the next best thing to unconscious, aren't you? You selfish little turd! You haven't heard a single goddamned word I've been saying to you, have you? I've been wasting all these pearls of wisdom on the desert air, haven't I? Hello? Hello? Anyone in there? *Peter*! YOUR FATHER IS TALKING TO YOU.

"Nothing, eh?

"The motor's run down, has it?

"Ah, well . . .

"I suppose it makes a change, though. Your not answering back. I ought to be grateful, really. You've got a mouth on you like a barrack-room lawyer. Always arguing the toss, aren't you? Black, white. Day, night. Left is right and vice versa. I ought to be grateful for brief mercies. I've daydreamed sometimes of having myself surgically deafened.

"You're always bleating about social justice and revolution—and look at you! Purple hair and vintage puke-slobbered clothing. Let me tell you, my little chickadee, that any self-respecting revolutionary would shoot you *on sight*. Thus displaying both acumen *and* taste.

"Some revolution you'd run. You and Munchy and Bunchy and Drippy and Droopy. What would you do after you'd liberated Baskin Robbins?

"That's a nice touch. Doing your face purple as well. Suits you.

"Neat but not gaudy.

"And to revert for a moment to the subject of music. You, my dear boy, and your fellow-members of The Virgin Exterminators, are about as much musicians as is my left bojangle. You'd be hard put to find middle C under a searchlight. Musically speaking, blood of my blood and bone of my bone, you couldn't distinguish shit from shinola.

"Hello?

"Yoo-hoo!

"Anyone at home?

"*You're an offensive little heap!* What are you? 'I'm an offensive little heap, Daddy.' Yes, you are! And you're also idle, soft, and spoiled. And in addition to that, you've spewed on my shoe.

"What do you imagine's going to happen to you? Who the hell's going to hire you when you leave school? For what? What can you *do?* You can't even cut the lawn without leaving tufts all over the place. And dare I ask you to trim the edges with a pair of shears? You were outraged, weren't you? 'By *hand*' you said. How do you think *I* do it? By foot? Wanted me to buy one of those ludicrous buzzing machines to save your poor back from stooping. And when you've chopped it to pieces so that it looks as if you've gone at it with a knife and fork, you have the nerve to demand two bucks. It's all so easy, isn't it?

"Just shake the old money tree.

"Well, life isn't like that, my little cherub. Life isn't a matter of rolling out of your smelly bed at eleven in the morning and lounging around sipping Earl Grey tea and eating nine muffins rich in fibre. Life, my little nestling, is tough bananas.

"And what are you doing to prepare yourself for its rigours? Studying hard? Mastering your times tables? Practising the old parlezvous? Getting a grip on human history? History! Dear God! Stone hand-axes, the Magna Carta, the Pilgrim Fathers—it's all the same sort of thing, isn't it? Events that took place in that dim and inconceivable period before the Rolling Stones. The glories of civilization—it's all B.S., isn't it?

"Before Stones.

"And math? You don't even know your tables. Oh, I'll admit you're very handy with the calculator on that fancy watch of yours but I'm afraid *you'd* have to admit that you'd be up the well-known creek if the battery gave out.

"In sum, then, you're close to failing in damn near every subject. And why is that? What was the reason you advanced? Something about school being 'a repressive environment.' I'm not misquoting you, I hope. And what was it you received a commendation in? A discipline I hadn't encountered before. 'Chemical Awareness,' I believe it was called.

"In which you have now moved on, I see, to practical studies.

“Pissed out of your mind at fifteen.

“What mind you have.

“And speaking of pissed, and I apologize for bringing this up, as it were, when you’re a little under the weather, but I’d be gratified if you could remember in future to raise the toilet seat before relieving yourself.

“I mention this because I am tired of living knee-deep in balled Kleenex, soiled underwear, crusted piss, and rotting tofu.

“I am, as a matter of fact, tired of a hell of a lot of things.

“Oh!

“Yes.

“I also wish you’d shave your upper lip every couple of weeks now you’re nearing man’s estate. You look like a spinster with hormonal imbalance.

“And another matter of petty detail.

“That cat.

“I don’t like it.

“That cat is going back to the SPCA *forthwith*. To be humanely electrocuted to death IN A WET STEEL BOX.”

Stooping and grabbing up a rotten branch which had fallen in the storm, Paul beat it against the trunk of the nearest maple until it shattered into fragments. He threw the pieces, one by one, as far as he could out onto the grass. He threw them with all the power and violence he could command. He threw them until his elbow joint began to hurt.

He turned and walked back towards the pedestal. The pool of vomit between Peter’s feet glistened. He sat on a nearby bench and spread his arms along the back.

He crossed his legs.

He breathed in deeply and then sighed profoundly.

He stared up at the great bronze bust of San Martin.

“*Well?*” he demanded of the moonlight touching the high military collar, the frogging, the star burst of a military decoration or Royal Order.

"What do you say, José? How was it with you? What do *you* have to offer? You wear your seventy-two years easily, I'll say that for you. You have that calm and peaceful look about you of the man who gets laid frequently. I'd lay odds *you* didn't live in an open-plan house.

"It's about all I *can* lay.

"Odds.

"And what about Mrs. José de San Martin? Doubtless a beauty, you salty dog. Veins surging with hot southern blood? Bit of a handful? I don't suppose *she* had to go out to work. Wasn't too tired at night? Wasn't worrying that the children might hear? That the tomato chutney in the basement might explode?

"Lucky man, José.

"And the kids? I expect they were tucked up in their nursery half a mile away in the East Wing?

"And *not* by you.

"Very sensible, too.

"And she adored you?

"Well mine adores me but she's got a lot on her mind. Is the gas turned off? Did she or didn't she put tooth fairy money under Jennifer's pillow? Will chutney attract rats? It takes the bloom off it, José.

"But I've always been faithful to her. Up till tonight, that is.

"What happened? That's a good question, José. I wish I knew. There's this girl, you see. Polly Ongle. And . . . well, I *wasn't* unfaithful. Though I could have been. Or maybe *not*. No. There's a thought. Maybe not. And anyway, this one turned out to be Norma. To tell the truth, I'm a bit confused about it, José. You see, I'm beginning to suspect it was all about something else.

"Can I put it more clearly? I'm not surprised you ask.

"No.

"But you. These campaigns of yours. When you were away from her. I expect you rogered your way across the continent.

I don't suppose you went short of a bit of enchilada, did you? Oh, don't misunderstand me! I'm not being censorious. If anything, I'm envious, José. It's just that it isn't so simple now. A lot of other things have been liberated since Chile and Peru.

"I wish I'd flourished then.

"It seems more vivid, somehow. Somehow simpler.

"Jingling home after you'd given the hidalgos a severe thumping about in the course of liberating this or that, clattering into the forecourt of the ancestral home, tossing the reins to one of the adoring family retainers, striding through the hall in boots and spurs,

"Coo-ee, *mi adoracion!* I have returned! It is I.'

"And then off with the epaulettes, down with the breeches, and into the saddle.

"*Whereas*, José, when *I* return—granted not from a two-year campaign but from a two-day business trip—there's no question of skirts up and knickers joyfully down. I have to suffer a lengthy interrogation about expenditures on my Visa card.

"Following which she promptly collapses.

"Why, you ask?

"Because, José, for two nights she has not slept. She has not slept because she has lain awake, José, worrying (a) that I might have been killed in any of an astounding variety of ways, and (b) that the burglars and perverts who surround my house would take advantage of my absence and kill *her*.

"After first buggering, of course, all the children.

"Talking of which, how did yours turn out?

"Children, I mean.

"A comfort to you in your old age? A source of pride? Or did they cause you grief? Blackballed from clubs? Welshed on debts of honour? Or did they rally round bringing Dad his cigar and nightly posset?

"Tell me, José, what would *you* have done with *this*? Head under a pump and a stick across his back, eh? It's an attractive thought. Very attractive. Bur he'd have me up in front of the Children's Aid soon as look at me. Probably argue his own case, too. With *his* mouth, he wouldn't *need* a lawyer. And I'd end up being forced to increase his allowance and buy him a colour TV.

"The army? Well, these days I'm afraid they don't take all comers. They tend to ask questions. Such as what's five multiplied by twelve. And I don't suppose they'd let him use his watch.

"I don't know, José. This one's bad enough. But I've got two more coming to the boil. What are *they* going to dream up to break my heart? Need I ask? I *know*. In the middle of the night, I *know*. My little daughter will get herself tattooed and fuck with unwashed, psychotic bikers. My other son will blossom suddenly queer as a three-dollar bill. What does one do? What does one *do?*

"You lived a long time, José."

Close ranks and face the front.

"Well, there's a gem from the military mind. *Very* comforting. But forgive me. I'm being rude. I'm forgetting. You *do* know more about fortitude than I do. I'd forgotten that. Was it a daily bitterness? All your titles resigned, your honours returned. Thirty-odd years, wasn't it? In France? Thirty-some years in voluntary exile. And all in support of a monarchy nobody wanted.

"I don't know, José.

"But on the other hand, it couldn't have turned out worse than generals in sunglasses.

"Was it worth it, José? Looking at it now? I've never been there. Argentina. Used to read about it when I was a kid. Gauchos deadly with knife and bola. That sort of thing. But if the rest of the world is anything to go by, the gauchos are probably wired to Sony Walkmans and the pampas is littered with Radio Shacks.

"Still, you did it when the doing of it was fun. Horses. Gorgeous uniforms and women swooning. South American heartbreakers all looking like Bianca Jagger with flowers in their teeth.

"'Was it worth it?'

"What a stupid question!

"Of *course* it was worth it.

"Before. After. All those years in bitter exile.

"Of *course* it was worth it. Leather, harness, steel, pennons snapping in the wind. For those eight years you were larger than life. Coming down out of the mountains, your columns trailing you, the guns bouncing on their limbers—you were living in a dream. Oh, don't think I don't understand!

"I envy you, José.

"You breathed an air I've never breathed.

"I envy you that, José.

"God! I envy you that.

"'*Was it worth it!*'

"Look at us!

"Here's me down here with puke on my shoes—ever tried to get it off suede?—and there's you up there growing greener every year.

"Ah, well . . .

"What can you do?

"As my father-in-law, the philosopher says,

"'What can you do?'

"What can you do, José?

"What can you do, flesh of my flesh?

"No contributions from you?

"No ready answers?

"Good.

"That's a relief.

"Come on, then. Heave! Up you come! Don't *step* in it! Beddybye time for you. Come on! That's it. We're going walkies. *Hasta la vista, José*. Come on, Peter. Say goodnight to the General. That's it. Christ, you smell revolting! Get your feet out of the zinnias, there's a good boy. *This* way! This way. Come on! Five more blocks. Walk *straight!* Come on, Petey. You can do it. Five more blocks and then you can sleep. Good! That's it. Good boy. Good boy, Petey.

"Left, right.

"Left, right.

"Not so *much* left.

"Right.

"Steady the Buffs! Steady! Correct that tendency to droop. And get your leg out of that juniper bush. What do you think this is, you 'orrible little man? A nature ramble? Now, then. Close ranks and face the front. *That's* the front—where the street light is. And on the word of command, it's forward march for us.

"Ready?

"*Forwaaard—*

wait for it!

wait for it!

MARCH."

FORDE ABROAD

ROAST PORK with crackling was repellent. Roast pork with crackling was *goyishe dreck*. Black Forest ham with Swiss cheese was, however, her favourite kind of sandwich. She loved even the greasiest of salamis. Sausages, on the other hand, were unclean. All Chinese food involving pork was perfectly acceptable, with the single exception of steamed minced pork, which was, apparently, vile *trayf* of the most abhorrent kind. Prosciutto she adored. But pork chops . . . *feh!*

Forde stared at Sheila in exasperation.

"And you can be sure they haven't changed," she said, "in their hearts."

"But how do you know they ever *were* . . ."

"But how do you know they weren't?"

"Well, I don't, but how *could* they have deported anyone? Slovenia was invaded by the Nazis. The Slovenians were a subject people. Slovenia was an occupied country just as—as France was."

"And look at *their* record."

"I don't think," he said, "that this is a particularly logical conversation."

Lines at the corners of her eyes tightened.

"So what makes you think they didn't collaborate? Like the whatnames."

"Which whatnames?"

"The French ones. Begins with M."

"The *milice?*"

"Exactly."

"Well, I *don't* know . . ."

"More likely than not, I'd say."

". . . but I'll look it up," he said.

She bent over the atlas again.

"Here's the Nazis immediately north of them, in Austria.

And then immediately to the right of them, in Hungary—what were those called? The Iron Cross? The Iron Guard?"

"I think it was the Arrowcross."

With her left shoulder she gave a quick, irritated shrug.

"And then *here* to the south of them you've got the Ustashi in Croatia. Why *should* the Slovenians have been any different?"

"Listen,' he said, "Sheila . . ."

"But, please,' she said, "it's your career. I know I'm just being silly."

She patted below her eyes with a tissue.

"If it's what you want, off you go."

She sniffed.

"Off you go,' she said, her voice breaking.

"Sheila . . . *please.*"

"No!' she said fiercely. "No! You can go there and you can do what you want. I don't care. I don't *care* if you choose to consort with Slovenians."

To her offended and retreating back, he said, "I hardly think the word 'consort' is quite . . . oh, *indescribable* BALLS!"

After she had left for work, Forde stood over the toilet in the second-floor bathroom. The intense, rich yellow, the Day-Glo brightness of his urine, gave him daily pleasure. The vitamins did it. He wasn't sure if it was the E, the beta carotene, the C, or the Megavits. He had read in a newspaper article that vitamins C and E "captured free radicals'; he had no idea what that meant, and wasn't curious, but he enjoyed the sound of it. It made him think of warfare against insurgent forces in fetid jungles, sibilant native blades, *parang* and *kris*.

Even the toilet itself pleased him. It was probably seventy or eighty years old. Against the back of the bowl, in purple script, was the word 'Vitreous.' And above that, in a wreath of what might have been acanthus leaves, was the toilet's name—'Prompto.'

He flushed the toilet and watched his brightness diluted, swirled away. He stood looking at himself in the medicine cabinet mirror as the plumbing groaned and water rilled and spirted, silence rising, settling.

He wandered into his frowsty study and sat at his ugly government-surplus oak desk. Beyond its far edge the scabby radiator. Then the blank wall. Two years earlier he had faced the window but had spent too much time gazing out, watching passersby and the busyness of dogs.

Usually he enjoyed the daily solitude and drew the deepening silence of the house around him like a blanket. But on this day the silence burdened him. He sat looking down at the gold-plated stem-winder, which always lay flat on the desk to his right. He wound it every morning, pleased every morning by the feel of the knurled winding knob. He had bought it at a pawn shop cheaply because engraved on the back of the watch were the words: *Presented to George Pepper in recognition of forty-five years' service to the Canadian Cardboard Box Company.*

It amused him to think that this was the only presentation gold watch he'd ever have. No such flourishes were likely to conclude *his* career. He kept the watch on the desk as a talisman, a spur to effort, as *memento mori*, as a reminder of the world to which he gratefully did not belong. He thought of the watch as 'George.' He sometimes talked to it.

This is a lovely bit of writing, George, even if I say so myself. And why not? No one else will.

I think we can get another hour in, George, before we're completely knackered.

He wound the watch.

He sighed.

He sat staring across his desk's familiar clutter. He had no appetite for writing necessary letters, for providing references and recommendations, for the fiddle of filing. His last novel was now six months behind him—almost a year since he'd written seriously—but he remained listless, uncommitted about what he might do next, bored.

When he was in the grip of first-draft writing, he risked nothing that might break the flow. Ritual and omen ruled. He laid in stocks of Branston pickle, wooden matches, tins of Medaglia d'Oro. His heart leapt at the cawing of crows. He did not like to leave the house, did not open his mail, did not shower, wash, or shave, slept in unchanged shirt and underpants, sat in his study smelling the smell of himself.

It was only on Friday mornings that this obsessive routine was interrupted. On Friday mornings the cleaning lady hired by Sheila arrived at nine and made his life unendurable until noon. He had begged and remonstrated, but Sheila had offered as the only alternative that he clean the house himself as she had neither the time nor the energy. And definitely no inclination. He saw fully the justice of her position but felt put upon.

He attempted politeness when he let the woman in, attempted conversations about the weather, the heat, the cold, the damp, but could never understand more than a word in five of anything she said. Although he closed his study door and put on his industrial ear-mufflers, he could still hear her imprecations and mad Portuguese diatribes, her crooning monologues punctuated by sudden squawks and screeches directed at vacuum cleaner or doorknob.

She had once left a note on the kitchen counter that read: *Mis mis erclen finisples.*

It had worried at him most of the afternoon.

Sheila had read it with impatient ease. *Miss. Mister Clean is finished, please.*

According to Sheila, Mrs Silva had an unemployed husband with three toes missing on one foot from an industrial accident, a son who was a bad lot, and was herself a devoutly Catholic hypochondriac whose spare time was divided equally between her priest and doctor.

He could not understand how Sheila had found any of this out, how she understood anything the bloody woman said, but he had come to suspect that Sheila's ability to understand Mrs Silva, bereaved Romanian upholsterers, and monoglot Vietnamese shelf-stockers in odoriferous Asian stores, had less to do with some rare linguistic talent than it had to do with the fact that she was a nicer person than he was.

He started to link up the doodles.

One of John D. MacDonald's thrillers came into his mind. He'd always admired the title: *The Girl, the Gold Watch, and Everything.*

He was supposed to be polishing an interview which was supposed to appear in the summer issue of *Harvest*, but *Harvest* was doubtless two issues behind where it was supposed to be so that all of its three hundred subscribers would have to wait with bated breath until the summer of *next* year before they could devour his profound and penetrating insights into this, that, and whatever, so that, all in all, six of this and half a dozen of the other, all things being equal, when push came to shove, polishing the bloody thing up did not seem an enterprise '... of great pith and moment,' he declaimed into the study's silence.

Who *said* that?

Fortinbras?

Hamlet himself?

He plodded downstairs to find a copy of *The Complete Plays* and to make a cup of tea. Better for his health, Sheila insisted, than coffee.

I must put my pyjamas, he chanted, *in the drawer marked pyjamas.*

I must eat my charcoal biscuit, he recited, *which is good for me.*

As he stood waiting for the kettle to boil, he looked at the *New York Times Atlas of the World* Sheila had left open on the counter. He took a roll of Magic Tape from the kitchen drawer and started to tape up the tears in the tattered blue dust jacket; he'd been meaning to do that for weeks. Often, after dinner, they sat over the atlas finishing the wine and squabbling happily over holidays they would never be able to afford. Sheila's most recent creation had been a trip up the Nile to see the temples, but without getting off the boat because Egypt was hot and smelly and every historical site was plagued by importunate dragomen, smelly and anti-Semites to a man, and one could surely get a *sense* of the temples while remaining in one's deck chair and being served large Bombay gin martinis.

A snort of laughter escaped him as he thought of the words "consort with Slovenians."

Her performance that morning had not, of course, been about Slovenians, World War II fascist groups, or deported Jews. It had been what he thought shrinks called "displacement." It was that, simply, she was upset that he was going away, and although she had not yet said so, she was even more upset that at the conference he would, for the first time, be meeting Karla.

Sheila did not like Karla. She had taken against her from the arrival of the first letter. She always referred to her as "your Commie pen pal."

The conference was to be held in the Alps at a lake resort called Splad. The brochure about the hotel and its services was written in an English that charmed him. He thought it strange that in a Communist country a hotel would offer to launder silk handkerchiefs; they also offered to launder Gentlemen Linen and Nightshirsts. He had studied the sample menus with fascination; he particularly liked the sound of National Beans with Pork Jambs. It seemed certain that the whole expedition would provide him with unimaginable comic material.

But he had scarcely bothered to glance at the programme itself when it had arrived from the Literary and Cultural Association of Slovenia, disliking the hairy Eastern European paper it was printed on and the fact that the paper was not the normal 8 1/2 by 11 inches, but 8 1/2 by 11 3/4, an intensely irritating deviation probably traceable, like the metric system, to the meddling of Napoleon.

From horrid experience, he knew that the papers would range, from deconstructionist babble to weird explications in uncertain English, of the profundities of Mazo de la Roche and Lucy Maud Montgomery.

Not that he would be caught listening to any of it; he would rather, he thought, sit and listen to a washing machine.

And ranged between the deconstructionists and the simply uncomprehending there would be interminable feminists in frocks and army boots, gay theorists in bright-green leather shoes, huddles of Slovenians in suits discussing Truth, the State, the Writer, smart-alec Marxist smarty-boots, chaps in tweed from New Zealand....

But looking on the bright side, his expenses in Slovenia would be covered by the Literary and Cultural Association, and his travel expenses to Slovenia would be covered by the Department of External Affairs, which was also to pay him a *per diem* and a small honorarium. This, together with another honorarium from the Slovenians for reading, might mean returning home five hundred dollars ahead.

And he'd be freed from his desk, from the chipped radiator, the blank wall facing; he'd be free of the house, he'd be out and about, out in the world, free of the weight of his numbing routines.

His spirits rose at the thought of leaving behind the wearying end of Ottawa's winter, the snow beginning now its slow retreat, revealing Listerine bottles and dog turds. He would be leaving behind brown bare twigs and flying towards a world in leaf, in the alpine meadows, gentians.

And, once ensconced in Splad, he would perhaps meet someone who would wish to write about his work. Perhaps a convivial evening in the bar might lead to further translation. . . . Nor could he deny that he enjoyed the attention, couldn't deny that it made him feel expansive to answer questions, pontificate, disparage Robertson Davies.

"What I don't understand," Sheila had said, probing at his contradictions to deflate and anger him in these last bickering days before his flight, "what I can't follow is why it gives you pleasure to impress people for whom you have little or no respect. Why *is* that?'

"Well, it's not so much the *people,*" he'd explained, "it's what they represent."

"And what's that?"

"Well . . . a certain interest, a respect even . . . these are academics from all over the world, you know."

"And according to you some of them can't speak English and the rest talk gibberish."

"I'm not saying it's a *desirable* situation, Sheila, but one's reputation rests to a certain extent on how much attention academics pay to one's work."

"One's reputation does, does it?"

He had shaken his head slowly to convey a weary dignity.

"And one doesn't feel," she'd probed further, "that disporting oneself in front of people one disdains is rather . . . well . . . *pitiable?*"

He sighed and sipped at the tea.

Lighted a luxurious cigarette.

Closed the atlas.

And there also awaited in Splad the pleasure of holding in his hands a translation, into Serbian, of his third novel, *Winter Creatures.* His translator was travelling to Splad from Belgrade bringing the book with him. At a conference two years earlier in Italy he'd been approached by a man—and actually he wouldn't swear to the *absolute* details of any of this because he'd been rather drunk himself and had not quite grasped everything the man was saying, what with the noise in the bar and the accent and the syntax—by a man whose father was Serbian and whose mother was Croatian—or possibly it was the other way round—who worked for a cultural radio station and magazine in Belgrade and who was an actor and impresario who translated works in English into Serbian on behalf of the Writers of Serbia Cultural Association, and who, when not involved in manifestations, worked by day as chauffeur to a man of extensive power.

After his return to Canada, Forde had largely forgotten this loud stranger with his winks and nods, his glittering gold fillings, his finger tapping the side of his nose, until the telephone calls began.

Ripped from sleep at 3:33, heart pounding, staring into the digital clock inches from his face, Forde croaked into the phone.

"Hello?" he repeated.

"Here is Drago."

"Who?"

"Drago! Drago!"

"Who is it?"

He flapped his hand shush at her.

3:34

"You will visit me in Beograd. We will have much talking."

"Beograd?"

"*Yes!* Yes, Robert Forde."
"Excuse me . . . you're . . . from Bologna?"
"Yes, *certainly* Bologna."
"I'm sorry. For a moment, I . . . ah . . . rather disoriented."
3:35
"In Beograd we will together drink Nescafe."
This had been the first of many calls.
All came in the small hours.
"Get *his* fucking number!" hissed Sheila, furiously humping the sheets over her shoulder. "I'll phone *him* in the middle of *his* fucking night, fucking Slav fuckheads."

Forde soon came to dread that ruthless, domineering voice. Drago bombarded, hectored, rode roughshod.
He was implacable.
He was impervious.
"Here is Drago. You have written: 'American students littered the steps.' This *littered* is not a nice word, not a *possible* word, it is meaning *excrement* and *rubbish* and so would *offend* the Americans, so we find a *compromise* word. . . ."
He wondered what the book would look like. He presumed it would be a paperback but didn't know whether they went in for the quality paperback format or whether they produced paperbacks in the utilitarian French style. He realized that he didn't even know if Serbian was written in the Roman alphabet or in Cyrillic. He wondered what Serbian readers would make of *Winter Creatures* given Drago's strange queries and frequent assurances that he would 'make things come nice.' He suspected that the novel had been less translated than traduced. So why was he so gratified to have his novel badly translated into a language he couldn't read?
Forde did not delude himself.
He had not forgotten the wellingtons phone call.
"Wellies," said Drago. "This means, I think, *venery*."
"*What?*"
"You *know*, Robert Forde, what I am saying."

"No, *no,* Drago! Wellies are rubber boots."

He had listened to the echoic international silence.

"Short for wellingtons."

"Never," said Drago, "in all my reading and my talking, *never* have I heard it called so."

"It?" he'd squeaked.

But he *was* gratified. As he sat doodling at his desk, he hummed. Had he liked cigars, he would have smoked one. Had there been a mirror in his study, he would have inclined his head with all the benign courtesy of a grandee.

"...consort with Slovenians...."

He grinned at the radiator.

He was even pleased by Sheila's moody assaults, pleased and a little flattered that after all the years they'd been together, she could still flame into jealousy. Not that she had the slightest cause for concern. As he'd told her repeatedly, his friendship with Karla was a purely literary friendship.

Her first letter had arrived some three years ago from the University of Jena in the German Democratic Republic. She had expressed her admiration of his novels—a colleague at the University of Augsburg had lent her some volumes—and although her syntax and vocabulary were sometimes peculiar, he'd been pleased to receive her praise. No one from East Germany had ever written to him before. She had ended her letter by saying that her great sorrow was that she had not been able to read his first two novels because she could not obtain them. Was it possible he could send her copies? For such a resolution of the problem she would be most grateful.

"Why has it always got to be *you?*" Sheila demanded. "Why should *you* have to pay for the books and postage?"

"Well, I've never thought about it before but I don't think their currency trades. They can't buy things with it in the west."

"Well, how did her letter get here then, with an East German stamp on it?"

"I don't know. I don't know how that works."

"Well," said Sheila. "I'd say there's something suspicious about it."

He had sent her the books and within weeks they were writing back and forth regularly. What other Canadian writers should she read? Who were reliable critics? Which books were most loved by the Canadian people? She loved to read about Red Indians and Eskimos and the North. Was Grey Owl thought a great Canadian writer? Canadians, as she had studied in Margaret Atwood's book *Survival,* had invented the genre of the wild-animal story. Should she read Ernest Thompson Seton? An anthology at the university contained an Ernest Thompson Seton story entitled 'Raggylug, the Story of a Cottontail Rabbit.' Was this one of his most loved stories?

Forde had dealt with all this misplaced enthusiasm firmly. He had explained that no books were beloved of the Canadian people with the sole exception of *Anne of Green* Gables, and that only because it had been on television. Most Canadians, he had explained, were functionally illiterate. No stories by Ernest Thompson Seton were 'most loved' because only academics knew who he was.

He explained that most Eskimos worked in collectives with power tools turning out soapstone seals. The North was actually a vast slum run by the federal government's Canadian Mortgage and Housing Corporation, the landscape littered with empty oil barrels. There *were* Red Indians but no longer of the bow-and-arrow variety. They were not to be called "Red' Indians. Indeed, they were not to be called 'Indians.' In Ottawa, people of the First Nations wearing traditional braids and cowboy boots were almost bound to be high-priced, hotshot lawyers.

He began to send her reading lists; in the library he xeroxed what critical articles he could stomach; he sent clippings and reviews. When he went out walking around Ottawa's used-book stores, he picked up inexpensive paperbacks and, from time to time, sent parcels.

After a few months had gone by, he felt bold enough to start correcting her English.

The more he moulded and shaped her, the larger the claims her letters made on him. She became increasingly confident of his attention. Her ardent engagement with his own writing slightly embarrassed him. It seemed a natural progression for his letters to move from *Sincerely* to *With best wishes* to *With warm regards* to *Affectionately*. He had hesitated before writing *With love* and had then delayed mailing the letter.

During the two weeks he waited for her reply he found that the letter and her possible reactions to it came often into his mind.

He asked no questions about her life but often, as he sat staring across the grain of the government-surplus desk made uglier by thick polyurethane, he found himself wandering, daydreaming.

He had gleaned some few facts about her. He imagined that she must be between thirty-five and forty because she had a son aged ten. She had not mentioned a husband; when she used the word "we" she always seemed to mean herself and the boy. She lived in an apartment in an old house. She used the spare bedroom as her study.

When Sheila commented on the flow of letters from the German Democratic Republic, he had explained to her that such contacts were simply a normal part of the literary life, a necessary part of the shape of a career.

After they had been corresponding for about a year, there arrived, in the week before Christmas, a padded airmail package fastened in European style with split brass pins. It contained between two sheets of cardboard a photograph of Karla and a Christmas card drawn by Viktor of the Three Magi and what was probably a camel.

The photograph was a glossy close-up studio portrait in black and white and lighted in a stilted and old-fashioned style. Karla was in dramatic profile gazing up towards the upper left-hand comer. It reminded Forde of a Hollywood publicity photo from the forties of some such star as Joan Crawford or Myrna Loy.

Embarrassed that Sheila should see it, he said, "What a strange thing to send someone!"

"Fancies herself, doesn't she?" said Sheila.

"But going to a *studio,*" said Forde.

Sheila tilted the photo.

"Probably air-brushed," she said, dropping it on the counter.

Pointing at the camel, he said, "What do you think that is?"

"I just wonder," she said, "what you'll get next."

What he got next was a request for three tubes of Revlon Color Stay lipstick: No. 41 'Blush,' No. 04 'Nude,' and No. 42 'Flesh.' He had lurked along the cosmetics counters in Eaton's in the Rideau Centre trying to avoid the eye of any of their attendant beauticians. He knew these supercilious women with their improbable sculpted make-up thought him a pervert, the Eaton's equivalent of the schoolyard's man-in-a-mac. He had felt uncomfortable and faintly guilty while buying the lipsticks, but later felt even guiltier about not telling Sheila.

But he had done no wrong. He had to insist on that. It was not being disloyal to describe Sheila as in certain ways excitable. There was simply no point in upsetting her needlessly. Where lay the fault in buying small gifts for a friend—a colleague—who lived under a repressive totalitarian regime that did not allow her access to such simple commodities as lipstick? Or the Ysatis perfume by Givenchy she'd later requested?

He opened his desk drawer and took out the calendar. He had put the photograph inside the calendar to keep it flat. He looked at the upturned face. He looked at the dark fall of hair. Her lips were slightly parted. Light glistened on the fullness of her bottom lip. It was as if seconds before the photographer had pressed the shutter-release button, she had run her tongue across her lip wetting it.

He put the photograph back in the calendar.

Tearing off the doodles page from his writing pad and the page beneath where the ink had gone through, he started to jot down all the words in German he could think of. He couldn't think of many. He arranged them into alphabetical order and sat looking at the result.

Autobahn	*Kristallnacht*
Blitz	*Luftwaffe*
dankeschon	*Panzer*
ersatz	*Realpolitik*
Flak	*Reich*
Fuhrer	*Stalag*
Gauleiter	*Ubermensch*
Gestapo	*Waffen SS*
Kaiser	*auf Wiedersehen*

Sheila was pretending to be concentrating on driving. From Ottawa International Airport he was to fly to Toronto on the Air Canada Rapidair service. In Toronto he was to board a Lufthansa flight to Frankfurt. In Frankfurt he was to board a JAT flight for Slovenia's capital, Ljubljana. He stared out of the window at the wastes of snow, the frozen trees, the roadside lines of piled crud left by the snowplough. From time to time Sheila sniffed.

"All this stuff's of your own imagining, you know."

She did not reply.

"Sheila?"

"I've said what I had to say, thank you."

"Yes, but it was untrue and unfair."

As the road curved round to the parking and departures area, Sheila said, "I'll drop you off at the Air Canada counters and then I won't have to bother with parking."

"And also," he said, "hurtful."

She pulled the car in to the curb and parked.

"Well..." said Forde.

"Have a good trip," she said.

"Aren't you going to kiss me goodbye?"

She inclined her head towards him and he found his lips brushing her cheek.

He gathered his carry-on bag, umbrella, and briefcase and, opening the car door, said, "Really, Sheila, you're being ridiculous."

She sat staring ahead.

He got out and shut the door.

Stood for a moment.

Started across the sidewalk to the revolving door.

Sheila leaned across the passenger seat and wound down the window. She called out to him.

"Pardon?'

"*Az der putz shtait . . .*"

"What?"

"*Az der putz shtait ligt doss saichel in tuchus.*"

"What's that mean?"

She turned the key in the ignition.

"What did that mean?"

He reached for the door handle.

She pushed down the button locking all the doors.

He banged on the roof of the car with the flat of his hand.

She rolled up the window.

"*I demand to know what that meant!*"

A small male child with a suitcase on wheels stopped to gape up at him.

A Blue Line cab driver parked behind them had lowered his window and was staring.

"What. Did. That. Mean?"

He emphasized each word by accompanying it with a bash on the car's hood with the malacca handle of his umbrella.

The taxi driver started honking his horn.

Sheila stretched across the passenger seat and opened the window two or three inches. Hoisting the strap of the carry-on bag higher on his shoulder and jamming the briefcase under his arm, Forde stooped to confront her through the narrow slot.

"It's an old Yiddish saying."

Forde glared.

"*Az der putz shtait* . . . When the prick stands up," she said, ". . . *ligt doss saichel in tuchus* . . . the brains sink into the ass."

* * *

THE ORNATE iron lamp posts along the lake's margin speared light out on the water. Gravel crunched under their feet. Somewhere out beyond the reach of the lamps, a waterfowl beat a brief commotion in the water. After the heat and the blare and the smoke of the crowded bars in the dining room, the breeze from the lake smelled invigoratingly boggy.

"Intrigue," continued Christopher, "will be rampant."

He wiggled his fingers like fishes.

"Aswirl with currents."

"But who's listening? Does anyone really *care* what academics say?"

"*Everybody* is listening, Robert. This isn't Canada. Much of what's going on here you won't be able to understand. But the Party is listening, the factions of the separatists are listening, the Croatians are listening, the Serbs, the Macedonians, a positive *stew* of intelligence people. . . . And there are Slovenian writers here, too. They're important political figures, spokespeople. You see, writing here *is* politics."

With Christopher Harris, Forde felt he had hit the mother lode. They had sat together on the bus, which had carried the party from the Ljubljana Holiday Inn to Splad and had quickly fallen into delighted conversation. Christopher was, Forde assumed, gay, about Forde's age, his nose blooming with drink-burst veins, and his fingernails all bitten to the quick. He was a British expatriate who lived and taught in Lund, in

Sweden—*Provincial. Something of a backwater of a university, really. I'm suited*—but who was an expert on all things Yugoslavian. His passion in life was the celebration of Slovenia and the Slovene language; he had translated most of the significant literature; he was working on a history.

Slovenians, Christopher had explained, considered themselves strongly European, a civilized, energetic northern people distinct from the increasingly dubious rabble to be found to the south, a rabble that culminated in the barbarism and squalor of Islam. This did not mean, Christopher had insisted, that the Slovenians were any more racist than anyone else. Exactly the same sentiments were openly expressed in Germany, France, and Italy. Try cashing a cheque issued in Rome in a bank in Milan without having to listen to an earful about the duplicity of idle southern monkeys.

Christopher had also explained that although the ostensible purpose of the conference was to discuss matters Canadian, much of the international presence was also intended by the organizers as a buffer and defence for separatist Slovenians who would slant their papers and statements in politically unacceptable directions.

Secession was in the air.

They turned back towards the hotel, Christopher sparkling off fact and anecdote—Saint Cyril, called in earlier life Constantine, the Glagolitic alphabet, the battles of Kosovo and Lepanto, the quirks of Selim the Terrible, the westernmost reaches of the Ottoman Empire, the karst cave system near Ljubljana, Chetniks, fourteenth-century church frescos—pausing only to sing sad stanzas from a Slovenian folk song about boys leaving their sweethearts to suffer their forced military service in the Austro-Hungarian army.

"Alf a mo', squire,' he said in a sudden Cockney whine.

He stood with his back to Forde and pissed loudly on a bush.

Forde suddenly felt shivery cold and quite drunk.

The verb 'to stale' came into his mind.

He had had some powerful short brown drinks commended by Christopher and two bottles of nasty wine.

Christopher's feet on the gravel again.

"That mansion set back there," he said, pointing, "was one of ex-King Peter's summer palaces. Do you know Cecil Parrott? Chap who translated *The Good Soldier Svejk* for Penguin? When he was a young man, he was tutor in that house to the two Crown Princes. Tiny, the literary world, isn't it?"

The bulk of the hotel was looming in the darkness. It was a strange building, its central block the remains of a massively built castle which, according to Christopher, dated from the fifteenth century. In the nineteen-thirties, an architect had joined onto the existing structure three huge concrete-and-glass wings. They rose up into the air like birds' wings, rather like, Forde thought, three immense upside-down Stealth aircraft. The castle part was divided up into a reception area, kitchens, and a variety of bedrooms on different confusing levels and up and down small stone stairways. The three concrete-and-glass wings contained most of the bedrooms and an auditorium, conference rooms, and the vast dining room, which was cantilevered out over the lake's edge.

"So as the Nazis withdrew," Christopher was saying, "the only organized force able to step in was the communists. But they'd been a military force, a partisan force, there was no *civil* organization. So inevitably there was great civil confusion. It was a sad period. The communist peasants went on the rampage. The churches, of course, took the brunt of it. Paintings, carvings, tapestries . . . so much of it smashed and put to the torch . . . so many beautiful things lost forever."

He sighed.

"To them, of course," he said, "it was nothing but capitalist trumpery."

Forde stopped and put his hand on Christopher's arm. He was overcome by a sudden warmth of feeling. With the earnestness and grave courtesy of the inebriated, Forde said, "That is the first time in my life, Christopher, that I have heard the word "trumpery" used in conversation."

"And you are the first person I have met," said Christopher, "to whom I could have said it *secure,*" raising his forefinger for emphasis, "*secure* in the knowledge it would be understood."

They crunched on towards the hotel.

Forde's room was in the warren of rooms in the castle part of the hotel. He had been in and out of it three times now since arriving at Splad that afternoon but was still uncertain of his route. He knew that he had to make a first turn left at the painting of the dead deer.

The corridors, staircases, and walled-in embrasures were hung with *nature morte de chasse* paintings. Early-to mid-nineteenth century, most of them, he thought, though a few might have been earlier. It was a genre he'd always avoided, disliking the lavishing of such formidable technique on the depiction of wounds. There was something unsettling about the best of the paintings. He sensed in them a sexual relishing of cruelty and death. He felt repelled in the same way by what he thought of as the Mayan element in Mexican cruifixes, Christ's wounds shown to the white of the bone, shocking atavistic inlays of ivory.

He bent to peer at the small brass plate at the bottom of the frame but all it said was: 1831.

The deer was lying head down across a rustic bench. Two tensely seated hounds with mad eyes yearned up at it. In its nostrils, blood.

As he walked on down the silent corridor, he found himself groping for the name of Queen Victoria's favourite painter. The man whose animal paintings had got nastier and nastier, the cruelty coming closer to the surface, until his mind gave way entirely and he'd died years later barking mad. The man who did the lions at the foot of Nelson's monument in Trafalgar Square, the *Stag at Bay* man.

It was on the tip of his tongue

Began with 'L.'

Lutyens?

Battues of grouse and pheasants. A gralloched deer. Hecatombs of rabbits, grouse, partridges, snipe, and ducks. In some of the paintings, for no obvious reason, greaves, helms, gorgets, a polished-steel cuirass inlaid with brass, a drum bright with regimental crest and colours amid the piled, limp bodies.

He had to go up a short flight of stone steps just after a painting of a dead hawk and rabbit hanging upside down from a fence. Highlights glinted on the rabbit's eye and on the hawk's curved talons. The rabbit's grey fur was wind-ruffled to show the soft, blue underfur pocked where pellets had struck, each swollen puncture dark with gore.

At the top of the steps he turned the wrong way. The short curving corridor terminated in a dead end. He stood in the stone embrasure staring at the ice-making machine.

It rumbled and hummed.

"Landseer!" he exclaimed. "Sir Edwin Landseer."

He followed the corridor in the opposite direction and, recognizing the red brocade curtains partially drawn across the entrance to the recess, finally gained his room.

He felt relieved to lock his door. It had been a long day and he felt tired and crammed with undigested new experience. The bedroom had an antique look, the furniture old and heavy, the walls covered in some kind of grey material, slightly furry to the touch, velvet perhaps. Off the bedroom to the left was a bathroom and to the right a separate little room intended, perhaps, as a dressing room. It contained a chest of drawers and a long mirror in a gilt frame. He had been pleased to discover, in what had seemed to be a cupboard, a TV set and a mini-bar.

The thing Forde loathed most about travelling was *carrying things*. He hated lugging heavy cases about. He hated luggage itself. Luggage, he had often proposed to Sheila as she sat on her case to get it to close, reduced people to being its ill-tempered guardians. Who would wish to stand with the anxious herd watching tons of luggage tumbling onto carousels? Who would wish to share in that mesmerized silence as luggage trundled round and round?

Forde travelled only with a carry-on bag. He never carried more than two shirts, two pairs of underpants, and two pairs of socks. Sheila made up for him little Saran Wrap packages of Tide, each secured with a garbage bag tie and each sufficient to do one wash. Every night he washed his clothes in the wash-basin, scrubbing clean the collars and cuffs of the shirts with an old toothbrush, and then hung everything over the bath to dry.

He lay in the dark, letting his mind run back over the last two days to his landing in Ljubljana. Thought of his surprise at seeing booths at the airport for Avis and Hertz. At the taxi, which accepted Visa and on whose tape deck the Stones were singing 'Midnight Rambler.' At the opulence of the Ljubljana Holiday Inn. Hardly the grim face of Godless Communism he'd been looking forward to.

It had all been much like anywhere else.

He'd wandered the streets of the old city, the buildings distinguished but shabby, the river running through the centre of it all, graceful bridges, churches, and nuns everywhere, the castle at the top of the hill boarded up because of the danger of falling masonry, no money, Christopher told him later, for renovation or repair.

But there was certainly money in the new part of the city. Most shop doors carried Visa and American Express stickers. Familiar names in windows—Black & Decker, Cuisinart, Braun. Parked along the streets, Audi, BMW, Volkswagen. In a bookstore window he'd seen translations of Jack Higgins, Wilbur Smith, Sidney Sheldon, Dick Francis and, to his mortification, an omnibus edition of three Jalna novels by Mazo de la Roche.

But the play of pictures in his mind kept going back to the taxi ride in from the airport. Woods. Small fields. Groups of men and women working in what he took to be allotments of some kind. A tethered donkey eating the roadside grass. In a vegetable garden, a woman working with a mattock.

Then a narrow stone humpback bridge, the road rising, and he'd been looking down over the side of the bridge into a meadow. And there he'd caught a flash of an enormous white bird standing.

He'd cried out to the driver to stop and back up. He'd pointed. The driver, rolling down his window and lighting a cigarette, said, "You like such?"

He'd sat staring.

"What is it? What's it called?"

The driver said something, perhaps a name.

Mist hung over the stream. He could not see the water. The stream's course was plotted by polled willows. The bird was taller than the three grey stacked bales of last year's hay.

He guessed it stood nearly four feet high.

"Cranes," Christopher had said on the bus from Ljubljana.

"I've somehow never really *warmed* to birds."

"Not storks?"

"No, these are rather famous. They'll have been here for about two weeks now. They spend the winters in North Africa. Morocco, somewhere like that."

"And they nest here? In Slovenia ?"

"And always in the same place. They just pile new stuff on top of the old."

"You mean the same birds go back to the same nest?"

"They mate for life, apparently. Some pairs have been together for fifty years."

He pulled a face.

"Not really my cup of tea."

As he slipped towards sleep, just conscious of the irregular dripping sounds from his shirt in the bathroom, he imagined himself in the meadow trying to get closer to the crane without frightening it. The bird was aware of him and walked away keeping the distance between them constant. It walked slowly and gracefully, sometimes hesitating before setting down a foot, reminding him of the way herons stalk. He could see it quite clearly. Its body was white except for the bustle of tail feathers about its rump, which were grey shading to black. Its long neck was black with a white patch around the eyes and, on top of its head, a cap of brilliant red. He edged closer. The crane was pacing along the margin of the mist, from time to time stopping and turning its head to the side as if listening. Past the old bales of hay and the field becoming squelchy, breaking down into tussocks and clumps. And as he looks up again from the unsure footing, the crane is stepping into the mist, which accepts it and wreathes around it, hiding it from view.

Three waiters in mauve jackets and mauve bow ties stood beside the buffet tables impassively surveying the breakfasters. Their function seemed to be to keep the tables stocked and tidy. From time to time they flapped their napkins at crumbs. Two of them had luxuriant drooping mustachios, growths he thought of as Serbian.

He inspected the array of dishes. Cornflakes, muesli, pickled mushrooms, sliced ham, salami, liverwurst, hardboiled eggs, smoked fish, triangles of processed Swiss cheese in silver foil, a soft white cheese in liquid—either feta or brinza—and small round cheeses covered in yellow wax, which he suspected might be kashkaval—honey, rolls, butter. Juice in jugs. Milk. Coffee in thermos flasks.

No sign of Christopher, so he took his tray to an uncrowded table and nodded to a darkly Arab-looking man who promptly passed him a card, which read: Abdul-Rahman Majeed Al-Mansoor. Baghdad. Iraq.

"Hello," said Abdul-Rahman. "How are you? I am fine."

As Forde started to crack and peel shell from his egg, the other man at the table took out his wallet and extracted a card, saying, "I hope that my coughing will not discommode you. I cannot suppress it as the cough is hysterical in origin. My card. Dorscht. Vienna. Canadianist."

Pretending abstraction, Forde busied himself with his breakfast. Covertly he watched Dorscht. Dorscht had a black plastic thermos jug from which he was pouring . . . hot water. He was wearing a leather purse or pouch on a strap that crossed his chest. The archaic word "scrip' flashed into Forde's mind. From his purse Dorscht took a cracker, a Ryvita-looking thing, and started nibbling.

The hubbub in the room was rising to a constant roar. Three men and two women brought trays to the table. They seemed to be a mixture of Canadians and Americans and all seemed to know each other. They were arguing about a poet.

". . . but surely he's *noted* for his deconstruction of binaries."

". . . and by the introduction of chorus avoids the monological egocentricity of conventional lyric discourse."

Christ!

"Let me say," brayed one of the men, "let me say, in full awareness of heteroglossia . . ."

Christ!

Dorscht performed his chugging cough.

Abdul-Rahman Majeed Al-Mansoor belched and patted prissily at his lips with a paper napkin.

Dorscht had a little silver box now, which he evidently kept with his crackers. He was selecting from it three kinds of pills. One of them looked like Valium.

Suddenly Forde sensed someone close to him, was aware someone was staring at him. He turned his head and looked up.

Her arm was raised as though she'd been about to touch his shoulder.

"It *is* . . . isn't it?" she said.

"Yes."

He got to his feet.

"I'm so happy," she said.

"Karla," he said.

At the narrow end of the lake the water was shallow and choked with weed. The air was rank with the smell of mud and rotting vegetation. Karla stopped and pointed down into the water.

"What is the name of this in English?"

Floating there just a foot from the edge of the lake was a mass of frog spawn. He knelt on one knee and worked his hands under the jelly, raising it slightly. It was the size of a soccer ball. He was amazed at the weight of the mass, amazed and then suddenly not amazed, pierced by memory, transported back to his ten-year-old self. He saw himself crouching beside a pool in an abandoned gravel pit, which was posted with signs saying DANGER. NO TRESPASSING . On the ground beside him stood his big Ovaltine jar with air holes punched through the lid. It was full of frog spawn. He was catching palmated newts with a small net made of clumsily stitched lace curtain and placing them in his weed-filled tin. All about him yellow coltsfoot flowers.

"In German,' she said, "you say *Froschlaich.*"

Some of the intensely black dots were already starting to elongate into commas. As she bent to look, her hair touched his cheek. The mass of jelly poured out of his hands and slipped back into the water, sinking and then rising again to ride just beneath the surface.

Forde felt almost giddy. His hands were tingling from the coldness of the water. He felt obscurely excited by the memory the feel of the frog spawn had prompted. He felt he could not breathe in deeply enough. The sun was hot on his back. After months of grinding winter it was a joy not to be wearing boots, a joy not to be wearing a parka, a joy to see the lime-green leaves, the froth of foliage, to hear birdsong, sunlight hinting and glinting on the water, dandelions glowing, growing from crevices in the rock face the delicate fronds of hart's-tongue ferns.

He wanted to hold this place and moment in his mind forever.

Ahead of them a cafe bright with umbrellas. They sat at a patio table and drank cappuccinos, the lake's soft swell lapping at the patio's wooden pilings. Everything conspired to please, the sun, the water sounds, the stiffness of the foam on his coffee, the crisp paper wrapping on the sugar cubes. He watched her hands, the glint of transparent varnish on her fingernails.

Into a sudden silence, Forde said, "And . . . ah . . . Viktor?"

She raised an eyebrow.

"I suppose Viktor's with your husband."

"Oh, no," she said. "He's staying with a friend of mine from the university. He likes it there. She spoils him and she has a hound he can play with."

"Hmmm," said Forde.

"And he knows that when I return I will be bringing presents."

Forde nodded.

They walked on to finish the circuit of the lake. As they neared the hotel, Karla said, "Tell me about your name. I've often wondered about this. In English, people who are Robert are called Bob. So are you called Bob or Robert?"

"Well, sometimes Rob but the people closest to me seem to call me Forde."

She paused in the doorway.

"Then I, too," she declared, "will address you as Forde."

He sketched a comic caricature of a Germanic bow.

"My colleagues will be wondering where I am," she said. "I must go and hear a paper."

“We’ll meet for dinner?”

She smiled and nodded.

“But I must change my shoes.”

She put her hand on his arm and then turned and walked off across the hotel lobby.

He looked into the dining room in hopes of finding Christopher but the buffet tables had been stacked away and a lone waiter was droning away with a vacuum cleaner.

Papers were being delivered in all the conference rooms. He eased open doors.

“... his fiction is sociolect and foregrounds the process of enunciation.”

Christ!

“... the analytico-referential discourse reinstalls itself covering up a self-referential critique which ...”

Christ!

In the small bar just off the lobby he settled himself with a bottle of Becks and, writing on the blank pages of an abandoned conference programme, started to make notes. The feel of the frog spawn had unsettled him. He was startled by the intensity of the images and the spate of words he was dashing onto the pages. He had no idea what he might use it for, but he certainly wasn’t going to question the gift.

Around the top of the old gravel pit, bramble bushes grew in profusion. In late August and early September they were heavy with blackberries. He used the curved handle of a walking stick to draw the laden shoots towards him. He always took the blackberries to his grandmother, who made blackberry and apple pies and blackberry vinegar to pour on pancakes.

His maternal grandparents lived in a tiny, jerry-built, company-owned row house not many miles from the pit where his grandfather had worked all his life. The backs of the houses looked onto a squalid cobbled square where vivid algae slimed the open drains. In the centre of the square stood a row of outhouses and a communal stand pipe. Surrounding the square were tumbledown sheds in which were kept gardening tools, work benches, rabbits, old bicycles, junk. And towering above the houses and the yard up on the hillside stood an abandoned factory.

The factory was a classic Victorian building of iron and glass. Had someone told him once it had been a shoe factory? Every time he had gone out of the back door, there it was, derelict, looming dark over the yard. Many of the glass panels were shattered or gaped blank. The road that ran up to the front of it was disused and closed off by an iron gate hung with threatening notices. Brambles and nettles grew right up to the walls. The building both lured and frightened him. It was a place of mystery. His mother and his grandparents had told him constantly of its danger.

"You go there," his grandfather cackled, "and the tramps'll get you."

Falling glass. Rotting boards. Trespass.

The pencil racing.

He bore in on it.

(Why machinery not melted down in 1939 for munitions?)

Inside—very quiet, *still*. The floor loud with glass. The light is dim—gloomy—subaqueous. Yes. Factory like sunken ship. Silt and weed have blunted its shape. The machinery is actually *changing shape*. What was once precise geometry—straight lines of steel—is now blurring, becoming *rounded* by rust and decay. Furred. Dali. Pigeon shit growing like guano. Whitewash on walls leprous and swollen. Brutality of the shapes and spaces oppressive. Girders, I-beams—name of place Nazis hanged Bomb Plot people with piano wire? Check. Spaces have that kind of feel.

What is going to happen here?

"There's Karla on the left," Forde said to Christopher.

They watched the three women coming across the lobby.

"Which do you think's the heavy?" said Christopher.

“What do you mean?”

“The minder.”

“*What?*”

“Oh, really, Robert,” said Christopher. “Don’t be *impossibly* naive. Stasi informers monitor the political dependability of colleagues. *Inoffizielle Mitarbeiter*, they call them. And one of *them’s* bound to be one.”

The other two women went on into the dining room.

“Karla,” said Forde, “may I introduce you to Christopher Harris. Karla Schiff.”

“Enchanted,” said Christopher in a flat tone.

But the menu cheered him up. It was written in Slovene and English. It offered: Ham Dumplings with Fried Potatoes, Veal Ribs with Fried Potatoes, and Butter Pies with Chicken Pluck.

“That *is* rather good, isn’t it?” said Christopher. “The Slovene would suggest they mean what Americans call ‘chicken pot pie.’”

The din was extraordinary and, as wine bottles appeared, was getting louder. Waiters and waitresses were carrying plates on the largest trays Forde had ever seen. They must have been four feet across. The waitresses were wearing what he thought of as Roman-legionnaire sandals, straps wound up round the ankles and shin. Karla’s shoes were made of plaited brown leather and were narrow and elegant and seemed to him very expensive-looking. He still felt slightly dissociated, still a little dazed by that world of memory and imagination, and was content to watch Karla and let rain down upon him the sparks and boom and brilliance of Christopher’s performance.

Slovene wine production understandably collective rather than *Mis en Bouteilles au Château* so the height of praise would perhaps be the word *serviceable*. . . .

Forde smiled and sipped.

Karla was wearing a loose, white muslin blouse whose changing configurations kept his eye returning.

He wondered where Dorscht was seated; he sensed that Dorscht had immense possibilities.

He suddenly noticed that Christopher had tended to his nose with pancake make-up.

Frescos again. Mid-fourteenth century. The death of John the Baptist. A tiny, perfect chapel near Bohinj. The headless corpse gouting blood in three streams. Angels decorated the other walls. One angel had a triple goitre.

"If only Bernard Berenson had visited Slovenia," Christopher said, "our frescos would be famous throughout the world."

"The Master of Bohinj," said Forde.

"The Master of the Goitre," said Christopher.

"Master of the Goitred Angel," said Forde.

"Amico," said Christopher, "of the Master of the Goitred Angel."

Forde laughed delightedly.

"It isn't kind, Forde," said Karla, "it isn't being nice to talk at dinner about things I don't understand."

Her lips moved into the faintest suggestion of a pout and Forde was enchanted.

As he sluiced his shirt in the washbasin, he burped and the taste of tarragon cake revisited him. They had gone to the bar off the lobby after dinner and had drunk something Christopher claimed was a local specialty, a pear brandy, but it hadn't tasted of pears and was aggressively nasty, like grappa or marc, and the bar had been cramped and jammed with people talking about the materiality of the signifier.

Forde was beginning to feel rather peculiar. He felt hot and somehow bloated though he had not eaten much of the ham dumplings. The fluorescent lights in the bathroom were unusually harsh and turned the white tiles, chrome, and red rubber mat into a restraining room in a hospital for the criminally insane. He studied his face in the mirror. When he swallowed, his throat seemed constricted. He wondered if he was getting a cold.

He decided that he might ward it off by taking vitamin C and an extra aspirin. He took an aspirin every day to thin his blood. The heart attack that was going to fell him was never far from his conscious thought. He decided that if he took vitamin C with a Scotch from the mini-bar and added to the Scotch a little *warm* water, this would render the Scotch medicinal, but the drink burned and it felt as if he were pouring alcohol onto raw flesh. He had difficulty swallowing the pills.

He went back into the bathroom and took off his underpants to wash them.

He thought how very silly men looked naked but for socks. Pain was clutching his stomach. He sat on the toilet in the mad light, emitting high-pitched, keening farts, which culminated in an explosive discharge. He stood and looked in the toilet and then bent and peered. Finally, he knelt to look. Floating on the surface were three whitish things, each ringed with what looked like froth. They looked exactly like the water-steeped jasmine flowers in Chinese tea.

Florets, he thought.

An efflorescence in his bowels.

Benign?

Or cancerous?

Despite the aspirin, he still felt hot, feverish. He switched on the bedside lamp. He lay naked on top of the coverlet. The grey velvet on the walls was dappled with faded spots, which showed in this light like the subtle rosettes on a black leopard's flanks.

He switched the light off and lay in the dark, feeling ill and swallowing with difficulty. His head was aching. The room felt close about him, furry. He seemed to sense the grey walls almost imperceptibly moving as if they were breathing. He slept fitfully, dozing, waking with a start, drifting off deeper to lose himself in a chaotic and terrifying dream, the narrow beam of his flashlight cutting into the darkness, a trussed body hanging from a steel beam, the broken glass loud under his feet.

On top of the cliff that rose at the head of the lake stood another small castle. According to Christopher, it had been extensively altered in the eighteenth century, to turn it into something more comfortable, more domestic. The Nazis had used it as a recreation centre for army officers. Now it had been turned into a museum which housed an absolutely undistinguished collection of artifacts. Drinks and snacks were served on the ramparts.

It was possible to climb up the cliff on a wandering trail through the trees and then scramble the last fifty yards or so on scree, and skirt the parapet to come at a side gate.

Forde turned back and watched Karla scrambling up below him. As she reached the steepest pitch, he leaned down and extended his hand. She looked up at him, winded, a smudge of hair stuck to her forehead with sweat. She reached up and grasped his hand and he took the weight of her and pulled her up over the last of the scree onto the track below the wall.

The museum delighted him. It was exactly like one-room museums in provincial English towns, haphazard accumulations of local finds, curios brought home by colonial officers, the last resting place of the hobbies of deceased gentry.

They browsed over the glass cases of unidentified pottery shards, stone hand axes, arrowheads, bronze fibulae, plaster casts of Roman and Greek coins, powder flasks of polished horn, bullet moulds, bowls heaped with thirteenth-century coins of Béla IV of Hungary, fossils, Roman perfume bottles, stilettos, poniards, medieval tiles with slip decoration the colour of humbugs.

Forde stopped and exclaimed and bent over a display case.

"What is it?" said Karla.

"Look how pretty!" he said.

Forde stared at the leather object. He had never seen one before. The leather was rigid rather than pliable. It was a leather tube, which flared like a champagne cork at the open end. Three quarters of the way up, the tube bent over like a cowl and tapered slightly to a close. The stitching was precise and delicate, the leather dark with age, glossy, and chased with a wreathing convolvulus design. The whole thing was about the size of a shuttlecock.

"It *has* to be," said Forde. "It's a hood for a falcon."

He was moved by the craftsmanship, by the thought of the hands that had gentled the hood over a hawk's head, by the sudden opening into the past the hood afforded.

"I'd love to touch that," he said. "I'd love to hold that in my hands."

He tried the case but it was locked.

When they'd exhausted the possibilities of the museum, they wandered out into the garden and then climbed to the ramparts and sat under an umbrella, sipping lemonade through straws. The length of the lake lay silver before them, the hotel, the marina, ex-King Peter's summer palace. A small yacht was tacking up towards them.

"You see, Karla," he suddenly burst out, "*that's* where art comes from. That leather hood. It arises from the realness of the world. Of course, art encompasses ideas but it's not *about* ideas. It's more concerned with feeling. And you capture the feeling through things, through particularity. There's nothing *intellectual* about novels."

Suddenly embarrassed, he busied himself with lemonade and straw.

Karla was reading his face.

They strolled back towards the hotel, following the road which led gently downhill all the way. Forde, still ravished by greenness, growth, the lemon-green of leaves, stopped to pick some wild flowers. He presented the bouquet to Karla. Daisies, white cow parsley, purple vetch, and campion both pink and white.

The venison was tough and fibrous. It was accompanied by a compote of red berries. Nobody knew what they were called but Professor Dorscht thought that in English they might possibly be called cloudberries. Though he could in no way guarantee that that was so.

Forde had been studying the programme earlier and said to Dorscht, "So tomorrow's the day of your paper."

Dorscht inclined his head.

"About Lucy Maud Montgomery, isn't it?"

"Lucy *who?*" warbled Christopher.

"Specifically," said Dorscht, "the Emily novels."

"Emily?" repeated Forde.

"They are lesser-known works of her maturity."

Works, thought Forde, who considered it something of a national embarrassment that Canadian scholars and universities studied the output of a hack writer of children's books.

"This is another Canadian writer I do not know about it," said Karla. "There is so much for a Canadianist to learn."

"Oh, not really," said Forde who was tempted to express the opinion that the best Canadian writing could be accommodated on a three-foot shelf.

Christopher was beginning to slur his words.

"Lucy *who?*" he said again investing the word 'who' with patent incredulity.

"What I term the 'Emily' novels," said Dorscht, "is the trilogy of novels beginning in 1923 with *Emily of New Moon* and followed in 1925 by *Emily Climbs* and concluding in 1927 with *Emily's Quest.* My paper will—I think the most appropriate word is 'probe'—my paper will probe the trilogy's mythic aspects."

Mythic scrotums, thought Forde. *Mythic bollocks.*

Forde watched Dorscht peel his apple with a little silver penknife. His ability to digest was limited, he had explained, his health undermined by the tensions generated during the long years of study leading to his doctorate, years made unendurable by the psychological savagery visited upon him by his supervising professor.

"But what I mean *is,*" insisted Christopher, "who *is* she?"

"*So,* Robert Forde!" boomed a familiar voice.

He automatically started to get to his feet, but a heavy hand on his shoulder rammed him down again into his seat.

"May I introduce," he said generally, "Drago Tomovic."

"And who," said Drago, "is this most *beauteous* lady?"

He smiled a gold-toothed smile that was revoltingly roguish.

"Drago has translated my novel *Winter Creatures* into Serbian."

Drago, with mock flourish, handed a package across the table. Forde tore open the paper.

It was in Cyrillic.

It had no cover art.

The paper was hairy.

Karla suggested they celebrate the translation in the bar off the lobby. The evening wore on. Drago's flappy jacket was in huge checks, like the outrageous clothes worn by comedians in vaudeville or music hall. Christopher made it quite clear by grimace and the stiffness of his body that he found Drago appalling. Dorscht could not drink alcohol because of his ulcer. He also confided that he feared losing control. Drago flirted ponderously with Karla. Christopher started to read the translation, making loud tut and click noises.

Through the surf of conversation Forde kept overhearing snatches of astounding drivel from a bony woman behind him who was, apparently, uncovering a female language by decoding patriarchal deformation.

Christ!

"Winter," boomed Drago, "is not just *winter.*" He tapped his forehead. "*Think!* It *stands for* the coldness between the characters. Always say to yourself what is the *hidden* meaning of this book. Andrew is not *just* a bureaucrat. He works for the *government* and so *represents* ..."

"You mean," said Karla, "that you read the book as ..." She groped for the word. "... as an allegory?"

"*Certainly,*" said Drago.

Forde was horrified.

"I make everything," said Drago, "*crystal clear.*"

Dorscht went into another coughing fit.

When he'd finished and done the tic-thing with his left eye, Forde pressed him for details of the psychological savagery visited upon him by his supervising professor. Dorscht revealed that he had been commanded to write papers which his professor then appropriated and delivered at conferences as his own work. That the professor would only discuss his thesis in expensive restaurants, where Dorscht was always forced to pay the bill. That for years he had to take the professor's clothes to the laundry and dry-cleaners and then deliver them to the man's house.

Christopher interrupted Dorscht's lamentations by slapping shut *Winter Creatures* and walking round the table to hand it to Forde, saying, "Oaf and boor."

To Dorscht, Karla and Drago, he said, "I am now going to bed."

His leaving broke the party up. Dorscht went off to take a Valium and a mild barbiturate, Drago was swept up in the lobby by a noisy group of fellow Serbians who were all wearing what Forde took to be the rosettes and coloured favours of a soccer team, and Karla was claimed just outside the doors of the bar by her two friends from Jena.

She turned to look back at him; she smiled and shrugged.

Forde made his way up past the deer with blood in its nostrils, climbed the stairs at the pellet-pocked rabbit and the hawk with the shattered wing. His room felt stuffy and hot. He flipped through the translation of *Winter Creatures* but the only thing he could read was his name. But even if Drago had reduced a sprightly comedy to a stodgy allegory of his own invention, a book was still a book and it had his name on it. And if one thought of the Cyrillic as a kind of abstract art, the pages were not unattractive.

He filled the sink in the bathroom and poured in one of Sheila's Saran Wrap packages of Tide. He took off his clothes and immersed the shirt, pushing it down repeatedly to get the air pockets out. He was beginning to feel decidedly odd again. A band of constriction across his forehead. Difficulty swallowing. He wondered if there was something about the room itself. Outside it, he felt entirely normal. Perhaps he was allergic to something in the room. Though he'd never suffered from allergies before. And the first night he'd slept in the room had been uneventful.

His mouth kept filling with saliva, as if at any moment he might vomit. Perhaps they were using some devastating East European or Balkan chemical to clean the carpets or the bath.

He felt not only hot but distressed and confused by his discomfort. He wandered into the bedroom and sat in the armchair hoping that if he concentrated on reading he would be able to ignore or conquer the symptoms. He always travelled with a copy of *Hart's Rules for Compositors and Readers at the University Press Oxford* because it was small and inexhaustible. But the print swam and he kept putting the book down and staring at the furry wall, concentrating on not throwing up.

The venison?

But no one else had seemed affected.

And didn't it take twelve hours or more to incubate, or whatever one called it?

He forced himself back into the bathroom and scrubbed the shirt's collar and cuffs with the old toothbrush. He rinsed the shirt in the bathtub, leaving the soapy water in the basin to do his underpants and socks.

He sat on the toilet but nothing resulted. The fluorescent lights hummed. He thought suddenly of an eccentric landlady he'd once had when he was at university. She'd been having the house painted and had walked in on one of the painters who was on the toilet. In great embarrassment he'd said to her that he was having a pee.

"What kind of a man," she'd demanded, "sits down to squeeze his lemons?"

Why had *that* swum into his mind?

He lay on the bed and tried to sleep but under the covers he was too hot, on top of them too cold. The nausea had settled into uneasiness in his stomach and at the back of his throat. Pictures churned about in his mind. Karla looking up at him from the steep scree. The falcon's hood delicate and as light on the palm, he imagined, as a blown bird's egg. In the gilt cabinet, the plaited silk jesses with silver varvels. The roadside flowers. Pink and white campion.

He felt small cramps of pain in his stomach. He flung back the covers again and went to sit on the toilet. He strained briefly but nothing happened. He got up and realized immediately that something *had* happened. The toilet bowl was speckled with a fine mist of blood. Through the toilet paper his incredulous fingertips felt a lump, a lump with three—his fingertips explored that heat and hugeness—a vast lump with three.... What *was* this? A Pile? Piles? What *were* piles? Exactly? Such a thing had never happened to him before. His fingertips traced the dimensions and configurations of the horror. A lump with three ... *lobes.*

The very word filled his mouth with clear saliva.

His hand smelled and was sticky with watery blood.

He twisted round trying to look at his behind in the mirror.

He put one foot on the toilet seat and bent forward, separating his cheeks, but this position revealed nothing but redness.

A woman had once told him that, after giving birth, she'd had piles "like a bunch of grapes."

He waddled across the bedroom into the dressing room with its full-length mirror and contorted himself variously and ingeniously but could see nothing. He imagined it to be blue or purple. He didn't want to get too yogic in his postures in case the horror burst.

He began to feel panicky. He could not endure the embarrassment of requesting treatment. But he did not wish to leak to death in a Slovenian hotel. He made a pad of a dozen or so Kleenex and wedged it between his cheeks and over the thing. He eased on clean underpants to keep the pad in place. Then he put on a clean shirt and his trousers and, taking his key and the plastic ice-bucket, set off down the corridor, with tiny steps, towards the ice machine.

Back in the bathroom he leaned his weary head on his arm on the vanity and, with his right hand, held ice cube after ice cube against the hot, swollen lumps his body had extruded, ice water trickling down his legs into his toes, his scrotum frozen, fingers numb even through the flannel; weary, weary for his bed.

Forde was sitting with Karla. Christopher was sitting in the seat behind. The bus, one of four, was taking the conference people on this final day for a picnic in a village high up near Mt. Triglav in the Julian Alps.

Forde was feeling cheerful and restored. His piles had retreated entirely. His reading and lecture the day before had been well attended. Even Forde had been surprised by how rude he had been to an earnest man at the lecture who had put a question to him that had involved the name 'Bakhtin' and the words 'dialogic,' 'foregrounded,' and 'problematized.' Though he felt absolutely no contrition. That night he had again felt ill and feverish but suffered nothing worse than a rash over his torso and thighs, hot, white welts that itched and throbbed and bled when scratched. He had tried to soothe the itching by repeatedly applying a flannel soaked in ice-water.

He was sure he was suffering from an allergy either to something in the room or to food.

He had read from his last novel, *Tincture of Opium*. He'd done a restaurant scene involving the two lovers and a Chinese waiter who understood little English and whose every utterance sounded like a barked command. It was a set-piece, but it performed well, modulating from near-farce to a delicate affirmation of love. He particularly liked the way he'd cut the sweetness of the sentiment with comic intrusions.

At dinner that night Karla had arranged with the Oliver Hardy waiter for a bottle of champagne to be brought to their table. She had proposed a toast to Forde's wonderful reading, to his glittering novels, to his eminence in Canadian letters, to his generosity with his time to beginning Canadianists, to, well, *Forde!*

She had been flushed, her eyes shining.

"Bottoms up!" cried Christopher.

"Sincere felicitations," said Professor Dorscht.

"To Forde!" said Karla again.

"*Certainly* to Forde!" boomed Drago.

Now he could feel her thigh swayed warm against his as the bus made turn after turn climbing the narrow road terraced into the mountain. The buses parked outside the boundary of the Triglav National Park, and people set out to walk the mile or so through woods and meadows to the village. The sun was pleasantly warm, the surrounding mountains serenely beautiful. The mountains enclosed them, cupped them. It was, thought Forde, rather like being on the stage of a vast amphitheatre. In places, the path they were walking along ran over outcroppings of rock. They stopped to help an elderly couple whose leather-soled shoes were slipping on the smoothed stone.

"What are those wooden things?" asked Forde.

"They're racks for drying hay on," said Christopher. "Unique to Slovenia. They're called *kozolci.*"

"And look!" said Forde. "Cowslips and primroses. I haven't seen those for years."

"And here," said Christopher, "are some of our famous gentians."

Forde stopped. He stared down at the intensity of the blue.

"Oh, yes," said Karla. "In German we say *Enzian.*"

"This is a very special day for me," said Forde. He got down on his knees and brushed the grass aside. "I've never seen a gentian before. I read about them when I was in my teens. I used to learn poems off by heart that I liked the sound of and there was one called "Bavari:an Gentians" by D. H. Lawrence. Well, perhaps it's not such a good poem. Perhaps you're extra forgiving to things you liked when you were young."

He looked up at Karla.

He frowned slightly in concentration.

Reach me a gentian, give me a torch!
let me guide myself with the blue, forked torch of this
flower
down the darker and darker stairs, where blue is
darkened on
blueness
even where Persephone goes, just now, from the frosted
September
to the sightless realm where darkness is awake upon the
dark
and Persephone herself is but a voice
or a darkness invisible enfolded in the deeper dark
of the arms Plutonic, and pierced with the passion of
dense gloom,
among the splendour of torches of darkness, shedding
darkness on
the lost bride and her groom.

"Stone the crows!" said Christopher. "Do you do that often?"

"No," said Forde. "It's weird. Only with things I learned when I was about sixteen."

"Sort of idiot savant-ish," said Christopher.

"It *sounds* beautiful," said Karla.

"Well," said Forde, getting up and brushing wisps of dry grass off his trousers, "sometimes I think it's nothing *but* sound but then the old bastard gets off things like 'darkness is awake upon the dark' and you have to admit..."

The path through the meadow joined a wider path that led down into the village. A large banner was strung across the path. On it were the words:

WELCOME TO THE CULTURAL WORKERS.

The straggling procession from the buses was beginning to pool now around the village hall, where rustic tables and benches were set out. The villagers were greeting each newcomer with trays of bread and salt and shot glasses of slivovitz. The men were in Alpine costume: long, tight white pants, thigh-high black leather boots, embroidered waistcoats. Cummerbund things. Or lederhosen. The women wore layered skirts and waistcoats and bonnets. Forde found it oddly unreal. Slightly embarrassing. He felt it was like being on the set of a Hollywood musical.

Some of the men were carrying crates of beer and cases of wine from the village hall and setting up one of the tables as a bar.

"The best beer," said Christopher, "is this Gambrinus. And Union's quite good, too. They brew that in Ljubljana. And for wine, I'd stick to Refošk or Kraški Teran."

"Who's paying for all this?"

"The Literary and Cultural Association of Slovenia and the local Party boss."

"And what about..."

"The peasants?" said Christopher.

"I wish you wouldn't keep saying that."

"Why?" said Christopher. "Peasants are a recognizable class. In France, Germany, Italy, Spain . . . *everywhere*. Peasants are peasants."

"Oh, *very* much in Austria and Bavaria," said Karla.

On the concrete slab in front of the village hall three young men were setting up amplifiers and speakers and going in and out of the hall trailing wire. Lying on and propped against the kitchen chairs were a bass, two guitars, and an amplified zither. Another man arrived and started messing about with a snare drum.

A little girl of about four or five, dressed in skirts and bonnet, was wandering through the tables staring at the people. She clutched to her chest an enormous and uncomfortable-looking rabbit.

The drummer's peremptory rattings and tattings and paradiddles sounded through the roar of conversation. Two of the village women were spreading white linen tablecloths over three of the tables. As they flipped the cloths in the air, they flashed like white sails against the vast blueness, a sky so huge that it made him think of the word 'empyrean.' The warmth of the sun, the azure sky, the stillness of the mountains all around—a sigh of pleasure escaped him. Dishes, bowls, pans, and platters began coming out of the village hall. They strolled over to look. Fried pork. Sausages with sauerkraut. Pork crackling. Fried veal with mushrooms. Pork hocks. Beans and chunks of veal in tomato sauce. Pasta stuffed with cottage cheese. Hunks of bread in baskets.

"That's the only thing to avoid," said Christopher, pointing. "It's a sort of cheese pie called *burek* and it's *terminally* greasy."

They filled paper plates and Christopher exchanged pleasantries with the man behind the bar and snagged a bottle of Refošk.

The band started to play polkas and waltzes. An accordion came to join them. The music was just the thing for a picnic in the Alps, jolly and silly. Forde drank more wine and found himself tapping his foot in time to the rattletrap drummer.

He noticed some of the village men raising their hats to a man who had just arrived. He was wearing a black suit and a black shirt with a priest's white collar. But on his head was a bowler hat with pheasant feathers pinned to one side of it to form a tall, swaying cockade. He made his way through the villagers, shaking hands and slapping backs until he reached the bar where he was immediately handed, not a shot glass, but a tumbler of slivovitz. Forde had known some gargantuan drinkers in his day but he had never before seen a man *purple* with drink.

"He is both notorious and widely loved," said Christopher. "Later on—he always does—he'll sing a selection of sentimental and dirty songs."

When they'd finished eating, Forde volunteered to fetch beer. The slow beer line-up brought him alongside a table of cultural workers who, seemingly oblivious to meadows or mountains, were locked in earnest discussion. As he stood there he heard a man say 'univocal discourse.' He looked with loathing upon these money-changers in the temple.

As he put the three bottles of Gambrinus down on the table, Christopher was saying, "Well, the high point of the day for me is the absence of that hulking *Serb.*"

"Drago is not my fault," said Forde.

"He certainly isn't mine."

"Certainly!" said Forde. *"Certainly!"*

The crowd around the food tables was thinning out. Some of the conference people had drifted away higher in the meadow and were lying down sunbathing. The band had returned after a break and was playing waltzes. Forde had had enough to drink for the day to feel dreamlike and desultory. Some couples were waltzing in the village street. Forde idly watched the swirl of skirts. The sun was getting hotter. He started to peel the label off his beer bottle.

Karla got up and, pointing down the street, said, "Forde! Take me dancing.'

He looked up at her.

He hesitated.

"Karla," he said. "I have eaten sausage and sauerkraut. Fried potatoes. Fried mushrooms. And that sheep cheese. I must have drunk a bottle of wine. And beer. I *might*," he said, "just might be able to manage a slow stroll in the meadows."

People started to crowd around the band.

"Must be Father Baraga," said Christopher.

They walked over and joined the crowd. Father Baraga was sitting on a wooden kitchen chair, hands on his thighs, beaming and purple. The zither man was lowering and adjusting the microphone. The musicians conferred with Father Baraga and a song was agreed upon.

It was obviously a kind of patter song, and the priest accompanied it with exaggerated facial expressions indicative of leering surprise, outrage, shock. Everyone who understood Slovene was laughing and grinning.

"What's it about?"

"Oh, this is a mild one," said Christopher. "It's all innuendo and *double entendre.* Like old music-hall songs." He thought for a second. "You know—

'In the spring, my Auntie Nellie,

Dusting down her Botticelli'

—that sort of thing."

Watching the rubbery lips, the sweat running from the bags under his eyes, the spittle, the purple flesh bulging onto the white collar, the yellow stumps of his teeth, Forde felt again how dreamlike, even nightmarish, the world so often seemed.

His novels were often criticized for containing what reviewers and critics described as 'grotesques' and 'caricatures.' What world, he wondered, did they live in? They carped and bellyached that some of his scenes were 'improbable' or 'strained credulity,' yet Forde knew that this was the way the world *was.* The world was bizarre. The word "normal' was simply a notion.

He shrugged as he thought about it.

He was more than halfway up a very high mountain listening to a Fender bass being played by a man in thigh-length leather boots, to two guitars being played by men in lederhosen, to an amplified zither being played by another man in thigh-length leather boots, and to the singing of a drunken Roman Catholic priest wearing a bowler hat with feathers in it. *And* he was in the company of a woman Christopher had implied might well be a Stasi informer.

Karla caught his eye and motioned with her head. He followed her, working his way out of the crowd. They strolled up through the meadow, past the sunbathers, past hay racks, until they were high enough on the narrow trail to look down on the roof of the village hall. Karla was wearing her hair in a ponytail that bobbed as she walked. He thought of the photograph she'd sent. The photograph that was inside the calendar in his desk drawer. In that picture her hair had been short and helmet-shaped.

They could see only three houses on the main street, with another set back from it by about fifty yards. Not that the street was really a street. It was just an unpaved, sandy path. The rest of the houses were dotted about the meadows. As they stood there, Forde was very aware of Karla's toenails. She had painted them a silvery colour.

The path they were walking along ran in front of three houses, grouped together. The house in the centre sported a frieze of stylized flowers painted just below the eaves. Outside the house stood the little girl in skirts and bonnet they'd seen earlier lugging her rabbit about.

The rabbit was lying in the grass, unmoving except for one ear, which turned to monitor its world. Karla smiled at the child and bent down to pet the rabbit.

"Das ist doch ein hübscher Kerl!"

The child laughed and swooped on the rabbit, hauling it up to her chest, its hind legs dangling. Just as Karla reached out to stroke it, the rabbit squirmed and raked the inside of her forearm with its back legs. She cried out in surprise. The little girl dropped the rabbit and squatted beside it and seemed to be scolding it. As Forde watched, blood welled into the two scratches, rose into large beads, ran.

"Animal things are always bad news," said Forde. "Dog bites, that sort of thing. They're always dirty. You probably ought to get a tetanus shot, but for now..."

He took her arm. He held her with his left hand just above her elbow. With his right hand he held her hand. He bent over the inside of her forearm. On her wrist he could smell the fragrance of Ysatis. He sucked the length of the two scratches, filling his mouth with blood and spitting it out onto the grass. Suck and spit. Suck and spit.

Karla laced her fingers with his.

His mouth tasted vile and he could hardly get his eyes open. He'd obviously slept for far longer than the nap he'd intended. His watch had stopped. He went into the bathroom and looked at his puffy face in the mad fluorescence. He'd caught the sun.

He went down to the dining room. The lobby was deserted. He heaved open the door to the dining room. The vast room was empty and silent. The chandeliers blazed light on the emptiness. By the trestle tables used as a service station, two of the waiters were silently folding a tablecloth. Arms raised above their heads, the corners of the cloth held between thumb and forefingers, they advanced upon each other. The corners met. The fat waiter stooped and picked up the bottom edge. He retreated until the cloth was taut, then advanced again to meet and make a second fold. They looked as if they were performing an elephantine parody of a courtly dance.

The door thunked shut behind him.

He went into the bar off the lobby. There were three people there. He supposed some of the conference people had already left. He discovered that it was nearly nine thirty. The buses had arrived back at Splad at about six thirty, so he'd been asleep for nearly three hours. He wound his watch and reset it.

He wondered if he ought to call Karla or Christopher.

He stood in the silent lobby in indecision.

Then he turned and started up the stairs, left at the deer, up the stone steps at the rabbit and hawk, hardly noticing them now they were familiar. He felt quite groggy from the unexpectedly deep sleep. He sat in the armchair in the bedroom and immediately started to feel even worse. His mouth was filling with saliva. He was feeling waves of nausea. He mastered the surge of vomit long enough to get into the bathroom, where he vomited copiously and uncontrollably. He braced himself with both hands against the wall and stood, head hanging over the toilet bowl, breathing through open mouth, drooling, strings of saliva and mucus glistening from his lower lip. His stomach seized again and again and he vomited until he was vomiting nothing but bile and his throat was raw. He was in a cold sweat and his legs were trembling. He could feel the sweat cold on his ribs.

When the nausea faded, he brushed his teeth and cleaned the rim of the toilet and the underside of the spattered toilet seat. As he was doing so, he realized that something was happening to his vision. Bright white sparks seemed to be drifting across things, the sensation intensifying until there was a gauze obscuring things like the snow of interference on a TV screen. He felt quite frightened, and went back into the bedroom, feeling his way along the walls. He got himself onto the bed and lay there wondering what was happening to him, what he ought to do.

He opened his eyes again, but the silent crackle of white dots still veiled the bedside lamp, the occasional table, the bed itself. He closed his eyes and tried to think calmly about his situation. Were the vomiting and the white dots related? Could they have the same cause? Why might he have vomited? Wine? Extremely unlikely. Might he be suffering from sunstroke? Might the white dots be a migraine headache? Though he'd never had one before and his head wasn't aching.

He lay on the bed and tried to relax. He breathed as slowly as he could, trying to slow the rate of his heartbeat. Despite his anxiety and the churning question and formulations in his mind, his head turned into the pillow and he drifted some of the way towards sleep.

And on the threshold of sleep, he sees himself walking along a hospital corridor. As he passes each open doorway, the sudden warm smells of sickness, of food and faeces. He is standing near a bank of elevators looking out of the window onto the flat, gravelled roof. The roof is mobbed with pigeons and seagulls screeching and squawking and fighting for the scraps thrown out of windows by patients and orderlies. The roof is seething with the bodies of birds. They tread upon each other. Pigeons are pecking cigarette butts and a dead pigeon. The gulls are threatening each other, pumping up raucous challenges. One rises to a piercing crescendo only for another to start over again. The screeching of the gulls heard through the glass merges with geriatric wailing further up the corridor, a cacophony of aggression, fear and despair.

He goes into the room. It has two beds in it but only one is occupied. The nurse is bent over the person in the bed. The sheets and blankets are pulled back off the bed and trail on the floor. The nurse *plaps* a sanitary napkin onto the polished linoleum. It is bloody. She withdraws a syringe and caps it, and puts it on a stainless-steel tray on the bedside table.

He goes around the bed and looks down at Sheila. Her eyes are closed. He puts his hand on her arm. It is cold and clammy. Karla is wearing a stethoscope. She looks up at him across the bed.

She shakes her head.

The room is silent. The only sound other than Sheila's rapid, shallow breathing is the screeching of birds.

The bus that had been laid on for Ljubljana pulled out of the hotel car park onto the road that led to the highway. There were a dozen or so passengers from the conference, none that he'd spoken to before. He was returning to the Holiday Inn.

He'd woken only half an hour earlier and, in a panic to catch the bus, he'd forgone a shower, stuffed his possessions into his bag, paid the mini-bar bill at reception, and, standing in the bar off the lobby, had gulped down a tepid, black coffee.

The bus had been his only chance of getting into Ljubljana in time. He had agreed to give a lecture that afternoon at the University of Ljubljana; yet another honorarium had been mentioned.

A few introductory . . . the professor had said . . . *and such and so.*

He gazed out of the window. His stomach was empty and rumbling and he still felt flustered from rushing about, but at least he could *see*. The screen of white dots had disappeared entirely. He had Christopher's address in Sweden and he would write to him—and to Karla—to explain his disappearance the night before, and his unceremonious departure.

The journey took just over an hour. The room that had been reserved for him was actually vacant and ready for occupation. He poured a package of Tide into the washbasin and washed the shirt he'd been too ill to deal with the night before. His flight the next day to Frankfurt left at eight in the morning. The trip to the airport took some twenty minutes to half an hour. He liked to be early so he would need a taxi at six thirty. The hotel could doubtless supply one, but he had accepted a business card from the driver who had driven him in from the airport and had promised to phone him. He suspected the man was desperate for the business. The switchboard got him the number and eventually he made himself understood and completed the arrangements.

He went downstairs and ate breakfast in the Holiday Inn restaurant in solitary state. Four unenthusiastic waiters stood about. He worked his way through a mushroom omelette and three rolls with butter and plum jam and felt soothed and restored after the purging his stomach had suffered in the night. The morning fog was dispersing, the sun burning through. He decided that he would go for a walk along the Ljubljanica River and then devote the rest of the morning to finding presents for Sheila, Chris, and Tony. As he strolled out into the plaza in front of the hotel, he was feeling a lightness of spirit, almost a jauntiness.

Presents for Chris and Tony would prove far more difficult than finding a present for Sheila. They seemed to be interested only in rock bands, basketball, and strange fantasy magazines involving dragons, mazes, dungeons, and monsters. Pleasant-enough boys, but he found them rather blank. Sheila said they'd turn out just fine, that all boys were like this. What he was seeing was just adolescent conformity. Beneath were two sturdy individuals. Forde trusted Sheila's understanding of people and did not doubt that she was right. What troubled him was what they didn't *know.* Things like History and Geography. Sheila had told him he was becoming cranky.

Two years previously he'd taken the pair of them to England to visit their grandparents. He had shown them Buckingham Palace, the Tower of London, the British Museum, Westminster Abbey, all the delights of London. He had taken them to Warwick Castle. To Stratford to see Shakespeare's birthplace. To Oxford. Through the Cotswold villages. Chris had been—he thought for a moment—eleven, and Tony thirteen.

He had tried to give them a sense of the past, to connect them with it. He'd pointed out tumuli in the fields and medieval strips and baulks still visible under the turf. He had taken them through an iron-age hill fort. He'd marched them along the Ridgeway from the White Horse at Uffington to the megalithic long barrow called Wayland's Smithy, rhapsodizing the while that their feet were treading the same ground that tribes and armies had marched on since prehistory.

On their return to Canada, Chris had confided in Sheila that the place he'd liked most, the very best place they'd visited, was Fortnum and Mason. The high point of the expedition for Tony, apparently, had been the purchase of an extra-large T-shirt on the Charing Cross Road, a T-shirt bought without consultation, on which was printed, front and back: Too Drunk To Fuck.

It was in the bookstore where he'd seen, in the window, the omnilius edition of the Jalna novels by Mazo de la Roche, that he happened upon the perfect gift for Sheila. The book was a facsimile edition, in superb colour, of a famous medieval Jewish book in the collection of the National Museum in Sarajevo. The book was in a slipcase, which also contained a pamphlet in English detailing the book's history.

It was known now as the *Sarajevo Haggadah.* One hundred and forty-two vellum pages. The text was illuminated lavishly, initial words in gold and a blue so intense it might have been made with powdered lapis lazuli. Hebrew characters became flowers; heraldic and fanciful beasts stalked the intricate foliage. Just as beautiful was the chaste, unadorned calligraphy of the prayers. The stories of the Exodus were illustrated with nearly a hundred miniature paintings.

The *Sarajevo Haggadah* was thought to have been written and painted most probably in Barcelona shortly after 1350. When the Jews were expelled from Spain in 1492, the book had started its journey eastward. There was a record of it in Italy in 1609. It was carried into the Balkans, most probably to Split, or Dubrovnik, by a family called Kohen. The book was sold to the National Museum in Sarajevo in 1894.

He was touched that reproduced on some pages were the spots and blotches from wine and food spilled on the book during Seders over the centuries. And it pleased him to think that next Passover, when they went to Toronto for the Seder, Sheila would be able to read along in something more sumptuous than the prayer books her father handed out and that her father would be able to pontificate on the historical prohibition against art in sacred texts in the Jewish tradition and when he discovered the book was Sephardic he would launch into rambling assaults on Ladino as a language and the eccentricity, if not impurity, of Sephardic rites and Sheila's mother would either contradict him or introduce a new topic of conversation she'd derived from TV talk shows, such as the spontaneous combustion of human beings, and within minutes everyone would be shouting and on it would go, on and on it would go....

At six thirty he was waiting in the lobby with his carry-on bag, his briefcase, and his furled umbrella. The night had passed restfully and without incident. He had not bothered with breakfast as it would be served on the plane and he'd be able to get coffee at the airport.

He was brooding about his carry-on bag. Because he was up early, the collar and cuffs of his shirt were still slightly damp and clammy. He had worn the same shirt every day, except for the day before, when migraine or whatever it had been had prevented his washing it. But it was obvious that, normal circumstances prevailing, one shirt would suffice. If he were to cut out seconds on socks and underpants as well, it might be possible to get essentials into a briefcase alone. He stood looking out of the plate-glass window. It was slightly foggy again. Not enough to delay take-off, he hoped. Checked his watch. He thought it would be something of a triumph if he could dispense with a carry-on bag, if he could get into his briefcase alone any necessary papers and the essentials—toothbrush, toothpaste, hairbrush, *Hart's Rules,* razor, cellophane twists of Tide, aspirins. Light glowed on the fog. The taxi turned into the plaza and drew up under the porte-cochère.

The driver greeted him warmly, and they shook hands. As they cleared Ljubljana itself, the fog seemed to be thinning. They'd been driving along for about fifteen minutes when the car slowed and the driver signalled a left turn. Forde listened to the click-click-click of the indicator. The driver turned off the main road and into a narrow side road.

"Is this the way to the airport?' said Forde.

The driver raised his forefinger and nodded, a gesture obviously meaning: Just be patient. Wait for a minute. At the bottom of the hill, the driver pulled up onto the grass verge. Forde felt slightly apprehensive. He hoped he wasn't being set up. He looked at his watch. They got out and Forde followed the driver along the road until they came to a stone bridge. The driver put his finger to his lips and then gestured for Forde to stoop. They approached the centre of the bridge, bent almost double, and then rose slowly to peer over the side.

The river was quite wide and mist hung over it. In the middle of the river was a long, narrow island. Standing at the near end of the island were two cranes and some little distance behind them a nest, a great platform of gathered sedge and reeds.

The cranes were bowing to each other, their heads coming down close to the ground. One of the birds fanned out its bustle of tail plumes and started to strut circles around the other, every now and then leaning in towards it sideways, as if to gather or impart intimacies. Then the crane with the raised plumes walked over to the messy nest and began to parade around it, pausing from time to time to bow deeply towards it.

The other bird raised its great wings over its back and jumped into the air. The other responded by launching itself sideways, a collapsing, hopping jump. The jumps looked like the hopeless efforts of a flightless bird to take wing. They started jumping together. There was something comic in the spectacle. It was as if these huge and stately birds were being deliberately juvenile and ungainly. The way they trailed their legs suggested the way dancers in musicals jump and click their heels together in the air. Their antics were oddly incongruous. The birds were so regal, so dignified, that to see them flap and hop and topple was as if two portly prelates in gaiters suddenly started to caper and prance.

One of them stretched its long, heron-like neck straight up into the air and gave forth a great trumpet blast of noise, harsh and unbelievably loud.

Krraaa-krro.

The other bird straightened the S of its neck and replied.

Krraaa-krro.

And then the two birds paced towards each other until their breasts were touching and began to rub each other's necks with their heads, long swooping-and-rising caresses, their beaks nuzzling at the height of the embrace.

The driver took out a packet of cigarettes and lit one. Forde realized that his fingers were clenched over the edge of the stone block. The smell of tobacco hung on the air.

The driver grinned at Forde.

Forde smiled back.

The cranes trumpeted at the sky, first one then the fierce reply, reverberating blasts of noise bouncing off the stonework of the bridge, filling the air with the clamour of jubilation.

Forde felt …

Forde exulted with them.

John Metcalf was Senior Editor at the Porcupine's Quill until 2005, and is now Fiction Editor at Biblioasis. A scintillating writer and magisterial editor and anthologist, he is the author of more than a dozen works of fiction and non-fiction, including *Standing Stones: Selected Stories*, *Adult Entertainment*, *Going Down Slow*, and *Kicking Against the Pricks*. He lives in Ottawa with his wife, Myrna. His new collection, *The Museum at the End of the World*, is forthcoming in Fall 2016.